Crossing into Spain

An explosion of sound and light awoke her. Kate sat up, blinded by a beam of light directly in her eyes. Icy air was gusting into the hut through the open door. At her side Tony spoke first in halting Spanish, then tried French.

The light beam left Kate and went to Tony's face. He was trying to stand up, but a dully gleaming length of metal shoved him back down. The shadows shifted and Kate's eyes focused on the man with the rifle . . . Tony looked up at the intruder and said in French, "We must get across the border into Spain!"

Kate gasped. "Don't tell him anything!"

Tony said, "It's all right, Kate . . . Smile sweetly at the nice gent . . . He's going to guide us over the pass to the border. . . ."

"KATE IS A WONDERFUL HEROINE . . . READERS WILL SHED SOME TEARS, BUT THEY'LL BE UPLIFTED BY THE COURAGE AND LOYALTY SHOWN BY JOAN DIAL'S CHARACTERS."
—*Romantic Times*

Most Pocket Books are available at special quantity discounts for bulk purchases for sales promotions, premiums or fund raising. Special books or book excerpts can also be created to fit specific needs.

For details write the office of the Vice President of Special Markets, Pocket Books, 1230 Avenue of the Americas, New York, New York 10020.

ECHOES OF WAR

JOAN DIAL

PUBLISHED BY POCKET BOOKS NEW YORK

This novel is a work of fiction. Names, characters, places and incidents are either the product of the author's imagination or are used fictitiously. Any resemblance to actual events or locales or persons, living or dead, is entirely coincidental.

POCKET BOOKS, a division of Simon & Schuster, Inc.
1230 Avenue of the Americas, New York, N.Y. 10020

Copyright © 1984 by Joan Dial
Cover artwork copyright © 1986 Roger Kastel

Published by arrangement with St. Martin's Press, Inc.
Library of Congress Catalog Card Number: 84-12715

All rights reserved, including the right to reproduce
this book or portions thereof in any form whatsoever.
For information address St. Martin's Press, Inc.,
175 Fifth Avenue, New York, N.Y. 10010

ISBN: 0-671-60357-4

First Pocket Books printing July, 1986

10 9 8 7 6 5 4 3 2 1

POCKET and colophon are registered trademarks
of Simon & Schuster, Inc.

Printed in the U.S.A.

For Paul . . . to keep a promise

[BOOK ONE]

[[1]]
Berlin, Spring 1939

The crowd suddenly fell silent, but the pulsing excitement remained, electrifying the air. Kate Kieron felt the press and sway, the pounding heartbeats as chests swelled with national pride; the catch in ten thousand throats. Then a blinding white halo of light exploded into the gray darkness as a hundred giant searchlights pierced the sky.

Directly in front of her a tall row of blood red swastikas stirred as though the breath of the waiting hordes had moved them.

Fanfares blared, and Adolf Hitler strode into the glare of light, his right arm upraised. The response was instantaneous, deafening. The roar burst forth, rising to a crescendo *"Sieg heil! Sieg heil!"*

Behind Kate someone commented loudly about tall foreign women with too much flying hair who impeded the view of the Fuehrer. She felt herself being shoved forward, but there was nowhere to go. A solidly built burgher stood in front of her, feet planted in the attitude of an unyielding oak. Feeling trapped and claustrophobic, she thought perhaps she'd have been wiser to remain at the hotel with her elderly tourists.

The pressure on her back eased. She felt an arm slide

across her shoulders. A voice close to her ear said in English, "It's a bit like watching a volcano erupt, isn't it? Knowing we're all going to boil in the rush of lava, but fascinated by the glimpse of doom."

At the same instant, Hitler ranted about stolen German territory, Danzig, and the Polish corridor. As Kate turned in the direction of the English voice, a wave of mass adulation washed over her and rode forth to spend its energy on the man Germany had proclaimed its savior.

The protective arm across her shoulders was clad in well-cut tweed and was attached to a man carelessly elegant in dress, with that certain composure derived from background and breeding. Despite his apparent youth, his expression managed to look weary and disillusioned, while at the same time his fiercely gray eyes and symmetrical features expressed a controlled energy. Caught in the brilliant light, the effect of this paradox was intriguing. Kate felt as if she were examining him under a microscope.

The immediate impression was of his height, since few men were so much taller than she. The second was that he didn't wear a hat and his slightly tousled brown hair gave him an appealingly nonchalant air that contrasted pleasantly with his immaculately tailored clothes. But that accent was unmistakably upper-class British.

The crowd quieted again as the Fuehrer resumed his speech. Hitler's pictures had not captured fully the intense, burning quality of his eyes. The Charlie Chaplin mustache and errant lock of hair on his brow that in photographs had seemed comical trademarks now appeared more sinister than amusing. His words hurled his hatred at the crowd like a whip, and the effect of his invective was obvious in the frenzied response: *"Sieg heil!"*

Kate's heart began to hammer against her ribs, as if she'd stopped suddenly after a hard run. She felt threatened, violated in some way by Hitler's overwhelming magnetism. She had the unnerving feeling that had anyone uttered a single word of dissent the crowd would have torn the offender to pieces.

The Englishman whispered, "Do you understand German?"

"Enough to know I've seen and heard all I care to. Is there a way out of here?"

"Aha! An American. I thought so."

The burly burgher in front of them turned and scowled a warning to be quiet. The Englishman took her arm and led her through the tightly packed ranks, shouldering his way with an authority that made those in their path move grudgingly aside.

When they reached the thin edges of the Fuehrer's audience, Kate said, "Thank you. I can find my way from here."

He looked at her with an amused, slightly questioning expression that would no doubt wither tradespeople and instill fear into the hearts of scullery maids. To Kate it was a typically supercilious aristocratic stare, but she had to admit that on this handsome face it acquired another dimension. A challenge perhaps. She had a sudden wild notion that it would be interesting to see that face vulnerably asleep, or contorted with passion.

He said, "I hope you're familiar with the streets of Berlin. There are dangers for the unwary here. I doubt that everyone in the city is in the square listening to Herr Hitler's speech. The SS and the Gestapo often use such occasions to remove dissidents."

"I'm a tour guide," Kate answered, and immediately wondered why she felt it necessary to justify herself. "I've taken people all over Europe. Believe me, one learns caution."

"Good. I'm here on business myself and getting more uncomfortable every day with the excesses of the Third Reich. I can't believe the business-as-usual attitude of the rest of the world, in view of the inevitability of war."

"Your Neville Chamberlain doesn't seem to think there'll be a war. He's promised 'peace in our time,' hasn't he?"

"At the moment my countrymen are divided on the issue of Nazi Germany. There are even a few who endorse Hitler."

"Well, be that as it may, thanks for the rescue." Kate started to walk away.

He called after her, "Would you care to join me for a drink? There's a little cabaret I found—"

"No, thanks. I've a big day tomorrow. We're leaving for Switzerland." She felt his eyes on her back as she walked away.

Now why did I do that? she asked herself as she went down the Wilhelmstrasse, turned the corner, and headed for the hotel. He was young, good-looking, and seemed to know his way around. A couple hours' entertainment would be a welcome break from the now tedious round of museums, art galleries, and historic buildings.

> *'Tis fine to see the Old World, and travel up and down*
> *Among the famous palaces and cities of renown,*
> *To admire the crumbly castles and the statues of the kings,*
> *But now I think I've had enough of antiquated things.*

For once she recalled all of the opening stanza of Henry van Dyke's poem.

The street was deserted and she groped for the second stanza as she hurried along. *So it's home again, and home again, America for me—*

But of course it wasn't. Not for another couple of weeks, and then when she returned there would be all the reminders of Wade. No, don't think about him now. Damn him. Damn every man who ever humiliated a woman.

She could no longer hear the loudspeakers blaring forth the Fuehrer's diatribe against the enemies of the Third Reich. Her footsteps rang with a lonely echo among the shadows. She had a foolish desire to whistle the darkness away.

Glancing over her shoulder, she decided the Englishman had been wrong. Everyone *was* in the square. The street was empty. Yet an uneasy feeling persisted. A sixth sense told her she was being followed.

Half a block ahead of her a black Daimler turned the corner. Before the car came to a complete stop the doors opened and four shadowy figures hurtled across the sidewalk toward a darkened shop. The sound of their pounding on the door reverberated down the street.

Kate stopped, unsure whether to proceed.

Seconds later the door yielded to the boots of the first man. They crashed into the shop. Kate hurried on, wanting to be gone before they reappeared. As she neared the shop she saw the window was boarded up. A crudely painted sign explained why: JUDEN.

She was parallel with the shop doorway when two of the intruders dragged an old man into the street. A trickle of blood ran down his forehead, seeping into deep crevices in his cheek. His eyes were bewildered, glazed with pain and shock. He wore a nightshirt. One of his captors shoved a polished boot in front of him and the old man sprawled on the pavement, showing spindly legs and a shriveled torso.

Kate gasped, almost feeling the shock of the impact on frail bones and tired flesh. She reacted without thinking, bending to grab his arm to help him to his feet. At the same time she pulled his nightshirt down over his pathetically defenseless buttocks in an attempt to restore his dignity.

She whispered to the old man lying on the sidewalk, "Are you all right? Can you get up?"

He moaned uncomprehendingly. Kate felt her arms grasped from behind, and she was pulled roughly away from him. The man holding her spun her around. His breath smelled sour. Kate looked into the livid face and yelled, more from fear than bravado, "Let me go. I'm an American citizen."

In reply, she was flung back against the boarded shopwindow. A sharp pain shot down her spine. Dazed, she looked around the group, their attention now riveted on her. The old man still lay where he had fallen, mumbling what could have been a prayer for deliverance.

The four men barked orders at her in unison. "Don't move. Stay where you are. Where are your papers—your passport? No—give me your purse. Keep your hands in sight."

The nearest man snatched her purse and rifled the contents, producing her passport. He flipped it open, held it under the streetlight, and read, "Katherine Kieron, Brooklyn, New York, U.S.A. Occupation, tour guide." He paused, then jerked his head in her direction. "Search her."

"No!" Kate screamed as two of the others closed in. This

isn't happening, she thought as she fought groping hands. None of the accounts of Hitler's Germany appearing in newspapers back home had prepared her for this reality, or for the fact that her American citizenship would not somehow protect her. A quick vision of the German-American Bund marching proudly down American streets to show their support of their Fatherland flickered through her mind like a fragment of an unbelievable nightmare.

She broke away, was caught again, slammed into the wall. Her skull cracked horribly and bile rushed to her throat.

All at once she heard a shouted command, and the melee subsided. She leaned back against the wall trying to catch her breath. As the street came back into focus, she saw that a fifth man had joined the group. He stood in quiet conversation with their leader. Kate recognized him as the tall Englishman. So he *had* been following her.

The two men who had tried to search her now turned their attention to the old man on the ground. They hauled him to his feet and pushed him into the back seat of the Daimler. The Englishman moved to Kate's side, slipped his hand under her elbow. "My dear, this is not the way to meet Heinrich. If you're so intent on it, then I'll give in and take you to meet Herr Himmler tomorrow evening." His tone was amused, but Kate saw a spark of fury in his eyes. He added under his breath, "Are you all right?" She nodded. He said brusquely, "Come on then."

The Germans made no move to stop them as they walked away, Kate supported by the Englishman. "What about the old man?" Her voice was hoarse.

"We can't help him. Keep walking. Don't look back."

"Who are you anyway? My guardian angel?"

He smiled ironically. "I've always admired you Americans for your sense of humor under trying circumstances. My name is Anthony Winfield. Tony to my friends."

"Kate Kieron."

"Well, Miss Kieron, that was a gallant but foolhardy gesture. You must know the situation here regarding the roundup of the Jews. Hitler has made them the scapegoats for all of Germany's woes."

"That was a frail old man. How could he be an enemy of the Reich?"

"You're lucky you're not accompanying him to Gestapo headquarters. American passport notwithstanding."

"Did you follow me from the square?"

"Yes. Some premonition told me you'd get into trouble. Perhaps it's that outraged expression you wear."

"What did you say to make them let me go?"

He hesitated a fraction of a second too long before answering. "Oh, you heard . . . I resorted to name-dropping."

"You don't really know Himmler?"

"I do have a gilt-edged safe-conduct pass I showed their leader." He glanced at her as though assessing her reaction as he added, "An invitation to dinner at the Grand Hotel tomorrow night with several high-ranking party members. You see, my mother has a rather odd coterie of friends, one of whom happens to be Sir Oswald Mosley."

Sir Oswald Mosley! The infamous Nazi sympathizer. Of course, Winfield must be one too. How else could he have rescued her from those beasts?

"This is my hotel," Kate said coldly. "Good night, Mr. Winfield."

As she reached for the door, his hand closed around her wrist. "You're still shaking, and with good reason. A cup of chocolate would help you relax. Come on, there's a little cafe not far away."

Kate's first instinct was to pull away, but he was right. She was too wound up to sleep. Telling herself that if he were a British Nazi it might be satisfying to bait him a little didn't quite disguise the spark of interest, perhaps even attraction, she felt, despite his loathsome politics. There was something about Anthony Winfield that demanded investigation. Some hint of intrigue or mystery that aroused more than curiosity in her. She said, "Okay. You can explain to me how a British aristocrat can possibly admire the sheer brutality of the Nazis."

Ignoring the personal innuendo, he said, "I'd rather talk about you than Mosley." He slipped her arm through his, and she walked beside him, their steps perfectly matched, as

ECHOES OF WAR

if they'd strolled together many times. "You're the first woman I've ever seen try to tackle four men—Nazi or otherwise. I'm impressed. We get the impression in England that America's isolationism borders on the hysterical. That the majority of your people fear involvement in another European war more than they fear that jackboots will march down Fifth Avenue."

"We had to bail you out the last time, remember? At considerable cost to American lives. You're right, we'd prefer to stay out of your territorial squabbles. Especially as they seem to erupt every twenty years—an interval guaranteed to decimate every generation."

"One war, twenty years ago," Tony murmured, opening the door to a nearly empty cafe. He greeted the lone waiter in flawless German, ordered chocolate and cheese, then pulled out a chair at a window table for her. "You're of Irish extraction, of course?"

"Why 'of course'?"

"Auburn hair that shines like a beacon, warning of a temper to match, I daresay. The Irish are the only race who ever achieve that particular shade of fiery splendor."

"I'm American. Third generation. What are you?"

"What indeed. A question I've pondered unsuccessfully for years."

"Are you one of Mosley's gang?"

A mug of steaming chocolate was placed in front of her, along with a plate of bread and cheese. Tony watched her with paralyzing intensity for a moment, as though trying to assess the extent of her interest. "His *gang?*"

"Well, you're in Berlin. You have some influence with the bully-boy storm troopers—or Gestapo or whatever they were—and an invitation to dine with high-ranking Nazis. Back home we have a saying: If it looks like a duck, walks like a duck, swims like a duck, quacks—"

"Yes. I follow your line of reasoning." He sipped the chocolate, grimaced, and said, "Too sweet. I could use a brandy. How about you?"

"No thanks. This is fine. I wonder if we got our Fifth Amendment from your Magna Carta?"

"Fifth Amendment?"

"To the Constitution. The right not to incriminate yourself."

He regarded her with amusement. "I have a feeling I'm going to learn more about the United States than I really wanted to know."

"I guess it wouldn't appeal to you. We don't have anything like the sheer drama and viciousness of the Nazi party to offer. Just Roosevelt's New Deal. We're clawing our way out of the Depression without resorting to an arms buildup."

"So you've made up your mind that I'm pro-Nazi?"

"You haven't denied it."

"No, I haven't. Now let's discuss something more interesting. You, for instance. Are you married, engaged, attached, traveling in tandem, meeting anyone?"

She wasn't aware that she'd looked away from his questioning gaze until he said, "I'm sorry. I'm being presumptuous. I suppose it's the atmosphere in Berlin. The doomsday tension in the air. Makes one cast discretion to the wind and follow wild impulses before it's too late."

"And what wild impulse have you followed?"

"Pursuing an auburn-haired American with sparks in her eyes, for one thing. Common sense tells me this is neither the time nor the place for such encounters, but spirited women have always been a weakness of mine."

Kate was too on edge to flirt. "I hope you find yourself one." She sipped her chocolate. "You're right about the tension. There's an overwhelming feeling of evil here since the Nazis took over. I'll be glad to get the tour group safely home."

"Your last tour to Berlin, I hope. I may not be here to keep an eye on you next time."

"Lucky for me you happened along."

"You think we met by random chance, do you? I'd prefer to believe it was ordained by fate."

There was a certain disarming honesty in his light tone that soothed her Wade-bruised ego. Too bad she was leaving tomorrow. Pro-Nazi or not, Tony Winfield was a damned attractive man. She said, "I'm not much of a believer in fate. We make our own, I think."

"Oh, not entirely. We're all victims of our ancestry, in one

ECHOES OF WAR

way or another. Tell me, which part of America are you from?"

"New York."

"An exciting city. I had a too-brief visit a couple of years ago. I'd like to see it again without the heartbreaking hordes of unemployed. We have the same problem in England, of course."

"But not here in Germany," Kate responded, watching for his reaction. None showed in his expression. He murmured, "No."

The cafe door opened, admitting a gust of night-chilled air and two uniformed storm troopers. They laughed noisily as they sat down and ordered schnapps.

Kate rose abruptly to her feet. "Would you walk me back to my hotel, please?"

They went silently out of the cafe, Kate's mood swinging back to tense edginess. Outside her hotel she stopped and offered her hand. "Goodbye. Thanks for the chocolate."

"May I see you again?"

"What would be the point?"

"I'll think about that and let you know." He smiled suddenly, and all of the cynical weariness vanished from his face, leaving almost boyishly unblemished integrity in its wake. Leaning forward, he brushed her mouth lightly with his lips. "Meantime, try to stay out of trouble, will you?"

[2]

Kate awoke from troubled, half-remembered dreams to the sound of nervous rapping on her door. She sat up trying to recall where she was. She wasn't usually so disoriented first thing in the morning.

As she got out of bed a quick vision of yesterday's trip to the Tiergarten returned, along with the snapping cameras in front of the Brandenburg Gate. The memory of her encounter with the Gestapo agents restored her sense of surroundings more completely, but was quickly eclipsed by the dashing image of Tony Winfield. She allowed herself a small sigh of regret.

Pulling on her robe, she opened the door. Outside, Mrs. Radner, still clad in her nightgown and a woolly robe, regarded her with frightened eyes, lips moving soundlessly.

"What is it? Are you ill? Here, sit down. Now take a deep breath." She helped the old woman into a chair. Mrs. Radner's shallow breathing and dilated pupils were cause enough for alarm, but what she held in her tightly clasped fingers was worse. A yellow arm band adorned with the Star of David. The mandatory accessory worn at all times by German Jews.

Kate pried open Mrs. Radner's fingers. "What's this? Where did you get it?"

Radner? Was that a Jewish name? Would any Jews in their right mind visit Berlin now, even if it was only one stop on a European tour? "Mrs. Radner, where is your husband?"

The woman was a feisty New Yorker, not given to complaints. Her husband was a quiet, withdrawn man, but normally Mrs. Radner made up for both of them when it came to verbal appreciation of their vacation abroad and the "quaintness" of the Old World. Now she appeared drained, lifeless. She whispered, "He never told me. . . . I didn't know. He went to see them late last night. Came back with this arm band. . . . Said their house was deserted, but he was going back to a friend who might be sheltering them."

"Oh, God," Kate said. "You have Jewish friends—relatives—here? Is Mr. Radner Jewish?"

She shook her head. "Not him, no. But his first wife was. He was very fond of her family. They visited each other. Then when his wife was dying, he promised her he'd try to get them out of Germany." She held up the arm band. "I found this stuffed in his coat pocket a little while ago. I'm so afraid."

Kate was already throwing on her clothes. "Where did he go? Do you have an address?"

Mrs. Radner nodded. "He said he'd be back before morning."

"Okay, now listen to me. First write down the address. I suppose there was no phone. Go back to your room and pack—for both of you. The coach will be here in an hour. If I'm not back, I'm counting on you to help get everyone aboard. You're not to wait, you understand? I'll leave Michelle in charge. Under no circumstances are you to let that coach leave without you. I don't want to have to chase you down too. If Mr. Radner and I miss it, we'll catch up with you in Zurich."

"But, what will you do? How—"

"I'll try the address first. If I can't find him there, I'll go to the American Consulate. Don't worry. Your husband is an American citizen. They can't keep him here just because he's got Jewish relatives." She gave Mrs. Radner what she hoped was a reassuring smile. "Chances are, he'll be back before you've finished breakfast."

Mrs. Radner scribbled a name and address on a sheet of hotel stationery and handed it to her. Kate ushered her out into the hall.

Michelle Larson was in the next room. Kate hammered on her door. Michelle was along to learn the ropes, and Kate didn't dwell on the fact that Michelle had been hired as her replacement when she announced her impending marriage. Only now there wasn't going to be a marriage. Formerly, Evans European Tours supplied a male and female guide, but the company, having survived the worst of the Depression years, was now in financial trouble, and women came cheap.

A minute or two elapsed before Michelle opened her door. She always looked as though she should be reclining under the magnolias of some Georgia mansion, surrounded by adoring swains, and this morning was no exception. Kate was irritated by the fact that Michelle had obviously taken time to comb her hair. "What's up, honey? My alarm hasn't gone off yet."

"Trouble." Kate pushed her back into the room and told her in swift whispers what had happened.

Michelle flopped weakly to her bed. "Oh, mercy! I knew we should've skipped Germany. Whatever shall I tell them if y'all don't get back before the bus leaves?"

"Just say Mr. Radner was taken ill. I'm staying with him, and we'll catch up with you in Zurich."

"What about Mrs. Radner? Is she staying with you?"

Kate pondered. That was a problem. A wife wouldn't go on without a sick husband. "No, she's going with you. Better say he has some business. Say anything, Michelle, for God's sake, just get them on that bus."

Michelle chewed on her full lower lip. "I think we should stick together."

"What if Radner has been arrested? What if he had some crazy idea he could get his relatives out with our group? The Gestapo might think we're all in on it, using the tour as cover for a smuggling ring. No, you've got to get them to Switzerland." The vision of Radner as some latter-day Scarlet Pimpernel was ludicrous, but people had a habit of fooling you.

"I don't like it, hon," Michelle was saying as Kate disappeared through the door.

The address Mrs. Radner had given her proved to be in a run-down section of the city: a grim row of older houses with age-darkened bricks and sloping roofs. She was deposited in front of a house that seemed normal, unviolated. She had half expected to see splintered wood and broken windows. There was no response to her knock. After a few minutes she went to the house next door. The lace curtains at the window moved almost imperceptibly. Kate felt the scrutiny of unseen eyes. A moment later the door opened a crack. A middle-aged woman regarded her suspiciously. Without waiting for Kate to ask, the woman said, "They're gone away. I don't know where."

She began to close the door, but Kate's hand stayed its progress. "Please, Fraülein, a moment. Did you see a friend of theirs—an American—last night? Did he come over to inquire about them?"

The woman shook her head and slammed the door, missing Kate's fingers by a fraction of an inch.

A harried young consular official was trying to answer the telephone and sort through a stack of official documents while at the same time dealing with Kate's frantic pleas. "Yes, Miss Kieron, I understand your concern. But you've very little to go on. Under normal circumstances, the first thing to do would be to file a missing persons report with the police, but in view of what you've told me—"

"You're afraid the Gestapo have him."

"No, no. Nothing like that. We need to find out where he is. We can't do anything until we know for sure where he went. He may have committed some civil crime."

"He's a well-to-do retired executive, not some criminal. When will you know something?"

He shrugged helplessly and said into the phone, "Yes, yes, I'll do what I can. We've been inundated with requests for visitors' visas."

Replacing the receiver, he looked at Kate. "File a complete report with my secretary, then take my advice and get

ECHOES OF WAR

your group the hell out of Germany. There's going to be a war soon. I can't believe how blind everyone is. We've watched Hitler gobble up Austria and Czechoslovakia and know damn well he wants Poland."

"But we're Americans. We won't be involved in a European war."

He gave her a pitying glance. "That's what we thought last time."

"I can't leave Berlin without Mr. Radner. I'm responsible."

"I'll try to get some information for you by tonight. You understand that we have to go through diplomatic channels? But I'll get some unofficial inquiries started too. Where will you be?"

Fighting a rising sense of frustration, Kate gave him the name of her hotel, filled out a form for his secretary, and left.

She stopped for breakfast at a small cafe and spent twenty minutes watching the passing parade. So many uniforms, so many swastikas. Yet there was a sense of order and purpose that had been missing the first time she visited Berlin. Could that have been six years ago? Like Michelle, Kate had been an eager young apprentice on her maiden voyage. She smiled wryly at the thought. She'd been eighteen, passing herself off as twenty-one.

Sipping the scalding black coffee, she willed herself to remember Berlin rather than Wade, but of course that was impossible.

He'd been traveling with his aunt. Wade Lowery at that time was a student at the Sorbonne but confessed to being more interested in the American literary and artistic expatriates of the Left Bank. He had taken great delight in getting Kate to slip away late at night for private tours of the seamier Berlin cabarets. She had been shocked by the glimpses of depravity he'd shown her: a transvestite ball; the leather-clad, whip-wielding prostitutes of both sexes parading their wares openly; cabaret waitresses who allowed customers to slip their hands into their silk panties in full view of other patrons.

Hitler had swept all of that away with his New Order.

Kate wondered what Wade would think if he could see his

decadently wicked Berlin now. The pain was still almost unbearable when she thought of him. If only that long-ago tour had been the end of it, she could have remembered him with sweet nostalgia as her first, lost love.

But they'd met again three years later when he returned home to New York. There'd been a brief, intense romance that ended when she refused to have an affair with him. After he left, she thought the pain would never end, but it eased with the passing of time. Yet when she ran into him again—was it only six months ago?—all the old magic flared to life.

Walking back to the hotel, Kate tried to concentrate on the missing Mr. Radner, but Wade's image kept intruding, his voice whispered at the back of her mind: "Okay, Kate. I guess I've got me an old-fashioned girl who won't give in without the orange blossoms and ring. Let's set the date."

It was a date he hadn't kept. But he'd at least had the decency to tell her in time to cancel the church ceremony and return the gifts. She'd been grateful for the opportunity to escort this tour to Europe. Time to sort things out before she had to face family and friends.

Back in her room she paced restlessly. The day was overcast, with rain clouds nudging the tops of buildings. Michelle had evidently been successful in getting everyone, including Mrs. Radner, aboard the coach. Kate felt deserted, isolated, somewhat martyred.

At four o'clock in the afternoon her phone rang. It was the consular official. "I'm afraid Mr. Radner was picked up by the SS for questioning. We're in touch with the Embassy."

"The SS? Oh, no!" Kate heard the rising panic in her voice.

"Please, keep calm. No charges have been filed yet. Miss Kieron, we strongly urge that you rejoin your tour group. Let us handle this matter."

Kate stared at the telephone for a minute after she replaced the receiver. He was right. What could she do? Perhaps if she waited until morning, the Consul would know something.

At five-fifteen the phone rang again. The resonant voice and Oxford accent were unmistakable. "Tony Winfield here.

You know, I did tell those Gestapo blokes we'd be dining with the top Nazis tonight. You're not going to make a liar of me, are you? You may never have another opportunity to see the German leaders at play. I could pick you up in an hour."

The thought that this man had friends in Nazi high places who might be able to help Radner stifled the refusal that came automatically to her lips. She paused, wondering if she'd be able to keep from telling Tony Winfield and his Nazi buddies what she thought of them. At length she said, "I'll meet you in the lobby in an hour."

She looked at her suitcases and thought about the wrinkled results of her hasty packing.

Her white silk jersey probably wasn't too crushed; it would have to do. Peering at herself in the steamy bathroom mirror, she decided she looked too pale, so she dabbed lipstick on her little finger and outlined her cheekbones. "You've got good bones, Kate," Wade had told her. "You'll improve with age, like good wine."

She sat on the edge of the bed and carefully rolled her stockings up her legs. Very good legs, long and slim and well shaped, complementing a good figure. A figure that was her undoing. Men looked at it and wanted to get her into bed. If that was what Mr. Nazi Sympathizer Winfield had in mind, he was out of luck.

Grabbing her wrap, she went down to the lobby. He was standing near the elevators, under a chandelier of cut crystal that blazed its brilliance over a scrolled ceiling.

Tony Winfield in evening dress was attracting the attention of every passing female. Even standing still, he conveyed a sense of movement and vigor that contrasted in a strange and exciting way with his wearied expression. On those sculpted features the apparent exhaustion had the effect of arousing immediate interest. Kate wondered how many women had sought to assuage that spiritual weariness only to find themselves overwhelmed with animal energy.

His hair gleamed, light brown with gold lights, and there were gold flecks in his gray eyes, flickering like sunspots, she realized as she drew closer. Had he taken pains with his appearance in order to present that immaculately handsome facade? Was he bent on seduction? Berlin was full of flaxen-haired beauties. Why would he bother with a snub-nosed upstart from Brooklyn?

"Good evening, Mr. Winfield."

He raised her outstretched hand to his lips, and the gesture almost disarmed her. Drawing her arm through his, he said, "Might we get on a less formal footing? Tony and Kate? After all, I told our hosts that we're old friends."

"Sure, but I have to be honest. I'm here with an ulterior motive. I'm hoping you can use your Nazi connections to help me with a little problem.

"I've lost one of my tourists," she said as the waiting Mercedes glided away. "He's been picked up for questioning."

Tony gave her a quick sideways glance. "How very careless of him. So that's why you accepted my invitation. Tell me about your missing tourist."

Kate explained, and he said, "I'll see what I can do. Now tell me about Kate Kieron. You evaded my questions rather skillfully last night."

"Me, evade? Next to you I'm Miss Blabbermouth of 1939. Besides, there's nothing to tell. I leave for Switzerland tomorrow, all being well, then on to England."

"Ah, so you'll be in my homeland. Where will you be staying?"

"We'll be on the move and I won't have time for personal gallivanting. The only reason I'm not working tonight is because of Mr. Radner."

"Must you be so distressingly blunt? Couldn't you at least pretend you're here because I invited you—perhaps even acknowledge that glimmer of attraction that took place when we met."

"What glimmer? You picked me up."

He winced. "So be it. I'm not sure why you're being so hostile, but I suspect I'm catching it for someone else's misdeeds."

That hit too near the mark. Kate said quickly, "Who's giving this party we're going to? Himmler?"

"The Goerings, actually. Himmler will be there, and there's a possibility the Fuehrer himself will drop in. The guest of honor is Sir Oswald Mosley. Too bad you're leaving, or I could perhaps have wangled a weekend at Obersalzberg—Hitler's Eagle's Nest. A wonderful spot: backdrop of mountains, clean air. Only his closest friends are invited there."

"And you're one of them, I take it."

"He'd like me to be. And at present it suits my purpose not to discourage the overtures. I have business to conduct here."

"Tell me, what do the Nazis hope to get in return?"

"If Hitler can get those members of the British aristocracy who are sympathetic toward him to pledge their support before he grabs any more territory, he won't have to worry about England being a thorn in his side. I might add that there are Englishmen of even greater stature than Mosley involved—whom I'd better not name. Not to mention some leading Americans who have been vocal in their pro-Nazi support—your aviator-hero Lindbergh for one."

"I hope you're not comparing yourself to Lindy."

Tony smiled. "Hardly. But I do share his love of flying. Been a member of the Aero Club for years."

Superimposed over his evening clothes, Kate envisioned flight jacket, helmet, goggles, and a white silk scarf flapping in the breeze. Yes, it was exactly the right image, and damn him for being a Nazi and spoiling it for her. "Well, I want you to know I wouldn't be hobnobbing with any Nazis if it weren't for Mr. Radner."

"You've already made that abundantly clear. I trust, however, you'll keep your political opinions to yourself this evening."

She looked at him curiously. "If you were afraid I'd put my foot in it, why did you invite me?"

"You mean apart from the fact that I'm attracted to you? I suppose because I detest Mosley's radical females and am intimidated by most German women, but dislike being an odd male at a dinner party. There, how's that for honesty?"

"Fair enough. Although I can't imagine you being intimidated by anyone. Do you really think Hitler will drop in? I may make some faux pas if he does, out of sheer terror."

He smiled. "He's not quite as dynamic when he doesn't

have a crowd in front of him. It's incredible how he whips a crowd into a sort of orgy. A pent-up sexual tension that builds to a cataclysmic climax—a kind of oratorical ejaculation."

Kate swallowed, somewhat dismayed by the turn of the conversation.

Tony went on: "He draws his dynamism from the mobs of people. René Schnickele, the writer, once compared Hitler's speeches to sex murders. He uses speech as a sexual surrogate and once referred to the masses as his 'only bride.' "

"But you said he's quite different away from them?"

"Left to himself, he exists on dull films, endless performances of the *Meistersinger,* and positive gluttony when it comes to chocolate confections. His conversation is mostly about architecture."

"Sounds like you know him well," Kate said uneasily as the Mercedes stopped before the canopied, red-carpeted entrance to the Grand Hotel. "Are you sure they'll let me in? I mean, who am I to get to meet Hitler?"

"They'll let you in. I told you, Hitler has an all-out campaign on to seduce the British aristocracy into supporting him. He mistakenly believes I'm a member of that aristocracy."

"Are you saying you're not?"

"No, I'm not." A faint pulse flickered in the region of his temple, as though the admission was painful. Kate wanted to ask what it was that troubled him and why he was involved with these gangsters when he was so obviously a decent and honorable man. But he was already out of the car, coming around to open her door, and the moment was lost.

[3]

A polite murmur of conversation, unpunctuated by laughter, and muffled by thick carpets and the paneled walls of the banquet room, floated over Tony's head. He felt the tenseness that preceded any appearance by the Fuehrer. It was evident in glances darted toward the double doors, in surreptitious straightening of ties and uniform tunics. The women patted their hair nervously and moistened their lips.

Tony watched the doors too, waiting for Kate to return from the powder room. Frau Goering, an attractive former actress, appeared. Kate was behind her.

For Tony, only Kate was distinct. Beside the solidly built German hausfraus and the thin, intense British fascist women, Kate was a sleek racehorse, beautifully formed, long-legged, tossing her fiery mane impatiently as though prancing at the starting line. After a man recovered from the impact of her figure and graceful carriage and managed to tear his eyes away from her body to her face, he supposed her eyes were her best feature. Kate wasn't beautiful, but there was an appealing vigor about her, an eagerness in her expression and blazing honesty in her dark blue eyes that would be more enduring than mere beauty.

At his side, Sir Oswald Mosley said, "Who is that Amazon in white, Tony?"

"My companion for the evening. An American. I'll intro-

ECHOES OF WAR

duce you later." Tony moved toward Kate, not wanting to discuss her with Mosley, and caught a warning glance from Charles Morcambe indicating that Charles felt he was again showing his dislike of Mosley and his fawning over Nazis. Which, of course, he was. Sir Oswald's intellectual and rhetorical skills were undeniable, but Tony abhorred the direction they had taken.

Goering regaled Mosley and his entourage with boastful descriptions of the Luftwaffe, while they listened with their usual wide-eyed wonder. A jovial man, Goering was more interested in his airplanes than party ideology. Later, after the new acquaintances had been accepted or rejected, the chosen would repair to Goering's fairy-tale estate, Karinhall, to continue the party, probably through the weekend.

Kate moved among the uniformed Nazis and expensively gowned women with an air of bravado. Only a slight downward cast to her eyes betrayed her real feelings. Tony had already assessed her as being a woman recklessly brave, hot-tempered, but a champion of underdogs and the helpless. Lord, he thought, does she need someone to look after her, protect her from her own valor. At this point in my life, he decided regretfully, I'm the last man on earth for the job.

"I was afraid you'd draw me into that circle around Goering," Kate said when he reached her. "He's the best of the bunch, but what a windbag. Himmler and Goebbels give me the creeps."

"Better keep your voice down. Some of the Germans and one or two of the Englishmen understand American."

She laughed. Charles Morcambe pushed through the crowd to her side and said, "Glad someone is happy. The rest of the guests seem afraid to laugh aloud. If they don't serve dinner soon, I for one am going to end up blotto. I simply can't keep up with our hosts."

Tony said, "There'll be an end to the drinking once the Fuehrer arrives. He doesn't drink or smoke but usually arrives late enough to give everyone a chance. If he's coming for dinner, don't expect much until we get to the dessert. He's a vegetarian."

Charles turned to Kate. "Is this your first visit to Berlin?" His eyes were extraordinarily pale and seemed to vanish behind his steel-rimmed glasses. With his slight build, rounded shoulders, and somewhat crumpled air, he gave the appearance of a contented professor. Which, Tony reflected, was probably why he'd got the job he had.

Kate replied, "No. I've been here several times. Are you and Tony old friends?"

Charles said brightly, "Oh, yes. We go back to Eton—winning battles on the playing fields and all that rot. Of course—"

Tony decided he'd better cut that off right away. He said, "Kate and I have a favor to ask of you. She's a guide and one of her tourists seems to have got himself in a spot of bother. I'll give you the details later." He added to Kate, "Charles is with the diplomatic corps, presently attached to the Embassy here."

Charles peered at her. "Yes, of course."

One of the uniformed German officers edged through the guests toward them, smiling in recognition as he caught sight of Tony. The young officer's features appeared more French than Aryan, with a strongly dominant nose and hooded eyes.

"Wolf!" Tony exclaimed in genuine surprise. "When did you join the army?"

"Quite recently. It seemed to be time. Besides, I was getting bored with my civil service job. And you, Tony Winfield, what have you been up to since we met at that somewhat memorable cabaret? Aha! What's this?" He reached behind Tony's ear, and a large silver coin appeared in his fingers.

Tony laughed and turned to Kate. "May I present Wolfgang von Klaus—Oberleutnant von Klaus, I see. Wolf, this is Miss Kieron. I believe you already know Charles." The German clicked his heels and bowed to Kate.

Charles had enough aplomb not to show any surprise at Wolf's unexpected appearance in uniform.

Tony said, "We met Wolf when he managed to quell a near riot in a cabaret one night. The patrons didn't care for the entertainer, a rather vapid tenor with a wobbly voice, and

ECHOES OF WAR

Wolf took over with a dazzling display of magic tricks—for an amateur." He glanced sideways at Charles, wondering what he would do now for a civil service contact.

Charles said, "Wolf, if you've got a minute later on, I'd like to have a word with you—" He broke off as all conversation around them died. Hitler had arrived. The room seemed to reverberate with a silent fanfare.

Kate watched, mesmerized, as Adolf Hitler moved toward her, shaking hands and smiling. Hermann Goering presented his guests to the Fuehrer. Oswald Mosley was evidently an old friend; Charles Morcambe was a newcomer. What am I doing here? Kate thought. I must be dreaming this. Me, Kate Kieron of PS 32, whose old man was a cop, and who never made it past high school.

In the instant before Hitler reached them, Kate wished passionately that Tony Winfield would not prove to be, like Oswald Mosley, an old friend of the Fuehrer. But Hitler shook Tony's hand, murmured that he was glad to see him again. Kate didn't offer her hand when she was presented to Hitler. She'd seen him kiss the hands of the other women and was filled with revulsion. If he touches me, I'll shudder for sure, she thought.

Luckily she was the last person to be introduced, and since the first course of the dinner arrived at the same moment, she was spared more than a perfunctory greeting.

Seated between Charles Morcambe and Wolfgang von Klaus, now a model of decorum in his Fuehrer's presence, Kate was scarcely aware of what she ate.

As conversation around them grew more animated, she whispered to von Klaus, "Does Herr Hitler always come alone? Doesn't he ever bring a girlfriend?"

He gave a particularly wolfish leer and replied, "He's got a bit of stuff he keeps out of sight. Her name is Eva Braun. A rather vacant young woman. Personally, I'd make her disappear in a hurry."

"I'll take that as a magician's turn of phrase, rather than a literal one," Kate said.

Tony, across the table, caught her eye and smiled. Her reaction to seeing him chat amiably with Frau Himmler and

Frau Goebbels, on either side of him, elicited a sense of unreasonable disappointment, considering her own exchange of small talk with Wolf von Klaus. Telling herself she had no real interest in the man and that it wouldn't matter if he turned out to be one of Mosley's lunatic fringe did little to ease her disillusionment.

When the meal ended she dutifully trooped behind the women as they departed for an adjacent lounge, leaving the men to their cigars, brandy, and politics. Adolf Hitler's departure had taken place the second after a spectacular chocolate dessert was finished. Kate noticed Wolf von Klaus had disappeared too.

One of the women asked if Kate was a member of the German-American Bund in America, and she replied that she was a dyed-in-the-wool Democrat and hoped Franklin Roosevelt would live forever. The woman gave her a blank stare and began to gush about Frau Goering's gown. Kate escaped to the rest room. She hoped Tony was briefing Charles Morcambe on Radner's predicament.

Emerging, she found Tony waiting for her. "Where's your wrap? We're leaving," he said as soon as she appeared.

"No goodbyes? Isn't that a bit gauche?"

"I've already explained that you have to catch up with your tour group."

Kate's Spanish wool shawl was easily found among the furs in the cloakroom.

When they were in the Mercedes speeding through the city, she asked, "What about Mr. Radner?"

"I'm taking you to him."

"Now?"

There was an unexpectedly harsh note in his voice when he replied, "Now. I hope you're as cool and collected as you were at dinner."

"Why?"

He didn't answer as he jammed on the brakes, turned off the ignition, and jumped from his side of the car. The building they had parked beside looked ordinary enough. A downtown office building. Then she saw two uniformed men come out of the front doors and caught the lightning flashes of their shoulder insignia. SS. The building, with its brightly lit windows, suddenly took on the appearance of a chamber of horrors. But perhaps that was her imagination. It hadn't occurred to her that Tony would actually take her to Gestapo headquarters. She'd had some vague idea that Radner would meet them somewhere, perhaps at the hotel.

She went reluctantly into the building at Tony's side. Music was coming from a radio somewhere. Wagner, she thought, but wasn't sure, because her heart had begun to pound.

Tony ushered her into a waiting room on the ground floor: fairly comfortable-looking chairs, end tables, lamps. "No magazines?" Kate asked with a faint grin.

"Wait here." He gave her a hard sideways glance before leaving and closed the door firmly behind him.

Too nervous to sit down, Kate walked small circles around the room, remembering every dentist's waiting room she'd ever been in, all at once amazed that she had believed she knew dread before this moment. She was hard put to remember that *she* hadn't done anything, wasn't awaiting interrogation. The minutes dragged by.

When the door opened again at last, she was ready to scream with tension. Tony held Mr. Radner's arm. The old man looked pale, his eyes sunken and smudged with fatigue, but he was apparently none the worse for his encounter with the Gestapo. He nodded to Kate in dumb acknowledgment of her presence. She didn't have to be invited to leave. Taking his other arm, she almost yanked him out into the corridor.

There was a staircase leading to the upper floor, just a few feet from the waiting-room door. Someone was crashing down the stairs screaming—an inhuman cry of terror that assaulted every nerve in Kate's body. She stopped and turned toward the sound, her mouth open, winded as though from a blow to the stomach.

If he hadn't been stark naked, she wouldn't have known the sex of the creature falling down the stairs. His face was a pulpy mass of bone and tissue, hair covered with blood. He was bruised and burned all over his body, and one arm hung at an odd angle. Hard on his heels were two men in civilian clothes. They grabbed him and dragged him back up the stairs.

Frozen to the spot, Kate thought she would either faint, vomit, or scream. Perhaps all three. Waves of dizziness washed over her and she gasped for breath.

Then Tony was half carrying, half pulling her through the doors into the reviving air. No words were exchanged until they were in the Mercedes. Kate leaned back against the upholstery fighting for breath, her tears drowning her. In the back seat Mr. Radner muttered, "Monsters. They're not human. Oh, God . . . they're monsters."

Slowly Kate's head rolled around until she was looking at Tony. "You . . . you filthy . . . rotten . . ."

He looked at her out of the corner of his eye. "Me? I'm the one who got your tourist out of there, remember? Now, I'll drive you to —"

"To our hotel, to get our bags," Kate snapped. "Why should we be grateful for being allowed to leave? Why should we be grateful to you? You're a friend of those murdering thugs."

"I'm as appalled by the brutality as you are," Tony began, but Kate was too angry to let him finish. "Tell me, how did you get Mr. Radner out of there?"

She saw Tony's hands tighten on the wheel. His jaw moved slightly. "What does it matter? He's free, isn't he?"

"A note from Himmler maybe?" Kate suggested. "As a favor to his English fascist friend. You're a bloody Nazi yourself. Go ahead, deny it."

"Why bother? You've already made up your mind."

Kate slumped back in her seat, feeling sick to her stomach as the reaction to what she had accidentally witnessed set in. Neither Tony nor the interrogators at Gestapo headquarters could have known that one of the prisoners would break free at that particular moment, or she would undoubtedly have been left to wait in the car. But to Kate the incident was another sign that she should end her brief acquaintance with this man. Tears scalded her eyes and she choked them back, along with the knowledge that if it hadn't been for Tony, Mr.

Radner's visit to Berlin might have ended tragically. She said heavily, "You could at least say you're neutral."

He gave her a hard sidelong look. "I'll do better than that. I'll tell you what you want to hear. Yes, I'm definitely pro-Nazi."

Never force a showdown, Kate thought. You never get what you want when you do. Damn, how could a man who looked so good be so rotten at the core? Worse, how could she have been so attracted to him?

He stabbed the brakes and the car stopped abruptly. Kate looked out of the window. "This isn't our hotel."

"It's the railway station. Charles Morcambe is waiting for you. He has your tickets."

"I can't travel in these clothes."

"He also has your baggage. Don't argue. Go." He reached across and opened her door, turned to the passenger in back, and said, "There isn't much time, Mr. Radner."

Kate suddenly felt the tension and sense of urgency between the two men. Mr. Radner scrambled out of the back seat as Tony shoved her out of the car.

The Mercedes slid away as Charles Morcambe materialized at Kate's side. He flung a raincoat over her shoulders, linked his arm through hers, and propelled her rapidly into the station. Despite his age and recent shattering experience, Mr. Radner was a couple of steps ahead of them.

Before a burst of steam from an incoming train obscured her view, Kate had a quick glimpse over her shoulder of a second car as it turned the corner and followed Tony's Mercedes. "Is that—" she began.

"Tony can handle it," Charles said. "Look sharp now. Your train's in."

Yes, Kate thought, Tony Winfield could certainly handle anyone who was tailing him. All he had to do was call one of his party-boss friends. Still, he'd been gentleman enough to lead their pursuers away from herself and Mr. Radner. For that Kate could be grateful even to a pro-Nazi Englishman.

[4]

The rolling meadows of southern England were a welcome respite from the glare and glitter of London. Kate leaned back, head on a starched white antimacassar in the first-class railway compartment. She watched the pastoral scenes flit past the windows, glad she was done with cities for a while.

The English itinerary included Stonehenge, Stratford-on-Avon, a castle, and a stately home. As usual, too much in too little time. But Kate had been glad of the hectic pace of Switzerland and London. She hadn't had time to dwell on the nightmare of Berlin. When Tony Winfield intruded into her thoughts, she merely reminded herself of her propensity for finding unsuitable males.

Opposite her, the Radners sat close together, still clutching hands as they had since they were reunited in Switzerland. Mr. Radner hadn't said much about his brief incarceration, but he still seemed shaken by the experience.

Two of the male tour members in the compartment were arguing about the situation in Germany. A raised voice cut into her thoughts. "... And I say Hitler's got the right idea. You can feel the sense of order there—the riffraff off the streets. And damn it, what's wrong with that? So he's a military dictator. We've got a benign dictator in power back home."

"Christ! Some of you Republicans are nearly as far to the right as Genghis Khan, never mind Hitler."

"You don't really believe Roosevelt can keep us out of a war?"

"Sure. Didn't he cable Hitler and Mussolini asking for a pledge not to attack any European or Middle Eastern country for ten years? In return he promised a world conference on disarmament and international trade."

"Uh-huh, ignoring the fact that Hitler and Mussolini have already made conquests. Besides, there's been no response. And won't be. Hitler knows he's got Roosevelt bamboozled, and Daladier and Chamberlain are fools hell-bent on appeasement."

Kate tried to shut out the voices by concentrating on the peaceful beauty of the English countryside. Time enough to listen to the strident voices of isolationism when she returned home. American eyes were fixed on Europe with both dread and fascination. Few people expressed admiration for either England or France, perceiving them as decadent colonial powers, but there was openly expressed wonder at how Hitler had ended Germany's economic woes. She wished some of Hitler's admirers back home could have been with her in Berlin to witness the price Germany was paying for economic recovery.

As the train began to slow down, the conductor walked along the corridor, announcing that they were coming to the village of Middle Knole. "That's our stop," Kate said, and stood up to begin retrieving bags from the overhead rack.

Michelle informed the group that they were in the county of Buckinghamshire, north of the Thames, known for the fertile Vale of Aylesbury. "William Penn is buried at Jordans, John Milton wrote many of his lyric poems at Horton. Oh, yes, and Stoke Poges was the scene of Thomas Gray's 'Elegy Written in a Country Churchyard.' "

As the train came to a halt, Kate went to the carriage door to be the first to alight so she could help the others down to the platform. The incident in Germany had been horrifying, but she suspected her irritability had its roots at least partially in her encounter with Tony Winfield. There'd been a moment, when he rescued her from the storm troopers, that she'd realized, for the first time since Wade, that there were other men on earth.

Bright spring sunshine washed the walls of Cardovan House, with its bay windows and raised stone terrace running along the east wing. The tour bus was a jarring note parked under the trees bordering the drive. Hundreds of bright yellow daffodils nodded on a steeply sloping bank to the left, while beyond the trees Kate could see the turrets of a medieval church.

She stood staring at the house as the group uncoiled arthritic limbs and proceeded to inch their way down the aisle of the coach.

Since Cardovan House had not been on any of her previous tours, she was unsure how to proceed. Her tour group had been scheduled to visit another of Buckinghamshire's stately homes, but that had been cancelled because of restoration work in progress.

By the time the crocodile of tourists was wending up the driveway, a uniformed footman had appeared at the top of the terrace steps. They were conducted into the north hall. An awed gasp whispered through the group as they were confronted by a staircase of inlaid oak with a delicately wrought balustrade of a floral design that was repeated in wall designs of stucco in surrounding alcoves and above a fireplace. The floor was black and white marble.

A woman wearing a black dress with a lacy jabot at the throat awaited them, scrutinizing each member of the group as though they were in a police lineup. As the footman departed, she announced, "I am the housekeeper here at Cardovan House. I'll be conducting you on your tour. Please stay together and remember that the family is in residence. I'll tell you which rooms you may enter."

They dutifully trooped after her in tight formation as she went on: "This is the home of James Philip Barry Richard, Sixth Earl of Hardmoor. There are a hundred rooms and an indoor staff of thirty-nine."

Following her group into the library, Kate was as overwhelmed as any first-time tourist. She'd seen plenty of other stately homes, some even grander than this, but there was an atmosphere here as though the house beckoned to her alone, laying out its glory for her approval.

She moved through the library almost in a daze, trying to make sense of her feelings, and eventually found herself lingering on the flagged terrace, ostensibly waiting for the stragglers, but actually reluctant to leave the serenity of the setting. She walked slowly, trailing her hand along the cool smooth stone of a giant urn filled with as yet unblooming roses. The air tasted of dew-washed grass and wood smoke and was filled with the fragrance of spring blossoms and trees stirring from winter slumber in cool dark woods.

At the end of the terrace she stopped and looked across the rolling lawns to a geometric placement of topiary shrubs. A pathway winding through a rose garden ended at a copse of sycamore and elm.

The strangely disturbing feeling persisted. Contentment, peace, sadness, joy—a yearning for something that had no name. Not exactly déjà vu, but a feeling that all her life she had been waiting to stand on this very spot, feeling that particular breeze ruffle her hair, tasting the clean gentle air. Spring, she told herself sternly. That's what it is. That and what Wade Lowery did to me.

Behind her a voice said softly, "At least you find my home attractive. Could you be persuaded to return this evening and meet what I laughingly call my family?"

She spun around and looked disbelievingly at Tony Winfield.

He wore gray flannel slacks and a white shirt, no coat or tie, and looked more handsome than any man had a right to be. There was no surprise in his expression, he looked at her as though he had been expecting her.

"Your home? But I thought the Earl of Hardmoor—"

"Lord Winfield. My father."

"Then you also have a title?"

"No, I'm . . . his adopted son. We're a somewhat unusual family. You might find us interesting if you'd do us the honor of joining us for dinner this evening."

"Are you telling me you somehow contrived to have our

tour switched to Cardovan House, just so you could see me again?"

His smile was warm, frank, and totally disarming. "I did indeed."

"Then you wasted your time. My feelings about Nazis haven't changed since Berlin. If anything, I feel more strongly than ever. You're a bunch of slimy sadists, lower than a snake's belly—"

Tony held up his hand in mock alarm. "Please! I loathe Nazis as much as you do, if not quite so eloquently."

"That wasn't what you told me in Berlin. You said you were definitely pro-Nazi."

"In Berlin I'd have told you anything to protect your pretty hide. And, I might add, mine. So long as they—and you—believed I was one of Mosley's boys, neither of us was in danger."

"But . . . I saw you . . . talking to Goering and Hitler."

"The only reason I went with Mosley that night was because you'd tangled with the Gestapo, and they had your name. What do you suppose would have happened had you then barged in—forgive me—in your rather hotheaded fashion to try to rescue Radner?"

"You didn't know about Radner when you called me."

"Oh, didn't I?" He smiled enigmatically. "Kate, you never gave me a chance to explain that while on the surface I appeared to be consorting with the Nazis, in actual fact I abhor their doctrine. I'm not even a political animal. I'm a banker."

Kate looked into his eyes and saw absolute sincerity there. She felt a rush of relief and at the same instant a snapping of her self-imposed restraints on her feelings toward him. Tony Winfield was a man who could make a woman forget every other man she'd ever known. At the back of Kate's mind hovered a wild desire to cable Evans European Tours and tell them Michelle was bringing the group back while Kate remained in England.

Tony said, "Mosley is an intellectual who probably could have done great things in England politically if he hadn't been sidetracked into fascism and anti-Semitism. He's my mother's friend, and she rather enjoys shocking everyone with her Bohemian coterie. Anyway, I looked up Mosley in Berlin because my friend Charles Morcambe wanted to meet him. Look, it's a bit complicated. You'll understand in time."

"In time?" Kate repeated, liking the feeling of continuity in his tone, flattered by the way he looked at her, and overwhelmed by the amount of trouble he'd gone to in order to meet her again.

"I hope we'll see one another frequently in future, Kate. I'm not usually this impulsive, and Lord knows your arrival in my life isn't quite as convenient as I'd have liked, but I've thought of you constantly since Berlin. I want to get to know you. I want you to know me. If I'm wrong in assuming that you do have a bit of interest in me, then please forgive my diverting your group to my home. Although I believe you'll find Cardovan House most interesting. We still have secret rooms where the Royalists were hidden in Cromwell's time, while all they have at your scheduled stop is haunted plumbing."

Kate laughed, thinking that she could go on listening to his resonant baritone forever. He lounged against the great stone urn on the terrace, the sunlight outlining breeze-tossed brown hair and emphasizing tautly muscled forearms where he'd rolled up his shirtsleeves.

The collar of his shirt was open, and Kate caught herself glancing at the blond hair that curled against hard pectorals. The occupation of banker didn't fit. His body was too well tuned for a sedentary life. He looked capable of climbing a mountain or running a marathon. Adventurer, explorer, aviator—spy? Now where did that idea come from?

Misinterpreting her appraisal, Tony said, "Excuse the casual attire. I went for a walk to pass the time while you toured the house."

"I'd love to come to dinner," Kate said quickly, "but I'm a working woman."

"By the time your old ladies have staggered back to the charabanc they'll be done in. We can trot them around the topiary garden to make sure, if you like. Then your assistant can supervise high tea and tuck them in their beds at the inn. Say you'll come, please. I'll send a car for you at seven."

"Well . . ." Kate had already capitulated in her mind, but she enjoyed keeping him waiting one more second before agreeing, mostly to keep that eager expression on his face.

Out of the corner of her eye she could see Michelle herding the last of the group toward the bus, but Kate lingered, reluctant to leave.

Following the direction of her glance, Tony said, "Kate, you won't be going back to Germany, will you?"

"I go where I'm sent. If enough people want to go—"

He caught her hands in his, and the pressure of warm fingers against hers sent a flood of awareness through her body.

"Don't go back," he said with an urgency that surprised her. "We're possibly only weeks away from a war—three months at most. The whole damn world is ignoring Hitler's threats, even though he's spelled out his goals very clearly in *Mein Kampf*. He'll gobble up continental Europe. The Maginot Line is a relic of another time. Goering's Luftwaffe will strike at France and the Low Countries by air, and there isn't a country in Europe capable of stopping them."

"What, not even England?" Kate's tone was light, because she didn't want to contemplate the inconceivable horror of war.

"Well, a rather remarkable aircraft designer has come up with a superb plane called a Spitfire—quite revolutionary in design. Unfortunately, we only have eight or nine of them built so far and nothing in the way of anti-aircraft guns to speak of. And if there was mass mobilization of an army, there wouldn't be enough rifles to arm them. We have the Royal Navy, of course. But that's all we have."

An uneasy picture of Tony issuing a sharp command to the storm troopers to release her—moving among the Nazi leaders, completely at ease—flashed into her mind. The information about England's inadequate defenses, Tony's insistence that war was imminent . . . Would an ordinary citizen be privy to such inside information? A faint suspicion that Tony Winfield was not what he seemed again flared to life.

ECHOES OF WAR

"I'll try to avoid Germany," Kate promised. "But right now I'd better go count my tourists, in case any of them are hiding in your secret rooms."

At six o'clock that evening, while Michelle was pressing the wrinkles from her evening skirt, Kate tried to tame her hair. "It's no use. I need a whip and a chair," she groaned.

"With your gold lamé blouse and my moiré skirt, no one is going to notice anything but the *color* of your hair," Michelle said. "The gold lamé will make you look like a warrior maiden."

"You don't think it will be too much? Maybe my white jersey—"

"No. You wore that in Berlin. He's seen it."

"He knows I'm a working girl." Kate fingered her blouse.

Michelle sighed with extravagant abandon. "The prince and the pauper. It's so romantic."

"He's only the son of an earl and I'm not exactly a pauper. He doesn't seem to use a title. What do you call the son of an earl, anyway?"

"Kate, you'd better get into this skirt if you want to be ready in time. Personally, I won't relax until you're on your way. One of the group is sure to come down with galloping plague if you try to take another night off."

Precisely at seven, Kate was assisted into a Rolls-Royce Silver Ghost by a uniformed chauffeur. Michelle's evening skirt was too short, ending well above Kate's ankles. She was acutely aware that her own peau de soie pumps were a different shade of black and slightly scuffed.

The chauffeur's attitude and disdainful glance confirmed her fear that the evening was going to be a disaster.

[5]

Cocktails were being served in the drawing room. Waiting to enter, Kate was grateful for the reassuring pressure of Tony's hand under her elbow. A uniformed footman, splendidly medieval, had taken her shawl, laying it across his arm with the same care she saw him give a sable coat slipped from the shoulders of a guest ahead of her. Shimmers of light from the chandeliers picked out diamonds adorning elegant throats, danced on champagne glasses, and added sheen to satin gowns as women moved about the room greeting friends.

Feeling like Cinderella at ten past midnight, Kate had a wild desire to hitch up her skirts and flee, convinced she stuck out like a duck among the swans. She was surrounded by doll-pretty faces, sleek coiffures, and real gemstones. Apart from her ill-chosen outfit, her hair was a mess, but she couldn't wear the smooth short styles. On her they turned into a bush. Only by allowing her hair to grow at least to shoulder length did the frisky curls fall into softer waves. Her features, she'd long ago decided, were beyond the help of cosmetics.

Incredibly, Tony didn't seem to notice her shortcomings. He whispered, "You're going to enchant them. Especially Cecilia."

"Cecilia?" It came out somewhere between a croak and a hiss.

"My mother. Here she comes."

A tall woman with magnificent upswept hair, set off by a simple black gown, detached herself from a trio of intensely conversing men and skimmed across the polished oak floor toward them with a dancer's grace. Twinkling hazel eyes were taking in every detail of Kate's appearance, but Lady Winfield wore an approving smile. She seized Kate's hand in a warm clasp even before Tony finished introducing them.

"Delighted you could come, my dear. Anthony told us you're brave, witty, and charming; but he didn't tell me you're *tall*. Thank God I'll have another woman around at last who can look me straight in the eye!" Tony's mother laughed, a full-bodied sound that warmed the heart.

Kate felt some of her trepidation vanish.

"My dear Kate, you must call me Cecilia. Everyone does, including Anthony here, who hates to be called Anthony. Come along, I'll whisk you around for introductions. You won't remember a soul, but don't worry about it, because they certainly won't forget you."

Kate followed in a pleasant daze, smiling and offering her hand, since it seemed to be expected. On closer inspection, she saw that the other guests were a diverse group, despite their well-dressed appearance. Kate had been around enough people to realize that Tony had been right about his mother's friends. She evidently collected interesting characters.

There was a brooding-eyed poet, sundry members of the aristocracy, several shifty-eyed young men who looked as though they were planning to blow up the Houses of Parliament, and an assortment of Cecilia's relatives, including a handsome fiftyish man, introduced as her cousin Clive, who apart from Tony was one of the few men taller than Cecilia. There was also Sir Oswald Mosley, several of his English fascists, and the pale-eyed Charles Morcambe.

Tony hovered near, and when the introductions were complete, he placed a glass of champagne in her hand. Raising his own glass, he said, "To the fates who ordain first meetings."

Crystal rang as they touched glasses lightly.

Tony added, "Now, having been given the opportunity to know you, I intend to take full advantage of my good luck. Tell me about your family and home and—Oh, damn it, what I really want to know is is there a fiancé lurking on the horizon?"

"My father was a New York City cop—policeman—retired early because of illness. Mom thinks I'm an old maid." Kate took another sip of champagne. "Incidentally, I'm the world's easiest woman to ply with liquor. Only trouble is, I get belligerent rather than romantic usually. So please don't let me get into any fights."

Tony smiled. "Sounds like a clear case of Irish ancestry."

"Uh-huh. Want to get into the home rule question?"

"Absolutely not. Better men than I have spent seven hundred years on it without coming up with an answer. You carefully avoided my question about a fiancé."

Kate studied a large painting hanging over the fireplace, a portrait of Cecilia in her youth. Stunningly pretty, her theatrical presence was almost captured on canvas. Kate said, "There was someone. It's over now. How about you?"

"*Amourettes,* as the French call them. No one who stayed."

"Your father isn't here. Will he be joining us later? I've never met a real live earl."

Tony's jaw moved slightly, as though to stifle a comment. "No. He doesn't care for Cecilia's friends. Nor does he spend much time here. My sister will be here soon, however. She's quite an accomplished pianist and has been giving a charity concert up north."

"What about you? What do you do at your bank? Foreclose mortgages on widows and orphans?"

His eyes rolled upward. "I work for a merchant bank, sometimes known as an acceptance house. It's rather complicated and quite boring. We carry on transactions in the monetary settlement of foreign trade. I work in several continental countries, not just Germany."

A butler announced dinner, and they followed the stream of guests into a dining room where even larger chandeliers spotlighted silver dishes and crested cutlery.

Tony belonged in this house, she decided: it was both as handsome and substantial as he. The house and the man gave the impression they would always be there, strong and protective. She decided to forget her probably unfounded suspicion that international banking was a good cover for the movements of a spy. He ignored Mosley and his fascists completely. As they took their places at the table, she said, "You're very lucky to live here."

"It is a rather gracious old house, isn't it? Kate, I should explain about my father . . ."

Whatever he was going to say was forgotten as a young woman ran into the room, clouds of delicate purple chiffon floating behind her. "Sorry, Cecilia, I honestly intended to be here an hour ago."

Kate's first thought was that, judging by the jewels, makeup, and hairdo, the woman could have pared an hour from her primping time. She was startlingly pretty, with yellow-gold hair and a complexion that bespoke misty English rains and absolutely no exposure to the sun.

"My sister, Ursula," Tony murmured as the vision in purple bent to kiss Cecilia's cheek, then whirl into a chair. He called to his sister, "Ursula, say hello to Kate. You can meet her properly later." They exchanged nods in the second before the first course was served.

Several times during the meal Kate felt Ursula's eyes on her, and although the glance seemed almost accidental and was fleeting, it somehow made Kate again aware of her unfashionable hairstyle and slightly tarnished lamé blouse. She had the feeling that when she stood up, Ursula's eyes would go immediately to the gap between her hem and shoes.

Dinner was delicious, belying the reputation the English had for incessant boiled potatoes and overdone beef. Kate was hard put not to smack her lips over salmon in aspic, spring lamb with new peas, as well as a succulent ham.

When they were finished, everyone drifted back into the drawing room. There was no separation of male and female guests. When Cecilia finished eating, she led the way. Her cousin Clive was at her side, and Kate saw her laugh delightedly at something he whispered to her. Brandy and liqueurs were served and the conversation grew more animated.

Ursula was quickly surrounded by young men, and when Tony drew Kate into the circle around his sister it seemed to Kate that a spark of frost appeared in Ursula's eyes.

"Are you on holiday in England?" she asked, and Kate guessed from the quick sideways glance Tony gave that Ursula was well aware why she was in England.

"No, I'm working. Tour guide. My group's staying at the inn."

Ursula looked at Tony. "Surely you're not planning to take a tour. What a busman's holiday that would be!"

Everyone except Tony smiled. Kate felt as though her face was permanently frozen into an inane grin. Tony said, "With Kate as my guide, I'd be tempted. But I'm going back to Berlin next week."

Behind them voices were suddenly raised in argument. Sir Oswald Mosley said loudly, "You, sir, are an anarchist. You have a hatred of *all* governments—all government policies."

"And you, my friend, have been bamboozled by that strutting little dictator."

"Have you visited Germany lately? Have you *ever* visited Germany? Do you know what it used to be like—the currency fluctuations, the utter debauchery—"

"And are you aware what replaced the utter debauchery, as you call it? Storm troopers, book burnings, a shackled press. Now Hitler's locking up minorities, homosexuals; and, it's rumored, the mentally and physically handicapped are being put to sleep like unwanted animals. I know all about the Fuehrer's New Order."

Cecilia moved swiftly to join the group. She was like a referee, Kate noted, keeping the lid on tempers, conceding points, thoroughly enjoying herself. Clive watched her as an indulgent father might watch a precocious child.

Tony said to Kate, "Would you like to see the gardens? Sounds like the oldest ploy known to mankind, I know, but the grounds are particularly lovely in the moonlight. The topiary shrubs especially."

Kate quickly agreed. She wasn't comfortable with political arguments, which in her family often led to brawls. Tony slipped her arm through his and led her from the room. Kate noticed the frown that appeared on Ursula's lovely face as they left.

In the hall a footman was dispatched to bring her shawl to ward off the night chill, and as Tony wrapped it carefully around her shoulders she thought it might be easy to get used to such pampering.

Strolling through the shadowed grounds, past the carved topiary shrubs that seemed like real animals silently keeping vigil, Kate was overwhelmed unexpectedly with sadness. They walked through the rose garden, which was not yet in bloom, but she seemed to sense the memory of its fragrance from past summers.

Tony said, "I ordered a nightingale to sing in the woods, but apparently he's forgotten. Come back in a month or two and the roses will break your heart."

There had been the scent of roses in the air the night Wade had asked her to marry him. Had he asked, or merely conceded? Kate turned her head so Tony wouldn't catch the tear that glistened suddenly on an eyelash. "It's so peaceful here." There was a slight catch in her voice. "It would be easy to stand on this spot and imagine the earth's as lovely as God made it."

She felt his hands on her shoulders turning her gently to face him. He raised one hand and wiped away her tear with his thumb. "Whoever he is," he said softly, "I want to kill him."

"Who?" The word trembled on her lips.

"The man who hurt you. I recognize fresh wounds when I see them."

"Oh, I've managed to staunch the bleeding. I wasn't thinking about Wade, honestly. I can't explain what it is about Cardovan House. It seems to have cast a spell over me."

"Then you must come back soon. So his name is Wade. And although you weren't thinking about him, your voice breaks when you say his name."

She tried to think of a way to change the subject, but when she looked up into his face he lowered his head and kissed her.

ECHOES OF WAR

His lips were warm, only slightly parted, questioningly. The kiss wasn't passionate, yet she was aware of passion held in abeyance. Their lips touched for only a moment, but she was breathless when he released her. His hand traveled to the nape of her neck, and he ran his fingers through her hair.

"I love your hair, Kate. How wonderful to be able to grab a woman's hair in this age of shorn locks and Eton crops. Will you come back, please?"

"I'll be sailing on the *Queen Mary* next week, and I'm not scheduled for another European tour for months. I expect I'll be spending my time in the New York office trying to drum up business."

"Is there a possibility you'll see Wade when you go back? Should I try to put you out of my mind?"

"No to the first and probably yes to the second. But thank you for inviting me tonight. In the future, whenever I have insomnia, I'll think about the gardens—the sense of tranquility here."

He played with a strand of her hair. "There's a better cure for insomnia and for what ails you. When you fall off a bicycle, it's best to get right up and ride again. Why don't we begin an *amourette* to take your mind off Wade?"

"Is *amourette* a euphemism for affair?"

"Sometimes. Or it can become a grand passion, or a lasting friendship. In your case, I suspect you're not ready for more than an *amourette* just now, and under normal circumstances I'd court you with subtle finesse. Unfortunately we don't have time for that. Don't go home, Kate. Stay with me. Let's find out what's causing this magic when we're together."

Kate had a sudden notion that it would be nice to lay her head on his shoulder, to trace with her fingertip the smoothly chiseled contours of his face, to say, Yes, to hell with convention, let's find somewhere private and make love. Slow down, a warning voice insisted, don't let Tony sweep you away, you're too vulnerable yet.

"Tony, I—"

She didn't get a chance to finish, as footsteps clicked across the terrace above them and high heels ran down the steps. Ursula called breathlessly, "Anthony, where are you? Oh, there you are. Listen, there are two men here who insist on seeing you. They're in the library and they look suspiciously like CID men to me. You haven't been—" she broke off, peering through the darkness at Kate, still in the circle of Tony's arms.

Embarrassed, Kate pulled free, feeling more like she'd been caught in a stolen kiss by Tony's wife than his sister. But perhaps it was only the pale moonlight that seemed to etch those lines of jealous disapproval on Ursula's face.

Tony laughed. "CID? Hardly, old girl. Did they give their names?"

"I don't know, Cecilia spoke to them. She told me to find you. But I saw them. They looked horribly official. And Charles tried without success to talk them into coming back tomorrow."

Tony linked arms with the two women and walked them back up the terrace steps. Kate was aware of the slight tenseness in his arm, despite his unhurried pace. CID? Criminal Investigation Department? No, Ursula would be wrong about that. But official-looking men? Could they be from the English equivalent of the State Department; and were Tony's Nazi connections the reason for the visit? With Mosley and his gang of fascists present, why was Tony being singled out for questioning?

[6]

Kate rejoined Cecilia and her guests, who seemed unaware that Tony was closeted in the library with two official-looking men. Or perhaps they were merely exhibiting typical British control. Mosley was still arguing with the anarchist. Ursula went to a grand piano in the corner of the drawing room and began to play a Chopin waltz.

Cecilia drew Kate aside. "Come and sit on the sofa with me, my dear. I've been dying to talk to you all evening, I mustn't miss this opportunity. I'm quite sure my son will monopolize you again when he comes back."

"He isn't in some kind of trouble, is he?" Kate asked.

"Oh, I shouldn't think so. Anthony is the most stable member of the entire family."

It wasn't the most reassuring of statements, in view of the missing earl, his wife's odd friends, and the fact that Ursula had abruptly switched from Chopin to jazz and was now on her feet, dancing wildly up and down the length of the piano as her hands flew over the keyboard. Cousin Clive was stacking crystal wineglasses in a precarious pyramid on a glass-topped table. A young man leaned on the piano and watched Ursula with adoring eyes.

Cecilia glanced in the direction of her daughter and said, "Rodney Davenport is going to propose to her, but she

ECHOES OF WAR

won't marry him. Tell me, Kate, are you going to marry my son?"

Startled, Kate replied without thinking, "I was going to be married to someone back home, just before I came on this trip. He . . . We cancelled the wedding at the last minute."

"But how wonderful!" Cecilia exclaimed.

"Wonderful?"

"Catastrophically wonderful. Dissolutions always are. Endings signify new beginnings."

"I suppose you're right, in some strange way." It was the first time anyone had so casually dismissed the aching void Wade had left. Curiously Kate felt comforted.

"How *do* you feel about my Anthony?"

"We've only just met. He helped me out of a fix in Germany. Frankly, I didn't expect to see him again."

"But you must know how smitten he is with you?"

"I'm afraid you're imagining more to our acquaintance than there really is. Besides, I'll be three thousand miles away in a couple of weeks."

Cecilia seemed to be gazing at some point beyond Kate, perhaps into her own memory, as she said softly, "It's so terribly easy when one is young to let love slip away unnoticed. I'm afraid it's one of the crosses we bear in our maturity—recognizing it too late."

Kate knew her cheeks were scarlet, not so much from the older woman's assumptions about Tony and herself, but from the acute pain that flickered briefly in Cecilia's lovely eyes. Kate felt like an unwilling witness to something intensely private.

Sensing her discomfort, Cecilia laid her hand on Kate's arm. "The Winfields have the perfectly dreadful habit of saying exactly what's on their minds. Forgive me, my dear, but do try to accept it as more a deep concern with the state of humanity than any social eccentricity."

"I'm fairly outspoken myself," Kate responded smiling. "I believe we'd get along just fine. I'm sorry I probably won't see you again."

"But surely you'll be back with your tourists. If not to see Anthony, come to see *me*, Kate."

ECHOES OF WAR

"I have a feeling that Americans won't be doing much touring in Europe soon, thanks to Herr Hitler."

"Oh, the fascists are just boys, playing at their martial games. Overgrown boy scouts. Men are obsessed with finding new ways to govern themselves. Fascists, communists, anarchists—they come and go. Look at Sir Oswald. Everyone laughs at him behind his back. It's the reason I invite him to my parties; we have such lovely arguments, quite entertaining."

"Hitler's fascists don't seem quite so benign," Kate began, but there was a hideous crash from the direction of Clive's pyramid of glasses. Cecilia rose reluctantly. "Oh, dear, I must go and commiserate with Clive. He'll feel terrible. He doesn't usually drink—and shouldn't—but he's been acting strange lately. *Everyone* has been acting strange. I mean even more than usual. Excuse me, Kate."

The instant Cecilia left her, Ursula ended her piano recital and walked across the room to Kate. "Are you staying overnight?" The inquiry seemed abrupt.

"No, I'm not. I have to get my tour group on a bus early tomorrow morning."

"I was just thinking, if Anthony's going to be busy for a while and you wanted a car to take you to the inn, I could send for one."

The dismissal was obvious. Up close, Ursula's prettiness was marred by a downward turn to her mouth and a certain lift to her chin that suggested vanity. Kate usually avoided snap decisions about people, but decided it would be easy to dislike this woman. She said, "No, thanks. I'd like to see Tony before I leave."

Ursula shrugged. "Up to you." She remained standing, looking down at Kate. "He doesn't usually go for your type."

"Oh?" Kate felt her hackles twinge slightly. "What type is that?"

"No offense, but Anthony likes beautiful women."

But I *am* offended, Kate thought. Over Ursula's shoulder, she saw Tony reappear. He smiled and waved to her, then went to Charles Morcambe and whispered something to him.

Morcambe nodded and left the room. The incident was over in a minute, but Kate thought, Conspirators, those two are up to something. At the same instant the image of Tony shaking hands with Hitler, moving easily among the Nazi leaders at the Grand Hotel flashed into her mind.

The frown on Ursula's face vanished as her brother approached. "Glad to see you two getting to know one another. Hope you've managed to show Kate we can act like normal people when we choose. I've been on pins worrying about Cecilia's menagerie scaring her off. Good lord, what happened to all those glasses?" He was looking at a maid clearing the remains of Clive's pyramid.

Ursula gazed adoringly at her brother. Pity the woman he marries, Kate reflected. Ursula will devour her. Tony said, "We're going to roll up the carpet and put on some gramophone records. Do you like to dance, Kate?"

"Love it," Kate answered, jumping to her feet. "I do a wicked rhumba."

Except for a slow waltz with his mother, Tony danced exclusively with Kate. He was easy to follow. Smiling down at her, he said, "People will swear we choreographed this. You're a wonderful dancer and you've no idea how marvelous it is to dance with a woman of the right height. I have a theory that height matching should be a prerequisite for lovers too."

At midnight she regretfully announced she'd better get back to the inn. She made her goodbyes, and Anthony took her to the garage. She was glad when he opened the passenger door to a modest-looking Morris and then got into the driver's seat himself. They drove slowly down a moonlit country lane.

"I'd have picked you up myself too, but I'd been warned I might have a visit from those two blokes. I'd hoped it would be over before you arrived. I'm sorry for leaving you to the tender mercies of our friends. They're a circus, aren't they? And Cecilia is the ringmaster. Poor old Clive would have to pick tonight to fall off the wagon, as you Americans say."

"Who were the two men? Or isn't it any of my business?"

"Just a little business matter. The way things are in

Germany at the moment, my bank has to be extremely careful."

"Ursula seemed worried that you were being investigated in some way."

"Ursula lets her imagination run away with her." His mouth clamped shut in a way that disturbed her. *He's hiding something, and why am I so curious about what it is?*

Parking the car in the courtyard of the inn, he shut off the engine and turned to look at her. "Let's not just be ships that pass in the night, Kate. Let's decide here and now that we met for a reason, and see each other again so we can discover what it is."

This time she was prepared for his kiss. She leaned forward and felt his breath against her face, his hands in her hair. She parted her lips and responded in a way she would have thought impossible only hours ago. A moment later she resisted a sudden impulse to guide his caress to a more intimate spot. A clamor of warning voices in her mind restrained her.

Too soon after Wade. This is the proverbial rebound. You'll be hurt again. Why would someone of Tony Winfield's background want you for anything beyond a brief affair? Run, you fool.

Pulling away, she said in a shaky voice, "Good night, Tony. Thank you."

"The evening isn't over yet." His hand lingered on her cheek, tracing small circles with a gentle finger.

"Yes, it is. It has to be. And so is our brief but exhilarating acquaintance. I'm sorry. I'm just not ready for a new man in my life yet, even if there wasn't such a distance involved."

She fumbled under her seat for her purse and her fingers closed around a piece of cloth. Pulling it slowly into the light, she held up a yellow arm band marked with the Star of David.

There was an awkward silence. Then Tony said, "Now where the devil did that come from?"

Kate said in a small tight voice, "Since you're not Jewish yourself, it was obviously worn by a German Jew. And as it's no longer on his arm, I guess the Gestapo have him. I

ECHOES OF WAR

was right about you all along, wasn't I? You are a Nazi, just like Mosley. How else could you have gotten Radner out of Gestapo headquarters? You probably picked up the arm band on some occasion you went along to see how they handle their scapegoats."

She flung the arm band in his face and shoved open the car door, all of her horror and revulsion over the Nazi treatment of the Jews returning.

He caught her before she reached the inn door. "Kate, you're dead wrong about me."

"Yeah? What about the men who came to see you tonight? Can you deny they were from your Foreign Office? That you were questioned about your activities in Berlin?"

"No, I can't. Nor can I tell you where I think that yellow arm band came from. All I can do is ask that you trust me and not ask questions I'm not at liberty to answer."

"What you do is your affair, but the people I choose to associate with is mine."

"You're surely not going to end a promising relationship because you found an arm band in my car? What has it to do with us?"

"Everything, Tony. I can't separate a man from his philosophies; and yours don't seem too reassuring. You're either a Mosley or a Chamberlain—neither of whom appeals to me—so let's call it quits right now."

"As you wish," he responded stiffly. "I'm not ready to explain my every action either. Perhaps it's as well we've revealed our flaws before we get too hopelessly involved. Have a safe journey home."

He turned and walked back to his car, and Kate had to force herself to go into the inn. Damn, *damn*. All he had to do was explain how that yellow arm band got there. Sometimes principles were a heavy burden to carry. She knew that if she hadn't still been aching somewhat from losing Wade, she could have cried over Tony. But perhaps she'd already exhausted her supply of tears.

[7]
August 1939

Ireland was a misty green smudge along the horizon. Kate stood on deck in a light drizzle and watched the land draw closer. She hoped France would be basking in summer sunshine. They'd be in Cherbourg tomorrow.

Her fingers drifted to the collar of her raincoat, slid inside, and found the cool gold of her locket. It was an antique, heavy, ornate, with unused places for pictures inside. It had arrived just before the *Queen Mary* sailed to take her home last spring, along with a note:

Kate, Cecilia would like you to accept this as a token of Winfield friendship. She says only a tall woman can wear it and that she no longer cares to draw attention to the wrinkles in her neck. Incidentally, it's supposed to be a good luck piece, guaranteed to ward off danger. (If you'd like to hear the entire legend, drop in at Cardovan House next time you're in England.) Meantime, remember what I said about choosing your destinations carefully. Bon voyage,

Tony

Funny how three months later Tony's face was still so clear in her mind. Kate had given up speculating as to why Tony had written the note rather than his mother, or whether the invitation to return to Cardovan House was from him or Cecilia. Kate was so confused about him. Apart from his unacceptable politics, she was convinced she would be asking for another dose of heartache. Tony wasn't likely to want a permanent arrangement, and she was afraid she wouldn't be able to back away first, to avoid the hurt.

Preparing for this new tour, Kate had worn the locket. It was a lovely piece that seemed to go with everything, and besides, it was a gift from Cecilia, who, Kate felt, didn't quite understand the true nature of fascism. She merely found Sir Oswald Mosley an interesting dinner companion.

Then too, if the locket really was a talisman to ward off danger, well, it wouldn't hurt to have it along on a trip she was more than apprehensive about. Despite Hitler's assurances that he had made his last territorial claim in Europe, storm clouds continued to gather there.

"Miss Kieron, there you are. I've been looking all over the ship for you."

The voice belonged to a Midwestern widow on her first voyage. Mrs. Myrna Maynard clutched the polished rail as the liner rolled slightly. "I was wondering about France. My late husband was there in the Great War, and he told me . . ." —she paused and looked around— "that the French don't have separate toilets for men and women. . . . And you know I've not been well."

Kate put Tony Winfield out of her mind and turned her attention to business. Mrs. Maynard, a gauntly handsome woman, had been marking time since leaving New York rather than enjoying the crossing. Kate worried that the woman's present problem with her bowels as they neared landfall was a symptom of nervous anticipation. But of what?

At the same time Kate was standing on deck watching the Irish coastline, Tony Winfield was aboard a German train thundering through the night toward the Belgian border. Beside him sat a woman dressed in a black cloth coat, wearing a felt hat with veil, beneath which her face was pale, haggard.

The other passengers in the compartment dozed or swayed, mesmerized by the movement of the train and the staccato rhythm of wheels on track. Belgian and German newspapers, tucked into bags and coat pockets, headlined the announcement of the Russo-German Pact and Ribbentrop's impending visit to Moscow. Since the French and British military missions were still in Moscow trying to avert this dreaded development, Tony avoided looking at newspaper headlines, knowing they would cause a spark of anger that might diffuse his concentration on the problem at hand.

He glanced sideways at his female companion, sending her a silent message of encouragement. Her eyes, heavy with fatigue and glazed with memories too frightful to contemplate, beseeched him, *Don't let it happen to me.*

She seemed more elderly than middle-aged, although he knew she was barely fifty. Her oval face and great haunted eyes had once been beautiful but now were blurred with pain and bewilderment. How could this be happening to her, to her family and friends? What had they done to deserve such hatred? How could human beings do this to one another?

Tony was well aware of how much it had taken to shatter her faith in humanity. That was what amazed him most about these particular German citizens. The fact that they refused to believe that what was happening was real, until it was too late. Or almost. He leaned close to her and whispered in German, "We'll cross the border in ten minutes. Are you all right?"

She licked her lips nervously and nodded.

Tony fixed his gaze on the empty blackness of the train window. Charles Morcambe would have been furious if he could see him now, risking their operation for this woman, whose name certainly wasn't on Charles' list; especially now that Wolf was no longer able to supply travel documents.

Musing silently on the circumstances of this trip, Tony told himself again that he wasn't really risking his hide to prove something to Kate Kieron. God knew he might never see her again. But if they made it across the border tonight, wasn't it possible that the American, Radner, would let Kate

ECHOES OF WAR

know that Tony Winfield, her Nazi sympathizer, had rescued his sister-in-law from Berlin? Probably not. Kate and Radner's guide-tourist relationship had been a tenuous one and no doubt long since severed.

The irony of the situation was that the yellow arm band Kate had found in his car had been pressed into Tony's hand by Radner that night in Berlin. Radner had whispered to him, "There's only my sister-in-law left. Her husband and son are gone to work camps. Please, you have friends in authority. Help me get my sister-in-law out."

Radner had taken her to a safe place and then made the mistake of returning to her house to pick up some of her personal belongings. That was when the Gestapo picked him up.

The train had begun to slow down. Frau Mermelstein looked ready to faint at any moment. Tony squeezed her arm reassuringly and she attempted a small smile.

Recalling Kate's outrage at his Nazi connections, Tony wondered again why he hadn't simply told her, Look, we aren't all oblivious to what's happening to the Jews in Germany. We're getting as many legal emigrants out as possible, and more than a few are being smuggled out illegally.

It wasn't just that he'd sworn an oath of silence about their operation, delicately fronted as it was by Charles Morcambe's diplomatic status and Tony's international banking connections. There was also a perverse desire to have Kate recognize him for what he was, without explanations on his part. Tony had never expected to fall so suddenly or so hard for a woman, and when it happened he found himself wanting more from her than it was probably possible for any woman to give.

The train's wheels squealed on the tracks as the brakes were fully applied. Frau Mermelstein jumped, startled, and cast a frightened look around the compartment. The other passengers were fishing in pockets and handbags for their papers.

"Steady," Tony murmured. "Remember what we rehearsed."

ECHOES OF WAR

She nodded, pulled a man's handkerchief from her purse, and clapped it to her mouth and nostrils.

The train door was yanked open, sucking in a blast of night-chilled air. A nervous-looking conductor climbed aboard, closely followed by two men in dark uniforms.

Damn, they were still on the German side of the border. Those were SS, not the expected Belgian customs officials. Why the hell were they stopping the train, unless . . .

The conductor demanded everyone's papers, took them without examining them, and passed them to the two Germans. Tony waited until they were only one seat away from him before casually pulling two passports from his inside pocket. Frau Mermelstein coughed into her handkerchief.

The first German scrutinized both passports, glanced at Frau Mermelstein, then back at Tony. "Your destination, Herr Winfield?"

Tony replied in German, "My mother and I are returning from a holiday in Berlin. We planned originally to visit friends in Belgium before returning home, but my mother became ill. How long will the train be held up here? I'm quite anxious to get her to our doctor."

The German was examining Cecilia Winfield's passport and glancing up, trying to peer into Frau Mermelstein's face. He had already studied them longer than previous passengers. Between the veil and handkerchief, Frau Mermelstein's face was effectively hidden. The first German handed back the passports and began to move on, but the second said quietly, "Herr Winfield, will you please ask your mother to remove the handkerchief from her face?"

Frau Mermelstein began to cough harder. Tony said in English, "Mother, I'm sorry, dear, but they can't see your face." He flashed the Germans a hard, exasperated look.

All attention in the compartment was now focused on them. Frau Mermelstein went into a paroxysm of coughing, choked, then flung the handkerchief down on her lap. It was smeared with blood. At the same instant, Tony reached into his pocket for a clean handkerchief, pulled it out, and spilled the contents of his wallet. Two snapshots fell to the floor.

The closest German bent to retrieve the pictures. One

showed Tony standing to the left of Sir Oswald Mosley, who was gazing with admiring eyes at Hitler and Goebbels. The second showed Tony in conversation with Goering.

The other German tugged at his sleeve and jerked his eyes in the direction of the bloodstained handkerchief. Tony thought, That's right, you fine specimens of Aryan manhood, translate the coughing and blood to tuberculosis and get the hell off the train.

For a moment nobody moved except Frau Mermelstein, who snatched Tony's clean handkerchief and dabbed her nose. A second later there was a commotion outside, shouts from further down the platform.

Their passports were flung at them as the conductor and the two Germans leaped from the train. Minutes dragged by before the conductor returned, slamming doors. The whistle blew and the wheels again began to grind down the tracks.

Tony let out his breath slowly and said a silent prayer for the poor devil for whom the SS had been searching. At the same time he made a mental note to tell Charles Morcambe that one of his much-maligned plans for all contingencies had at last been put to use.

Charles Morcambe was waiting for Tony when he reached the Croydon aerodrome. Charles' eyes behind his steel-rimmed spectacles glittered like cut glass. "I hear you added an uninvited guest to our list."

They walked behind the disembarking passengers headed for customs.

"You never cease to amaze me with what you know," Tony responded.

"It's immaterial now. You've made your last run. I suppose we should be thankful it wasn't your last in more ways than one. You were a fool to risk it without Wolf's help. That damn fool shouldn't have given up his cushy civil service job to join the army. Wonder what came over him?"

"You mean my services are to be dispensed with just because I—successfully—brought out a personal friend?"

"The woman in question was met in Brussels by an American named Radner. The same Radner extricated from

Gestapo headquarters last spring. You got her out to impress your American girlfriend."

Kate Kieron in all her fiery splendor—impudently curling lips that begged to be kissed, long legs that Tony had fantasized gripping his body—materialized again in the part of his mind she had made uniquely her own. After three months' absence she still ignited unbridled lust in him that perhaps would have diminished had he not also been intrigued by her personality. He'd once been privileged to meet the American aviatrix Amelia Earhart, and he recognized the rare adventurer quality she possessed as being present in Kate.

"As a matter of fact," Tony said aloud, "I haven't seen my American girlfriend, as you call her, since last spring."

"I see. It's strange that she's docking at Cherbourg tomorrow aboard the *Ile de France,* isn't it?"

Surprised, Tony asked, "How do you know?"

"I checked on her whereabouts after I learned your Frau Mermelstein had been met by Radner. I wondered about the extent of your involvement with the Americans."

"Kate's arrival now is a coincidence. I didn't know, Charles, honestly. But in any case, surely a successful escape isn't sufficient reason to get rid of the best man you've got? How many of your other people not only have international banking connections but also Nazi and neo-Nazi acquaintances?"

"Beside the point now. We've run out of time."

"What do you mean?"

"Hitler's going to march on Poland. It's almost a certainty, despite Chamberlain's views to the contrary. We expect we'll have to honor our Polish treaty within days."

"I wonder where Kate's taking her tour group," Tony mused.

"She's American. She won't be in any danger."

"Bombs and bullets don't discriminate between enemy and neutral. And Kate's fighting Irish blood is sure to get her into trouble. Listen, Charles, can you get me an itinerary of her tour?"

"If you wish." Charles gave him a particularly penetrating

sideways glance. "I remember your mother making a remark at that dinner party last spring. She watched you and Kate disappear into the garden and said, 'I was always afraid this would happen; and now that it has, instead of anxiety I feel only envy.' "

"Did Cecilia explain herself?" Tony asked lightly.

"Oh, yes. She said you were a man born out of your time. She felt you were too much of a swashbuckler for modern times. Too reckless, too brave for your own good. For a split second I was afraid you'd told her about your activities in Germany. Then she said, 'Ursula and I always knew that if Tony found a woman as full of daring as himself, we'd lose him. God help him and Kate. I hope they survive knowing one another.' "

"That remark sounds more like a product of Ursula's imagination than Cecilia's."

"Tony, you do understand that I'm here to tell you that my organization no longer requires your services?"

"I've been duly sacked, never fear."

"What will you do now? You won't have much to do with German banking any more."

"Join the RAF, if war comes. His lordship might as well get something in return for all those expensive flying lessons."

"It's none of my business, but why do you treat him like some kindly guardian who is completely unrelated to you?"

Tony's fist clenched around the handle of his travel-worn bag. He knew better than to give Charles the satisfaction of getting a reaction out of him. He said indifferently, "You're quite right, Charles. It's none of your business. Why don't you wait in the car while I go through customs?"

The conversation with Charles Morcambe returned to Tony's mind when the Royal Air Force recruiter looked up from his application and said, "You haven't stated your father's name."

There was no one else in the office. Behind the recruiter, on a file cabinet, a battered-looking wireless played dance music by Ted Heath's band. The recruiter looked scrubbed-clean and eager.

"I don't know it," Tony replied. "I was born to my mother before her marriage. My birth certificate bears only her name."

There had been a time when he would have died a thousand deaths before admitting it. When he cringed every time Cecilia referred to him as her "love child." Oddly, it had been her husband who put a stop to it. "Don't punish the boy for his parents' misdeeds, Cecilia," he'd said.

They hadn't been aware that Tony was in the hall below as they walked along the gallery. The seven-year-old boy had frozen in the shadow of an alcove and listened.

His mother's voice had been icy. "I don't know what you mean, James."

"There's no need to constantly remind the boy of his illegitimacy. Can't you see how confused he is? You insist that he calls us both by our first names and keep reminding him that I'm not his father. He'll be going away to school soon. I believe it's time I formally adopted him, don't you?"

"Is it Anthony you don't want reminded, or yourself, James?"

"For God's sake! Can't you see what you're doing to him? To you he's a badge of honor, the symbol of your flouting of convention. Woman in charge of her own fate, an end to double standards. But the world isn't ready for it, Cecilia. Don't make the child suffer because you don't want to conform to society's standards."

The brief illuminating scene had taken place so long ago. Tony believed he had shown them both how little his beginnings mattered by living his life as if he'd been nobly bred—striving to be best, first, the instigator, the innovator, the leader. As if being a bastard guaranteed a charmed existence. He had never understood his feelings toward his parents, wondering why he didn't love his mother more and his adoptive father less. But Tony was never able to resolve his ambivalent feelings toward Cecilia, or his desperate need to have James admire him.

Ted Heath's dance music intruded into his reverie. Blinking the RAF recruiter back into focus, Tony wondered if he should produce his adoption papers. "Is illegitimacy a problem? Does it void my pilot's license?"

ECHOES OF WAR

Embarrassed, the recruiter shook his head. He began to write something on the forms Tony had completed. Behind him the music on the wireless suddenly stopped. A dispassionate BBC news announcer stated that the program was being interrupted to inform them that the German Luftwaffe was bombing Warsaw.

[8]

Michelle hopped from one foot to the other, hands on the window ledge as though she were contemplating taking flight and soaring out over the Seine. "Honey, I'm scared out of my wits. What are we going to do?"

Kate continued to unpack her suitcase, placing folded underwear into a dresser drawer. "We're going to show them the Eiffel Tower and the Arc de Triomphe and the Louvre, just like we planned."

"But what if the Germans come?" Scarlett O'Hara's weaker sister probably wore an expression similar to Michelle's, Kate thought, when contemplating the arrival of the Yankees.

"The Germans are a long way from here, Michelle." On the dresser in front of Kate lay a copy of the London *Times*. The headline read: INVASION OF POLAND. GERMANS ATTACK ACROSS ALL FRONTIERS. WARSAW AND OTHER CITIES BOMBED. WAR WITHOUT DECLARATION. The date was September 2, 1939.

"I've wired the home office for instructions. I don't know what else to do except carry on as planned. It might be hours or even days before we get a reply. Do you want to huddle in a hotel room with two dozen anxious tourists?"

"I reckon not. But France and England have declared war on Germany. What if the German bombers hit France too?"

"Michelle, finish unpacking," Kate said firmly. "I'm going to check on Mrs. Maynard. I didn't like the look of her when we checked in."

"Her bowels again," Michelle said, grimacing.

"More than that. That's just a symptom. Back in a minute."

Walking down the hallway to Myrna Maynard's room, Kate reflected that if the woman was another Radner with Jewish relatives, at least the outbreak of war had put a stop to any plans to try to smuggle them out of the country.

She had to wait for Mrs. Maynard to finish in the bathroom. As soon as the woman emerged, it was obvious there would be no tour of the City of Light for her. She was deathly pale, her eyes dull, and her face sagged in dehydrated folds.

Kate went to her to help her back to the bed. "Mrs. Maynard, you've got to let me call a doctor. I must insist. This is no mild case of the tourist trots."

Mrs. Maynard nodded weakly and lay back on her pillow. As Kate pulled the covers over her, the woman grabbed her hand. "Promise you won't leave Paris without me."

"We're going to take good care of you." Kate picked up the phone and asked the switchboard operator to find a doctor. Her French was good, but they always recognized her accent.

"I saw the papers," Mrs. Maynard said. "France declared war. Does that mean we'll have to leave?"

"Don't worry about that now. Let's get you well first."

"I can't leave. There's someone here I have to see."

Kate sat down. "Perhaps you'd better tell me all about it."

"It's my sister. She calls herself Marie now; she used to be Mary. Marie Allegret. She married a Frenchman. We quarreled. I wrote, but she never replied. We haven't seen or heard from her for years. When my husband passed away, I decided I'd come and see if I could find her. But I was too afraid to come alone, so I booked with the tour."

Kate patted her hand, relieved. "Just relax. If she's still here, we'll find her."

Word came from New York the following day that any of

ECHOES OF WAR

the tour group who wished could immediately return home and obtain a refund of the tour package cost.

It was unfortunate that news of the torpedoing of the British passenger liner *Athenia* came at the same time. There had been twenty-eight Americans among the casualties.

All members of the tour, except Mrs. Maynard, elected to fly home, despite the added cost and roundabout routes involved. Mrs. Maynard was in the hospital with suspected amebic dysentery. Kate agreed to remain in Paris while Michelle accompanied the others home.

Marie Allegret was quickly located, and Kate decided to go and visit her rather than discuss the matter by phone.

Paris had never looked lovelier. The sky was a fragile blue over the trees of the Bois de Boulogne, and a gossamer mist rose above the Seine. Kate felt a keen sense of disappointment that she would have to leave so soon, not only because she loved the city, but because of what she knew she faced at home. That continued wake her mother insisted on holding over Kate's dead hopes of marriage to Wade Lowery. Funny how her mother had quickly adopted the attitude that it was all Kate's fault. Not only that, but Kate got the impression her mother thought she'd lost her *only* chance for marriage. Damn the Germans for starting a war, but oh, how remote it seemed on such a day.

The cab dropped her at Claridge's on the Champs-Elysées. Marie Allegret proved to be an older version of Mrs. Maynard, but with twinkling eyes and a Parisienne's chic.

"Come, a glass of wine in a sidewalk cafe is essential on a day such as this," she said when Kate had introduced herself. A slight French intonation had crept into her speech over the years, and on observing the Frenchman's widow more closely Kate noted other subtle differences between her and her sister. Whereas Myrna Maynard, when not bemoaning her illness, was a rather dull and self-absorbed woman, Marie Allegret had the lively step and inquiring gaze of one more interested in those around her. There was also a certain mysterious glow in her eyes that suggested she was a woman who had been much loved and much desired.

ECHOES OF WAR

Ten minutes later they surveyed one another across a canopied table and both began to speak at once.

"I didn't tell you on the phone, Madame Allegret, but your sister is—"

"I'd forgotten how good it was to speak English again, Miss Kieron, to hear a voice from home—"

They both broke off, laughed, and apologized. There was a moment of silence as each waited politely, then Kate said, "I'm afraid your sister is ill. She's in the hospital, but they expect she'll be all right in a week or two. Will you come with me to visit her?"

Marie Allegret stared into space for a moment. "I suppose one must forgive and forget. Yes, I will go to her. But sit a minute and talk. You're a New Yorker, aren't you?"

Kate smiled. "Brooklyn. How long since you were home?"

"France is my home, has been for twenty years. I never went back. But, of course, I devour all the news about America." She paused. "You should have been a model. Have you ever thought of it? The French couturiers would go mad over those long legs of yours."

"But I'm not pretty enough to be a model."

"Nonsense!" Marie Allegret exclaimed. "Do forgive me for making such personal remarks. It's one of the indulgences of age—or perhaps one of the vices—insatiable curiosity about people. You make me feel young again, just looking at you. There's a wonderful sense of vitality about you that—But here's our wine. My dear, a toast to you and to Brooklyn."

She and Marie chatted companionably over their wine until Kate realized with a pang of guilt that they had both forgotten poor Mrs. Maynard, languishing with her bedpan. Kate decided she hadn't had such instant rapport with anyone since she met Cecilia Winfield.

They hailed a taxi and went to the hospital. Kate remained in the waiting room during the reunion of the two sisters. An hour later Marie emerged red-eyed and beckoned for Kate to go into Mrs. Maynard's room. "She wants to speak with you. And so do I. I'll wait here for you."

Myrna Maynard was also weeping. Kate sat beside her

ECHOES OF WAR

bed and waited for her to compose herself. She was looking considerably better since she had been admitted to the hospital. "Thank you for bringing my sister to me. You'll never know what it meant."

"I'm sorry she had to see you here, but perhaps you'd like to stay in Paris for a while when you get out of the hospital?"

Mrs. Maynard twisted the sheets nervously. "You did promise to stay with me. You won't leave, will you?"

"Of course not. Not until you do. You're my last and only tour member." Kate felt a twinge of guilt that another week or two in Paris meant she was doing herself more of a favor than Mrs. Maynard.

Mrs. Maynard said, "Thank you. My sister is going to see if I can be released earlier, into her care. We'd like you to stay with us." She added as an afterthought, "Marie is quite wealthy."

Since the death of her businessman husband, Marie preferred to live in hotels. She insisted that Kate move in with her immediately and together they would await Myrna's release from the hospital. Kate accompanied her to a lavish suite of rooms at Claridge's, feeling as though a shroud had been lifted from her shoulders, even though her return home was only delayed for a week or two.

The day after she moved in with Marie, there was a call from the desk for Kate. She had a visitor. Tony Winfield awaited her in the lobby. She slipped his mother's locket from around her neck before going down to meet him.

She had almost forgotten his dazzling good looks, his deceptively languid gaze, and how effortlessly he dominated his surroundings. She asked, not rudely, "How did you know I was here?"

"Well, a little bird told me your tour group left yesterday, without you. When I inquired, I was told you remained behind with one of your tourists who was ill in hospital. I visited Mrs. Maynard, and—*voilà*." He smiled disarmingly. "Come on, Kate, say you're glad to see me and then let's have a friendly drink. It might be one of the last we get in Paris."

"Okay, a quick *café au lait*. How's your mother?"

67

"Cecilia's fine. Furious with Mosley because the Nazis weren't playing games after all."

"I notice you're still in civilian clothes." Kate couldn't hold back the observation. "Even though your country's at war."

Tony didn't appear to be ruffled. "Would I endear myself to you if I were to don a uniform?"

"Probably not. Especially if it was field gray."

He laughed. "Battling Kate never lets an opportunity go by without reminding me she believes I'm on the Nazi side, does she? Ah me, and here I am worried to death because she's still in France with the German armies at the door."

"What's happening? I haven't seen a paper today."

"Luftwaffe planes are smashing Poland. Massed panzer divisions are across the borders. The Poles are resisting, but they've been thrown into confusion by the blitzkrieg. Warsaw is a heap of rubble, and all the industrial and mining regions in the south are in Nazi hands."

"Oh, God! What next?"

"Well . . . since I don't have to leave right away, I thought we might go on a picnic."

"Are you nuts? Or just incredibly unfeeling? Or maybe the collapse of Poland is good news to you?"

"Kate, once and for all. I'm not a Nazi. You goaded me sufficiently at our last meeting that I told you what you wanted to hear. But I'm telling you now I hate fascism. I hate everything the Nazi party stands for. I have many German friends, some of whom have joined the party and others who are aghast at Hitler's excesses. This isn't your Wild West. Don't try to determine who the good guy is by the color of his hat."

She was surprised at how much she wanted to believe him, but was not yet ready to concede. "You seem to change the color of yours to suit the convenience of the moment."

"Look, there's not much we can do, the two of us, about the advancing German armies. So let's go on a picnic. Believe me, our turn will come soon enough."

"Not mine. I'm an American." The echo of what the consular official in Berlin said rang uncomfortably in her mind: *That's what we thought last time.*

"Hitler's ambitions extend beyond Europe. He's bent on world conquest. And even if Germany doesn't draw America into the war, then probably England and France will."

"That sounds slightly traitorous on your part."

"I'm afraid the Winfields tend to be somewhat reckless in dispensing unpopular views."

Kate sipped the deliciously creamy coffee and was idly amused by the way two Parisiennes at the next table were eyeing Tony. *Lord,* she thought, *please find me a nice ugly man to be my very own.*

"Are you going to stay in Paris until Mrs. Maynard recovers?"

"Yes. I'm still on the Evans Tours payroll."

"And then?"

"Home again, it's home again, America for me."

"Oh, Kate, why couldn't we have met at a more opportune moment? Where *were* you?"

I was falling in love with Wade Lowery and making a complete fool of myself.

She lowered her eyes in case he read her thoughts. Had he just inadvertently given the reason for his interest in her? Was she desirable only because she was unobtainable? She said, "I have to go. My hostess will think it rude of me to disappear for so long."

"What, no picnic? Dinner then. If necessary, we'll invite Madame Allegret too."

Kate considered for a moment. Had Wade left her so vulnerable that she was afraid of any kind of relationship with a man, even friendship, in case it led step by step to that unbelievable pain of rejection? If so, it was time to heal her wounds. "Call me later this afternoon. I'll see if I can get away."

Marie Allegret's household included a personal maid, a quiet woman about Marie's own age, and a chauffeur, a sullen-looking man in his early thirties with the shiftiest eyes Kate had ever seen. His name was an unpronounceable double-barreled one, but Marie called him Bruno. He was short, with powerful shoulders and bulging muscles.

Kate's first vision of Bruno was when she saw him casually crush a portion of the fender of a car that had inconsiderately parked too close to Marie's Citroen. Kate decided not to mention the incident to Marie, but it bothered her. As did his insolent attitude toward Marie.

Marie explained this by telling Kate, "I never learned to drive, and frankly, Paris traffic terrifies me. My late husband hired Bruno's father and we called him Bruno because I couldn't pronounce his name. When the first Bruno died, I sort of inherited his son."

"I see," Kate replied, thinking privately that she wouldn't trust Bruno II as far as she could throw him.

Evidently the feeling was mutual, judging by the jaundiced eye he cast in her direction whenever their paths crossed.

An hour after she returned to Marie's suite in the hotel, a bouquet of roses arrived with a card from Tony: ". . . *until tonight. T.*"

After Bruno dumped the flowers in front of her, glowered, and left, Kate said to herself, Oh, Tony, don't be so damn nice. I can't stand it.

Marie came into the room and admired the roses. *"Chérie, a beau so soon!* Wonderful! Listen, I'm going to the hospital; and tonight I have a tête-à-tête with an old friend. You won't be lonely, will you?"

Okay, Kate thought, so it's meant to be. "No, I have a dinner invitation," she said, feeling a surge of anticipation.

That evening Kate studied Tony across their table in a crowded little cafe on the Left Bank, struck again by his charm, his self-deprecating humor, his apparent total unawareness of his own magnetic personality and good looks. Any woman in her right mind, she told herself, would accept any little bit of Tony Winfield he was willing to give.

Tony leaned forward and touched her left hand as it lay curled around her wineglass. "What beautiful hands you have." His forefinger moved to her third finger and she momentarily froze, although the imprint of Wade's engagement ring had faded along with the summer's tan.

Their glances locked, perhaps in astonishment that the simple contact of fingertip against knuckle could generate such intense awareness. Tony said softly, "The whole damn world is going to blow up in our faces, Kate. You know that, don't you? Lord, listen to me, I'm using the oldest line known to man, but it's true. We may not have much time together. Couldn't we make a happy memory or two before it's too late?"

She felt her hand tremble slightly under his. All at once her fiercely Catholic upbringing and her pious refusal to sleep with Wade before marriage seemed ludicrous. Could she really have been that naive such a short time ago? Had she actually believed the conditioning—if you sleep with a man before marriage, he'll lose all respect for you, and your soul will be damned for all eternity. Not that the views were confined only to the Catholic church. The mores were hammered into the heads of all "decent" girls by mothers terrified of premarital pregnancy. After all, even for Protestants there was no reliable method of birth control.

She said, "Why am I even considering making any kind of memories with you?"

"Because you're as aware as I am that we'd be fools not to snatch a moment's happiness while we can. I believe we need one another, Kate. In each other's arms we could forget the world's madness for a little while."

"Yes," Kate said softly. "I knew there had to be a reason other than the peculiar physical sensations I'm feeling." She drained her wineglass. "Do you have a place in mind where we can make that memory?"

Smiling, Tony motioned for the waiter. "I'm staying at a *pension* not far from here."

His room was small but filled with moonlight, and the sky glittered with a million stars. Kate stood at the window remembering how beautiful the city lights used to be before the blackout. But the artificial brilliance had obliterated the starlight. Sometimes, she thought, it's necessary to give up one thing in order to have another.

Tony came to her side and slipped his arm around her. "Would you like a drink? I have some cognac."

Turning, Kate placed her arms around his neck and burrowed her face into the hollow of his throat. "No, thanks. I want to be held, touched."

"Kate, oh, Kate," he whispered against her hair, then his

hands were on her face, tilting her mouth upward. Their lips blended with a hunger honed to a sharp edge by every moment they had been together wanting this to happen but fighting against it.

She felt both shy and happy, proud and humble. It was right that she should be here in Tony's arms, kissing him and slipping her hands inside his shirt to feel the warm vibrance of his muscled back as he strained to pull her closer.

Their kiss went on and on, and she wanted it to never stop. She felt his fingers on the buttons of her dress, then moving to slide it from her shoulders, and it was she who twisted impatiently out of her underwear. He drew back, his hands still on her shoulders, eyes sweeping the length of her body.

That he found her beautiful was evident in his eyes and in the way he caught his breath as with one finger he traced the hollow of her throat and the swelling of her breast. He bent and kissed her nipple and she felt his lips encircling, drawing her into the sweetness of his mouth.

She looked down at the gold lights in his hair, and her hands went to his head to keep him there, close to her heart. She heard him murmur, "So lovely . . . you're so lovely."

She felt a rush of emotion that had its origin in some hitherto untapped portion of her awareness. She felt a need to reveal more to him than her naked body. To tell him hopes and dreams and even fears and weaknesses. To know his. They hadn't had enough time; perhaps there'd never be enough.

Raising his head, he said, "I've wanted you so much. I can't believe you're here in my arms. Kate, I want you to know that you've become very important to me. Making love is only one of the things I'd like to share with you."

"I know," she whispered. "Perhaps if we'd met earlier, before—"

"We're together now. That's all that matters."

Dropping to his knees, he pulled her to him so that he could kiss her midriff, then move downward, finding each curve and hollow. Each fleeting touch of his lips lit new fires, tingled in nerve endings, so that her longing ran in molten flows through her veins until there was no longer any sense of shyness or shame, nor even awkward anticipation. She sighed in sheer sensual pleasure.

She felt herself tremble with a need for even greater closeness; and sensing this, he slipped his hands under her knees and lifted her to the bed.

Lying back, she watched as he discarded his clothes. She had never seen a completely naked male before, and her first reaction was surprise at his unexpected masculine beauty. She wondered if he'd be shocked if she touched, explored. He stretched out beside her and drew her back into his embrace. She felt his heart beating and the powerful surge of his desire.

He touched her lightly, and the hot rush of her own passion caused her to shiver involuntarily. Instinctively, she parted her legs so that he could kneel between them.

The pain as he entered her was momentary, gone before she was really aware of it. He was gentle, building slowly upon her rising desire, caressing her breasts, exploring her mouth with his tongue, withdrawing in order to slow his own blinding need so that she might catch up with him.

Kate felt as if she were rising and falling in some mystical ballet of the senses, whirling somewhere far out in the universe without any feelings of time or place. There was nothing more, nothing beyond their own fused flesh in this, the most magical and mystical of all human bonding. Pleasure was the feeling he inspired in her, and in knowing that his delight in her was as great.

Somewhere, far below on earth, she could hear Kate whimpering small sounds of passion and love as her hips moved to a rhythm as old as humanity, drawing him more deeply inside her, while on the other plane—that indescribably beautiful place she hadn't known existed—the parts of them that were separate from their bodies were meeting also, in mutual joy.

At the moment of climax she called out his name and heard the echoing cry of her own name on his lips.

But as passion subsided and she lay panting against his chest, she slowly realized that he was silent, contemplative, slightly tense. "Tony . . . ?"

"There's blood on the sheet, Kate. You should have told me. I thought—you were engaged and—"

"Is it a crime to be a virgin? What difference does it make? I wanted this, Tony. I really did." She snuggled closer. "I just wish I'd known what I'd been missing all this time."

Awakening in her room in Marie's suite the following morning, since she'd been afraid Marie would worry if she stayed out all night, Kate ran her hands over her body. It felt the same, and upon arising there didn't seem to be any telltale signs on her face either. Still she felt like whistling as she went to bathe.

Tony had been vague about his plans, but had said he had to return to England that day and would be back in Paris as soon as he could.

She and Marie had just finished breakfast when an enormous basket of flowers arrived. Tony's note read:

Have a pleasant sojourn in Paris, but don't be seduced by the apparent calm. It's the calm before the storm. If you need me for anything, any time, wire me at Cardovan House. You're wonderful, Kate. Thank you, my love, for the happiest of memories.

Marie watched her as she read the note, then, eyes twinkling, inquired, "A serious suitor, yes? He brings a soft glow to your eyes that I recognize only too well."

Kate felt her color rise slightly, knowing that her eyes reflected her initiation into womanhood more than anything else. "Oh, no, we're just friends."

There was no further word from Tony, and as several days passed Kate felt more and more disappointed, but she told herself she shouldn't be surprised. He'd gotten what he wanted; as far as he was concerned the chase was over. Well, so be it. She'd gotten what she wanted too, and there were no regrets.

By the time Myrna Maynard was released from the hospital, Kate felt as though she and Marie were old friends, and she was sorry when Myrna began to panic about the German successes and announced she wanted to go home right away, before they marched on France. "Come with us, Marie," she urged her sister. "You can't stay here with a war going on."

Marie shook her head. "I can't leave. I don't believe the Germans will get this far. You must understand, Myrna, Paris has been my home. I have so many happy memories."

"It isn't because of . . . what happened long ago?" Myrna asked anxiously. "Everyone's forgotten by now, you know."

Realizing that the conversation was veering toward personal matters, Kate stood up to excuse herself, but Marie said, "Don't go, Kate. You might as well know what we quarrelled about. Myrna married my fiancé. I was, quite literally, left at the altar."

Kate felt the color flood up over her face. No wonder they'd been drawn to one another. They probably sensed a similarity in the hands each had been dealt by life.

"What Myrna doesn't know," Marie went on, "is that it turned out to be the best thing that ever happened to me. I met Henri Allegret, and we lived happily ever after. Not only was he handsome and madly in love with me, but he was also wealthy. When I think how close I came to marrying Herb Maynard . . . Not that there was anything wrong with him. It's just that he never left the small town where we were born, and I'd have shriveled up and died living the life you lived, Myrna. Here you are, on your very first trip abroad, and you had to wait until he was dead to do it. Henri and I traveled all over the world, and, oh, how we loved one another! No, it was all for the best in the end."

Myrna gave a sour smile. "Then why didn't you answer my letters? Why did you let our feud go on all this time?"

Marie's eyes flashed with sudden fire. "Because what you did was unforgivable. You and Herb didn't just decide on the day of our wedding that you wanted each other. You could have warned me—spared me the humiliation of going to the church to explain that my fiancé had eloped with my sister. I'm sorry, I didn't intend to bring this up. I suppose the one thing we can't forgive those we love is betrayal."

"Kate," Myrna said in a small tight voice, "can you make arrangements for us to leave for home right away?"

"Yes, of course. I'll see if I can get us on—"

"Just a moment, Kate," Marie interrupted. "The other day you mentioned that you probably don't have a job waiting for you when you get home. Why not stay here as my companion and—when I get up the courage to get rid of Bruno—as my chauffeur? He's been stealing me blind for years, and I've had enough of his surly disposition."

Kate was surprised, pleased, and excited by the offer. If she stayed in France, she'd be within visiting distance of Tony. But she was uneasy at the prospect of replacing Bruno. She hesitated, and Marie, mistaking the reason, went on quickly: "I know we're at war, but if worst comes to worst, we can go to Spain. I have friends there."

A fleeting image of what awaited her at home flashed through Kate's mind: joblessness, Wadelessness, her mother's endless litany about Kate's spinsterhood. At the same instant her Berlin memories of Nazi brutality tugged at her conscience, as well as the blind isolationism of most Americans and her own feeling of shame that her countrymen wanted to pull the covers over their heads and sleep through the coming struggle. But the factor that decided her was that if Tony was going to fight fascism, then so was she; and as allies they would surely be able to get together occasionally.

With that thought in mind, she accepted Marie's offer.

[9]

Carefully holding a crystal vase filled with autumn flowers, Kate opened the door to Marie's bedroom. Her former personal maid had left to go north with her husband, and the young girl hired to replace her was fluttery and anxious to please. Kate eased the girl's burden as much as she could. This afternoon Marie was having her hair done, and Kate had just returned from a shopping expedition.

The scene in the bedroom etched itself vividly in horrid detail in Kate's mind. In her fright she dropped the vase and the sound of shattering crystal rang in her head like a thousand cries of anger. Bile rushed into Kate's throat at the sight of the naked haunches of Bruno, dark, mottled, rigid with muscle, his knees buried in the white satin of Marie's quilt.

She couldn't see much of the young maid under him, but her piteous cries, the limp resignation of helplessly splayed legs, the frantic clawing at the air of one hand, told the whole story.

Bruno's animal grunting and heaving stopped at the sound of the breaking vase. He glanced over his shoulder, his face sweat-streaked and ugly; then, seeing it was only Kate, he turned and rammed into the girl again.

Kate was scarcely aware of what she was doing. She scrambled over broken glass and hurled herself at Bruno's back, punching and tearing at his flesh. "Get off her. Leave her alone. Oh, God, *stop* it!"

She saw now that his hand was clamped firmly over the maid's mouth, allowing only tiny cries of pain to slip between his fingers. The girl's eyes were wide, pleading, her face swollen and tear-stained.

A shuddering climax went through Bruno's stocky body, and he collapsed, giving Kate a malevolent grin. "You jealous, *chérie*? You want your turn too, eh?"

Kate was sure she would burst with anger. She wanted to hurt him, humiliate him as he'd humiliated the maid, who was little more than a child. Kate's fists pounded his shoulder, and he laughed as she sobbed with rage.

There was a telephone on the table beside the bed and Kate grabbed the receiver. She yelled into it, "Get me the—" Before she could say another word, Bruno batted the telephone out of reach. He stood up, only inches away, regarding her with small crafty eyes.

The young maid rolled to the floor and crawled away, clutching the torn remnants of her clothes to her bruised body. Kate looked at Bruno, knowing she was no match for him physically, and the realization that they were alone stayed the urge to slap his grinning mouth.

He said softly, "Her word against mine, Katerina. She tempted me, wanted it, asked for it, and pretended I attacked her only because you arrived. You think the police will believe you if you call them? This is France. *Cherchez la femme*. Ask the girl. See if *she* wants you to call them."

He was right, of course, and knowing that made Kate even more furious. She said, "Get out. You're fired, you hear?"

His eyes went over her contemptuously. "You don't have the right to dismiss me. You're just jealous because it wasn't you. Who'd want you—a great long pole of a woman, like a giant. You should have been a man. Where were you when they were handing out looks? You've as much style as a barge pole." Bending, he retrieved his trousers and wiggled his hips suggestively as he put them on.

Kate turned and ran from the room. The maid had gone to her tiny room adjacent to Kate's bedroom. The door was locked and Kate couldn't persuade her to open it. She heard the hall door slam and knew Bruno had gone to pick up Marie at the hairdresser's.

Marie returned just as Kate was picking up the last of the broken crystal. Bruno was putting the car away. Marie took one look at Kate's face and asked quietly, "What happened?"

Fifteen minutes later when Bruno came up from the garage he was confronted by his employer, Kate, and the burly assistant manager of the hotel.

Marie said icily, "Your termination pay is in this envelope. Your personal belongings will be packed and sent down to the lobby shortly. If I ever see you again, I shall have you arrested. Now get out of my sight."

Bruno's fury was written on his face, but it was at Kate he flung his words. "Bitch! Yankee bitch. You've done this. But your turn will come. I promise you that." He turned and went through the door, slamming it.

Kate let out her breath slowly.

The image of Bruno gradually faded after they heard that he had joined the army. The maid left, and Marie decided not to replace her but to hire hotel maids when she entertained.

A note arrived from Tony saying that he was sorry he couldn't return to Paris right away, but would drop in "one of these days." Kate wondered somewhat resentfully why he bothered writing at all. Funny how easy it was to steel herself against pining for him, but then she supposed Wade had taught her that particular skill.

Kate gradually became aware that Marie was conducting a subtle campaign to make her over. It began with the offer of accessories with which to enliven her wardrobe.

"Here, Kate, this scarf will be perfect with that sweater. Wear it loosely around your throat. See how the color sets off your hair?" Or, "Wear my long strand of pearls with that dress. Knot them . . . so. See how they make your skin glow?" Then progressed to "Kate, you have magnificent eyes. You should emphasize them. Let me show you. Now be still. It's just kohl, been around since Cleopatra's day."

ECHOES OF WAR

The natural progression was a visit to Marie's hairdresser, then her dressmaker. "No arguments, my dear. After all, I practically kidnapped you from your tour with only the clothes in your suitcase. Winter is coming on, and you'll need warm clothes. Don't worry, I'll deduct the cost from your salary."

Kate laughingly protested but she was grateful for both Marie's generosity and her Parisienne chic. When she looked in the mirror she hardly recognized herself in sleek suits with tight skirts, high-heeled shoes, her hair swept up on top of her head to reveal a graceful neck.

"But I'm too tall. I've always worn low heels and full skirts and plastered down my hair."

"None of which made you any shorter. Kate, dear, your height is majestic. Flaunt it. And, you know, you have wonderful cheekbones. A touch of rouge . . ."

The subtle enhancing of cheeks and eyes certainly did work wonders. Kate still didn't see a beautiful face in the mirror, but even she had to admit it was an arresting one.

Marie hugged her impulsively. "You know, I've loved my life here, my Henri, living in Paris, traveling. I missed only one of life's blessings. I never had a daughter, to dress, to confide in, to laugh with and cry over. Indulge me, Kate. Be my long-lost daughter."

The change in Kate's looks and dress and the obvious impression she made on the men she met restored her self-confidence to the point where she could look back on being jilted by Wade almost as dispassionately as if it had happened to someone else.

As winter approached, Kate decided she loved her new life and freedom, and ignored desperate commands from her mother that she leave the war zone immediately. For all that was happening of a military nature, there might not have been a war, except for the tragedy of Poland. Newspapers were calling it the "phony war." Except for some shortages and all the young men in uniform, life went on as usual.

Marie had legions of friends of all ages and gave frequent parties, and since she was generous with time off, Kate had plenty of time to make friends of her own. She told herself that as soon as she found an attractive man she intended to indulge in an *amourette,* but somehow no one quite inspired her erotic longing the way Tony Winfield had.

She sent a picture postcard to Cecilia Winfield, who responded with a long letter telling of the phony war in England—how ludicrous it was to see elderly Home Guards drilling with broom handles, because there weren't enough rifles to go around; and preparing to beat off possible invaders with pitchforks or golf clubs. She fretted about how tiresome it was that all of the servants were being called into the armed forces. "We're turning over much of Cardovan House for storage of national treasures," Cecilia wrote. "Museums in London are preparing for German air raids, although personally I think Hitler has realized he's bitten off more than he can chew. He's certainly been quiet since we declared war on him. I'd rather give up the space for museum pieces than have a couple of dozen rowdy evacuees from the East End billeted here, the village is full of the little horrors."

There was no mention of Tony, but just before Christmas a note came from him telling her he'd see her soon but couldn't give an exact date.

A young captain in one of the newly formed French armored divisions named Jean-Louis Jourdain, who was an admirer of all things American, especially Kate and American music, had discovered that Marie had a collection of old American records. One Saturday evening when the suite was crowded with friends, he persuaded Marie to play a breezy rendition of the Charleston.

Marie, recalling her flapper days, immediately rolled up the rug and began to dance. Kate had always loved the dances of the twenties and was fairly proficient at the Charleston herself, so she joined in. They were surrounded by a laughing, clapping circle of admirers when the hotel maid admitted Tony.

Kate was glad that the wild dance called for her to shimmy and fling her arms in the air, so that her delight at the sight of Tony would not be quite so obvious. An inner voice—the echo of another time, another man—warned her not to show all her feelings or appear too eager. After all, Tony just

ECHOES OF WAR

dropped in on her when it suited his convenience. She managed a smile and a wave without missing a beat of the music.

Tony stared at her, surprise and obvious admiration on his face. Kate had a momentary vision of herself as he remembered her: untidy hair she'd cut herself, clothes never quite right, her only makeup a dab of powder on her nose and a smear of lipstick. Tonight she wore a deceptively simple jade green jersey gown that flowed over her body, with Marie's emerald ear studs sparkling on her ears, her hair swept into a burnished coil on top of her head. Carefully applied kohl made her eyes look enormous.

She had kicked off her shoes for the Charleston, but slipped them on before walking across the room to greet Tony. He wore a Savile Row suit of gray wool that was in sharp contrast to all the French uniforms present.

"Hello, Tony, how are you?" *You look wonderful. Oh, am I glad you're back. I want so much to hold you, touch you, kiss you.* She offered her hand and he took it and held it.

"Very well, thank you. You look bloody marvelous," he said in a small awed voice. "War or no war, Paris agrees with you." His eyes never left her face, even when first Jean-Louis and then Marie moved protectively to either side of her.

Presenting Tony to them, Kate was amused at the way Jean-Louis' deep-set eyes glittered darkly as he was introduced to the Englishman.

Marie said, "Come, Tony, let me get you a drink and introduce you to our friends."

When Tony was ushered away, Jean-Louis commented, "His country is at war, but he is not in uniform."

"No," Kate said, feeling oddly let down, as though Tony's civilian status was a personal affront. She wanted him to appear to the rest of the world as he did to her, a shining knight, no matter what he wore.

When Tony rejoined her, Jean-Louis was wrestling with Marie's ancient gramophone. Taking Kate's arm, Tony led her to a settee. "I've missed you, Kate, more than you'll ever know. I really hoped to catch you alone. Could we—"

"No," Kate said. "I can't duck out on Marie's party."

Sitting next to him, she could feel the muscle of his arm through his jacket, pressing against her bare shoulder.

His eyes traveled over her hungrily and he picked up her hand again. "I haven't much time and there are so many things I want to tell you, but I'll have to confine myself to the most urgent."

"And that is?"

"Your continued presence in Paris. How long do you intend to stay? I don't want you to get trapped here when the Germans invade; and Kate, make no mistake, they will invade."

So he had merely dropped in to suggest she leave the war zone. Her letdown feeling intensified. "You really are the limit, you know that? Who appointed you my keeper? I haven't seen you since last September, and now you barge in here—"

"I'm sorry I couldn't get back before now. I wish I could tell you I've been languishing in jail and unable to come to you, but the truth is I just haven't had time. But I've thought about you constantly, worried incessantly. I'm the world's worst letter writer, or I'd have sent you poetic missives to keep my image fresh in your mind."

"A note might have helped. Or a card with your name on it." In her mind she was lying in his arms, their naked bodies fused.

He glanced about the room. "I'd say, from the way your friend Jean-Louis looks at you, that you haven't lacked male attention."

She felt a glimmer of satisfaction that he'd noticed. She said in a studiedly offhand tone, "How about you? Is there a current *amourette* in your life?"

"If there was, would you care?"

She was tempted to say, Yes, damn it, I'd care a lot. But Tony didn't give her a chance. He added quietly, "Why are we playing these games with one another?"

How could she tell him that she was afraid she'd been used and then forgotten? She wanted to blurt out her true feelings, to say, You're so secretive about your life. Where do you go and what do you do and why can't I be a part of it? Yes, there's a war, but everyone's saying it's a phony war. It

ECHOES OF WAR

hasn't changed anything. You could have come back before now. You're a civilian. Instead she shrugged and said, "What games?"

"All right, Kate. Perhaps you're right to keep me at arm's length. It looks as though we're all going to have to put national concerns ahead of personal ones for a time. But I am truly worried about you. I'm begging you to leave Paris."

There was genuine concern for her in his eyes, and it was difficult to be indifferent to such sincerity. Some of Kate's hurt vanished. "I'm touched that you're worried about me, but there's no reason to be. I'm having a wonderful time with Marie, and we've made plans to go to Spain if things get unpleasant here. But it's not going to come to that. Jean-Louis was just saying that the French armies are ready for the real fight to begin now, that the Germans have lost their impetus and it will soon be all over."

"That's not quite the way I see it." Tony's voice was low, urgent. "Hitler will march again, probably in the spring. You saw the lightning blitzkrieg of Poland. When it happens, it's too fast to react. You should go to Spain now, while there's still time, or better still, go home to America."

Kate cocked her head on one side disbelievingly. "For someone who professes to think about me constantly, you sure want to get rid of me."

He squeezed her fingers. "I want you to be safe, so that when the war's over I'll know where to come looking for you. I'd ask you to come back to England with me, but I'm not even sure you'd be safe there. Some English families are evacuating their children to America. Kate, my dearest, I need to know you're not in danger."

The look in his eyes was one of raw longing, and she wondered about the depth of his feelings for her. Was it possible he did really care? Could she reciprocate? She thought, Why, men are just as vulnerable as women. He can be hurt as easily as I was. She was fiercely attracted to Tony, but what if it was only physical attraction? Strangely, she at last understood Wade. He simply hadn't loved her the way she loved him. She wondered how two people ever got their feelings synchronized. Could they ever be equal?

ECHOES OF WAR

Disconcerted, she said, "I'm flattered by your concern, but I make my own decisions. I'm staying in Paris. Tony, please don't read more into our *amourette* than there is. That's the right word, isn't it, for what we are to one another?"

He stared at her and she recognized the pain in his eyes and felt guilty about it. He said slowly, "I see. I'm to be hanged with my own rope."

To cover her feelings, she snapped, "Where have you been, anyway, and what have you been doing? Why aren't you in uniform?" She hadn't intended to sound so accusing but was confused by the paradox of his long absence and lack of correspondence and now this near declaration of love.

Releasing her hand, he leaned back against the satin upholstery of the settee, his world-weary and slightly cynical mask back in place. Why, why did he wear one with her? What was it he wanted so desperately to hide? Why did he come so close to confiding in her and then back off? If she wasn't worthy of his confidence, then clearly she was just a body to him. He said, "Why do you ask? If I don't have a good enough reason not to be in uniform, will you send me a white feather?"

"Damn it, Tony, you know I've always been bothered by the fact that you were so chummy with der Fuehrer and his buddies in Berlin. I just want to know, once and for all, which side you're on."

"But my dear Kate, you've just told me my concern for you is wasted. Why do you care about such trivial matters as national allegiance if that's so? Or can it be that you do care a little?"

"Okay, forget it. Just be sure I get an invitation if they decide to shoot you as a traitor, okay?"

The room was suddenly filled with the strains of "All the Things You Are" as Jean-Louis got the gramophone going again. Tony said, "Would you dance with me? I don't know any other way to get you into my arms."

"Sure. It will be a treat to rest my head on a shoulder of the right height."

Tony rolled his eyes. "I'll take that as a back-handed compliment." He rose, offered her his hand, and led her to the small square of polished parquet, then held her much too closely for Jean-Louis' liking, as he glared at them from the sidelines.

The foxtrot came to an end, but they lingered, eyes locked, acutely sensitive to the parts of their bodies still touching. Tony said quietly, "Let's get away from here."

"I can't leave now. Where are you staying? I'll come later, when the party breaks up."

"At the *pension*. I'll be waiting. I have some things to do, and I'll get them out of the way so we won't be interrupted later."

Foolishly, she remained at the open door after he left, until Marie's voice brought her back. "Kate, what a divinely good-looking man. He's coming back, isn't he?"

"No . . . no. He asked me to thank you for your hospitality. He didn't want to take you away from your guests. He thought he'd just leave unobtrusively."

Marie squeezed her arm. "I think he would have—if you hadn't stayed here staring at the empty hallway."

Kate flung her head back on the pillow, a gasp of pure pleasure torn from her lips as the convulsive spasms of release rippled through her body. Tony shuddered and collapsed onto her, his mouth finding hers in a slow kiss that conveyed his own fulfillment. He rained small kisses on her chin and nose and eyelids, then rolled onto his side, pulling her with him; his hand found her breast and held it tenderly.

"Oh, Tony," Kate murmured, sated, caressing him without shame. "I've longed for this. Why did you stay away?"

"Places to go and things to do," he quoted lightly. "If you won't go back to America, will you come back to England with me?"

"No, sorry. I've made a nice little life for myself in Paris. Why can't you come to me a little more often than every three or four months?"

"Kate, don't ask me questions I can't answer, please."

She sat up in bed, pushing her hair back over her shoulder. "Damn you to hell. I'm getting tired of your enigmatic

ECHOES OF WAR

Englishman pose. What am I, anyway? A body to sleep with but not a woman to confide in?"

He sat up and put his arms around her. "You're very dear to me, Kate. Someday I'll be able to tell you how dear, but not now."

"Uh-huh. I guess I realize why we had that little chat about birth control when I first got here."

He flushed slightly. "Forgive me, but when a man deflowers a woman he feels a certain responsibility for her. Especially if she happens to be a Roman Catholic and guided on such matters as family planning by a single and celibate Pope."

"That does it," Kate said, jumping out of bed.

He caught her by the wrist. "Please, let's not quarrel. I have to leave before dawn."

"I'm leaving right now. I must've been crazy to have anything to do with you in the first place."

[10]

Tony vaulted from the cockpit of the modified Spitfire, type B, and walked through a vaporous ground mist toward Charles Morcambe, who waited beside the landing strip.

Charles spoke through an oversized woolen muffler swathing his neck and lower face. "Any luck this time?"

"I should have some fairly clear shots of Wilhelmshaven. What's the word on the type C's?"

"Not ready yet. Let's get your film developed and then I want to talk to you about another little job I have in mind."

Sighing, Tony fell into step beside Charles as mechanics moved in to take care of the Spitfire. "Do you know how much leave I've had since I joined up? Hardly a bloody weekend pass. My duties with the PDU were supposed to be temporary. You know, the fact that I'm making these reconnaissance flights doesn't mean I've changed my mind about getting involved in that imbroglio of yours. Christ, you've so many different departments handling intelligence gathering I don't know how you keep from spying on each other by mistake."

"Oh, it wouldn't be by mistake." Charles smiled behind his muffler, pleased at his attempt at wit. "By the way, in addition to the Photographic Development Unit, we'll soon have a Photographic Interpretation Unit. A private company is using a Swiss device to calculate the dimensions of even small vessels from vertical air photos."

"Glad to hear it. But snapping pictures is only slightly less boring than Bomber Command's present job of supplying leaflets for the Germans to use as toilet paper."

"I did offer you more excitement," Charles pointed out mildly. "But you're bound and determined you want to get into dogfights with German aces. You've seen too many of those old Great War flying films."

"I don't want to be one of your operatives. The business of spying and counterintelligence doesn't appeal to me. Sooner or later we're going to clash with the Luftwaffe. The doldrums can't last much longer."

"Actually," Charles said, "I'm not here to recruit you for MI Five. I want you to fly some people to France and back. I thought you'd be interested because of your American friend in Paris."

Tony turned and studied Charles' face, looking for the inevitable catch in the offer. Charles returned the glance with an innocent shrug. "A few generals and diplomats for conferences with our French allies, that's all."

It was almost too good to be true, Tony decided. Having known Charles Morcambe since their schooldays, there was one characteristic of his that was unfailingly consistent. The man had absolutely no qualms about using anyone, including friends and relatives, in any harebrained scheme he devised that might produce information. From Charles' earliest days as embassy attaché to his present position in the SIS—and Tony wasn't even sure what that was, except that Charles seemed to have a sphere of influence that extended everywhere—he was a man who couldn't even drink a glass of ale without having three ulterior motives and two contingency plans. Tony was well aware that the Jewish refugees they had smuggled out of Berlin were all selected for escape by Charles because of some specialized knowledge they possessed. It made their gratitude a little hard to bear.

Still, a chance to get to Paris and see Kate wasn't to be sneezed at.

The flights to France proved to be to remote airstrips, and Tony was required to wait with his aircraft refueled and ready for immediate return to England. He spent a couple of nights in drafty hotel rooms while a field marshal argued strategy with his French counterpart, and at least one, he suspected, while a general visited his girlfriend. There was no time to get to Paris to see Kate.

He did manage to get home to Cardovan House one weekend. Traveling to Buckinghamshire on a slow-moving train packed with servicemen and a contingent of parents visiting their evacuated children, Tony thought about Kate again, wondering for the hundredth time how to tell her of his illegitimacy. How did a man offer his name to a woman when he had no name to offer? Unsure of her feelings for him, and with the world in its present mess, perhaps it was easier to simply evade the issue.

Entering the front door of Cardovan House, he heard the sweet sad strains of Liszt's *Liebestraum*, played as only Ursula could. Tony sighed, knowing that his half-sister played that particular piece when she was in the throes of another grand passion.

Handing his bag to the waiting butler, he went into the drawing room.

Ursula, looking almost ethereally beautiful in a white and gold evening gown, was seated at the grand piano, upon which leaned a darkly intense man in civilian clothes. Cecilia, Clive, and a couple of Guards officers who looked familiar and were probably the sons of friends of Cecilia listened in rapt silence.

"Anthony!" Ursula cried, catching sight of him. She stopped playing and ran to fling herself into his arms. Tony kissed her cheek, disentangled her arms, and went to kiss Cecilia.

"Darling, why didn't you let us know you were coming?" his mother demanded. "We'd have saved dinner. Cook is downright miserly nowadays, because of the rationing."

"I've had dinner. Hello, Clive." Tony nodded to the other men and turned as Ursula dragged her civilian across the room to meet him.

"Anthony, this is Albert Weales. He's a conscientious objector," she announced proudly.

Tony managed a handshake, recalling that Ursula's last

boyfriend had been one of Mosley's fascists, and, in fact, it was Ursula who first introduced Cecilia to that crowd. Albert regarded him warily, then retreated behind Ursula.

Taking a seat beside his mother, Tony asked, "Have you heard from James?"

Cecilia's lovely eyes clouded momentarily. "Yes. He used his influence with you-know-who and expects to be back in uniform any day. I'm so worried for him. He's too old for active service, but he's adamant he won't take a desk job at the Admiralty."

"He's not all that old—still on the right side of fifty," Tony said. "The navy can't be all that inundated with men clamoring to join up who have his experience."

Careful, Tony told himself, catching a note of annoyance in his voice. His father had been a much-decorated naval hero of the Great War, commanding a light cruiser, and Tony resented his mother's assumption that only his father's connections to the royal family could get him back into service.

Ursula resumed playing, and Albert, looking soulful, took his position beside her.

"Where does she find them?" Tony asked under his breath.

Clive leaned closer. "This one has a runny-nosed evacuee child billeted in the village. She met him at the Rose and Crown."

"He's married?"

Cecilia said uneasily, "Please don't be cross with her, Anthony."

"Not only a conscientious objector, also a socialist," Clive went on. "Writes pieces for the *Daily Worker*."

"Clive, please, let's not spoil Anthony's evening," Cecilia pleaded.

Tony leaned back and studied his sister. Damn, he thought Ursula was past this nonsense.

"Albert is a widower," Ursula informed him icily. They were the only two in the breakfast room. "You don't think I'd go out with a married man? I loathe that kind of thing.

God knows, we've seen enough of it with Cecilia and Clive."

"Let's not cast stones," Tony said. "Albert is a totally unsuitable companion for you. Do you go out of your way to find these people?"

Ursula's mouth opened in indignation. "Me? What about yourself? You brought that common American woman here and flaunted her."

"Kate is a dear friend. If you make any more remarks like that about her I'll be very angry. Now, what about Weales? Will it be necessary for me to play the outraged brother with him, or will you give him his marching orders yourself?" Tony stood up. "I must catch the afternoon train, so I don't have much time. Come on, let's take a stroll. It's time we had a serious talk."

They put on coats to ward off the morning chill and went outside. Walking slowly through the topiary garden, savoring the thin sunshine that gilded the shrubs but did not warm the air, Tony remembered the evening Kate had spent here, and his sense of loss was so acute that he stopped abruptly, staring at the ground.

Ursula put a small cold hand into his. "I've missed you so. I hate it when you're away. There's no one to look after me."

"Ursula, Ursula. What am I going to do with you? You're a grown woman now. You don't need anyone to look after you."

"Yes I do. I get mixed up with men like Albert if I'm left to my own devices."

"Why, do you suppose? Have you ever thought about it?"

"I know why." Ursula moved in front of him, her other hand reaching up to touch his cheek. "It's because they're the exact opposite of you. You're so fine, so noble, but you won't love me the way I love you."

Before he could stop her, she had her arms around his neck, trying to pull his face down so that she could kiss his mouth. The struggle was brief, ending with Ursula bursting into tears as he pushed her away from him.

He handed her his handkerchief and she blew her nose.

"Oh, Anthony, I'm so miserable. I love you so, want you so. I don't care if we are blood relations. I can't help my feelings."

Tony let out his breath, feeling both guilty and angry. He'd assumed she'd stop this nonsense eventually, and as there'd been no further declarations of love since the night he'd thrown her out of his bedroom after a tearful midnight visit, he'd assumed all was in order.

"Ursula, you've got to pull yourself together. What you feel for me is sisterly affection, nothing more. You're exaggerating your feelings because you have some misguided sense of hero-worship, which I can assure you is totally unjustified. Ordinary men can't compete with your fantasy image of what you *think* I am. If James had been on the scene more, no doubt you'd have gone through a perfectly normal crush on him."

"I love you," Ursula whimpered into his handkerchief.

"And I love you. As a sister. We'll have no more of this, or I'll simply stay away from you."

"You do the same thing when it comes to women as I do with men. You find all the wrong ones, because you really love me."

"We'll leave my love life out of this discussion. Come on, I want to ring James before I leave. I hope he's still at his flat."

"Are you going to patch things up with him? What did you quarrel about? You never told me."

Ursula's tears stopped and Tony thankfully changed the subject, vowing that from now on he would show his sister a side of him she wouldn't find so appealing, even if he had to invent one. "The last time he was home I asked him why he allowed Clive and Cecilia to deprive him of Cardovan House. I thought James was going to strike me."

"I think he's quite mad. I think we all are. Riddled with twisted passions."

Tony laughed, in spite of his concern for her. She was still such a child. "You've been reading your nineteenth-century novels again. Life just isn't dramatic enough for you, is it? You want to turn it into a melodrama."

"And you want to turn it into an adventure," she said with sudden insight. "Which of us will be more in jeopardy?"

The telephone was ringing as they entered the hall and the call was for Tony. Charles Morcambe's flat voice came over the wire: "Can you get back to the field right away? Oh, and Tony, bring some civilian clothes. We want you to fly some people in and out, and we don't want anyone to know the RAF is involved."

[11]

Marie came into the room just as Kate finished reading the return address on a newly arrived letter. She looked up, her eyes wide and a trifle damp. "Why, Kate, what is it?"

"It's from Tony, or maybe I should say Pilot Officer Winfield. He's in the RAF. I guess he was when he visited us. Just like him to come in civilian clothes."

"Why don't you open it?" Marie suggested gently.

Kate tore open the envelope and read the brief note, feeling her expression harden. "He wants me to—" She broke off.

"To go to him?" Marie asked simply. "Do you want to?"

"What, and become a camp follower?" Kate said lightly. "No, I don't think so. What would I do in England?"

"Your feelings toward him are very ambivalent, aren't they? Pity you couldn't have seen more of him. That's the only way to resolve such uncertainty."

That morning as the two women had their hair done, Kate reread Tony's letter for the sixth time.

Kate, love, sorry I haven't written. I warned you I'm the world's worst correspondent, but we've also been rather busy. You'll note my new address. I found a nice little cottage nearby. How would you like to live in it? I don't get much time off, and it's going to be awkward for me to visit Paris, but try as I might, I can't seem to live without you.

Kate felt a chill. He'd sent her not a declaration of love or a proposal of marriage but an invitation to be his mistress, available when he got a weekend pass. He wanted to provide a love nest.

No, damn it, she thought, if I'm going to play the game at all, I'm going to play it by my own rules. No love nests, no sitting around waiting for crumbs. A hurried evening here, a few minutes there, a fast romp in the hay when you're free. And in between an aching void. No, thanks. I'll call the shots. You feel free to move in and out of my life without giving up one bit of your own. That's what I want too.

Still in the heat of anger, she scribbled a hasty reply: "Tony, love, you must be kidding."

The phony war came to an abrupt end in the spring. In April Hiter sent his conquering legions into Denmark and Norway and was master of both countries within hours.

In May it was the turn of Belgium and Holland. Rotterdam suffered an appalling blitzkrieg, which was shown to the world in films shot by German cameramen who had parachuted in with the invaders. The threat to French and British cities was clear.

On May 11, Kate took Marie's breakfast tray to her bedroom, along with some grim news. "I just heard that German panzers are on French soil."

Marie pursed her lips thoughtfully. "I suppose we'd better wire my friends in Spain. We'll start sorting out things to take with us today. You can check on trains. Damn the Germans. How I hate to leave Paris in the spring."

Kate didn't want to leave either. She wasn't sure about her reasons, but suspected they had a lot to do with both the impending confrontation with the Germans and the fact that with the RAF flying air cover over the British Expeditionary Forces there was a slim chance Tony might show up in Paris.

In any case, the Germans were a long way away, and it

was difficult to conjure a sense of urgency when the city trees were bursting into new leaf and the soft May days bore the imprint of approaching summer. They spent a leisurely day deciding which clothes to pack.

In the afternoon Marie made calls to her friends to inform them she planned "a little vacation in Spain." Several of them were nervous about the fighting in the north and also planned to evacuate.

Late that afternoon Kate and Marie decided to visit Jean-Louis' mother. They hadn't heard from Jean-Louis for weeks.

They climbed the hill of Montmartre to the Rue Gabrielle, where the modest home of Jean-Louis' mother nestled under Sacré-Coeur, taking her a basket of artichokes and oysters, a long French loaf, and a wedge of cheese.

Annette Jourdain offered them wine, and they chatted under the beady and watchful eyes of a photo of Jean-Louis prominently displayed on the mantelpiece.

When the conversation began to flag, Kate glanced at Marie and she nodded in silent agreement. A clock ticked loudly beside Jean-Louis' portrait. Marie said, "Goodness, look how late it's getting. We must be on our way."

Annette said, "I'm so glad you came. I've been thinking of coming to see you, but I didn't want to alarm you. I wanted someone else to tell you first. But I've been worried ever since I saw him back in the city and out of uniform. Someone said he'd been dishonorably discharged."

"Who?" Kate asked, but she knew the answer. The room closed in suddenly and the ticking of the clock was deafening.

"Marie's ex-chauffeur—Bruno. I was most concerned when I ran into your hotel doorman and he said Bruno had been skulking about your hotel. Didn't the doorman tell you? I asked him to. I should think Bruno must have done something very bad to get kicked out of the army in these times, wouldn't you?"

Unless he's a deserter, Kate thought. She stood up, wanting the day to pass, and the night, so that she and Marie could be aboard the southbound train. Her heart was thumping uncomfortably against her ribs. Funny how the menace of one man was more frightening than the specter of legions of enemy soldiers.

That evening the two women had room service send up dinner and then they carefully locked their door. Kate even checked the window, but decided only a bat could gain entry that way. Still, she closed and locked the window, despite the warmth of the evening.

Suitcases and trunks stood about in varying stages of readiness, along with formidable mounds of clothing and personal possessions still stacked on beds and dressers. Kate's gaze kept drifting to the closed door as if she were expecting Bruno to materialize right through it.

Evidently Marie was worried too, for she came into the room carrying a tray upon which stood two glasses and a decanter. "Cognac, Kate. I think we need it to get us through the night." She negotiated the clutter of baggage carefully, then placed the tray on a table. "I wonder if we should call someone to come and stay with us."

Kate wondered who. All the young men were with the army or air force. There were only frail old men and boys left in their circle of friends and acquaintances. She said reassuringly, "Oh, that won't be necessary. We just won't open the door to anyone. I think we're exaggerating the danger. And we'll be on our way to Spain tomorrow." She picked up a satin lingerie bag and began to stuff silk stockings into it.

Marie said, "Maybe I'll call that nice assistant manager anyway and see if he'll come up."

"He left two days ago to join the army," Kate said.

Marie was shocked. "But he must be past forty."

"Forty-four, I believe. He served in the last war."

Marie went to the telephone. "Madame Allegret here. I need a bellboy—or any male on your staff—up here right away." She glanced at Kate as she replaced the receiver. "They owe me this much. I've lived here for years."

There was no response to her call for nearly an hour. Marie paced angrily. "When I think of all the money I've spent, the tips—"

A knock on the door interrupted her. Relieved, Kate said, "I'll go."

At the instant she opened the door she realized her foolishness. Through the crack she saw Bruno's grinning gargoyle face. She screamed and tried to slam the door shut, but his foot was in the way. Straining against the door, Kate yelled over her shoulder to Marie, "Call for help. It's Bruno."

Behind her there was a sudden crash and a gasp. At the same time the pressure on the door eased. Kate turned to see that Marie had collided with an open steamer trunk and fallen to the floor, where she lay writhing with pain, her hands clasped to her left hip.

Bruno's foot disappeared from the door and Kate slammed it and locked it. She ran to Marie's side, pulling a pillow from a sofa for her head. Marie looked up, ashen-faced. "My hip . . . *Dieu*, I think I've broken it."

While Marie was in the hospital, Kate shipped the trunks to Spain and moved with the lighter luggage to a hotel in the Place Louvais, registering under her own name rather than Marie's, in the hope that Bruno would not remember that her last name was Kieron.

She visited Marie daily, always careful to look around as she entered and left the hotel, in case Bruno's squat, apelike figure was there. The doctors weren't hopeful for a speedy recovery, because of the severity of the injury and Marie's age.

The trickle of refugees into Paris was rapidly becoming a flood. First the wealthy Belgians in their large cars, then young men on bicycles and families by train, and finally groups of hitchhikers on trucks. Kate was careful not to mention this to Marie.

Feeling suddenly very much alone, Kate listened to news broadcasts, read the papers, and questioned every American and English journalist she came across, trying to determine just how serious the situation was. No one seemed to know for certain. There were rumors that Britain's newly appointed Prime Minister, Winston Churchill, was in France meeting with Reynaud, Pétain, Weygand, and a general named de Gaulle.

Looking withered and fragile in her hospital bed, Marie asked Kate, "What news from the north?"

"Well . . . there's a time lag between what happens at the front and the arrival of news in the city," Kate answered truthfully. "People exchange rumors and whispers. Some are optimistic and some warn of dire peril. I guess it depends on their personalities."

Astute as ever, Marie said, "I suppose there's little immediate danger, unless the city is bombed." She gave Kate a wan smile. "You've been wonderful, staying with an old lady, but it's time for you to go home."

"No!" Kate interrupted. "I'm taking you to Spain as soon as you're back on your feet. What kind of long-lost daughter do you take me for?"

She was adamant, despite arguments that exhausted both of them. They would leave for Spain together as soon as Marie could travel. Kate held the older woman's hand until she fell asleep, then tiptoed out of the room and went back to her hotel.

There was a lull in the bad news from the front for a few days, but the pause was stifling, pregnant with terrible possibilities. The influx of refugees had dissipated since the beginning of the offensive, and the business streets were deserted.

Kate walked up and down the boulevards, where the remaining people seemed to gather in some natural herding instinct, drawing comfort from one another. There were plenty of tables in the sidewalk cafes, and when she stopped to eat or drink she was usually taken for an American journalist, since all other foreigners had left.

One morning just before dawn she awoke to the sound of anti-aircraft guns pounding the distant skies. Late that day she learned there hadn't been a bombing raid; the planes being shot at were only reconnaissance aircraft. But now sleep was disturbed every night by gunfire, especially just before dawn, and she dragged herself wearily out of bed to go visit the hospital.

May twenty-first was a black day, for both France and

Marie. The Germans were at Arras, and now France was in real danger. Marie had developed pneumonia and was in serious condition.

Overcome with despair, Kate walked back to her hotel. There were few taxicabs on the streets, and besides, she was in no hurry to return to her lonely room.

In the Place Louvais a gardener was weeding a bed of petunias in the tiny park near her hotel. She stopped, incredulous, and wanted to shake him and say, "Don't be a fool. You're making them pretty for the Germans." But of course she didn't.

Dragging herself into the hotel lobby, she was confronted by Tony Winfield, clad in the uniform of a Royal Air Force officer, sporting the wings of a pilot.

After one gasp of delight, she flung herself into his arms and gave him an ecstatic hug.

He smiled down at her. "If I'd known I was going to get this enthusiastic a welcome, I'd have been here long ago. Can we continue this somewhere private?" He indicated with a sideways glance several hotel guests and staff members who were watching with the unabashed delight of the French for displays of emotion between handsome men and chic young women.

Kate slipped her arm through his. "I have a suite. Come on. By the way, how did you find me?"

"When I couldn't get anyone at Claridge's to tell me where you and Madame Allegret had gone, I started calling every other hotel in the city. I might add that I wasted a lot of time looking for you under her name. I wasn't even sure I'd be welcome after that rotten little note you sent me."

"Let's not talk about rotten notes," Kate said as she led the way into the sitting room. She kicked off her high-heeled shoes, tossed purse and gloves onto the coffee table, and flopped onto the couch. "What are you doing here anyway?"

"I managed to wangle escort duty. Flew in a squadron of Spitfires accompanying a Flamingo carrying a very important person."

"Churchill?" Kate asked, impressed.

"Ask me no questions and I'll tell you no lies."

ECHOES OF WAR

"Let's have a glass of wine and a long talk," Kate said. "All at once I feel a great need to converse in my own language—or at least in your version of it. I haven't dared tell Marie how bad the news really is." She told him briefly about Marie's accident and the postponed trip to Spain, and about Bruno.

Tony listened silently, and when she finished he said, "That bloody little swine. I'd like to break his neck." He paused. "But Marie was right to urge you to leave. The situation up north is deteriorating almost as rapidly as Anglo-French relations. I know for a fact that Georges Bonnet—he's a representative of the banking house of Lazard Frères, if you haven't heard of him—anyway, he and Laval and the socialist Paul Fauré are planning to get rid of Paul Reynaud and put Daladier in his place in order to liquidate the war as quickly as possible."

"You mean they plan to sell France down the river?"

"Yes. Laval doesn't want to be premier himself, because then everyone would realize he'd try to make peace with the Germans. The army would revolt. So he'll get Daladier to do his dirty work for him."

"Politicians," Kate said, with all the disgust she could muster. "They got us into this mess in the first place."

"Not entirely unaided by arms manufacturers. You know, the Germans couldn't build good tanks. Now the Skoda tanks, which were built according to French design in Czechoslovakia, are ripping apart the French armies."

"Isn't that *wonderful*. And I was having such a lovely life in Paris." She picked up a wine decanter and filled two glasses, mainly in order to keep from adding, Except that I missed you like crazy.

"How would you like to have a lovely life in Buckinghamshire? Cardovan House is far enough out in the country that it should be safe."

His voice was carefully casual, but Kate's heart suddenly skidded across her ribs. Surely an invitation to live in the ancestral home was a different proposition from occupying a cottage near his air base?

Luckily, before she put her foot in her mouth by misunderstanding the invitation, he went on. "And before you tell me

ECHOES OF WAR

where to go, let me hasten to add it was Cecilia's idea. She said you told her in a letter you had no intention of going back to New York. As she put it, England is the lesser of two evils for you at present. She also said to tell you she'd be delighted to have the old lady as a guest too. Cecilia misses her hordes of houseguests now that everyone is busy with the war effort."

Feeling deflated, Kate made a vow never again to jump to any conclusions where Tony Winfield was concerned. "Marie has developed pneumonia. She can't travel, and I can't just walk out on her."

"Your loyalty is commendable, but I think a little foolish." He moved closer to her on the couch, took her wineglass from her hand, and placed it on the table. "Now, if I don't take you in my arms and kiss you, I'm going to explode."

Feeling his hands in her hair, looking into his eyes, aware of their intermingled breath, hearing her heart beat a tattoo in tune with his, Kate was lost. She sighed, slid her arms around him, and offered her parted lips.

When she came up for air she murmured halfheartedly, "I hope you don't expect me to hop into the sack with you whenever you happen to show up on my doorstep."

He uncoiled her arms from his neck, peeled his body away from her. "Absolutely not. What sort of cad do you take me for? Go and powder your nose and I'll take you out to dine."

Rising on slightly shaky knees, Kate complied. In her room she changed into a brilliant blue taffeta dress, cut low to show shoulders and a little cleavage. She picked up a white satin bolero embroidered with blue sequins and tiny seed pearls, just in case the warm evening turned chilly later.

Tony's eyes lit up when he saw her. "You look . . . quite magnificent."

"Thank you," she mumbled, tripping over her own feet. He put out a hand to steady her and she felt his touch rush up her arm in little shock waves. She wanted to tell him what an exciting man he was, that he could convey more with a word, a glance, a hand under her elbow, than many men were able to with a kiss. But instead she made a wisecrack about wearing her mother's high heels.

Smiling, he said, "When I'm away from you, I try to picture you in my mind. That funny wonderful way you have of smiling, the way sparks ignite in your eyes when you're angry. Last time I saw you I was going to ask for a photo. But even if I had one, it couldn't capture your essence, Kate. Sometimes I look into your eyes and imagine I'm seeing right into your soul. And a very noble soul it is."

She looked at him, bewildered again by his switch from casual to serious.

Perhaps, she decided as they went out into a heartbreakingly beautiful Paris evening, it was Tony's ultra-composed demeanor, his coolly unperturbable presence, the slightly amused expression he usually wore, as though life were only a game, that caused such a devastating transformation when he showed a serious glimpse of what lay beneath the surface. Under that calm exterior was a deeply passionate man, capable of great love and, perhaps, enormous rage. Kate wondered what would happen if she were ever able to unleash the emotions he concealed behind the carefully fashioned mask. Even when he made love to her she knew only his body was hers, and she found herself wanting his mind too, and was determined not to give all of herself until she was sure of his total capitulation.

Their evening together took on a fairy-tale quality. She sat across from him in a candlelit restaurant, with the sad sweet strains of a saxophone playing softly in the shadows. They could have been two people in love with each other and with Paris. Their conversation was filled with nostalgia and undercurrents so strong that it was as if he had reached across the table and touched her.

Somehow, for this one evening, they wrote a different past for their relationship, a different future. Kate thought perhaps it was because of the wine, the music, the sense of everything slipping away.

She asked passionately, "Why do human beings do it? Why are we so determined to tear down all we've built? It's almost as if we can't stand to be happy for long. Have you ever noticed how people say, Oh, everything's going so well, I know it can't last?"

"True. Then they set about making damn sure it *doesn't*

last. But I don't think there's a collective urge to destroy the world. No rational being wants war. Our problem is that we simply refuse to acknowledge the existence of pure evil. We prefer to believe there's some good in the worst of us. That Hitler will repent."

"What's more important to you, Tony, love or honor?"

"That's easy. Love. Without it, how can there be honor?"

"And what's your definition of love?"

"Commitment, joy devotion, fidelity. Between a man and woman, love is what fuses two imperfect halves into a perfect whole."

"Have you known real love?"

He smiled sadly. "That's like asking if I recognize the oak by looking at the acorn. I know only the beginning of love."

"When the world's sane again, perhaps there'll be time for the oak tree to grow."

"I hope so, Kate."

"Tony, are you a patriot?"

He considered. "If you're asking if I'd die for my country, I have to admit I'd rather live for it. But dying would be preferable to the alternatives."

"You mean living under a Nazi regime?"

"Yes. Or being horribly maimed. I'd rather die than that."

She shivered. "Let's talk about something else. About what it's going to be like when all the lights go on again."

Later, they walked along the blacked-out streets, stopped to enjoy the sight of the Seine flowing peacefully by, as it always had and always would, no matter what the foolish inhabitants of its banks wrought.

Tony said, "I'll keep tonight next to my heart and treasure it. A few hours I'll pluck from memory again and again. I'll try to recapture how the breeze felt as it ruffled your hair and then touched my face. Or how the scent of night blossoms blended so perfectly with the fragrance of your skin."

Kate turned to face him, feeling both sad and romantic and more than a little reckless. As she hoped, he kissed her.

Kate was magically enveloped in an awareness of the moment so acute that every other thought and sensation fled. She felt Tony's arms around her, tight, possessive; and his body pressing hers, while his mouth did wonderful things to her lips and teeth and tongue. The tight coil of yearning she felt caused her to melt against him, her legs numb. She parted her lips, closed her eyes.

He murmured against her mouth, "Kate, darling, let's go back to your hotel."

They walked with his arm around her waist. Beside Tony's height she felt small, almost dainty. She laid her head against his shoulder, allowing him to guide her steps, feeling completely protected and safe from harm.

Dreamlike, she walked into the lobby, not speaking, not wanting to break the spell, wanting only to be back in his arms, kissing him with all the abandon she felt.

The lobby light against her half-closed eyelids and a sudden tingling sense of danger broke the spell. Her eyes flew open and she saw, leaning against the desk waiting like some predatory beast, the figure of Bruno.

[12]

Seeing Tony with her, Bruno immediately turned and spoke to the desk clerk. A small cry escaped from Kate. Tony asked, "What is it?" His eyes followed the direction of her horrified stare and he said, "Is that the man?" She nodded.

"Go on up to your room. I'll have a word with him."

"No, please, come with me."

"Go on, Kate. Don't open the door until you hear my voice."

She knew by the look on his face it would be useless to argue.

In her room she paced anxiously, wondering what was happening down in the lobby. Although the wait seemed interminable, she supposed only minutes passed until Tony's voice called to her from the hall. She opened the door and admitted him.

"You talked to him?"

"Yes." She could see that he was angry and frustrated. "Technically, of course, he's free to come and go, even to register at this hotel, which is what he claims he was doing, unaware that you were here. I accused him of following you, harassing you, trying to break into your room, all of which he denied. He claims Madame Allegret owes him back wages and that he's just trying to collect."

"He's a damn liar. Marie paid him. What am I going to do?"

"You're going to get a good night's sleep, and tomorrow we'll find a new place for you to stay."

She was shaking uncontrollably. Tony drew her into his arms, but the passion had gone from their embrace. She leaned against him, drawing comfort, waiting for her terror to pass, hating the feeling of helplessness.

After a moment he said, "I won't let him near you, Kate. Come on, let's turn on the wireless and see if there's a late news broadcast. We'll get your mind off that ugly little brute."

The voice of the radio announcer crackled into the room as they sat close together on the couch, fingers intertwined.

". . . and whatever the result of the battle in Flanders, the high command has made provision that the enemy will not profit strategically by its result."

"What does that mean?" Kate asked, nestling even closer to Tony.

"It means," Tony said slowly, "what I've expected since I found out how bad things are on the front. That they're going to try to evacuate the army to England. If the Germans don't capture the army, their victory is only tactical."

"But if the army goes to England . . ."

"Yes," Tony answered quietly. "Now the Germans are coming to Paris."

Kate awoke at dawn the following day, feeling as though a lead blanket were pressing down on her. The unfamiliar room came into focus, then the open doorway. A shadowy figure moved in the adjacent room and it was a heart-stopping second before she realized it was Tony, and that she'd fallen asleep in his arms.

He turned and smiled, dark smudges under his eyes testifying to the sleepless vigil he'd kept over her. "Morning, Kate. I've dreamed of having breakfast with you, but the rest of my dream differed slightly from the reality of last night."

Kate stretched, marveling at how daylight could drive

away fear. "You could come back to bed and we could make up for lost time."

He crossed the room and sat on the bed, bent, and kissed her with lingering precision. She placed her hands on the back of his neck and murmured against his mouth, "How much time do we have before you have to rush off and do God knows what it is you do in your airplane?"

Stretching out beside her and wrapping her carefully into the closest possible embrace, he replied, "I don't have to report until this evening. We have all day." His hands slid down the length of her naked body and her response was instantaneous.

They made love as the sun came up and flooded the room with brilliance and warmth. There was no place in their thoughts for enemies, national or individual. There was just Tony and Kate, lost in sensual surrender and unable to think or feel beyond the realm of their own tingling flesh and soaring emotions.

It was Kate who unwittingly broke the spell when she whispered, "Why didn't somebody tell me about *amourettes* long ago?"

Tony swung his feet to the floor. "The literal translation, Kate, is 'little love.' Is that what I am to you—a little love, a passing fancy?"

Kate pushed her hair out of her eyes. "You're angry. Why?"

Tell me you love me. I dare you to admit it, and then perhaps I can too.

He stood up. "I'm not angry. But time is passing and I want to get you moved into my friend's *pension* for tonight. Later you can go to the hospital and say goodbye to Madame Allegret, then tomorrow you're off to England."

"Damn it, don't give me orders." Kate jumped out of bed and headed for the bathroom.

When she emerged, Tony was fully dressed and had coffee and croissants waiting. She drank some coffee as she packed and he went to try to find a cab.

By the time they reached the *pension* on the Left Bank a slight thaw between them was setting in. Tony said, "You'll be safe here. Bruno will be prowling the hotels that Marie would use—nothing so modest as this. But you've got to leave Paris. You must see that. Not even my battling Kate can take on Bruno *and* the Germans."

Kate was silent, still vaguely disappointed that she and Tony could be so close physically yet unable to share their deepest feelings. Besides, foremost in her mind was the vision of a frail old lady lying all alone in a hospital bed. To hell with Bruno and the Germans. She'd worry about them later. First there was a debt to repay to Marie.

Tony introduced her to the concierge, a big tough-looking man with an impatient manner, as "Miss Clifton." To Kate, Tony added under his breath, "Just in case anyone inquires."

That afternoon they strolled hand in hand around the Place Vendôme. Kate remembered thronging tourists and happier times as she looked into the windows of the luxury shops. Sunlight flashed on a jeweler's window, catching a gold chain from which dangled a crucifix. On the velvet backdrop the shadow of the cross was distorted by the draped cloth and the twisted result reminded her of the swastika and the shadow it had cast over all of Europe.

They went back to the *pension*, overcome with sadness, and made love with fierce desperation. As the afternoon shadows grew longer, Tony said, "If we're going to have dinner together we'll have to go now."

They dined at a restaurant on the Rue Montmartre and were the only customers. Tony reached across the table and picked up her hand. "We'll remember that tonight we had *rouget* cooked in brandy . . . and knew that for France the war was lost."

"Oh, God, is it?"

"I heard a news broadcast while you were bathing. The French army and British Expeditionary Forces are trapped on the beaches at Dunkirk. The German radio threatens that every ship that tries to embark troops will be sunk."

Kate stared at her barely touched plate, trying to comprehend that the unthinkable had happened. "Why are you here then?" she asked, frightened and angry. "Why aren't you flying over Dunkirk?"

ECHOES OF WAR

"Because I have orders to follow. I have a rendezvous in an hour. I doubt I'll be going anywhere until tomorrow. Wait for me at the *pension,* and I'll get back to you as soon as I can. You've run out of time, Kate. Do you really want to stay in Paris and greet the German conquerors?"

"Marie . . ." she said dully. "I must go and tell her."

"We'll have time to stop at the hospital if we leave now."

Marie was asleep, approaching the crisis of her illness, and couldn't be disturbed. Tony rushed Kate from the hospital to the *pension,* kissed her a hurried goodbye, and told her to be packed and ready to leave when he returned.

Tony's patience was about to evaporate. At his side, Charles Morcambe's steel-rimmed eyes peered into the pitch black street as they waited at the curb for their driver to bring their car. Tony said, "To hell with all of that. I've got to get Kate out of Paris. Just give me a couple of hours."

"It's out of the question. You're to go directly to the airfield. There'll be chaos when the word gets out. You'd never get through the mobs."

"Didn't you hear a word I said? There's a former chauffeur who—"

"Tony," Charles interrupted, "do you want to be courtmartialed? Look, for old times' sake, I'll take care of your lady friend, I promise. You're needed for some important flying duties."

"By God, I should be flying cover over the beaches at Dunkirk, where I'd do our own people some good. You promised me, Charles. You swore I'd be back in a Spitfire long before the German offensive."

"For the last time, you and several other pilots have been placed at the disposal of de Gaulle. He and certain of his people are to be flown to England. You're to stand by at designated airfields and wait for orders. No messages to *anyone* under *any* circumstances. No goodbyes before you go. But as a concession to our friendship, I'll go and see your American girlfriend and make some excuse for your not returning."

"That's not good enough. I want her out of France."

"You have my word on it."

Tony fumed silently, wishing now that he'd told Kate of his duties these past months, ferrying key men back and forth across the channel on sundry secret missions.

A yellow glow moved along the street toward them. It proved to be a pair of policemen carrying lanterns. They stopped and demanded to see papers. Tony waited impatiently until they were done and turned to Charles again. "It could be days—weeks perhaps—before de Gaulle is ready to go. You know what a stubborn bastard he is, especially if he thinks we're trying to give him orders."

"I quite agree. But when he or any of his aides need a plane, it's to be ready at a moment's notice."

Something blew against Tony's leg and he bent to pick up a creased piece of paper. It was a German leaflet threatening to bombard Paris. Tony crumpled it and flung it into the gutter under the wheels of the approaching car. There was nothing he could do but obey orders. After all, they had come from the Prime Minister himself.

Kate tossed and turned all night, unable to sleep, making plans and then rejecting them. If Marie shook off the pneumonia, could she be transported—possibly in a wheelchair—to England? With Tony's help, Kate decided it could be done.

When the darkness was eventually replaced by a gunfire-shattered dawn, Kate rose to go to the hospital. Please, dear God, she prayed as she dressed, let Marie be out of danger and let her agree to the plan.

Kate met the concierge on her way down the stairs from her room. *"M'sieur, s'il vous plaît,* if M'sieur Winfield comes before I get back, will you give him this note?" She had scribbled a few lines telling Tony where she had gone and why.

The concierge looked preoccupied and nodded absently, but took the note and shoved it into his pocket.

German bombers had bombed the huge Citroen factory on the Quai de Javel and knocked down some apartment houses nearby, but the bombs were dropped from too high an altitude to be really effective. Still, as Charles Morcambe arrived at the *pension* where Kate was staying, he was anxious to get out of the city as quickly as possible. If he was to be killed by Germans he wanted a more glorious end than suffocating in the rubble of a bombed building.

The concierge looked at him suspiciously when he asked for Kate Kieron; then he corrected himself and said, "I mean, Miss Clifton."

"There's nobody here by that name."

"Oh, come on, man, I'm a friend of Tony Winfield and I have a message for her."

The concierge placed his formidable bulk between Charles and the stairs leading to the guests' rooms.

Charles said, "Very well, I haven't time to argue. Will you please tell her that Tony can't get back to see her but he urges her to leave Paris immediately."

Watching Charles scurry through the door and jump into the waiting car, the concierge considered the warning Tony had given him to beware of a man who might come looking for his lady friend. The description he'd given didn't match the man in the steel-rimmed glasses, but perhaps he had disguised himself. The concierge decided that when Miss Clifton returned he would say there'd been a visitor and perhaps she should leave his establishment. After all, he had enough to worry about, with the Boche smashing toward Paris, without having some woman attacked on his premises.

Marie was sitting in a wheelchair at the window of her hospital room, looking considerably more lively than she had for weeks, although far from strong. She smiled as Kate came into the room carrying a small bunch of daisies. "Isn't the news wonderful?" she exclaimed, turning her cheek for Kate's kiss.

"Yes . . . it is." Kate tried to sound cheerful. A wave of exhilaration had rippled through Paris as friends and relatives began to receive telegrams from men who had been safely evacuated from Dunkirk to England. It was clear the northern armies were neither dead nor captured by the Germans. Vast numbers of them had miraculously been plucked from the beaches of Dunkirk by an armada of small boats.

But today the surge of high spirits was dampened by the news that Belgium had surrendered. Kate decided not to mention this. She had moved from the *pension* after the concierge told her about a strange man asking for her, but had left her new address, to be given only to Tony. Not that she expected him to return. He had probably been ordered to Flanders the minute he left her, and was too busy to get in touch. But his silence nagged her. She could hardly show up at Cardovan House with Marie without him. If she didn't hear from him soon, they'd have to revert to their plan to go to Spain.

Kate had moved into the Hotel Continental, which was packed with foreign journalists and where press conferences were held almost daily. She felt safer among large numbers of Britons and Americans, and besides, she was able to get the news firsthand.

"I spoke to your doctor," she said to Marie, pulling a chair closer to the window. "He says you can leave the hospital. You'll have to come back as an out-patient for a while, and we'll need a place where we can use the wheelchair."

"You don't have to worry about the wheelchair. This morning I went around the room on crutches."

Kate's spirits lifted. Perhaps they'd still be able to get out of the city before the Germans arrived.

They checked into adjoining rooms on the ground floor of the Hotel Continental, and Kate was glad to be busy again. She found she had a knack for caring for an invalid and the more she had to do, the less time there was for the persistent nagging question of why there'd been no word from Tony. She never mentioned him to Marie, afraid if she talked about him she'd break down and give voice to the fear that he'd been shot down, wounded, or worse.

Now there were definite changes in the daily life of the city. There was no telephone service in the hotel, many floors were closed, taxis were ever harder to find. Guests and staff dwindled. "Perhaps, if the line holds, they'll come back," the optimists said.

Restaurants closed. There were rumors of German infiltration among the refugees. A press conference was called by the Ministry of Information to announce that safe conduct passes would be provided to the foreign correspondents. Garbage trucks were left parked in the middle of streets to prevent airplane landings.

When Kate heard the sound of muted roars unlike the customary anti-aircraft fire and inquired about it, an American journalist told her, "Naval guns mounted on railroad cars. The Germans can't be far away. Hadn't you better get the hell out of here?"

Kate had a full tank of gasoline in Marie's Citroen and kept the car in a locked garage. They had decided to wait as long as possible to allow Marie's strength to return, but Kate knew they had about run out of time.

Kate went to the Prefecture of Police for visas for them to leave France. A harried woman official told her, "Leave your passports and come back in four days."

"But the Germans could be here by then."

The woman shrugged. "You're an American, what have you to fear?"

Kate decided against leaving the passports.

She walked the streets blindly, trying to decide what to do, whether to risk leaving without visas. In the Champs-Elysées the terraces of the cafes were jammed with people, as though nothing were amiss, but Kate saw sailors carrying boxes and papers from the Ministère de la Marine. She stopped one sailor and asked him, "Are you evacuating?"

"The Boche are at Nantes and Pontoise," he said, hurrying away from her.

That was half an hour by car from the city. They had to get out now. Everywhere Parisians seemed to be gazing at their city with tears in their eyes. Kate ran into a couple of British correspondents who said they were going to say goodbye to Notre-Dame and look at the golden trophies of the Eglise du Dôme at Les Invalides one last time.

Trying to compose herself, she went into Marie's room. The old lady was dressed in her street clothes, packing toilet articles into a bag. A wicker hamper filled with food stood ready.

Marie said, "The hotel is closing. The cable office and wireless have already moved south. Did you get the visas?"

"Yes," Kate lied. "I'll go and get the car while you settle our bill." She squeezed Marie's shoulder. "We'll be on our way before you know it."

[13]

The roads leading out of Paris were shockingly congested, the weather was hot and thundery. Most of the cars were driven by women and were full of old people and children. There was a marked absence of men.

Kate was at the wheel of the Citroen. She had tried to make Marie as comfortable as possible in the back seat, propped with clothing stuffed into pillow cases.

They caught up with the great army of refugees outside the city limits. Apart from the column of vehicles, there appeared to be thousands of people on foot with packs on their backs. A continuous river of humanity more wretched and despairing than Kate could have imagined in the worst nightmare. What struck her most forcibly was their terrible, overwhelming silence. They simply trudged south, forcing numbed feet forward; without food or water or hope, and probably, she thought dejectedly, without a place to go. Some pushed handcarts, while occasionally a bicycle whizzed around the creeping cars, making better time. Kate had to brake frequently and came to a dead stop several times as a car ahead of her ran out of gas or a truck broke down.

As night fell, it started to rain, and once again the traffic came to a stop. Kate got out to see what was wrong and was confronted by the pitiful sight of a farm wagon with a broken axle. A woman holding a baby, three young children clutching her skirts, watched with despairing eyes as an old man begged passersby for help.

Returning to the car, Kate said tearfully, "We couldn't possibly get all of them into our car, could we?" Marie, understanding, said, "Someone will help them."

Voices suddenly yelled, *"Alerte! Alerte!"* Kate stuck her head out of the window and shouted, "What is it? What's wrong?" The reply came: "Boche bombers coming. Switch off your lights."

They could hear the drone of aircraft growing louder. With every vestige of light extinguished, the darkness pressed in as clammy as a shroud. The roar of aircraft engines grew louder. Kate couldn't tell if they were French or German or how high they were flying. Flashes lit the horizon from distant gunfire. Watching, Kate felt a sense of unreality, as though it were all happening to someone else.

The drone of planes faded, but the car ahead still didn't move. Kate could dimly see the bottleneck of a bridge, just ahead of the broken-down farm wagon. She snapped on a flashlight and looked at her map. The road from Paris to Bordeaux was three hundred miles long, and in seven hours they had covered only fifty miles.

Marie said fretfully, "I feel so guilty, knowing we have food when people around us must be hungry."

"We've a long way to go," Kate reminded her gently.

Marie continued to stare with tears in her eyes at the throngs of refugees.

This time they were held up for three hours. Marie slept after a while, but Kate only dozed fitfully. At last they began to move again. Now there were women crying on the roadside, begging for gasoline. There was nothing to do but look straight ahead and keep going.

The rain continued to fall and the night was very dark, offering protection from bombers. Kate began to sing softly to keep herself awake. She hadn't realized what she was singing until Marie joined in for a rousing rendition of the "Marseillaise."

The burst of defiance didn't last. A man went running past

banging hysterically on every car window. "My daughter! Where is my daughter? Have you seen her?"

He was gone before Kate realized he had spoken in English. In the back seat Marie began to cry softly.

A little later she said, "There's a side road ahead. You need to rest. You can't drive all night."

Kate was too exhausted to argue. She turned onto a dirt road bordered by fields, put her head back, and slept.

She awakened to a murky dawn. Marie was handing the last of their food through the window to a woman with small children, who stammered, *"Merci, merci . . ."* and stumbled off to rejoin the weary column of marchers.

Kate climbed out of the car to stretch her aching limbs. Through the open window Marie said apologetically, "I have to go to the bathroom. I can't hold it any longer."

Kate went to the trunk and got out the bedpan she had packed. She put a towel over it and handed it to Marie. "Can you manage? I need to go too. I'll go over to those bushes. I'll be back in a second to help you."

"Go ahead. Don't hurry."

Walking across the field, Kate felt every constricted muscle in her body protest. There was a slight hollow filled with trees and bushes, and she dropped out of sight of the never-ending stream of refugees.

Almost at once she heard the drone of an approaching plane. She didn't even bother to look up, since it was obviously just a single aircraft, not a bombing squadron. A reconnaissance plane probably.

She emerged from the bushes as the plane began its dive earthward. There was a black cross on the fuselage. People on the road were hitting the ground, going down like dominoes.

There was a burst of gunfire, sounding no more formidable than a series of firecrackers. She heard the ping of bullets striking metal, then the plane soared upward, skimmed the trees, and was gone. Several cars had been hit, including Marie's Citroen. Kate could see the shattered rear window as she ran across the open field feeling as though every step was mired in mud.

ECHOES OF WAR

A man stumbled from the car in front, blood running down his face. Kate ran past him to yank open the door of the Citroen. Marie, in a reclining position, was gasping and clutching her blood-soaked shoulder.

"No!" Kate screamed. "No, no!"

There was at least one bullet embedded in Marie's shoulder. The bullets had also penetrated the fuel tank, and the remainder of their precious gasoline was running into the dirt. A truck driver offered to take Marie into the next small town, but he had no room for Kate.

Now she was part of the silent, trudging army—hungry, frightened, wondering what would become of them, praying that Marie, who had already suffered so much, would live. She carried only their money, abandoning everything else with the car. She passed many stranded cars. Kate reflected that the events of the past days were like Chinese boxes, each one opening to reveal another unpleasant surprise.

Just before noon she reached the next town, coming first to a railway station. A long freight train was pulling in from Paris, every car packed tight with people, at least a hundred in each. The doors were opened for five minutes and people stumbled out, telling of being machine-gunned by German planes.

Kate wearily went looking for the stationmaster to get directions to the hospital.

"She's lost more blood than she should have," the doctor told Kate. "And obviously the trauma of the journey—shock—as well as her previous fracture and illness . . ."

Kate wasn't listening. Marie lay in bed, her shoulder bandaged, arm in a sling, obviously fighting to stay awake, when she caught sight of Kate in the doorway with the doctor. But it was Marie's face that shocked Kate. Apart from her gray pallor and bruised eyes, there was an air of hopelessness and utter defeat that hadn't been there before.

As soon as Kate reached her bed, Marie whispered, "Thank God you came before I . . . Kate, I want to go back to Paris."

"Back?" Kate repeated blankly, thinking of the hours she'd spent at the wheel of the Citroen.

ECHOES OF WAR

"Yes. It can't be any worse than that sea of humanity on the road. Since everyone is trying to get out of the city, I should think the trains going back in will be empty. I'm going to sign myself out of here. We'll leave tomorrow. Kate, please, take me home, then you can go back to America. You're a neutral; you won't be detained. Please say you'll do this last thing for me."

She was becoming visibly agitated. Kate wearily agreed.

[14]

The city seemed utterly deserted. No honking cars circling the Place de la Concorde, no yelling news vendors, arm-waving policemen, chatting pedestrians, or meandering tourists.

Just an occasional German car en route to the Hotel Crillon, which housed the hastily set up headquarters of the occupying forces. A swastika fluttered from the flagstaff where once the stars and stripes flew to welcome President Wilson, to the cheers of the French crowd as he waved to them from the balcony. On the Eiffel Tower the tricolor had been replaced by a swastika.

A ghost town, Kate thought as she left the hospital and headed for the Rue Gabrielle. She was stopped twice by German patrols, who gave her passport a cursory check and sent her on her way. The soldiers seemed polite enough, but they were combat troops, not Hitler's secret police or storm troopers. She carried her American passport in her pocket now and touched it frequently to reassure herself that she was only a temporary observer of this nightmare.

With Marie back in the hospital, Kate was without a place to stay and again alone. The hotels were closed. Everything appeared to be closed. She decided to go to Jean Louis' mother and see if she would put her up until she could make other plans.

ECHOES OF WAR

But on that particular Sunday morning the goose-stepping German conquerers, led by horsemen, held a triumphant parade up the Champs-Elysées, past the Arc de Triomphe, and into the Avenue Foch, where Kate found herself standing with a silent and tearful group of spectators.

She tore her eyes from the marching Germans, who were fulfilling every nationalist's dream since the Treaty of Versailles, to study the faces of Parisians. Young and old alike wept, and she felt their utter humiliation and despair. But Kate shed no tears. She was too angry. Her hands clenched into fists and she shook with the effort to keep from hurling something, anything, at those arrogant goose-stepping soldiers.

Madame Jourdain welcomed Kate as warmly as if she were a daughter-in-law. Of course Kate must stay with her, as long as she wished. There had been no word from Jean-Louis. She was to call his mother by her given name, Annette.

"Tell me, how is Marie?" she asked when Kate explained how their evacuation plans had gone awry.

Kate felt a frown of tension knit her brows. "Not very well. The bullet wounds weren't really life-threatening. She lost some blood, but . . . I don't know, it's as if she's given up."

"Perhaps it is the sickness that attacks her beloved Paris that is the real malaise," Annette suggested.

The two women were keeping a vigil. Annette for the return of her son, and Kate for Marie's recovery. Only as the days passed, hope for both eventualities dwindled. It became clear that Marie had no intention of recovering. She wasted away visibly, and nothing Kate said or did distracted her from willing herself to die.

"She's dying, just like her beloved City of Light is dying," Kate said despairingly after visiting the hospital. "I feel so helpless. I can't save her: she wants to die."

"You're a good girl to stay until the end," Annette said.

But Kate wasn't just keeping a death watch. She knew that. Some vague idea that there was something she could do—some gesture of defiance—lurked at the back of her mind. Along with the knowledge that as an American citizen

ECHOES OF WAR

and a neutral she was perhaps in a unique position to strike back at the invaders in some way. How, she wasn't sure.

"If only Jean-Louis would come home." Annette sighed. "Once I hoped that you and he—"

"We're good friends," Kate said. "Nothing more." And she allowed herself to think about Tony and pray that he was safe. France had fallen, England would be next in line for conquest. But somehow, somewhere, she and Tony would find each other again. That belief was all that kept her going through that summer of indignity and defeat.

One day an army truck stopped on their street and German soldiers went to every house collecting bed linen. Householders were allowed to keep two sheets, one blanket, and one mattress for each bed in the house. The rest were to be donated to the German hausfraus who lacked them, since the German looms had been working only for the army.

The blackout was more rigidly enforced than previously. A warning was given if a light showed, then a pistol shot fired into the offending window.

A permit was required for everything. A vast bureaucracy of forms and files and printed permission slips became a part of daily life, stapling Parisians in place like insects in an entomologist's collection. Kate had to report once a week to the local police station to sign an aliens' register.

Annette wailed, "The Boche are looting *everything*. What a mania for carrying things off they have."

For Kate, the worst part of the Nazi occupation was the strangling grip of censorship. No news or letters got in or out of the French capital. Kate had no idea if her last letters home ever reached her family. She had also written to Tony at Cardovan House, since she hadn't kept his air force address, telling him she was staying with Annette Jourdain. She didn't really hope for a reply.

She ran into several American journalists she had known while staying at the Continental, and one, a quiet-spoken Southerner, told her, "I watched them sign the armistice. They'd hauled the same railway carriage where Marshal Foch dictated peace terms to the Germans in 1918 out of a museum so that Hitler could sit in the same chair Foch used.

Hitler was in uniform, wearing an iron cross. Goering carried his jeweled baton and was surrounded by members of the high command. What a cunning moment of revenge! Hitler's expression was a chilling mixture of triumph and scorn and hate. He placed his hands on his hips and planted his feet wide in a defiant gesture that expressed his contempt more than any words."

"So France is split into two countries," Kate said. "Why did he do that?"

"To prevent a unified France from rebelling or cooperating with England, I'd guess. Hitler wants two Frances, in conflict with each other. He wants an immediate agreement with England, so he can have a free hand in the East."

"What about England? Will they fight on alone?"

"You didn't hear their new Prime Minister's speech? Churchill has declared that they'll fight on the beaches and in the streets and never surrender. He made a farewell speech to the French. Sounded like a father giving comfort to an adopted child, and even though Churchill's French is excruciating, it brought tears to my eyes. He said, 'Good night, then, sleep to gather strength for the morning. For the morning will come. Brightly will it shine on the brave and the true, kindly upon all who suffer for the cause, glorious upon the tombs of heroes. Thus will shine the dawn. *Vive la France!*' "

Kate was silent, still unable to grasp that the most civilized country in Europe had been surrendered to such utter defeat by an eighty-four-year-old, nearly senile marshal, prodded by a few defeated generals and defeatist politicians.

One morning Kate awakened to a shriek from downstairs. She sat up, heart thumping, and called, "Annette?" Stumbling out of bed, she grabbed a small ceramic lamp, the only possible weapon she could see, and went to the top of the stairs.

At the front door Annette was sagging into the arms of a roughly dressed stranger, who was attempting to drag her plump body into the kitchen. Kate flew downstairs to Annette's defense, then skidded to a stop.

Coming slowly through the street door after the stranger

was a barely recognizable figure. Jean-Louis looked haggard, travel-stained, but the first thing Kate saw was his empty coat sleeve.

Wordlessly she put down the lamp and went to him, wrapped her arms around him, and stood very close. The other man had helped Annette to a chair and then gone to close the front door. He looked as though he was fresh in from the country, a farm laborer perhaps, from his clothes. He stood waiting, cap in hand.

Jean-Louis kissed Kate lightly on the cheeks, then went to kiss his mother. His eyes were burning with an even more fierce flame than Kate remembered. As Annette started to weep, he said, "I'm alive, Mama. *Alive.*"

Kate turned to the other man and said, "Come into the kitchen, I'll get you something to drink."

He had a tense, watchful expression. He replied in English. "I'm sorry. I don't speak French." From his accent, he might have been from the north of England.

Kate's mouth must have dropped open in surprise, for he added, "Jean-Louis insisted I come. But if you don't want me here, I'll be on my way."

They sat around the kitchen table and drank ersatz coffee, which was all that was now available, and Jean-Louis explained about his companion, who was an RAF pilot who had been shot down in Flanders. His name was Gerald.

Jean-Louis had been in a military hospital recovering from the amputation of his left arm when the evacuation from Dunkirk began. The hospital had been bombed and the surviving patients were scattered to various farmhouses. Gerald's plane was shot down and he parachuted to the farmer's field, where the farmer helped him bury his parachute, then hid him. They'd been there since the French collapse.

"I can't fight any more," Jean-Louis said. "But Gerald is a pilot, and God knows we need all of the pilots we can get. We've got to get him back to England somehow. I thought there must be many like him, soldiers and airmen who were left behind. And there will be more when the English planes come over to bomb the Germans. We need a chain of safe houses, and guides to send them south to the unoccupied

ECHOES OF WAR

zone, then over the Pyrenees into Spain. But first I need to talk to him! So far we've got by with sign language and odd words. Kate, tell him we're going to help him escape."

Marie died a month after Paris fell. Gerald and two other RAF pilots, as well as a British soldier who had escaped the German net, had all been sent south. For Kate, her role of interpreter in the smuggling operation accomplished a dual purpose. It made her a part of the struggle against the Nazis and, because she helped RAF pilots, it made her feel closer to Tony. After all, he could have been one of them.

Kate shared Annette's room and bed and pretended not to see the longing glances Jean-Louis bestowed on her. One evening when they returned after delivering the last of the current batch of escapees to the next safe house in the suburbs, they found Annette had already retired for the night.

Alone for the first time since his return, Kate and Jean-Louis faced one another, unsure of their new relationship. Was it friendship? It certainly wasn't the lighthearted flirtation of the months of the phony war, yet it was based on genuine affection and caring. Jean-Louis slowly reached for her, pulled her into a rough embrace. "Kate, *chérie,* you are brave and beautiful and I don't want you to pity me. I see you evading my eyes. I know you are afraid I'll make some romantic overture. But you need not fear. You are too valuable to our cause and to me for me to scare you away."

She leaned closer and kissed his mouth lightly. "Nobody's going to scare me off. Not until everyone who wants to go to Spain is safely there."

"And then?"

"I don't know. I gave up planning beyond tomorrow a long time ago."

"A wise decision in these times."

The silence of the night was abruptly shattered by a pounding on their door. Kate jumped and Jean-Louis said, "Go on upstairs. I'll see who it is."

Kate had barely reached the top of the narrow flight of stairs than the front door yielded to heavy boots. She crouched in the shadows as someone—it sounded like at

ECHOES OF WAR

least three men—burst into the house. Annette stumbled from her bed. Kate caught her and placed her hand over her mouth to keep her quiet.

The voice that addressed Jean-Louis down in the parlor was unmistakable. Kate's blood froze as she heard the grating voice demand to know if Jean-Louis and a woman companion had not just been seen on the street, in defiance of the curfew.

Bruno! There was no doubt. So he had been a deserter and now he was a collaborator. If he was working for the Nazi invaders, God help them if that little fiend had any authority over them whatsoever.

"You must have seen someone else." Jean-Louis' voice sounded bored, indifferent. "I've been home all evening."

There was a muffled sound, then a grunt of pain. Annette struggled, but Kate held her fast. Jean-Louis sounded winded when he went on. "You're brave, taking on a one-armed man. Too bad you weren't so brave when you were on our side—or were you ever on our side?"

There was a crash that sounded like breaking furniture. Then Bruno's voice again. "I know the American woman is living with you. I know you're up to something, the pair of you. I'll catch you one of these days. You tell Katerina that being an American isn't going to help her if she runs afoul of the Gestapo."

Kate held Annette until they heard the footsteps fade into the night, then they both rushed downstairs to help Jean-Louis, who lay on the floor, a trickle of blood running from his mouth, but a sardonic grin on his face.

Tony and the other pilots of A Flight stamped their feet and swung their arms as they moved around their Spitfires, trying to come fully awake and loosen their limbs before fitting them into the cramped space of the cockpit. Dawn was breaking clear and silver along the horizon, where land and sea met at the English Channel.

Across the field, B Flight was being refueled, and the delivery pump's thumping sounded vaguely like a heartbeat. A large convoy was coming through the Straits of Dover and it was certain the Luftwaffe would have a crack at it. Tony felt a combination of tense excitement and curiosity, wondering what his first taste of aerial fighting would be like and, more particularly, how he'd handle himself.

The crack of a Very pistol and the flight of two fiery balls over their heads sent the pilots racing for their planes as an orderly shouted, "Scramble, A Flight. Angels-ten."

As they climbed in formation toward ten thousand feet, the ground controller's voice crackled over the radio: "Ninety bandits approaching from Calais, Yorker Blue Leader. Twenty-plus at Angels-six, remainder Angels-twelve, over."

Six of us against ninety doesn't seem like reasonable odds, Tony thought, at the same time reminding himself that prior to his next scramble he was going to take a pee.

Twenty Heinkel 111 bombers came into view, which were to be intercepted by the other section. Above the bombers he caught a glimpse of the ugly outlines of the Messerschmitt escort that his flight was to intercept. Thirty Me 110 twin-engined fighters and, higher still, another formation of at least forty Me 109s. Tony swallowed, searching his mouth for nonexistent saliva.

Their flight commander dived into the attack and, peeling off with fan-shaped precision, the others went after him. Below, the 110s were forming a defensive circle above the bombers.

He pressed the firing button and the machine guns in the wings chattered in response. Almost instantly his plane was surrounded by orange-red globes that hung in the air, and it was a moment before he realized that the enemy rear gunners had opened up and he was their intended target. The pretty little glowing globes were hundreds of rounds of cannon fire.

After that there was no time to think. The skies seemed to be filled with flashing wings painted with iron crosses, and streaks of tracer ripping the heavens apart. He cursed as he fired, because he kept hitting the button too late and never saw his bullets strike home. A pair of 109s came zooming toward him on a collision course, and he roared between them with inches to spare.

Then all at once he was alone over the channel, except for

two parachutes hurtling earthward. He wasn't sure whose pilots had bailed out, but he hoped they made it, whoever they were. He radioed their position to the launches and turned for home, disappointed he hadn't shot down an enemy plane, but rather glad to be alive.

That evening he finally managed to reach Charles Morcambe by phone. "Charles? I thought you'd dropped off the earth. I've been trying to get hold of you for weeks. Why didn't you return any of my calls? What happened in Paris? Where did Kate go—to Spain or home to America?"

"Sorry, we've been busy. Total reorganization of our department. The PM has instructed us to set Europe ablaze, and that's what we're going to do." There was suppressed excitement in Charles' voice, which he must have heard himself, as he added quickly, "Just between ourselves, of course."

"Did Kate give you a message for me?"

"As a matter of fact, I never got to talk to her. She wasn't at the *pension* where you said she'd be. I did leave a message with the concierge that you felt she should leave the city."

"You mean she may still be in Paris?" Tony swore for a full minute before slamming the phone down in Charles' ear.

[15]

Tony was home on a weekend pass, listening to Cecilia complaining that tea had been rationed and from now on butter and fats would be cut to six ounces a week, when Ursula came flying into the drawing room.

"I just came back from Holloway Prison and I'm appalled!" She collapsed weakly to a divan, leaned back, and closed her eyes.

"Why, dear?" her mother inquired. "I mean, I thought prisons were *supposed* to be appalling."

"Who did you visit?" Tony asked sharply.

"A girl I knew who lived in Germany for a while. I mean, good Lord, all she did was to sleep with a German. She only lived with him for a couple of months."

"They locked her up?" Cecilia too was shocked. "I did hear that Sir Oswald Mosley and his fascists had all been sent to Brixton."

"Oh, yes," Ursula said grimly. "Brixton is full of people who are being held with no charges filed against them, picked up on the flimsiest of excuses."

"Mosley's lot proclaimed themselves against the war," Tony pointed out. "They're a bunch of anti-Semites, blaming everything on the Jews. They should be locked up."

"And what about all the others?" Ursula asked heatedly.

"One man I talked to was Jewish. He was a German Jew, and the stupid officials at Brixton didn't know the difference between him and a Nazi."

"It's not too long ago that you were marching through the streets of London with Mosley's fanatics, and you didn't know the difference either," Tony said.

"I say, did you really march with Mosley?" Cecilia asked. "I thought you'd just met his Diana at a party."

Ursula ignored the question. "My friend Albert Weales gave a really smashing speech at Hyde Park Corner. He pointed out that Britain has also resorted to tyrannical methods. He told the crowd that the Magna Carta has been ripped to bloody pieces."

"Did it occur to either you or your friend Weales," Tony asked, "that the mere fact that he can stand on Hyde Park Corner making such statements tends to—"

He broke off as a polite knock on the drawing-room door was followed by the entrance of the butler. "A message for you, sir, from your flight commander. You're to report back at once." He paused, his face grave. "It seems the Jerries are bombing London."

In occupied France the Germans had decreed that only infants, pregnant women, and people over seventy were to be allowed to purchase milk. Annette Jourdain had become adept at stuffing pillows under already well-filled clothes and passing herself off as pregnant; or, when someone noticed she was a wee bit past childbearing age, she managed to borrow someone's elderly relative. She reasoned that any means was justified to obtain nourishment for the hungry men they hid from the Germans.

One afternoon shortly after their last batch of "Boarders" had departed on the underground shuttle south, Annette announced that she was going shopping.

"I'll go with you," Jean-Louis said. "I want to talk to the baker. I believe he might take in some of our boarders. The trickle seems to be turning into a flood, and we can't hide all of them in this tiny house."

Kate bade them a preoccupied adieu and went into the kitchen to wash the dishes. It was a relief not to jump at

ECHOES OF WAR

every sound on the street, or at the sight of a passing policeman or German patrol.

With the tension, grief over Marie, and the constant drama of the occupation, as well as the lack of privacy as she shared Annette's bed, Kate found she had trouble sleeping. She dragged herself through the day's chores in a perpetual state of exhaustion.

After drying the last of the dishes, she went into the living room. The afternoon sunlight was warm on the windows and the house quiet. She sat unmoving, in a hypnotic daze, listening to the ticking of the clock. At length she drifted off to sleep.

She awoke suddenly, startled by something that was gone before she could identify it. The room was filled with long shadows. She called out, "Annette? Jean-Louis?" There was no reply.

The mantelpiece clock said it was evening, but it couldn't be. They would have been gone for hours and the shops would be closed. Surely they'd be back, unless . . . From upstairs came the sound of the toilet flushing.

She stood up, feeling the hairs on the back of her neck tingle, and called again, "Jean-Louis?"

There was no reply. Footsteps creaked down the stairs. She stared at the doorway, her thoughts rushing in several directions. If it was the police or the Gestapo, wouldn't they have come bursting in? An entry by stealth suggested a burglar. Shortages and German looting were turning even ordinary citizens into criminals. But what about the toilet flushing? She glanced about for a weapon.

The next second a shadow fell crookedly across the living-room floor. She looked into Bruno's gargoyle face. *"Bon jour*, Yankee."

She drew herself to her full height. "You're trespassing, Bruno, not to mention breaking and entering. We can report you for this. The Germans are great believers in martial law."

He lounged in the doorway, hands in his pockets. He wore a new-looking brown suit of some hideous ersatz material. Since his previous visit they had learned he was working as a driver and general flunky for several German officers who were billeted at one of the hotels, but Jean-Louis suspected that Bruno's real function was that of informer for the Gestapo.

Slowly he withdrew his hand from his pocket and she saw with a jolt of fright that he held her passport. So that was why he came sneaking in. Without it, and without the safe conduct pass and other documents inside it, she had nothing to prove her identity or her American citizenship.

He laughed. "What is the saying, *chérie?* About revenge being sweet."

"Why, you filthy collaborator. You think I'm afraid of you? Go ahead, take my passport. I'll just go to the American Embassy for a replacement." She hoped the bluff would work, since it would mean wrestling with more than passport red tape to replace all of the other documents, and with her present activities it had been nice to know she could leave the country at a moment's notice.

He frowned, took a step toward her, and she added, "Your German bosses won't like you fooling with an American. We're not at war, remember."

In the next second two things registered on Kate's mind. Out of the corner of her eye she could see a glint of gold in the crack between the cushions on the couch. She knew instantly what it was. One of the RAF pilots who had just left had worn a gold wristwatch. Kate told him to get rid of it, since it was made in England and might alert someone to check his forged papers more thoroughly. Evidently he hadn't wanted to throw it away or bury it and instead had left it for his benefactors.

"They're watching you, Katerina. You're up to something. I expect they're finding out what right now." Bruno grinned. "They picked up Madame Jourdain for obtaining illegal milk. The Gestapo is interested in all the food you've been buying—far too much for three people."

"Jean-Louis—" Kate began, her heart pounding at the thought of his mother being questioned.

"He's also at headquarters, trying to convince them that his mother is guilty of only a petty rationing violation. But we know better, eh, Yankee?" He shoved her passport into his inside pocket and beckoned her with his finger. "Come and beg for your papers. Beg for your friends. I want to see you grovel."

Kate stared at him, anger and revulsion sweeping over her. His face seemed to have congealed into a permanent expression of vindictiveness. Hardly knowing what she was doing, she let out a yell of rage, grabbed a table lamp, and sent it crashing toward his face.

Taken by surprise, he staggered backward, howling in fury, but didn't fall. Kate wheeled around and ran into the kitchen, slamming the door after her.

Annette's carving knives were laid out neatly in a drawer near the chopping block on the sink. Kate grabbed the largest in the second before Bruno battered the kitchen door open. He stopped at the sight of the knife, then calmly reached into his coat and withdrew a Luger.

Kate looked into the barrel of the gun and let the knife slip from her fingers. He motioned for her to go back into the living room. "I've got you now, you Yankee bitch. You threatened me with a knife. Anything I do to you will be self-defense. Get over there. Take off your clothes."

Oh, Holy Mother, Kate thought, help me.

"This is going to end the way it began," Bruno said thickly, his cold little eyes savoring the length of her body. She backed away from him and he followed, grinning.

As she moved behind the couch he stepped over the broken lamp. At the same moment he saw the gleam of gold between the cushions. "Now . . . what's this?" Reaching with his left hand, he slowly pulled out the wristwatch.

For a split second she thought he would merely slip it onto his own wrist, but then he held it up and turned it over to read an inscription on the back. "Well, well . . . a message engraved on here. And guess what, it's in English."

Damn. Bad enough the watch was *made* in England.

Bruno chucked delightedly. "We heard rumors that English soldiers and airmen were being hidden in the city. Your goose is cooked now, Yankee. Yours and your one-armed friend and his mother. You'll all dead meat. The Germans shoot anybody caught helping the English escape." He dropped the watch into his pocket. "Now get your clothes off."

"Go to hell," Kate said. She moved along the back of the couch.

He advanced slowly, transferred the gun to his other hand, and vaulted over the couch. Kate tried to grab the gun, but he held it aloft and used his other hand to strike her across the face. She fell back against the lamp table, gasping with pain. The next moment he had his knee in her stomach and was tearing her blouse to shreds.

She struggled, trying to dislodge him, and he hit her again. Her head fell back and struck the floor and she fought to stay conscious, the silence broken only by her labored breathing and the animal panting of Bruno. She lay still, only vaguely aware of her clothes being removed. Then a key turned in the lock and the front door opened.

Bruno leaped to his feet, gun in hand, as Jean-Louis came into the room.

Kate stirred, raising heavy-lidded eyes. *Bruno had his back to her*. She forced herself up on her knees, the room fading in and out of focus. He was telling Jean-Louis something and Jean-Louis was answering angrily, but nothing they said registered on her numbed brain.

Her hands closed around the carved legs of the lamp table. It was heavy, solid mahogany. She rose slowly to her feet, picked up the table, and brought it down with all her remaining strength on the back of Bruno's head. He crumpled to his knees, then crashed to the floor.

Jean-Louis quickly pulled the gun from Bruno's limp fingers, then felt his neck. Blood was spreading in a pool on the floor.

Hanging on to the back of the couch for support, Kate whispered, "Is he dead?"

Jean-Louis nodded. He was going through Bruno's pockets and came to Kate's passport. Or at least the empty shell of her passport. Opening it, he showed her that all the pages had been torn out. The passport was just an empty cover. She remembered the sound of the toilet flushing.

"We've got to get rid of him," Jean-Louis said. His voice was flat, his movements robotlike. It wasn't like him to be so unnerved, and Kate suddenly came to her senses.

"Where is Annette? Where is your mother?"

"They said she had a heart attack. She died while they were questioning her this afternoon. She didn't tell them anything." He blinked tears of both grief and pride from his eyes. "I'm glad you killed this putrid little swine. He turned her in."

Tony and his fellow pilots sat in the dispersal hut reading, playing cards, napping, waiting for orders to scramble. The previous day they'd encountered thirty German bombers without fighter escorts, and the resulting turkey shoot had left Tony a little sick to his stomach. Flying home over a bombed airfield, with wrecked hangars and burning aircraft everywhere, the runways pockmarked with craters, helped ease his qualms about shooting down six of the bombers.

A lanky Australian who had been nicknamed Dusty Miller was patiently explaining to Tony the meaning of the lyrics of "Waltzing Matilda." "Now a 'swagman,' see, that's a sort of highwayman, and his 'matilda' is the bedroll on his back. It swings back and forth while he walks, so it's a 'waltzing matilda.' Y'know, Tony, for a pommie you're not a bad sort."

"And for a colonial, you're all right too," Tony said. He liked Dusty Miller. They'd been up to the "big smoke" together several times, and Tony had been impressed by the Aussie's capacity for Scotch whisky and beer. Dusty in turn was impressed by Tony's flying skill.

"Though you and the other blokes what don't wear gloves and goggles is asking for it," Dusty predicted. "Bloody fools, you are."

Many of the fighter pilots had discovered that the goggles prevented them from seeing enemy fighters out of the corners of their eyes, and the heavy gloves hindered the operation of controls and gun buttons.

"And you're a bloody fool for disobeying orders and chasing Stukas across the channel," Tony countered. "One of these days a couple of fighters will take off from France and you'll believe us when we tell you that the Stuka was just a decoy."

ECHOES OF WAR

His words came back to haunt him that afternoon when, losing sight of Dusty's plane in the smoke of battle, Tony found himself on the tail of a lone bomber retreating toward the French coast.

The day was unseasonably cool, with cloud patches, and Tony searched the sky for his friend, wondering if he'd spotted the lone bomber. Tony was about to turn back, but looked once too often at the tempting tail of the bomber. Another couple hundred yards and . . .

Two Me 109s roared out of the cloud cover toward him and he went into an evasive roll, then dived sharply. The German fighters wheeled after him, and he felt the shock of impact as bullets tore into the tail of his plane. At the same time the bomber's rear gunner opened up and Tony watched in incredulous surprise as his starboard wing was torn loose and seemed to hang suspended for an instant in midair.

It happened so fast that he found himself floating beneath the silk canopy of his parachute with no knowledge of leaving the plane. Below he could see a stretch of dun-colored sand marking the French coast. At least he was going to land on the beach rather than ditching in the channel.

[16]

The cloud cover had descended, and now a swirling misty rain obscured the beach. Tony hit the soft sand and rolled over, releasing his chute. As the mass of silk collapsed, two figures loomed over him.

He lay on his back for a moment looking at the craggy face of an old man and the smooth curious gaze of a boy of no more than fourteen. Wordlessly they pulled him to his feet. The boy began to gather up the parachute.

"Parlez-vous Français?" the old man asked. His eyes were the faded blue of a fisherman's. Tony replied in French that he would be most grateful if they would help him hide the parachute and himself before the Germans arrived to look for him.

"Come, the boy will take care of the parachute," the old man said. "We must get you away from the coast, as far inland as possible. The Germans are thick as fleas here. We've only got minutes."

Tony glanced at the gunmetal surface of the channel, now churning with whitecaps as the squall moved in. He wondered if a small boat could perhaps evade the Germans under cover of darkness, but perhaps not in those heavy seas.

Reading his mind, the old man said, "We are watched too

closely for that. Your only hope to get back to England is to get to Vichy France and escape from there."

They ran for the cover of the sand dunes. Tony slowed his pace as his companion began to fall behind. He had to make it back to England. Pilots were in even shorter supply than aircraft. But if evading the Germans meant going inland and heading south . . . The thought hovered that it might be worth the risk to slip into Paris and see Kate. After all, he was thoroughly at home in the city. He had plenty of friends there who would help him.

At his side, the old man panted, "M'sieur . . . don't worry. There are many safe houses now since the evacuation and so many Englishmen left behind."

Jean-Louis and Kate finished wrapping Bruno's body in a rug. Breathing heavily, and still in shock, Kate sat back on her haunches and said, "What shall we do with him?"

"You have to get away from here. Right now. Go to the baker. He promised to help us. Ask him to put you up for the night, and then send him back here right away."

"I can't leave you alone with . . . this. Let's get rid of him together now."

Jean-Louis' face was grim. "I want you to go *now*. The baker will help me. What we have to do . . . Well, just go."

Aware suddenly of her seminakedness, Kate rose and went to wash and dress. She shook uncontrollably as she realized she was covered with blood. She had pulled on a skirt and blouse and was reaching for a jacket when Jean-Louis appeared at the door.

"Kate, we don't know how much the Gestapo knows about us. It would be better for you to go to your embassy first thing in the morning. Tell them you've lost your passport and papers. Get out of the country as fast as you can. Let's say goodbye now. It would be better if we don't see each other again."

Tears ran down Kate's cheeks as she embraced him. There was a frightening lack of focus to her thoughts. She felt she should be making plans, decisions, but all she could think of was that she had killed a man and now she would surely have to pay for it.

Jean-Louis whispered, "You take care of *yourself*, you understand? If you're questioned about us or why you moved out, say we had a lovers' quarrel. Don't worry, your embassy will take care of you."

Kate spent a sleepless couple of hours on a couch in the living quarters over the bakery owned by Monsieur and Madame Deschamps, then went downstairs to watch the baker's wife begin the predawn bread-making. The smell of yeast and warm dough added to her sense of unreality.

Just before dawn, Monsieur Deschamps returned. Normally a florid and rotund man, he looked pale and scared. "It's done," he said to Kate. "Now you must leave here. As soon as I start my deliveries, we'll put you in the van and take you to a safe house."

By midmorning Kate had a room in a small *pension* known to be safe and had telephoned the American Embassy to report that she had lost her passport. She was left holding the phone for several minutes, then a clerk came back on the line and told her to come in and make a written report.

As soon as she arrived at the reception desk of the Embassy she was ushered into a private office. The man who faced her across a formidably large desk was silver-haired, fatherly. He shook her hand, introduced himself, told her he was from Connecticut.

A growing suspicion that he was trying to get her to relax and confide in him was confirmed when he suddenly said, "Is there anything you want to tell me, Miss Kieron? Have you been involved in anything that might be construed as a civil crime?"

She gripped her purse tightly. "Have the Gestapo been inquiring about me? Is that what you're trying to tell me?"

"The Gestapo? Now why would they be interested in you? No, the matter that has been brought to our attention is strictly a civil one." He paused. "There was a murder last night. A body was fished out of the river. A collaborator, an unsavory type, but still . . . The man was known to you and was seen entering the house where you were staying."

The room danced dizzily for a few seconds. "Did the police pick anyone up?"

ECHOES OF WAR

"If you mean Jean-Louis Jourdain, no. As a matter of fact, he seems to have disappeared. I'm afraid you are both wanted for questioning. The police are looking for you right now. Please, I can't help you unless I know the whole story."

"We don't know anything about it," Kate said in a tight voice. *At least Jean-Louis had got away.* "Please, I've got to get my passport and travel papers in order. I feel adrift and helpless without them."

There was a long pause. "Go back to your *pension*. I'll see what I can find out. I'll be in touch."

Tense and exhausted, Kate went back to her room to get her things, wondering how much time she had before the police found her there. She was gathering up her toilet articles when the telephone rang.

Jean-Louis sounded hoarse. "They've picked up the baker. I'm afraid he might talk. Get out now, any way you can. Oh, yes, a friend of yours showed up at one of the safe houses. I've told him of a possible escape route. He's on his way to you, but don't wait. Go now."

The phone clicked in her ear before she could respond. What friend? Who? And where should she go? How could she go anywhere without her passport? She was pacing the room distractedly when the phone rang again. It was the American Ambassador and he suggested she return to the Embassy immediately.

"You've got my passport ready?"

"No. I'm sorry. We can't interfere with a murder investigation. You'll have to give yourself up, but we'll do all we can for you. Come back, Miss Kieron, it will go better for you if—"

Kate slammed down the phone and grabbed her purse and small overnight bag. Yanking open the door, she almost collided with a man about to knock on it. For a split second she thought it was Jean-Louis, but the man standing in the hallway was too tall. He wore a dark pullover and a black beret pulled rakishly over one eye. He was badly in need of a shave and haircut, and if it hadn't been for his cool smile and familiarly handsome features, she would have thought he was some denizen of a waterfront bar.

ECHOES OF WAR

Kate's breath caught somewhere between her heart and her throat. A mixture of joy, relief, and racing excitement flooded through her, demanding expression, but she forced herself to remember the danger they were both in. She grabbed his arm and pulled him into the room, closed the door, and locked it.

Tony wrapped her in his arms, found her mouth and kissed it with passionate haste, then pulled away to look at her. "What a sight for sore eyes you are, Kate. Thank God I've found you."

Breathless, Kate asked, "What are you doing here, for Pete's sake—and dressed like that? So help me, you look like an adagio dancer."

"Much as I'd like to bandy repartee with you, love, there isn't time. We're leaving right now."

"Before you get bossy, tell me how you got here."

"I was damn careless. Ditched my plane on the wrong side of the channel."

"But, oh, God! If you're caught out of uniform, they'll shoot you on sight." Her own danger forgotten, she began to shake at the thought of his.

He pulled her closer to him. "Calm down. They haven't caught me yet. Your underground system for getting downed pilots out of the country has been working fairly well, I understand. Jean-Louis tells me the best way is to take a train to Lyons and get off before it crosses into the demarcation zone. That you know people who will help us with forged papers and so on. Do you have any money, by the way?"

"Marie gave me a great deal of currency before she died. Tony, did Jean-Louis tell you about Bruno?"

He regarded her with level gray eyes that had the flash of steel in them. "Yes. Don't think about it. From now on we have to concentrate on getting out of France with our skins intact."

[17]

Tony pulled her back into the shadows. Across the street at the entrance to the railway station several Germans stood talking to a group of French policemen.

"Don't panic," Tony whispered. "Come on, I know a place where we'll be safe until morning. Just walk. No need to run, but stay close to the buildings. Thank God for the blackout. What a boon it must be to criminals."

Kate knew he was talking to reassure her, but it didn't help much. Of course, the Germans and police probably weren't looking for them; it was just bad luck that they should be there. She wanted to run, oh, *how* she wanted to run.

He took her into a somewhat shabby neighborhood, turned onto a seedy street, and stopped at a house that even cloaked in darkness had a soiled and dilapidated facade. Tony rang the bell, and a moment later the door opened to disclose a darkened vestibule. They stepped inside and Tony put Kate's bag down on the floor.

There was the sound of the outer door closing, then a low-wattage light bulb was flipped on. Kate blinked at the vision of a heavily made-up woman, her blond hair a mass of untidy curls, dressed only in a flimsy black lace wrapper that clearly revealed everything beneath it. She looked at Tony and gave a little squeal of recognition, then flung her arms around his neck and kissed his mouth.

ECHOES OF WAR

Tony carefully disentangled her arms, giving Kate an apologetic smile over a plump and creamy shoulder as the black wrapper slipped. "Hello, Coco. Good to see you too. Listen, love, my friend and I need a place to stay, just until morning."

Coco glanced at Kate, then shook her finger playfully at Tony. "What's this, *chéri*? You bring your own girl? Would you take pâté to a cafe? Shame on you!" She giggled and slipped her arm through his. "But of course I put you up for the night. I see from these clothes you are in disguise. You are hiding from her husband, yes?"

Pushing open the inner door, she led him into a dimly lit hallway, and then through another door, chattering and giggling all the way. Kate followed, feeling like a fifth wheel.

They were in a large room softly lit with pink lights. A long bar was at one end, mirrors behind it. The brocade wallpaper was of a vaguely Oriental design in red and gold, and there were worn Persian rugs on the floor, several faded couches and chairs, and a couple of statues.

Kate was only vaguely aware of the background, because lounging about the room were several girls dressed even more skimpily than Coco. There were also a couple of men—businessmen, from their clothes—sipping glasses of brandy. Kate kept her eyes fixed on Tony's back and followed them to an arched doorway on the far side of the room. Beyond lay a staircase, and they went up the stairs. Kate tried to shut out the sounds coming from behind the doors they passed on the upper landing.

"There," Coco said, opening the last door. "No one will come looking for you here."

Tony said, "Go on in, Kate. I'll be with you in a minute." He turned on the light. She stepped inside and he closed the door.

Kate clapped her hand to her mouth, her cheeks flaming. There was a double bed covered only by a sheet; a chair, and a marble-topped washstand with pitcher and bowl. A wooden stand held towels and washcloths.

She was still standing just inside the room when Tony returned a few minutes later. She spun around to face him. "This is a . . . a—"

"Brothel. Yes. The Germans knew better than to close them down in France."

"And that woman is—"

"Coco is the madame here."

"And obviously an old friend of yours. How dare you bring me here?"

"Would you rather have gone to Gestapo headquarters? That's surely where we'd have ended up if we stayed on the streets after curfew. Look, Kate, I'm not going to apologize to you because Coco is an old friend of mine, nor am I going to listen to any complaints about the accommodations. I know I can trust Coco and her girls, and this may surprise you, but women like her are just as patriotic as any suburban housewife." He grinned. "Besides, I never pretended I was a saint."

Kate looked at the double bed. "I'd rather not sleep with you here, that's all. I'd feel like a—"

"No need to buckle on your armor. I've got things to do. Get you some sort of identity card for one thing, so you can buy a train ticket tomorrow. No doubt you'll be asleep by the time I get back."

After he left, Kate took off her shoes and skirt, snapped off the light, and crawled under the sheet. There was a strong smell of disinfectant clinging to the bed linen. She began to shiver as reaction to the strain of the day set in.

One shock had followed another: Bruno, and Annette's death at the hands of the Gestapo. Then tonight when they went to the man who had prepared forged documents for the escaping Englishmen, they learned he had been picked up, along with everyone else involved in the smuggling operation in Paris, except for Jean-Louis. Thank God, he at least had got away.

Ridiculously, all of her numb disbelief over these events was now overshadowed by her reaction to her surroundings. Muffled sounds came through the adjacent walls; and, listening, Kate asked herself if what she felt was revulsion or perhaps the curiosity all women felt about their sisters-in-sin.

Her thoughts pulled her this way and that, but returned to her fiercely Catholic upbringing eventually. There was no way she'd allow Tony to make love to her in this setting, despite her desperate need for the comfort of his arms tonight.

It seemed a long time before he returned. She heard him fumbling in the darkness. His shoes dropped to the floor. She felt him spread a blanket over her. Then the other side of the bed creaked. She feigned sleep.

"I know you're awake, Kate."

"Maybe I am, but I'm not feeling romantic. It's the effect this place has on me."

He sighed deeply, then muttered, "If I had amorous inclinations, all I'd have to do is walk downstairs. Kate, I swear I'll never tell a soul we spent the night together in a brothel."

The bed shook slightly, and, tense and irritable, she wondered if he was laughing at her. She rolled to the edge of the mattress. They lay untouching in silence.

After a time he said, "I doubt either of us is going to sleep. You know, in view of the somewhat precarious state of our existence, there are some personal matters I'd like to clear up."

"Did you get an ID for me?"

"Yes. Coco knew someone. Kate . . . do you want to tell me about the man back home who hurt you? Perhaps there's a way to prove to you that he and I are not the same."

"No. I won't discuss Wade Lowery with you. If you must know, he jilted me. I'll never trust another man as long as I live, even though I realize now I'm glad I escaped the marriage trap."

"You regard it as a trap?"

"For women, yes. It's fine for men. I mean, hell, I wouldn't mind having a wife myself. It wouldn't really interfere with my life, if I were a man."

"Would you like to be a man?"

"No. I like being a woman too much. I just envy men's freedom."

"Are you very tired? This may be our last chance for privacy. There's something I must tell you."

"From the sound of your voice it's pretty serious. Probably more serious than explaining about your friendship with the madame of a brothel, I'd say. What do you want to tell me about?"

"My pedigree—or lack of one. I'm a bastard. Literally, that is. I was three years old when Cecilia married the Earl. She had never been married. He adopted me some years later. I don't know who my real father is. As you know, my parents don't live together. There'll never be a divorce. Bad form, don't you know."

"Tony, why are you telling me this?"

"Because I don't want to fly false colors, at least as far as my family is concerned. There are probably episodes in my own life I'll never tell you about."

She was silent, trying to digest his somewhat startling piece of information. She wasn't sure how or even if she should comment on it. His carefully casual tone suggested that it was a matter of great personal concern, although Kate had always wondered why the children of such unions were called illegitimate, when in actual fact the parents were.

After a while she fell into an uneasy sleep. She dreamed Wade Lowery was running down a long dark tunnel and she was following him, desperately trying to catch up. She was sobbing, crying bitter tears she'd hidden behind wisecracks and flippant banter every moment since that humiliating phone call when Wade had said simply, "Kate, I'm sorry. I can't go through with it."

She awoke to find her pillow soaking wet and strong masculine arms around her in a comforting embrace. "It's all right. Just a dream, Kate."

Disoriented, her dream still vivid, she gasped, "Wade?"

"Sorry. Just me," Tony said, stroking her hair. "If I could bring him to you at this moment, I believe I'd do it. I see now why you didn't go home, why you shy like a wounded fawn from any emotional commitment. But give yourself time, the wounds will heal."

She lay quietly in his arms. Perhaps he was right about her fear of emotional commitment. But then, in that regard weren't they two of a kind?

They got off the train at a small town well inside the demarcation border between the occupied and unoccupied zones. There had been no problem catching the early morning train from Paris, although Tony warned Kate to keep her mouth shut, since her American-accented French was more noticeable than his. To which Kate retorted, "Wanna bet?"

"I was taught a simple way to speak a foreign language without an accent. Listen to a person from the country in question speaking English, and mimic his inflections. I've never been asked if I was English, but a couple of people did ask why I keep impersonating Maurice Chevalier."

Kate laughed. She felt considerably better this morning. "Too bad you don't know sign language. We could use that."

"Ah, but I do. Where did you learn it?"

"Had a part-time job at a school for the deaf while I was in high school. How about you?"

"One of my mother's friends. Looking back on my life, it seems there was always one or other of Cecilia's bohemian friends to teach me something. Some of the things I learned probably would have given my father a stroke, had he known."

"I can imagine."

"We'll save the sign language for real emergencies, however. It would call attention to us even more than your accent."

They were now walking down the main street of town. The day was serene and sunny, and it was difficult to worry about their loss of safe houses and guides. Since the Paris people had been arrested, there was no way for them to know all of the links in the chain, as the connections had deliberately been kept separate from one another to avoid a domino effect should one person be arrested. Kate asked, "Have you any idea where we're headed?"

"I can see a bistro at the bottom of the hill. We'll find out from one of the waiters if there's anyone around who will take us into Lyons."

"You're crazy! How will you know who to trust?"

"Waiters and barmen have already started a profitable business in purveying anti-Nazi necessities—BBC News, contraband goods, and introductions to border guides. For a price, of course. This much I learned while I was on the run up north. The usual question is *'Connaissez-vous un passage?'* We'll try it in the bistro."

"And probably get ourselves arrested," Kate said as they reached the bottom of the hill.

Tony paused, looking around. There was a church a little farther on, several shops, another bistro. He held the door for Kate and they went inside.

Kate was about to speak, when Tony's hand tightened on her arm. She followed the direction of his quick glance and saw three men drinking at the *zinc*. Two wore ersatz tweeds of a particularly ugly shade of brown, while the other was dressed in a murky gray. All showed shaved necks and carried briefcases. Gestapo, Kate thought, her stomach lurching. You can spot them a mile off. She gave Tony a sickly smile and raised her eyebrows questioningly.

Smiling, he guided her to a small table, slid her bag under it, and pulled out a chair for her. Kate admired his nerve. When the waiter came, Tony affected a hoarse whisper and ordered wine. One of the Gestapo men turned and idly looked them over.

Kate gripped the underside of the table to keep from getting up and running screaming from the place. Tony began to tell her a ribald joke, still in his hoarse-throated whisper, and Kate couldn't keep from laughing aloud. The Gestapo man frowned and looked away.

Careful, Tony signed with his hands. *He might think we're making fun of them. They can't stand that.*

Kate sipped her wine. Tony's attitude of absolute calm conveyed control of the situation, as if they were well-rehearsed actors. But the presence of the Gestapo was making her hair stand on end. She jumped with fright as she heard heavy footsteps and German voices growing louder. *Oh, God, they were coming over!*

Flight must have been written all over her face, because Tony, still affecting the hoarse whisper, reached across the table and grabbed her wrist roughly. "I'm sick of your damn moods. Nothing ever pleases you. Just sit still and let me drink my wine in peace, woman, or I'll turn you over my knee."

Kate, her eyes widening, made sputtering sounds. She

heard a German voice mutter, "Do it. I'd like to see that." A second voice said, "Let's check their papers. There's something about them—"

Tony jumped to his feet and rushed around to her side of the table. Seizing her arm, he pulled her roughly to her feet and shook her. "I've had enough. You're going home with me and I'll show you who's boss in this family."

Kate struggled, but Tony sat in her chair and pulled her across his knee. She couldn't believe it. He actually gave her a couple of whacks with his hand, not hard, but firm. Yelling in outrage, she jumped up and began pummelling him with her fists. In response he grabbed her in a bear hug, reached under the table for their suitcase, and started for the door, Kate's feet dragging on the floor.

The three Gestapo agents watched, grinning; but one of them suddenly moved to block their path. Tony snapped in German, "You can check my papers later. Don't ever come between a man and his wife—even in the line of duty—if you know what's good for you." Then he shoved roughly through the trio. The Germans fell back in surprise.

Kate didn't have to pretend; she was furious. When Tony put her on her feet outside, she swung for his jaw. He raised his arm to block the blow, grabbed a handful of her hair, and propelled her across the street.

A minute later he was dragging her up the steps and into the cool dimness of an old Gothic church. When she opened her mouth to speak, he said, "Hurry. We're not clear yet. I take it you're familiar with Catholic churches? Where will we find the priest? I hear they're even more reliable than waiters."

"You . . . spanked me." Kate choked to keep from giggling. "And I think you enjoyed it."

"Well, you do have an attractive *derrière*. Where shall we look for the priest?"

Approaching the altar, Kate genuflected and crossed herself. She whispered, "Let's try the sacristy."

They were lucky. The parish priest had handled similar requests. An hour later they were climbing aboard a hay cart on a country lane a short distance from the church. A red-faced farmer with a bulbous nose carefully arranged the hay over them before urging a muscular pair of dray horses forward. The priest wished them God-speed, and they lurched off down the lane.

Under the sweet-smelling canopy of hay, Kate felt Tony's hand find her thigh and squeeze slightly. She said, "Keep your hands to yourself, you wife-beater," and kicked in his direction, disturbing the hay. Muffled laughter was quickly stifled when the farmer cautioned, "Stop that! Do you want to bring Germans with pitchforks?"

The farmer took them to his barn, where they were to await the arrival of "Monsieur René," who would help them cross into the unoccupied zone. Tony gave Kate an affectionate pat on the rump and remarked, "So far, so good."

"Too good. When disaster strikes it'll be a humdinger."

"Now, now, let's not be pessimistic. You know, there's a streak of Irish melancholy in your makeup. You must squash it. People who go around expecting the worst to happen usually aren't disappointed." He sat down on a mound of hay and patted the spot beside him. "Let's have some of that bread and cheese."

Kate scowled but complied. They were both hungry and demolished the food. An hour after their arrival the farmer came back with a wiry little man with mournful dark eyes. "M'sieur René," the farmer said, and left again.

René walked up and down in front of them jabbing the air with nervous hands to punctuate his remarks. "You will need, first, papers. I will take you to a place where we can make them. You will cross the river into the unoccupied zone. We shall have to bribe the German patrol. Usually I take parties of several people to the river, but in the case of you two, I think it better not to risk the lives of others. My price for this service is ten thousand francs."

Kate had her mouth open to accept when Tony said, "Five thousand." Kate listened in silent amazement as Tony haggled over the price. He might have been arguing over a piece of fish instead of their freedom. Eventually they settled on seven thousand, which would include connections and accommodations on the other side of the river.

Satisfied, René led them out of the barn. A battered truck loaded with milk cans was parked beside the barn. They were to crouch among the cans for the short journey to the place where they would get forged papers.

Just inside what appeared to be a small village, the truck came to a sudden halt. A German-accented voice barked questions. They heard René's nervous reply.

Heart thumping, Kate flattened herself on the damp bed of the truck behind the milk cans and looked at Tony. He put his finger to his lips to signal silence, then gave her a reassuring wink. She thought, He was on visiting terms with high-ranking Nazis before the war. If the worst happens, maybe . . .

The German voice said, *"Heil Hitler und merci."*

"Phew," Kate breathed as they set off again. "That was close. He didn't even check back here."

"I expect he was thanking René for the bribe. Let's hope all of the Germans we run into are as susceptible to bribery."

"Don't count on it," Kate muttered.

Their destination proved to be a repair shop for farm machinery, with a small concealed room in the back that housed printing and photography equipment. Photos were quickly taken, and they were told to wait in a tiny cubicle of an office with a high boarded-over window.

Tony lifted his head toward the window, listening. "I hear water running over pebbles. The river must be close."

"The one we're to cross?"

"I should think so."

René stuck his head around the door and told them not to talk, because German patrols sometimes checked on the repair shop. He also brought a knapsack to exchange for Kate's suitcase.

They waited, Kate with mounting tension, as the light coming in through the window boards gradually faded and then the stars glinted in an inky sky. Finally René reappeared and said curtly, "Time to go. No talking. Once you are across the river, you will run across an open field until you come to a dirt road. That leads to the village. At the village go to the blacksmith's shop and ask for Georges. He will take you to Lyons."

"Uh . . ." Kate cleared her throat. "How do we cross the river?"

"There are stones for you to walk on."

So much for the nice little boat she had imagined.

Tony asked her, "Can you swim?"

As she nodded, René said, "There's no need. The river is no more than four feet deep where you'll cross."

Pocketing their forged French documents, they silently followed René out into a starlit night and walked quickly to the riverbank. Kate had visualized smooth stepping-stones upon which to cross, but straining into the darkness she saw instead jagged boulders, around which the water frothed and churned.

Tony leaned closer and whispered, "You go first. I'll be right behind to keep an eye on you just in case you slip. But if you do, for God's sake don't scream."

"Go," René rasped impatiently. "The German patrol should be a quarter of a mile away at this moment, but one can never be sure with the Boche."

Kate drew a breath and stepped carefully onto the first rock. The water splashed against her feet and she felt the sharp ridges of the boulder try to turn her ankle. Arms outstretched to balance herself, she moved to the next one, wondering how anyone with shorter legs would have reached it. Glancing back, she saw Tony behind her, and René's shadow racing back the way they'd come.

Two more rocks . . . She was beginning to get the hang of it, when the night was shattered by the roar of a motorcycle. Startled, she misjudged the slope of the next rock and her foot skidded down the slippery sides. She clutched at the air, then felt a sharp pain as her other knee slammed into stone. The next second she was in the water.

At almost the same instant a flashlight beam pierced the darkness and a voice shouted in German, "Who goes there?"

[18]

Shoulder-deep in the swiftly running water, Kate felt the current tug at her as she struggled to hold on to the side of the boulder. Her wool skirt weighed a ton, threatening to pull her down. Could she drown in four feet of water? Maybe it was better than getting shot.

The German voice yelled again in guttural French, demanding to know who was there. Another shot whined overhead.

Tony splashed down beside her. He threw one arm across her shoulders, covered her mouth with his hand, and pulled her down into the water until only their noses were above the churning surface. They were wedged between the boulder from which Kate had slipped and the next one in the rocky chain, out of sight of the bank they had just left.

Panicked because water was splashing into her nostrils and she couldn't breathe, Kate tried to fight free of Tony's grip, but he held her even more tightly, giving her a slight shake as a warning.

Ice-cold water had now invaded every part of Kate's body. Her feet, in their leather-soled shoes, skidded on the shifting stones of the riverbed. Why was Tony trying to hide? Surely the German would simply follow across the stepping-stones?

The flashlight beam swept the river again, and Tony

dragged Kate's head completely under the water. He's drowning me, she thought wildly, struggling harder than ever.

Just as she felt herself losing consciousness, her face was again thrust into the air. She couldn't even cough and choke, as she wanted to, because Tony's hand was still clamped over her mouth.

There was no sound from the German. Seconds, then minutes dragged by, but still Tony didn't move. Kate's body was numb.

At length they heard the growl of the motorcycle again. The engine revved as it roared off into the distance.

Tony released Kate, placed his hand under her knees, and lifted her back up onto the boulder. She was too exhausted to do anything but gulp in great mouthfuls of life-giving air. Besides, now that she could breathe again, she realized that he'd probably saved their lives.

The rest of the river crossing was a nightmare. Tony went ahead this time, offering his hand to help her to each slippery rock, although when her feet were barely in place he had to leap to the next one, since there wasn't room for both of them. She had stuffed her waterlogged shoes and stockings into Tony's pockets before starting again and found it slightly easier to grip the stones with bare feet, but after a while had no feeling in them.

She sobbed with relief when they reached the far bank, but Tony wouldn't let her rest. He seized her hand and dragged her across the open field.

Her feet came back to life as they were jabbed by the sharp stubble of the harvested field. By the time they reached the dirt road, Kate had decided that never before in her entire life had she felt so miserable.

Tony shook out her shoes and slipped them back on her feet. They walked down the dirt road to the accompaniment of water dripping from their clothes and squeaking in their shoes.

When they reached the village and found the blacksmith's shop, Kate's skin was rubbed raw and she was shivering from cold. The blacksmith, Georges, lived behind his shop. He took one look at his saturated visitors and led Kate to a bathroom. She was ecstatic at the sight of the tub.

They were given dry clothes, which in Kate's case belonged to Georges, since his wife was considerably shorter and wider than Kate. Then a delicious meal of soup, fresh trout, and home-baked bread. Afterwards Georges showed them to a long attic room with a sloping roof. There were three bare mattresses on the floor and a pile of pillows and blankets. Georges said, "Sleep now. Tomorrow I take you to Lyons."

A candle in a brass holder cast a rosy glow on the bare room. Tony looked at Kate as the trapdoor closed over Georges' head. "I must say, old girl, you look quite fetching in Georges' trousers. Lean flanks and—"

She picked up the nearest pillow and flung it at him. Laughing, he collapsed onto a mattress. Kate pushed a strand of still-damp hair out of her eyes. "I thought we were goners back there in the river."

"German patrols in the occupied zone probably have orders not to cross into the unoccupied zone. Lucky for us that German was alone. He was probably returning from a night in town. Or maybe our friend René forgot to bribe him."

"No doubt because you haggled over René's price. That'll teach you not to be so tight with my money."

He extended a hand toward her. "Come and relax. And bring that towel with you, I'm going to dry your hair. I once had a nanny who swore that going to bed with wet hair caused deafness. I know it's not feasible, still . . ."

Kate dropped down beside him and he began to rub her hair vigorously. She leaned her forehead against his chest and surrendered to the comforting feeling of being ministered to. Discarding the towel, he ran his fingers through the soft waves of her hair, separating the strands, and she felt him breathing more deeply. His voice was low. "I want very badly . . . to make love to you."

"Your timing is terrific, Winfield. Half the German army on our tails, and you get romantic." She could have kicked herself the moment the words were out. Looking up, she saw that his face, lit by candlelight, was boyishly haggard, stripped of all but a primitive need that she felt as acutely.

He turned his head and she thought he winced, but it

could have been a shifting shadow. "That's probably a better reason than any I could come up with."

"Yeah? What would your line have been? If we're going to get tortured and killed in the morning, we might as well have fun tonight?" She didn't really know why she was angry with him. Perhaps because she wanted him to make love to her so badly, a faint suspicion stirred that she was beginning to need him more than she should.

"Something like that." His lips brushed her forehead, touched the tip of her nose, and came to rest on her mouth. He gathered her into his arms and held her, rocking slightly back and forth.

Kate began to relax and then to give in to her aching longing. She unbuttoned his shirt and slid her hands inside, ran them over the dearly familiar contours of his chest. There didn't seem to be any point in denying herself the pleasure of his body simply because of some vague fear that the time would come when she'd lose him.

He eased her down on her back, removed Georges' shirt and trousers, and covered her with his body. Kate no longer was aware of the musty, unused smell of the attic as she inhaled the scent of his skin.

There was a hungry haste to his lovemaking tonight, but Kate was ready for him. When they lay still, he said, "Kate, I told you I was illegitimate. I have no real name of my own to offer a woman. I used to think I'd never want to get married, not only for that reason, but for others that don't seem to matter now. But, oh, God, the agonies I suffered when I had to leave you in Paris. The nights I haven't been able to sleep for wanting you. I just can't go on worrying about you like this. Could you bring yourself to marry a bastard?"

Kate felt all the air seep out of her lungs. She lay still, experiencing a reaction that was in sharp contrast to any she might have imagined. The sensual yearning she felt for Tony was acute, but did she love him? Was it possible to love anyone with the all-consuming passion she'd once felt for Wade, or was that reserved only for a woman's first love? In getting over the loss of Wade's love had she constructed too impenetrable a shell around her heart?

A small panic occurred in her mind. Am I ready for this? Is he? Is what we have here mutual love, or a rush of adrenaline because we were so recently in danger? Is there some way to say, Wait! This isn't the right time. Ask me again when we're really safe and secure. I can't answer sensibly now. In these circumstances we're equals. Fugitives, expatriates, maybe soon prisoners of war, or worse. But what about in a normal place and time? We're far from equal then.

Drawing a deep breath, she said, "I'm more than flattered, Tony. And who cares whether your mother was married when you were born? But I think right now you're feeling the same euphoria I am that we didn't get shot in the river, that we made it into the unoccupied zone."

"Kate—"

"No, hear me out. Sure, there's a war on now and everything's gone to hell. But peace will come again, and then what? Can you see me presiding over Cardovan House? I'd be terrified of your butler, never mind anything else. I've no education, no old family tree. I'm not even sure I could live in England. After the first flush of passion passes, you'd soon realize your mistake. Oh, I know you're sincere now, at this moment. But then men have always been more slaves to their urges than women, more impulsive with their promises."

"That's not fair, Kate. You're comparing me to Wade again. Maybe his proposal was a smokescreen to indulge his lust, but damn it, I love you. I've known for some time I was going to ask you to marry me. I didn't plan to do it yet, but—"

"You're afraid you'll get me pregnant." The words were out before she could stop them. She hadn't said, *And then there'd be two bastards in the family,* but the unspoken innuendo hung in the air.

Tony said stiffly, "A simple 'no thanks' would have done, Kate." He released her, blew out the candle, and turned on his side.

Feeling suddenly bereft, she lay back on her pillow. The darkness was a suffocating mass. She tossed and turned and grew more wide awake. She wanted more discussion, more persuasion. She didn't want him to give up yet. Why couldn't he see that it wasn't as easy for her as it was for him? He'd never made marriage plans and had them collapse. Nor was he being asked to give up his country, his family, his friends, as she was. As the wife of an Englishman, she'd never truly be a citizen of her own country, or a daughter, or a sister again.

There was no sound of deep breathing beside her. She whispered, "I don't know what you see in me. I'm not beautiful."

His reply was soft as a shadow. "Everyone appreciates surface beauty at first glance. But after the first impression, there has to be something more than mere physical good looks to set a man's blood racing."

"You know, I wish I hadn't told you about Wade."

"How so?"

"Because I'd have liked you to think of me without pity."

"I don't pity you. I pity him, for not knowing what he lost."

Speaking to Tony in enveloping darkness seemed to uncork memories and emotions long stifled. Their shadow-shrouded conversation suggested the sanctity of the confessional. She heard herself say, "It was like a comic opera. Bride left at the altar—well, not literally. He called the day before and said he couldn't go through with it."

"You don't have to tell me this, Kate."

"Bride's mother hysterical, father gunning for Wade. Wade's family is fairly well off. I guess it didn't occur to him that my folks had to get a loan to pay for the wedding, and some things couldn't be returned. I'd used every dime of my savings too. Only, you know, when it was happening, it was more *Pagliacci* than comic opera. It's just funny when it happens to somebody else. Of course, now I can laugh."

He turned over and pulled her back into his arms, and held her until she fell asleep. But he didn't bring up the subject of her marrying him again. Kate, she told herself in her last waking thought, you're a fool.

[19]

They took a train to Lyons the following day, accompanied by Georges, prepared to offer their forged papers to any Vichy official who demanded to see them. But they were in luck and reached their destination, a "safe" cafe, without being challenged. The journey for the most part had been accomplished in awkward silence.

Kate had awakened in the comforting circle of Tony's arms to the embarrassing realization that she had spilled the beans, and completely, about Wade. It was some time before she realized that Tony's silence was probably due to the fact that she'd turned down his offer of marriage.

The worst part of it was, she hadn't intended to turn him down flat. She'd merely wanted to say, Proceed . . . with caution, but instead, with her usual propensity for running off at the mouth, she'd tossed cold water in his face. Looking back on last night, she saw that in seeking her reassurances to counteract her own doubts, she had created some serious ones for him. Now he'd backed off, and she didn't know how to undo what she'd done. Well, they still had a long way to go. Perhaps she'd be able to think of a plan to steer him back to where she really wanted, very desperately, for him to be.

Trying to bridge the awkwardness between them, she made so many wisecracks that when they were shown to a private room in the cafe, Tony said, "We're still in France,

Kate. And even though we're out of the occupied zone, the *milice* here may have been alerted to keep a lookout for us, so don't get too cocky yet."

"They're probably looking for me. I'm an escaping felon. But all they'd want you for is impersonating an adagio dancer."

"It would be a good idea for you to lie low and let me take care of things here. We're going to have to obtain a visa from the Spanish Consulate, and I've had a little prior experience in handling such matters for people on the run. This is where we find out how good our forged papers are."

In the following frustrating days, Kate battled cabin fever as she stayed in their room, and learned that more would-be refugees were undone by permit-wielding officialdom than by the Vichy police.

Four permits had to be acquired and synchronized, since each one was good for only a limited time. They heard of people killing themselves when their first permit expired before the fourth could be acquired. As one refugee remarked despairingly, "We are no longer human beings . . . we are papers."

Tony was unfailingly cheerful when he sallied forth each day to try to get *permis,* asking only of her that she be careful and patient. But she heard the talk in the cafe and knew that Lyons was a nightmare bottleneck of refugees.

Still, she had every confidence in Tony. The combination of his flawless French, his aplomb, and that indefinable air of command he seemed to exude, would surely distract any official from questioning him too closely. Besides, Tony's incredibly cool demeanor in a crisis compelled one to believe his word—no one could be that calm while playing a part. It was a quality of his she both admired and worried about, wondering what had taken place in his life to produce it and whether, in fact, he'd been trained for just such a situation as they now found themselves in.

Days, and then a couple of weeks, slipped by. Kate began to worry that their journey would end in a Lyons jail. Luckily, unlike some refugees, they had enough money to keep them going.

One night when Tony returned, looking a little more strained than usual, Kate screamed at him, "Don't tell me everything's going fine—tell me what's *happening*."

He dropped into the nearest chair. "Well, love, we have *permis de séjour* from the Rhône prefecture which allow us to be here—though I don't know what they'd be worth if the police nab us. We also have a Vichy France *visa de sortie*. What's holding us up is paper number three—Portuguese visas."

"Portuguese? But I thought we were going to Spain?"

"The Spanish won't grant visas to foreigners unless they have stamped proof that they intend to hurry right on out of the country—usually to Lisbon and its airport, which is Europe's last exit."

When Tony announced, several days later, that they now had three of the four permits, Kate heaved a great sigh of relief. "All we need now then is the Spanish visas."

"Well . . . there's a problem with that. I've been informed by Consulate clerks that the border is either closed, or only open twice a week, or an hour a day. Depending on who I talk to, the situation changes by the minute. I heard that Spain has mobilized its army too. But—there's a ray of hope."

"And that is?"

"One clerk very kindly suggested that if I was to make a donation to the Spanish poor . . . we could have visas the day after tomorrow. He also suggested that we could then visit the French border city of Pau."

"Which is the place where mountaineer guides take refugees over the Pyrenees into Spain," Kate said. "What are you waiting for—go and bribe that clerk."

The eighteen-hour journey to Pau by train, despite the fact that they managed to get seats, was uncomfortable, exhausting, interminable.

Before leaving Lyons they acquired from a pawnbroker, at outrageous prices, knapsacks, hiking boots, wool socks, and men's trousers.

When they finally found a place to stay in Pau—a room in

ECHOES OF WAR

a third-class hotel—Kate collapsed into bed and slept. She awakened hours later as Tony was letting himself into the room.

Sitting up, she rubbed the sleep from her eyes. Tony's somewhat taut expression relaxed as he looked at her. "You look so vulnerable when you're asleep. Did I ever tell you that I watch you sleeping? And when you wake up, you're as guileless as a little girl. I always want to hug you and ply you with lollipops."

She ran her fingers through her tangled hair and said, "I could go for a lollipop right now. Or ham and eggs would be even better."

"We can get a meal, but I doubt they're still serving breakfast. It's nearly nine—P.M., that is."

"I slept all day? What did you do?"

"Tried in vain to find a guide to take us over the mountains. Not to worry. I'll try again tomorrow."

"Nobody willing? But I thought—"

He shrugged, unconcerned. "Plenty of guides. It's just that when I mention that you're a woman—"

"I see. Poor little old frail me would slow you down."

"It's a pretty arduous climb, Kate. Some of the passes are higher than the Alps. I think perhaps a prospective guide would be less doubtful if he were to meet you."

"You could have been on your way by now without me, couldn't you? I appreciate your staying with me, Tony, I really do." She didn't say so, but she felt that in turning down his proposal she had relieved him of any obligation toward her.

"Think nothing of it, old girl. After all, you're the one with all the francs—and guides don't come cheap. Tomorrow we'll find another contact man to take us to a guide."

Kate slid her feet to the floor, searching for her shoes. They had shared a room in Lyons too, but Tony had made no more romantic overtures, nor did he sleep beside her. Perversely, Kate was disturbed by this. She mumbled, "I see, it's just my money that binds you to me. Ah, me . . ."

Two weeks passed, and their precious francs began to diminish alarmingly; but still none of the contacts would

ECHOES OF WAR

jeopardize their position with the mountain guides by introducing them to a woman—and an American woman at that, who, as everyone knew, spent her entire life being whisked about in luxury cars and scarcely knew how to walk, let alone hike over a mountain pass.

At last it was Kate who came up with a plan. "Look, find a new contact you've not talked to before. Then tell him that you and your friend, a young man who is a deaf mute, need a guide."

Tony eyed her thoughtfully. "We'd have to cut off your hair. You might get away with it. We've got the men's clothes for you. Do you think you could do anything to—uh—flatten yourself?"

"Sure. I'll tear up a sheet and use it as a binder. Get the scissors and let's get started on my hair."

Tony groaned more than she did as her red-gold tresses drifted to the floor. Kate urged him on. "More. Cut it shorter, go on. It grows fast." Her neck felt curiously bare and undefended. She had fleeting visions of aristos being prepared for the guillotine.

"Can you keep silent for the whole trip, do you think? It's not as easy as it sounds."

"Don't worry. I want to get out of here as much as you do."

That evening Tony brought her a cloth cap to wear, and she turned up her coat collar, shoved her hands into her pockets, and sauntered around the room for his inspection.

"Not bad," he said grudgingly. "Shoulders and hips aren't quite right, and the walk is still too graceful, but perhaps your height will compensate. I think I'll say you're English, a student who got caught when France fell. If I say you're American they'll want explanations as to why you can't leave the country legally—like all those contacts who turned us down."

"Okay, fine—" she began, then stopped and said in sign language, *My big mouth is now officially closed*.

Tony learned of a woman who owned a secondhand furniture shop and ran a smuggling operation on the side. She was more intent upon setting a price than examining the silent young man who stood behind Tony, and she looked away in embarrassment when he communicated with his companion in sign language. Tony tried unsuccessfully to get her to come down from her 40,000 francs price.

"But, m'sieur, this is the deluxe trip. There will be donkeys to ride on the lower slopes, so you'll only have to promenade over the peaks. Just a couple of hours walking and you'll be free men."

Kate gave Tony a sharp kick on the ankle, and he reluctantly agreed to the price.

They were to leave Pau by train the following day in the company of the woman's husband, get off at a way station, and then proceed to a farmhouse where they would be met by their guide.

Arriving at a small farmhouse, Tony looked around for stables or corrals and, not seeing any, asked, "I take it that the donkeys are provided by the guide?"

The man avoided his eye. "Ah, no, not this time. This time there'll be a truck. But you'll only have a four-hour hike."

Kate rolled her eyes when they were introduced to their guide, a lean olive-skinned man with darting eyes, and he quickly informed them there would be neither donkeys nor trucks. They would cross the mountains on their own two feet, and furthermore they would make exceptionally good time, since a shepherd recently down from the uplands had reported that the first snow was expected within the week. When it arrived, the passes would be closed for the long mountain winter. They would travel with two other men, whom they would meet in the morning. They were given a supper of cold lamb and told to sleep soundly.

As they were shown their sleeping quarters in a hayloft, their guide, who had not given his name, looked sharply at Kate and said to Tony, "He's young—not even old enough to shave. And a deaf mute too. Is he strong enough for the journey?"

"Being deaf doesn't automatically make him an invalid," Tony said. "He's stronger than he looks."

"Hmm. I don't see much in the way of muscles."

"He's been growing too fast to acquire muscle," Tony said, shoving Kate ahead of him into the hayloft.

When they were alone, Tony said in sign language, *Do try to look as though you don't know what he's saying. That outraged scowl of yours is going to give you away.*

She signed back, *I could be a lip-reader,* to which he responded, *Not when someone's lips are moving* behind *you.*

The other two men with whom they would travel proved to be a young Polish officer who had now twice evaded capture by the Germans and who faced instant death for treason if caught—since Poland was now regarded as German territory and Poles fighting for the Allies were considered traitors—and a pallid young man with a look of exhaustion about him who said he was a French airman. Kate was relieved to see that at least one of the party looked even less up to the climb than she did.

They set off before dawn in eerie darkness, plodding up the foothills in a strung-out line. The slopes were steep, and dried grass made them slippery. Kate found it tiring to constantly watch her balance and footing, but she was determined not to call attention to herself in any way, so she kept pace with Tony, who walked behind their guide. The other two men trailed behind, whether out of a desire to be alone or because of shortness of breath she didn't know. None of them were inclined to talk.

Their guide had warned them they must hurry to the first stop, since they could be stopped by a French customs guard on this portion of the journey.

When the young French airman began to lag behind, the guide muttered a curse and went to urge him forward. Kate felt her breath grinding against her ribs, and her head ached; but she resolutely put one foot in front of the other and tried not to think about how far they'd come or how far they still had to go.

She wanted to cry with relief when they reached their first stop, a shepherd's hut, about noon.

They were all responsible for their own provisions and all

had bought food from the farmer, but only Tony and the guide remembered to obtain flasks of water. The guide sat in a corner on the floor and ate bread and cheese and slaked his thirst, ignoring them after telling them there were to be no fires. They could rest two hours.

Tony offered Kate a drink and she sipped the water, acutely aware of the longing in the eyes of the Pole and the Frenchman, the latter looking distinctly pale and weary. As though reading her mind, Tony took a single swallow himself and then offered the other two a drink. Kate smiled her approval at him.

The Pole said in French, "No, really, I couldn't take it. I should have thought to bring water."

"Nonsense, man," Tony said. "Drink. We'll find a mountain stream this afternoon and refill it."

The Pole politely took a small sip and handed the flask to the Frenchman, who drank thirstily. Behind his back, Kate signed to Tony, *That man is sick. He's going to hold us up*.

Tony nodded, looking concerned. The Frenchman slumped wearily to the ground, his back to the wall. His face lolled forward on his chest and he slept.

"He has a fever," the Pole said. "I don't like the look of him."

Their guide wiped his mouth with his hand. "We move on in two hours—with him or without him. We have to rendezvous with the Spanish guide. If we miss him, you're on your own."

Tony shook his flask. It was empty. He said, "I'll be back in a little while," and started toward the door. Alarmed, Kate grabbed his arm and stopped herself from protesting aloud in the nick of time. Before she could get her hands going, Tony signed to her, *Going for water. We'll all walk better if we get enough to drink, but the Frenchman needs it desperately. Don't worry. I'll be back.*

Kate signed, *What are you—some sort of Boy Scout?*

He grinned and asked their guide for the best direction to take.

Kate watched him leave, the granite slopes towering over his head like a fortress. He walked with a jaunty stride, as though simply off to the nearest pub. There was no sign that he'd had a grueling climb that morning. She felt a private thrill of admiration, proud that he was her friend, that they were traveling together.

Her feelings were so proprietary that she found herself looking around at the others, as if expecting some acclaim for her man. Several minutes passed and Tony was now out of sight, but still she stared in the direction he'd taken, thinking that some men were brave and some were strong, but there was a gallantry about Tony that few possessed.

The young Frenchman moaned and Kate dropped to her knees beside him. He'd started to perspire heavily, and when she touched him he was hot and clammy. She eased him down into a supine position and put his rucksack under his head. She wanted to peel off her jacket to cover him, but was afraid if she did her breasts might show through their casing of sheet-binding and wool shirt. Their guide stood up and walked over to them.

"We'll have to leave him here. I'll take the rest of you on to the Spanish guide and then come back for him. He'll have to go back to Pau until he's well enough to travel."

Kate sat down, stretching out her legs. She would have loved to pull off her boots. She was hungry, but too nervous without Tony to eat. The minutes dragged by and she tried not to constantly watch the slopes for his return. After an hour her anxiety began to mount.

There were only ten minutes of their rest period left when he came back, his flask filled with icy cold mountain water. Kate thought that if she weren't playing the part of a mute male she would either have hugged him or yelled at him for scaring her.

He went immediately to the young Frenchman, who now thrashed from side to side, turning his head and moaning. Their guide said, "He can't go on."

Tony said, "Take the other two. I'll stay here with him until you get back."

"No!" Kate shouted. "No, I won't go on without you." She broke off, her female voice echoing around the hills.

The Pole and the guide stared at her, while Tony rolled his eyes upward.

"So . . . a woman." The guide spat the words. "That

settles it. The Spanish guide would have my skin if I brought him a woman. She stays here with the sick man."

Fifteen minutes later the arguments were over, the guide and the Pole were on their way, and Kate and Tony were left with the Frenchman and verbal instructions for reaching the pass if they wished to go on alone. They moistened the sick man's lips and piled their coats and spare clothes over him.

Kate gave Tony an apologetic grin. "Another fine pickle you've got me into, Ollie," she said in a fair Stan Laurel whimper. Tony smiled, but he kept looking at the man on the floor, who was now lying quite still. "He needs a doctor. I don't think we can wait for the guide to get back. We're going to have to carry him back down the hill ourselves."

She knew he was right, but thought with dismay about the arduous hike of the morning. "I guess we should eat something first. I'll get the bread and cheese."

They ate quickly and were almost finished when Kate glanced in the direction of the Frenchman again. She jumped to her feet. "My God, I think he's in a coma."

Tony reached him before she did, placed his hand on the man's neck, lifted his eyelids. He looked up at Kate and said quietly, "I'm afraid he's dead."

"But—oh, God!"

Unbuttoning the man's jacket, Tony uncovered a thick wad of stiffened and darkly stained bandage just below his heart. "He'd been shot, and the wound is horribly infected. Poor devil must have been desperate to escape. I heard something in Lyons about some ex-army men blowing up railway lines in the occupied zone. I wonder if he was one of them."

"What shall we do now?" Kate asked.

"I think we should set off right away and see if we can catch up with our guide. You heard him say they were expecting snow soon. If we don't make it during the next couple of days, we're going to be stuck here all winter. I'm not sure we can evade capture that long. I heard in Pau that so many Allied escapees have come this way that the Germans are patrolling the area."

"What if we don't catch up with our guide? Can we make it on our own?"

Tony gave her arm a little squeeze. "We'll give it a damn good try."

"Tony—"

"Yes?"

"Remind me that if I ever need to escape from anywhere again to be sure to take you along."

[20]

Dusk came and they were still alone. Their guide had too much of a head start. Tony found an overhanging ledge that offered some protection from a rising wind and they crawled under it, huddling together for warmth.

Kate said, "I keep thinking of the Frenchman. Do you think we should have buried him?"

"No. The guide will take his body back. Someone, somewhere will want to know what happened to him. Try to sleep."

Sheer physical exhaustion brought sleep quickly. She awakened to feel Tony's hand on her arm, shaking her. Opening her eyes, she looked at the most magnificent view she'd ever seen.

Daybreak slipped over the hills and painted a soft glowing light on the valleys below. The vistas were cathedral-like in their beauty, but Tony had not awakened her to admire them.

He said, "I've been thinking. I don't want to force you to attempt to find the pass without a guide. We might die trying. Do you really want to go on?"

"You bet I do."

"Good show. I've a pretty good idea of where to make for. We might detour a bit because I don't know the best trail, but let's give it a go."

ECHOES OF WAR

They ate bread and cheese and drank the rest of their water. Kate asked doubtfully, "Shouldn't we save some water?"

Tony smiled. "You've watched too many Hollywood films. Party stranded in desert rationing water a sip per person per day. Better to drink all you want and carry it inside your body where it will do you some good, rather than on your back in a flask. Don't worry, we'll find some more."

They set off again, and after the first hour Kate found she was less winded than on the previous day. Although Tony warned her that talking would tax her strength, she couldn't help but observe, "You really are amazing. I mean, when I first met you I thought you were the typical foppish Englishman who'd be more at home in a drawing room making sophisticated small talk and looking bored."

He looked at her with his best bored expression. "I didn't know there was a typical foppish Englishman. That must be an invention of you Yanks. Still, that remark indicates that you've revised your opinion of me. Is that so?"

Kate gave him a wide grin. "You bet."

They left the plateaus and began to ascend the gullies that marked the upper reaches of the mountains. The ground became rougher and much more steep. Stones tumbled in little avalanches under foot where the spring rains and melting snow had carved crevices. Tony walked ahead of her, instructing her to watch where he put his feet and to follow in his steps.

"I feel like the page in 'Good King Wenceslaus,'" Kate grumbled, and Tony began to sing in a rich baritone, "'Mark my footsteps, good my page, tread thou in them boldly...'" until Kate swung her rucksack at his back and told him to shut up or he'd bring a Nazi patrol after them.

"I doubt the Germans are patrolling at this elevation, but you're quite right, we should be careful. The altitude must be affecting me."

Rain began to fall and by midafternoon had turned to sleet. They were quiet now, pressing ahead with greater determination. Only the sound of their labored breathing and boots crunching stones broke the cold silence.

They found a stream and drank thirstily. Threads of ice

were forming around a waterfall. As the day wore on, a bitingly cold wind rose, trying to sweep them off the slopes.

Kate was so lost in concentration that when Tony stopped suddenly she almost collided with him. He grabbed her arm to steady her and pointed to the left. She could just make out the shape of a shepherd's hut ahead, almost lost in the sleet-filled dusk.

Bending closer so she could hear over the howl of the wind, Tony said, "Wait here. I'll go and see if it's vacant."

Minutes later he was scrambling back down the slope to her, and she saw he'd discarded his rucksack. Gratefully, she started toward him, and he caught her hand to help her.

The hut was larger than the first one, and as Tony slammed the door shut against the push of the wind, the last remaining light revealed that the floor was swept clean and there were several casks standing in the corner of the single room. Kate sat on the nearest cask, panting.

Tony came to help her take off her rucksack. "Did you know what they used to smuggle over the Pyrenees before the war?" She knew by his tone he'd discovered something interesting. "Rum. And it seems that they still do. This is a rum-runners' hut. You're sitting on a cask of rum, love, and I suggest we splice the main brace immediately."

Kate jumped up as though bitten. "Splice the—"

"The Royal Navy term for issuing the rum ration. Come on, this will warm the cockles of your heart."

Half an hour later Kate munched the last of their cheese and sipped the fiery liquid from the flask. The rum sent its warmth coursing along her veins. Tony lit a fire, reasoning that in the dusk and sleet and at that elevation there was little likelihood of the smoke being seen. There was plenty of firewood stacked near a stone fireplace.

"Oh, it's wonderful to be warm again," Kate said, taking another sip of rum. At first she had coughed and choked, but now it just slipped easily down her throat.

"Everything's relative, isn't it?" Tony placed their rucksacks at their backs, so they could recline against them.

Kate lay in front of the fire and wanted to purr.

"I never forgot an old gardener we once had at Cardovan

House," he went on. "One day he found me in a miserable state of depression when I was a small boy. He was as bent and gnarled as an old oak, could barely move with arthritis, and was almost blind. He asked me why I was so glum, and I told him whatever inconsequential childish thing it was that ailed me. I can't even remember now. But I remember him saying to me, 'Aye lad, I understand. What you've got is the rich boy's gloom. Now sometimes I gets the glums that old rheumaticky gardeners get, but lad, when I does, I thinks about the glums that plague the poor people—the ones without food and shelter, or missing limbs, or ill, or just lost their nearest and dearest. Think now what it must be like to be *that* glum.' Kate, it was a lesson I never forgot."

Kate turned teary eyes in his direction, wanting to comfort a heartbroken little boy, and said, "Thash a lovely bit of homespun philosh—" She took another drink.

Tony slipped his arm around her shoulders. "Why don't you try to get some sleep now? I'm hoping to reach the pass tomorrow."

"I like you, Tony. Dish I tell you that?"

"I'm glad. Rest now."

"P'raps I'll just have a lil more rum."

"No more, Kate."

Almost with a will of its own, her hand went up to his face, pulled it toward her, and she kissed him on the lips. For a second he hesitated, surprised, then his other arm went around her and he returned the kiss, but not in the way Kate expected. She disengaged her mouth, puzzled, and stared at him in the firelight, unable to interpret the look on his face.

"I thought," she said—enunciating the words carefully, because as the numbed, chilled parts of her body thawed, it seemed that her mind ran in pools of melting thoughts all blended and blurred and coming out of her mouth in garbled sentences—"that you said you were in love with me. Thash you wanted to—wanted—"

"I did and I do. But not now. Not here. You've had a wee bit too much rum, Kate. All my fault. I shouldn't have been so generous with it. I don't want you to hate me in the morning."

ECHOES OF WAR

Kate drew herself haughtily away from him. "I've jush been . . . rejected again."

"No, not that. Never that." He leaned forward and unlaced her boots, slipped them from her feet. "Your socks are a bit damp. Let's put them in front of the fire."

He massaged her toes, and although her pride wanted to jerk her feet out of his reach, her physical pleasure wouldn't allow it. She put her head down on her rucksack and said, "I think I hate you, Wishfield."

"Alas, it seems to be my fate. Oh, well, I suppose the high drama of life is the battle between man and woman. Makes conflicts between nations seem like mere flashes in the pan."

Kate's eyelids flickered down. She decided she'd just rest her eyes for a moment and then think of some scathing remark to let him know what she thought of him, but she was too warm and relaxed to do anything but doze in front of the fire like a sleepy cat.

Just before she fell into a deep sleep she felt Tony put a coat over her.

An explosion of sound and light awoke her. She sat up blinded by a beam of light directly in her eyes. Icy air was gusting into the hut through the open door. At her side Tony spoke first in halting Spanish, then tried French.

The light beam left Kate and went to Tony's face. He was trying to stand up, but a dully gleaming length of metal shoved him back down. The shadows shifted and Kate's eyes focused on the man with the rifle. He stood over them, barrel pointed at Tony's chest, and for a moment Kate's imagination conjured up the tortured figure of the man who had tumbled down the stairs at Gestapo headquarters. Then Tony grabbed the rifle barrel and twisted it, catching the intruder off guard.

Instantly there was a low growl of warning and Kate saw the bared fangs of a dog as the animal leaped to his master's defense. Kate screamed as Tony grappled with the dog.

The man shouted something and a rifle bullet smashed into the floor beside Tony, sending splinters flying. The dog whined and backed away. Panting, his hand blood-smeared,

Tony looked up at the intruder and said in French, "We must get across the border into Spain."

Kate gasped. "Don't tell him anything!" The man was speaking again, and she realized now he spoke in heavily accented French.

Tony said, "It's all right, Kate. He's a Basque. Owner of the rum we helped ourselves to. Smile sweetly at the nice gent, Kate. He's going to guide us over the pass to the border."

BOOK TWO

[21]
Buckinghamshire, England, 1940

Kate ran her fingers through the shorn stubble of her hair despairingly. On the mad dash from France into Spain it had been the least of her worries. But now as she stood in front of the dressing table in a guest room at Cardovan House, her boyish haircut was a major disaster.

"You look like one of those male comedians playing the part of Cinderella's ugly sister in a British pantomime," she told her reflection, wondering if it was too late to plead temporary insanity and escape from the party Cecilia was giving in her honor that evening.

When their Basque shepherd/rum smuggler had led them triumphantly to the great stone monument and pointed to the side that read "España," Tony had whirled Kate in the air in a moment of elation and said, "Come to England with me. An adventure such as ours deserves a fitting finale." She had promptly agreed. It had seemed like a good idea at the time.

Cecilia had welcomed them with everything but the proverbial fatted calf, and even Tony's adoptive father, the Earl of Hardmoor, had arrived from London to congratulate his son on his escape.

Kate had been presented to the Earl, not knowing what to call him, wondering whether to curtsy and rejecting the idea,

ECHOES OF WAR

sure she would say the wrong thing. Hardie, as Cecilia called him, immediately put her at her ease. He was a handsome man, silver-haired like his wife, with engaging clefts in his cheeks and a ready smile. Oddly, he reminded Kate of a masculine version of Cecilia. They chatted briefly before Cecilia chased everyone to their rooms to dress for the party. As they went up the stairs Tony whispered to Kate, "Courage, love, you're a heroine to everyone here."

Kate wasn't sure that was true of Tony's half-sister. Ursula greeted him tearfully, and then regarded Kate as one might look at a bedraggled hound dog that followed an adored brother home. Ursula's hair was sleek and smooth and satiny blond, cut to the fashionable wartime chin length, making Kate even more aware of the fiery unkempt spikes standing up on her skull.

There was a knock on her door and Cecilia's voice called, "Kate, may I come in?"

Kate replied, "Yes, come in," and applied a quick stroke of pale coral lipstick. At least she knew how to subtly enhance her features with makeup now, thanks to Marie Allegret.

As Cecilia Winfield entered the room, Kate thought of a swan gliding regally on a lake, perfect and beautiful; aloof yet touchingly vulnerable. But despite the gloss of manners and charm, there was a curious emptiness to her, as though she were only a cardboard cutout of the real person she had perhaps once been. Kate was eager to further observe Tony's mother and adoptive father together.

There had been a tantalizing glimpse of the electricity that still existed between them when the Earl arrived that afternoon. Kate had watched as the Earl took his wife's hand and kissed her wrist lightly. For a split second the two had looked deep into each other's eyes, and it seemed to Kate that unspoken questions hung in the air between them, tangible as the wood smoke from the fireplace log that scented the air. Then the Earl had turned to Tony and clasped his hand, while Cecilia continued to stare at her husband. The tiny drama had been fleeting, but the memory of it haunted Kate.

Now as Cecilia came into the room, Kate saw she was

dressed even more magnificently than ever and her hair was arranged in a stunning cluster of curls around a diamond tiara, matching the diamonds that glittered on her ears. In the soft bedroom light, Cecilia looked young despite her silver hair. She said, "That dress might have been made for you, Kate. I knew it was too young for me. You know, I'm beginning to love your haircut. It's unique and devil-may-care and gives your features a gamine quality that's quite irresistible."

Kate wanted to kiss her. Cecilia went on: "And you're wearing the locket I sent you. Bless you!"

Fingering the locket, which had traveled from Paris in her most secure pocket, she said, "I never did hear the legend of the locket, but you were sure right about it warding off danger."

Cecilia's eyes twinkled. "Let's save the legend of the locket for later. I have a feeling it's going to come true again. I wanted to have just a private moment with you before the guests arrive. We've been in such a high state of excitement since you and Anthony arrived, I don't believe we've had a second alone, have we?"

"Not really. To tell you the truth, a few minutes ago I was wondering what on earth I was doing here."

Cecilia smiled. "I thought so. Sit down for a moment, Kate, I want to tell you something."

Kate sat on the dresser stool while Cecilia walked slowly about the room. "You're thinking that all of this"—she gestured with her hands—"the house, the servants, the grounds—that you couldn't cope. But you could. I did."

Wondering exactly where the conversation was leading, Kate said, "Yes, but you . . . you're to the manner born. Or is it the manor?"

"Actually, no, I wasn't. I was an actress. Not a bad one either—I suppose because I wasn't terribly clever and needed to have someone write my dialogue and direct my actions. I met a rather strong-willed young woman. Her brother was a playwright, and she and I became friends. She was politically active—an advocate of women's rights and so on. I hero-worshipped her. She was everything I was not: brilliant, educated, flamboyant, self-possessed. Funny, but I never really understood what she saw in me at the time. Through her I met so many stimulating people. I suppose I was like a piece of clay waiting to be molded. I parroted her ideas, tried to be like her. She was a great believer in free love, in an end to the double standard for men and women. She said marriage was a trap for women, bondage. She instilled in me the idea that I could do anything a man could do and get away with it." She sighed. "Poor brilliant, doomed Ella Fontaine."

Cecilia stopped by the window and stood for a moment gazing at the trees, which were losing the last of their autumn leaves. She added softly, almost to herself, "It seems funny to think about it now. But how I do run on. What I intended to say was that when I first came here as Hardie's bride, I was awed by the house, intimidated by the servants—went around addressing them all as Mr. this and Mrs. that—and I made every faux pas known to society. I didn't have anyone to advise me, because Hardie's parents were dead when I met him. But in your case, Kate, I'd be here, and on your side all the way, so please don't be intimidated."

Kate had her mouth open to say something, but Cecilia exclaimed, "Goodness, I must fly! The first guests will be here any second." She kissed Kate's cheek and hurried from the room, leaving Kate twisting the locket and wondering why she hadn't stopped Cecilia immediately and told her again that she was jumping to the wrong conclusions about Tony and herself. Was it because Kate was dreading parting from him? The odyssey was over. Her visit to Cardovan House had to end too. She'd go home to New York, and then what? Yet if she stayed in England . . . The Luftwaffe had already bombed London ferociously, and the entire island was braced for the expected German invasion. There would be no escaping the Germans from these shores, no borders to cross into neutral territory.

She sighed and turned again to the mirror. Perhaps Cecilia was right. The outlandishly short hair made her eyes look larger than ever and called attention to her cheekbones, which weren't bad. She went downstairs feeling less unattractive than before Cecilia came into the room. After all, Tony had accompanied a scruffy creature in men's clothes out of France, and tonight in the beautiful dress she was transformed.

The house was rapidly filling with guests, but still there was no sign of Tony. Cecilia stayed at Kate's side, arm slipped through hers, reintroducing her to people she'd met, presenting her to people she hadn't. The British fascists were conspicuously absent tonight. Cecilia had told her that Sir Oswald Mosley had been arrested at his home the previous May, his fascist party dissolved. Nor was there any sign of Clive. When Kate inquired about him, Cecilia said shortly, "He won't be here tonight."

The Earl, looking magnificent in naval uniform, was chatting with Ursula and several junior officers. Cecilia glanced at her husband from time to time, longingly, it seemed to Kate.

A footman approached bearing a tray containing glasses of champagne, the last of a precious supply, brought out in honor of the occasion. Recalling what a fool she'd made of herself by drinking too much rum, Kate took a glass of champagne and held it. Tony hadn't wanted to make love to her that night in the Basque's hut. Tony hadn't made love to her since she turned down his offer of marriage. It was something she wanted very much to discuss with him but didn't know how.

The buzz of conversation faded momentarily, replaced by a chorus of greetings. "Ah, here's Anthony. Welcome home!"

Kate watched him move through the room, shaking hands, returning greetings. He was back in his RAF uniform. At her side Cecilia whispered, "Doesn't he look handsome in his uniform? I'm so proud of him, and yet afraid too. I shan't survive if anything happens to him. I'm just not capable of withstanding that kind of grief."

Neither am I, Kate thought. Is that the real reason I refused him? Having lost one man, am I afraid I couldn't survive losing another? It was no secret the RAF pilots were suffering heavy casualties.

ECHOES OF WAR

Tony reached her, and Cecilia discreetly moved away. For Kate everyone else in the room had faded too. He said, "You look lovely tonight, Kate."

"You look pretty good yourself. I was just thinking how I used to bait you about not being in uniform. I really did think you were pro-Nazi once."

"I've been meaning to come clean, as you Yanks say, about that."

"You've watched too many gangster movies," Kate remarked. "About what?"

"My activities before the war. I worked with Charles Morcambe and an organization that smuggled Jews out of Germany. That was the reason I exploited Ursula's friendship with Mosley. We also had help from Wolf von Klaus, the amateur magician you met at the Grand Hotel. He helped us while he was in the civil service by misplacing files and so on. The last person I got out was the sister-in-law of your tourist—Radner."

"I see." Kate's voice was a small squeak.

"During the last days before the French collapse I was assigned to fly de Gaulle's people out of France. That's why I couldn't come back for you. Charles Morcambe was supposed to bring you a message, but I gathered you never got it."

"No, I never did. Why are you telling me all this now?"

"Because in two days I have to report to Biggin Hill, and I might not get another chance."

Two days. She couldn't believe how desolate she felt. Around them people talked, laughed, sipped champagne. Chandeliers blazed overhead. Kate blinked. She didn't want to say goodbye to him.

Tony took her hand and led her to a sofa in a corner of the room. They sat silently for a while, then he turned to her and said in a matter-of-fact tone, "You will agree that we get along together rather well."

She nodded. Two days, and then he'd be gone from her life.

"I believe, Kate, that if we'd had more time, you might have learned to care for me. If there wasn't a war on, I'd chase you back to the States and hang around until you changed your mind. But I can't do that. I know you don't love me, but I think I love you enough to make it work for us. Marry me, Kate. We'll have fun together, if nothing else."

Her eyes filled with tears. She looked down at her hands. All of her doubts came back, unbidden. "But you said you had to report back in two days."

"We can get a special license tomorrow. I'm afraid it would have to be a registry office wedding. We could have a church wedding later on if you like. I can't promise I'll convert to your religion, but naturally you can attend any church you wish."

The eagerness in his voice came close to breaking her heart. She bit her lip, wondering if she'd known since that night in France what her answer would ultimately be. She wasn't as wildly in love with Tony as she had been with Wade, but he was right, they got along, and their physical relationship was magical. She admired him tremendously. Wasn't that a good enough basis for marriage? It was probably more than many women settled for. Perhaps enough to even compensate for the loss of her country.

She turned and looked into his face, and at that instant the slightly wondrous revelation came to her that *nothing* could ever compensate for the loss of Tony. She wanted him to stay with her forever. She was so overcome with emotion that all she could do was nod wordlessly.

"Yes?" Tony asked. *"Yes?"* His arms went around her, and he was kissing her while the prisms of light over her head flashed like comets in the outer cosmos.

A little later when Cecilia happily made the announcement and the other guests chorused their congratulations, Kate noticed Ursula slip out of the room, her face contorted and tear-streaked.

They were married the following afternoon in a somber-looking office by a clerk suffering from a bad cold who sneezed his way through the brief civil ceremony. Kate wore a hastily purchased cream-colored wool dress and matching jacket and a rather jaunty cream felt hat that Tony said made her look like a buccaneer.

Ursula did not come to the wedding, giving the excuse that she didn't feel well. Cecilia and her husband stood as witnesses, and it seemed to Kate that she could almost feel the older couple reliving their own wedding. She was saddened when they both went their separate ways at the end.

There was so much to do—apply for ration books for Kate, get her a national identity card—that there wasn't time for the wedding breakfast that Cecilia wanted to give them. Tony persuaded his mother that the party the previous evening would suffice. The party had turned into a celebration of their engagement, and about midnight Ursula had reappeared, acting a little tipsy, and informed everyone that she too was going to be married—to Roderick Davenport, when he came home on leave. Kate wondered if Roderick was aware of this, but tried to be charitable and wished her future sister-in-law all happiness.

The early dusk of the English autumn was settling by the time all of their form-filling and registering was completed. They drove to a country inn where Tony had reserved a room for the night.

"It's not far from Cardovan House, actually," he told her. "We're a wee bit short of petrol now it's rationed. I understand the civilian ration is going to be eliminated altogether soon."

They drove along shadowed country lanes bordered by hawthorne hedges, the countryside shrouded and starkly beautiful in the fading twilight. Now that they were alone and all the rushing about was over, Kate at last had time to think.

Mrs. Anthony Winfield. Tony's *wife*. I'm *married*. We're about to have our wedding night. Will it be different making love to a husband? Less furtive perhaps, more secure. Lord, she was becoming obsessed with sex, anticipating the consummation of their marriage rather than piously contemplating a long and happy life together. Perhaps the war had done that—sharpened all the edges of things. Who wanted to see beyond today? Still, the vague menace of some sort of cosmic punishment for her carnal thoughts floated mistily through her mind. Remembering that she'd been too nervous to eat all day, she told herself she was probably just light-headed from hunger.

A cable was en route to New York. Her mother would no doubt take great delight in sending announcements to the newspapers, especially the *Morning Express,* which was owned by Wade Lowery's family.

Arriving at the inn, they found they were the only people in the old-fashioned dining room for an early dinner. The inn was Tudor-style, with aged beams and mellowed wood panels. The stone floor, from the iron-studded front doors to a mahogany desk, was worn concave in a path trod by countless feet over the centuries.

An elderly waiter brought them a bottle of sherry and they toasted each other. Kate said, "Promise me that you won't get involved in any heroics when you get into your Spitfire tomorrow."

"How about if they assign me to a Hurricane instead?"

"Be serious, Tony. You do have a tendency to think you're indestructible. I've noticed that about you. Don't take unnecessary risks, okay?"

"I've no intention of doing so, believe me. But thank you for your concern, Mrs. Winfield."

The unaccustomed name made her feel suddenly shy. She turned to watch the waiter hobbling across the room with a tray of food. They had delicious Dover sole and light crisp French fries, which Tony called chips, and got into a discussion about American and English words and phrases that had different meanings, sometimes hilariously so.

"Just promise me," Kate said, "that when I take you home to meet my folks you won't ask anybody to knock you up in the morning."

"Why?" Tony asked in sincere innocence. "That's an ancient term, harking back to the cotton mill towns when they started work before dawn and alarm clocks hadn't been invented yet. Each village had its own official knocker-up who went around with a long pole knocking on bedroom windows."

He couldn't understand why Kate was convulsed as soon as he mentioned an official knocker-up.

They lingered over their meal until the innkeeper came to say their room was ready, their bags in place. Then Tony took Kate's hand and led her up the stairs to a charming room with a four-poster bed, a blazing fire in a tiled fireplace, and a sheepskin rug in front of it.

Half an hour later when Kate returned from the bathroom, which was down the hall, Tony was standing in front of the fire wearing a dressing gown, his hair still damp and tousled from his trip to the downstairs bathroom. He said, "I should think this skin once belonged to an Australian sheep. I've never seen one that large in the British Isles."

She crossed the room to his side and studied the rug intently, kicked off her slippers, and wriggled her toes in the furry softness. "Mmm . . . sure feels Australian to me too."

"One of the pilots in my squadron is an Aussie. Dusty Miller his name is. I hope he got over his penchant for chasing Jerry bombers back across the channel."

Kate placed her hands on his shoulders. "Please . . . don't talk about the war, not tonight."

"Oh, Kate . . . my Kate," he whispered.

The wisp of filmy chiffon that was her nightgown slid to the floor and nestled against the sheepskin. The firelight felt both warm and strangely erotic on her bare flesh, as though the dancing golden light were artfully applied by some unseen sculptor, gilding her skin and glorifying her body for her husband's pleasure.

Tony buried his face in her neck and murmured, "I love you so much. How shall I ever be able to express it?"

As he drew her down to the rug and traced the long column of her throat with leisurely kisses, Kate found herself wanting to do more than simply accept his lovemaking. As her own passion flared to life, she returned his kisses and caresses with an abandon she wouldn't have thought possible. Those other times they'd made love had been exciting, but nothing like this. Tonight the last barriers between them fell, and for the first time Kate understood how two people could indeed become one.

[22]

Kate knew that for as long as she lived she would remember the lovely old inn where she and Tony spent the too brief hours of their honeymoon. The way the coal fire glowed in the hearth, the patter of rain gentle on the windowpanes, the cozy softness of the featherbed and faint lavender scent of a patchwork quilt made of squares of satin and velvet, very old and fragile as the memory of first love.

But most of all, her new husband. Tony's tenderness would have melted a stonier heart than Kate's. She was constantly surprised and moved by the way he could make love to her with fierce abandon, yet make her feel precious, beloved, as though her needs and sensibilities were his first concern and his could only be satisfied if first she was happy.

Lying in his arms, she felt that with him she didn't have to pretend or do anything, merely to be herself, because that was enough for him. She simply had to be. Within the security of marriage Tony also cast off his own defensive facade and revealed a deeply sensitive nature. Kate quickly realized he had cultivated that blasé exterior to hide his true feelings. It hadn't occurred to her to feel sorry for him, but a picture of a bleak childhood began to emerge that made her see both Tony and his mother in a new light. It hadn't been easy moving in the circles he moved in, attending the schools of the privileged few, yet being that pariah, a bastard

ECHOES OF WAR

in a time when society labeled the child rather than the parents. Remembering his story about the old gardener, she knew what had been troubling Tony when the old man urged him to count his blessings.

Tony was unstinting in his expression of love for her, which touched her deeply. He never demanded anything in return, but seemed content merely to give, of his words, of his body, of everything he had to offer.

As they lay curled up in each other's arms on the morning of the day he was to report for duty, he told her, "I think I fell in love with you that first night in Berlin. You seemed to radiate honesty and integrity and compassion. When you went to help that poor old man being dragged from his house by the Nazi bully boys, I could have wept with pride at your sheer courage."

Kate ran her hand across his bare chest lightly, marveling at the pleasure of touch. "You're the one who was brave. When I think of all the times I taunted you about being a Nazi, about not being in uniform . . ."

He pressed a kiss to her forehead. "I'd taken an oath of silence about our smuggling operation, so I couldn't tell you. And right after I finished my RAF training, I was reassigned to Charles' people and again on hush-hush work. But I suppose there's more to it. In some ways men are even more vulnerable than women. We want to be loved for ourselves alone. For our weaknesses as well as our strengths. I didn't want to tell you anything that might cause you to be impressed by what I was doing rather than what I was. Am I making any sense?"

"Yes. But you know, it amazes me that a man with your looks and charm should feel so hesitant about his chances with a woman."

"Tell me more about my looks and charm," he said, running his hand down her back, fingers gentle as the patter of raindrops on the windows.

She giggled and snuggled closer to him. "I've decided I like being married. It's lovely to have a warm body close in the night. I like making love before I fall asleep. I wish . . . I wish you didn't have to leave. Where is Biggin Hill?"

"About eighteen miles from London."

"Couldn't I find a place to live near the base so we—"

"No, Kate, I think not. I'd rather you stayed at Cardovan House. The air raids have been heavy down there, and besides, I'll be on call for long periods of time, and pretty tired when I do get time off. I'll come to you as soon as I can get a weekend pass. Besides, you love Cardovan House. Don't make some rash gesture just because you feel I expect it of you."

Afterwards, she wondered why she didn't tell him the truth, that she wanted to be with him, that she was going to miss him desperately, that her few hours of being his wife was like a tantalizing appetizer and she wanted more. Instead, in typical Kate fashion she said, "Oh, it isn't that. I'm afraid I'm not ready for Cardovan House. I wouldn't know what to do with myself there. I've always been a working girl. I'd like to do something useful. I thought I might volunteer at a hospital. I found when I was looking after Marie I seemed to have a knack for nursing."

It was true, of course, but the look of expectation he'd worn when she said she would like to live near his base faded slightly, and she wanted to kick herself for not sharing her feelings with him as generously as he shared his. He kissed her again quickly and said, "At least give Cardovan House a try for a while—until the raids ease up a bit around London."

Although he continued to caress her, she felt acutely aware of an opportunity lost. Damn, why did she still have to hide behind that defensive screen? Why couldn't she open up her heart as readily as she opened her body? Did she really believe that if she showed her feelings to Tony it would be the signal for him to turn away from her? She recalled her mother's theory that Kate had worn her heart on her sleeve with Wade, and men like the chase better than the surrender—that she should have held back, not letting him know how desperately she loved him. Perhaps that applied to men like Wade, but not to Tony, surely not Tony?

Kate threw her arms around her husband and hugged him fiercely, trying to convey by her touch how happy she was to be his wife, but he mistook the gesture for an invitation to make love again and his mouth sought hers eagerly, cutting off what might have been said. Moments later she was lost in the rapture of that most intimate joining, breathless and frenzied and sweetly urgent because their remaining hours together were so few.

That afternoon Kate stood on the railway platform in a gray drizzle of rain as Tony's train moved slowly away from her and was swallowed by the mist. Her tears blended with the raindrops, but she had fixed a wide grin on her face until he was out of sight. She felt as though part of her had gone too, leaving an empty place that would continue to ache until he returned.

The full fury of the Luftwaffe had now been unleashed on British cities. Daily and nightly air raids pounded civilian targets as well as military ones. Invasion was imminent, everyone agreed. Street signs were removed, and makeshift roadblocks put up. Church bells were silenced, as they would be the signal that the invaders had landed. And in the skies, a vastly outnumbered handful of British Spitfire and Hurricane pilots scrambled to intercept the bombers.

At Cardovan House there were changes too. Fewer rooms were used, because of fuel rationing and the fact that national museum treasures were being stored there to keep them safe from German bombing. Strict food rationing had ended Cecilia's dinner parties, but she still managed to gather a few of her friends and a sprinkling of servicemen and women for weekend parties. Small portions of wine were carefully doled out, and hors d'oeuvres were often simply chestnuts gathered in the woods and roasted, or crackers with a dab of fish paste that to Kate tasted like wallpaper glue.

Her mother-in-law couldn't have been kinder or more considerate to her, but on weekends the sight of uniformed men made Kate lonelier than ever for Tony.

One Saturday night she sat on the sidelines moodily watching Clive hover attentively about Cecilia. Kate wasn't sure how she felt about Clive. He appeared to be that species peculiar to the British upper classes, a totally useless but charmingly witty, good-looking creature, bred only for entertainment value. When he limited himself to a couple of drinks, he was the proverbial life and soul of the party, always the one to turn any serious discussion about the suffering caused by the war to light topics.

Someone mentioned the appalling civilian casualties in London, and he drawled, "Damnedest thing happened to a friend of mine. He paid up his club dues for a year and the next night the Jerries blasted the place to ruins."

Kate looked at him over the rim of her untouched glass of sherry. Clive in his dinner jacket, safe within the insulation of a country house far from the bombing, increased her irritation.

He went on: "Did you hear about the chap who was almost arrested as a German spy at the village pub? Seems he was making strange scrawls in a notebook, and when someone asked was he a stranger in those parts he answered, 'Ya.' Only it turned out he was an American correspondent writing in shorthand, and the 'Ya' was actually 'Yeah.' Fortunately the local constabulary . . ."

Kate stood up and walked around the edge of the room toward the door. Perhaps if she went upstairs and wrote to Tony it might prevent her from making some ill-conceived remark.

Before she reached the door, Ursula's ringing tones announced, "Hardie called me a few days ago. He thinks the Admiralty is at last going to give him sea duty. Shipping losses are so frightful. I do wish they wouldn't. Of course, we won't get the refueling bases we need so desperately from Eire. De Valera can't lead his people; he has to follow them. The stupid Irish can't see that if we go down, they'll go with us. But then, they've always rather enjoyed hating us, haven't they?"

Looking back over her shoulder, Kate saw Ursula's eyes were fixed on her, glittering with anger. Several people cleared their throats uncomfortably, and even Clive appeared taken aback. Cecilia stared at her daughter, horror written on her face.

Kate's glance went rapidly around the room. "I take it from the way I'm being stared at that Ursula is holding me personally responsible for Ireland's refusal of naval bases? Well, you're all correct in assuming my ancestry is Irish, but

ECHOES OF WAR

I'm American by birth and loyalty." She looked Ursula full in the eyes and added, "Maybe you should go and let them know at Buckingham Palace what you think about their German ancestors."

Afraid that if she lingered another second she might find herself in an ugly argument, Kate started for the door again. She almost collided with the Earl of Hardmoor. He was dressed in a naval officer's uniform and his appearance sent a ripple of surprise around the room.

Ursula cried, "Hardie!" and rushed to embrace him, while Cecilia rose slowly to her feet. Kate stood still, not knowing what to do. After he had kissed his daughter he turned to Kate and said, "How are you, my dear? I spoke with Tony this morning, and he's quite fit." He kissed her cheek and she murmured a greeting and her thanks.

Cecilia crossed the room and took both of his hands in hers. "What a nice surprise. Have you had dinner?"

"Yes, thank you. I—" He broke off, and Kate followed the direction of his eyes. He was staring at Clive. Neither man smiled or spoke. Kate felt a slight chill creep up her spine. Then the Earl said, "I just stopped in to say goodbye and pick up a few things I need. I have to be back in London tonight and I'll be off to Portsmouth in the morning to join my ship."

Although he shook hands with some of the men he knew and kissed the cheeks of the women, Kate noticed that he didn't go anywhere near Clive. Minutes later the Earl excused himself and left the room. Kate slipped out after him, a nagging suspicion tugging at the back of her mind. Was it possible that Clive wasn't Cecilia's cousin, that he was more than that to her?

She caught up with her father-in-law as he and his valet were about to enter a room upstairs. She said, "Sir, could I talk to you for a minute?"

"Of course, Kate. Come on in while my valet finds some of my traveling gear. And by the way, why don't you just call me Hardie like everyone else? My name is James, actually, but it's been a long time since anyone called me that." For a second his gaze went beyond her, as though remembering someone particularly dear to him who had called him by his given name. Then he went into the room to give his valet instructions and Kate followed.

"Can I go back to London with you?" she asked hurriedly, as though afraid he might leave immediately.

He stopped, one hand on a silver-framed photograph that stood on a dresser. From where Kate stood, it appeared to be a picture of two young women. He handed it to his valet, who dropped it into a suitcase along with a shaving kit. "Of course you may. But I must warn you, it's a bit noisy there."

"I need to see Tony," Kate said. "I need to very badly. I thought if I could call his base and tell him I was there, maybe we could get together—if only for an hour."

"You're tired of Cecilia's friends," he said with a slight smile. "Can't say I blame you."

"Oh, no, nothing like that. She's been wonderful to me, so kind. She shoots all of the old mother-in-law jokes down in flames."

"How are you getting along with my daughter?"

Kate felt her neck grow a little warm. "We . . . haven't really gotten to know each other yet."

He smiled. "How very tactful of you, my dear. She was always so exquisitely lovely, it was hard not to spoil her. I'm quite sure she's let you know that she doesn't relinquish her possessions easily, and I'm afraid she regards Tony as one of them. She absolutely hero-worshipped him when she was a child. I told myself it was just a phase, but it hasn't really lessened as she matured. Of course, soon she'll be married herself, and everything will be better for all concerned, I believe."

Kate shifted her feet awkwardly. Privately she thought Ursula was a brat and there was something a little unnatural in her attachment to her brother, but Kate would never have said so. She asked, "Are you going back tonight?"

"Yes. There's a midnight train." He stood looking around the room, as though committing to memory the stately Chippendale furniture, the paneled walls, and the Turner landscapes that adorned the wall behind a desk of heroic proportions. This was a man's room—wood and leather and uncluttered elegance.

Kate knew of the British aristocracy's habit of maintaining

separate sleeping quarters and wondered how they could bear to forgo the comfort of one another's arms in the lonely nights. She supposed the conjugal visits between Hardie and Cecilia had ended long ago. Would they perhaps have salvaged their marriage had they shared a bed? Silently vowing never to let Tony escape to another bedroom, Kate said, "It's so lovely here, how can you bear—" She broke off, knowing she'd overstepped the mark.

"Not to live here?" he finished for her. "A part of me will always live here. Just as part of me will always love Cecilia. I know you must feel you married into a strange family, Kate, but believe me, Tony is a good chap. You know, my dear, I'm not surprised he fell head over heels in love with you. You remind me of the woman I fell in love with so long ago. If only she hadn't been made angry at the world in general and mankind in particular. Contrary to popular belief, men don't really like the clinging vine. But she wasn't content with just being her own woman, strong and self-willed and independent. She had to punish us for setting the double standards in the first place."

"Maybe—" Kate began.

But he glanced at his watch and interrupted her. "Forgive me, but if we're going to be on that train I think you'd better change and pack an overnight bag."

Her father-in-law had a flat in Berkeley Square and insisted that she use it while she was in town and on any future visit. He gave her a key and made her promise that since the flat was on the fourth floor, she would go down to the ground floor if the bombs started to fall too close.

They traveled on a slow train that made frequent stops, one for a couple of hours, and it was almost dawn when they reached London. Since the Earl had to catch a train for Portsmouth, he put Kate in a taxi, kissed her cheek, and said, "Tony is a very lucky man. Take care of yourself, Kate. *Au revoir.*"

The taxi driver winked at her and said, "Not to worry, ducks. The Jerries have gone home. The all clear sounded a bit ago."

Emerging from the station to a smoky dawn, Kate was

ECHOES OF WAR

appalled by the destruction the bombers had wrought. Great piles of rubble, craters in the streets, blackened shells of buildings, pitiful remains of houses, some with the front walls gone, so that they resembled doll houses smashed by a careless child, revealing twisted floors and inner walls. One still had a brass bedstead perched crazily on half an upper floor, red roses on a strip of wallpaper left clinging to the plaster behind the bed. Kate thought of a man and woman and the intimacy of that room and looked away hastily.

On one corner a group of civil defense workers were digging in the rubble of a block of flats. As the taxi passed, Kate saw them haul an elderly woman from beneath the smoking bricks, her face soot-streaked, immobile, in shock. Two blocks later they came to a barricade and were ordered by a fresh-faced young army sergeant to detour another way.

"UXB," the taxi driver explained apologetically. When Kate looked blank, he added, "Unexploded bomb—they're digging it out. Big one hit St. Paul's Cathedral the other day, and I heard one bloke drove it out into the country for miles so they could defuse it away from the city. Some American correspondents wanted to interview the bloke, but the War Office wouldn't let 'em. They don't want 'em making individuals into heroes, see."

By the time he delivered her to the address in Berkeley Square, Kate was numbed by what she had seen. This wasn't a country simply at war, as France had been, this was a country under siege. She wondered how people could possibly live under such conditions. Then, alighting from the taxi, she saw a milkman delivering bottles of milk, and noticed newspapers were already lying on doorsteps.

She picked up her father-in-law's newspaper before letting herself into his flat, making a note to cancel the delivery. She had a telephone number where she could leave a message for Tony, but the line was either busy or down and she couldn't get through. She sat down at Hardie's desk with the telephone in front of her and idly glanced through the newspaper she had carried in.

There was an article about a session the American correspondents in London had had the previous day with the Minister of Information regarding censorship. Mr. Duff

ECHOES OF WAR

Cooper had made it clear that he would rather sacrifice a good headline than risk revealing information to the enemy. When some of the war correspondents' protests became unruly, one of their number had taken the Minister's side and pointed out that the American public was already receiving more information than the British were.

Kate leaned forward suddenly, her hands flattening the newspaper. The name of the American correspondent who had defended the censorship policy was Wade Lowery.

[23]

The sirens began their banshee wail at dusk. Kate's stomach lurched, but following her father-in-law's advice, she went as calmly as she could down to the lounge on the ground floor.

Several dowagers and a couple of elderly gentlemen were already there, sitting in overstuffed chairs and sipping brandies.

Bursts of anti-aircraft fire shattered the night. Planes droned in the distance. There was the whine of falling bombs and, seconds later, the sickening blast of explosions. Kate glanced about nervously. A waiter approached and, sensing her alarm, said, "They're mostly falling on the East End, I should think, miss. May I bring you something?"

Her throat dry, Kate ordered a sherry. When one of the bombs exploded even closer, there was a stirring of interest among the other patrons. One old gentleman observed, "Saville Row, I shouldn't wonder."

"No, I think it fell right in the square," a woman said. She smiled reassuringly at Kate. "This is one of the strongest buildings in London—all steel and concrete. We're safe enough here."

"Unless we get a direct hit," the man said testily, apparently irritated at being disagreed with.

Steel and concrete or not, Kate felt the entire building

sway under the impact of the next stick of bombs. She noticed that everyone sat well away from the windows, despite the blackout shutters shielding the glass.

There was a lull in the bombing and Kate dozed, all at once aware of her previous sleepless night. When the raid didn't resume, she decided to go to bed.

Hovering in the back of her mind as she lay on a luxuriously soft mattress listening to the distant thud of gunfire was the knowledge that what she was seeing and hearing was being reported to people back home by Wade Lowery. He was here in this city somewhere. Did he know she was here? Had he left New York before or after the announcement of her wedding? Chances of them running into one another were nil—unless one looked up the other. She wondered if she would tell Tony when she called. She was too tired and too tense to give the matter deep thought.

She awoke the following morning somewhat complacent that she had slept through most of a night of bombing. The popular phrase "London can take it" flitted through her mind just before she remembered Wade was here. She pictured him in some Fleet Street bar, dark eyes taking in every detail of his surroundings, scrutinizing everyone around him in the quizzical way he had, black hair windblown, boxer's shoulders forever squared expectantly, and always that cocky up-and-at-'em attitude, the restless where's-the-action expression on his ruggedly appealing face. He wouldn't be taking the air raids or the war or anything else for that matter too seriously. By the time she'd bathed and dressed she was able to stop thinking about him.

Trying the telephone number Hardie had given her again, this time Kate got through. When she asked to speak to Pilot Officer Winfield a crisp female voice asked if it was an emergency, and when Kate replied that it wasn't, she was told he was sleeping after having flown for sixteen hours straight. Feeling a little ashamed of herself, Kate said, "Don't disturb him. Just ask him to call his wife. I'm staying in his father's flat in Berkeley Square."

The day passed slowly. There was no call from Tony. Prowling the flat restlessly that afternoon, Kate wandered into her father-in-law's bedroom, fully expecting all of his personal belongings to be gone. She sat at a Sheraton writing table, fingers tapping on the surface, willing Tony to wake up and phone her. Idly her hand drifted to the single drawer and pulled it open.

Inside was a leather-bound album, its cover worn to a soft patina. Carefully she lifted it out and turned the pages, studying the photographs inside, intrigued that it was Hardie who kept the album rather than Cecilia.

The early snapshots were of people she didn't know, some against the backdrop of Cardovan House. She recognized a smaller topiary garden than the one now in existence, and other subtle differences the years had wrought.

Then suddenly she came to a series of pictures of two young women dressed in the hobble skirts and big picture hats of the pre-World War I era. Somewhere between 1910 and 1914, Kate estimated. Both girls were dazzlingly pretty and were about the same height and build, but upon closer examination Kate saw that one seemed to be a carbon copy of the other. She wasn't sure why this was so obvious. Perhaps because one young woman gazed at the camera with bold lively eyes, her pose suggesting a matador facing the bull or a duelist about to raise the pistol. The other girl, who was probably a few years younger, had a slightly vacant, dazzled-by-it-all look when she regarded the camera, but usually she stared in admiration at her companion.

A few of the snapshots included a flashily dressed young man who scowled or stared with brooding eyes at some unseen horizon. Then there was a dashingly handsome young naval officer that Kate recognized instantly: James, Earl of Hardmoor, standing at attention between the two women, then later on in cricket whites, arms carelessly around the shoulders of both women.

Turning the page, Kate came across one enlargement that showed the bold-eyed young woman alone on a platform, banners hung behind her. The words were faded, indistinct: ELLA FONTAINE FOR . . . something, something hidden behind an upraised arm: CHAMPION OF THE WORKING MAN.

Kate frowned, concentrating on the name. She'd heard it before. Of course, Cecilia's friend, the one she'd admired so much. So she'd run for government—the Labour party, by the look of it—in some small district. Had she won? What had become of her?

Flipping forward, there didn't seem to be any more pictures of her or the brooding-eyed young man. He must have been the playwright brother Cecilia had mentioned. Remembering her conversation with Cecilia, it was now clear that she had indeed been strongly influenced by Ella Fontaine, even to the point of mimicking her dress, mannerisms, and expressions. It was rather sad. Cecilia must have had quite an inferiority complex to have tried so desperately to be another Ella Fontaine.

The remainder of the photos were of Hardie and his bride and an appealing little boy. Kate smiled down at Tony's solemn innocence. The progression of pictures ended with Cecilia holding a new baby in a long christening gown, surrounded by guests and vicar, now looking less like Ella Fontaine and more like the Cecilia Kate knew. But perhaps that was because of the circle of friends forming the familiar protective barrier around her. It occurred to Kate that crowds were the enemy of intimacy, and she wondered again about the Winfields.

Lunch consisted of a couple of shortbread biscuits she found in a tin in the kitchen, and some weak tea made from the dusty remnants in a tea caddy. By now Kate was sure Tony would call at any minute.

The afternoon passed slowly. By four o'clock she decided to risk another call to the air base. This time she was told curtly that he wasn't available. She replaced the receiver, nagged by a premonition that something had happened to him.

What if he'd been shot down and they wouldn't tell her over the phone? She put a call through to Cardovan House, and the butler told her that Lady Winfield and her daughter had gone out and, no, there were no messages and no telegrams had been delivered.

Kate paced the living-room floor. What had Tony said—that Biggin Hill was only eighteen miles away? Not a great distance. She made a quick decision. To hell with it, she'd go there.

* * *

Searchlights crisscrossed the sky and an anti-aircraft battery opened up somewhere close by. The taxi driver said, "I'm not sure how far we'll get, miss, before we're stopped."

"Try to make it to the station," Kate said.

"Trains mightn't be running, you know."

"Please, keep going."

Aircraft engines throbbed overhead and a flare burst into brilliant light, illuminating the empty street. There was a whistle of falling bombs and a fearful *crump*. Glass flew across the street in their path.

Swerving, the driver called, "What'll it be, miss, a shelter or the nearest pub?"

"Make it a pub," Kate answered as the cab was shaken by the blast of the next bomb. The driver pulled over to the curb, jumped out, and yanked open Kate's door. Taking her hand, he dragged her toward an unlit door as the pavement trembled beneath their feet. He pushed open the door and they went inside.

The welcome glow of yellow light and aroma of malt liquor met her. A leaded glass inner door proclaimed the room beyond to be the "Saloon Bar." Two soldiers stood at the bar and a middle-aged couple were seated at a table. A young barmaid laughed loudly at something one of the soldiers said. Too loudly, Kate decided, noting the girl's wide eyes and nervous movements. Poor kid was terrified. Kate ordered a glass of dry sherry for herself and bought a pint of ale for the taxi driver.

The din of exploding bombs and staccato gunfire now sounded like a manic group of drummers pounding their drums in a closet. From time to time the windows rattled and walls shook from the blast. Snowflakes of plaster drifted down from the ceiling. Kate sipped her sherry and wished she'd gone to an air-raid shelter.

A young soldier in battle dress gave Kate a tentative smile. "Nice night out, isn't it?"

Kate raised her brows questioningly, and he added, "Didn't you see that bombers' moon coming up? I hope our blokes are using it to find their way to Hamburg."

There was no chance to reply as they heard an earsplitting

whistle directly overhead. The soldier grabbed Kate and shoved her down beside the bar, shielding her with his body. At the same instant she saw the barmaid disappear on the other side of the bar, while the middle-aged couple dived under their table.

The detonation of the bomb was deafening. The door with the leaded glass was ripped from its hinges and crashed atop the table sheltering the man and woman. All the lights went out and the floor rose up under Kate, smashing her knees. Behind the bar every bottle and glass seemed to be shattering.

Seconds later the darkness was broken by an orange glow from across the street. A voice at the end of a flashlight beam called out, "Is anyone in there hurt?"

Cautiously Kate felt her knees. Her stockings were in ribbons, but her bones seemed to be intact. The young soldier scrambled to his feet and offered his hand to help her up. Someone was coughing nearby. Silhouettes rose around her as people stood up, backlit by the light of a burning building across the street.

"The barmaid," Kate said, choking on the dust. "Is she all right?"

She picked her way carefully around the length of the bar, stepping over chunks of lath and plaster that had been blasted from ceiling and walls. There was broken glass everywhere. The young barmaid lay crumpled against the bar, her face covered with blood. Kate yelled, "Over here. Bring the flashlight."

Crouching down, she cradled the girl's head in her lap, feeling the warmth and stickiness of pumping blood. The flashlight beam swept over them and a voice said, "I'll try to get an ambulance."

The girl's body suddenly went limp.

Before Kate had time to react, a man's voice called hoarsely from the doorway, "I need some help next door. People buried in the rubble."

The flames burned more brightly, illuminating the barmaid's staring eyes. Kate eased her down onto the glass-strewn floor, feeling her throat. She wasn't breathing.

As if in a dream, Kate got up slowly and followed the

others into the street. Next door to the pub was a pile of bricks and mortar, wooden beams, doors, and, incredibly, an unbroken clock still attached to a piece of plasterboard.

The man with the flashlight wore the steel helmet of an air-raid warden. He and the men from the pub heaved aside bricks and broken furniture and Kate went to help them. Within minutes sweat poured from her face and her hands bled. She was vaguely aware of the others, the taxi driver slinging bricks back over his shoulder along with a continuous barrage of Cockney curses.

"Here," one of the soldiers said as he shoved aside a wooden beam and revealed two small bare feet.

They all went to the spot, working with a frenzy now. Moments later a small girl was carefully pulled from the rubble. Kate held out her arms to receive a dirt-streaked head of dusty gold curls. She screamed, "Where the hell is the ambulance?"

The child opened her eyes and looked directly at Kate. "Mummy, I hurt."

Holding the child, Kate rocked her back and forth, crooning a lullaby, because she didn't know what else to do and wanted to shut out the sounds of death falling from the sky.

The ground shook again as another bomb exploded, somewhere close. Kate flung herself across the child. When the smoke and dust settled, she saw another house on the opposite side of the street had collapsed. The men were frantically digging still and minutes later pulled the body of a woman from beneath the bricks.

Somewhere, distantly, Kate heard the clanging of an ambulance bell and thanked God that help was coming. The barmaid was dead and the little girl's mother was dead, but perhaps there was still time to save the child.

The ambulance came screeching to a halt and at the same time firefighters arrived to deal with the incendiary blazes on the street of modest houses. Figures materialized beside Kate, someone peeled her arms from around the child. "Sorry, love," a woman's voice said sympathetically. "There's nothing we can do for her. Lay her down over there with her mother, and somebody will be along to take care of them."

ECHOES OF WAR

The ambulance clanged off into the night to search for the living. Kate clutched the child more tightly and went on singing. She wasn't sure how long she sat on the cold pavement, or at what point the child was forcibly removed from her arms. She vaguely recalled later that the taxi driver wanted to take her somewhere but she refused to go.

She remembered walking, hearing the sounds of carnage continue, dropping to the ground when a bomb exploded too close, thinking that it was all a nightmare, a scene from Dante's *Inferno* from which at any moment she would awaken.

Mummy, I hurt. The little girl had said the words to Kate. Why did she have to speak to Kate? This wasn't Kate's war. What was Kate doing here anyway? Damn the limeys and damn their war. She should have stayed in Brooklyn where she belonged.

Stumbling around a dark corner, a steel-helmeted figure blocked her path. "Come on, ducks, you didn't ought to be walking about the streets now." She found herself escorted into a brick public shelter with a concrete slab roof. People were sleeping inside, propped against the walls, lying on the floor.

The air-raid warden who had intercepted her pulled her into a corner, which was evidently his station. He had a small table and an alcohol stove. "You're just in time for a cuppa," he whispered, as though the night were quiet. "The rest of this lot's asleep."

The hot sweet tea brought her back to her senses. With reality came unbearable pain, knifing into her heart, tearing at her vitals. It was like coming out of shock and finding every part of her body injured. But there were no physical wounds to deal with, rather a raging sense of horror at the injustice and stupidity of it all. What had the young soldier said? Bombers' moon . . . Hope it lights the way for our planes to Hamburg? She didn't feel anger at the Germans. Their children were suffering and dying too. She saw again the wide frightened eyes of the young barmaid, heard the child say, "Mummy, I hurt," remembered Marie willing herself to die along with her beloved Paris; and Kate was overwhelmed with pity for all of mankind, who had to battle a blind, unreasoning, all-powerful evil.

Her emotions tossed her this way and that, between anger and pity and frustration, because there was no clear resolution of all she felt. A small band of demons, anti-Christs, walked the earth, and everyone else had to suffer. How could the few have led the many to this cataclysm?

Realizing that she had actually resented the barmaid and the child for dying in her arms, had wanted them to leave her out of this war of theirs, made Kate bitterly, deeply ashamed. She put the cup back into the air-raid warden's hands as the all clear sounded its thin monotonous wail.

Stumbling outside into a smoke-filled dawn, she started to walk back to Berkeley Square.

[24]

Nineteen thousand feet over Biggin Hill, Tony flew steadily toward a flight of eighteen Dornier 215s escorted by twenty Me 109s heading for London.

At six hundred yards he opened fire, closing to two hundred yards before he saw his bullets strike home. A German bomber burst into flames and spiraled toward earth, smoke pouring from its tail. A couple of parachutes opened in the wake of the falling plane.

A quick glance over his shoulder showed that Dusty Miller's Spitfire was still with him. Tony and the Aussie always tried to keep an eye on each other, watching for enemy fighters in the other's blind spot. Dusty gave him the thumbs-up sign before zooming off in pursuit of his own prey.

Tony sent a fusillade of tracers streaking after the Dorniers before pulling up sharply to engage the fighters.

They'd learned a lot since the past summer of the Battle of Britain. No longer did they fly in formation, having learned that the ability to see the enemy and maneuver into attack position depended upon having enough space around their aircraft. Never for more than two or three seconds did they fly on a straight course, straightening up only to attack; closing in, holding the machine steady in the slipstream of the other plane, then hitting with all eight guns in snap bursts. Morale was high, despite the toll of pilots and planes, because the RAF knew they had two distinct advantages not possessed by the Luftwaffe: the Spitfire and that modern wonder, radar.

In the shrieking confusion of the dogfight, Tony saw Dusty's cockpit outlined in flame. The plane flipped over on its back, and Tony breathed a sigh of relief as Dusty bailed out. Thank God their squadron leader wouldn't be sending a letter to Adelaide, Australia. Every night he spent at least an hour trying to write letters to the next of kin of his dead fighter pilots.

The tail of a Messerschmitt was in Tony's sights now. The German pilot, sitting atop his fuel tank, went into an evasive action, a half-roll followed by a vertical dive. The usual rule was, Don't dive after them, but today Tony went anyway. There were too many of them and not enough Spits. He emptied the last of his ammunition as the ground swept upward. Banking sharply, he soared aloft again, heading for a cluster of clouds to cover his escape back to base.

Fifteen minutes later when he landed, his flight crew told him his engine needed repair, but that there were only ten serviceable planes left in the squadron, and the Germans were pouring across the channel to attack the coast and southern cities. They'd try to have his plane repaired and ready for take-off in an hour.

Tony crawled under the wing of the Spitfire, put his head on the ground, and slept.

Kate laid several folded sweaters and skirts on the bed in her room at Cardovan House next to her open suitcase. Cecilia, seated beside the case, said, "But I'm sure you could find some volunteer work to do in the village, the WVS, or . . ."

Bundling up clothes for evacuees or making cups of tea in service canteens, Kate thought. She said, "I really want to work in a hospital. I hear there's a need for nursing aides. What do they call them—VAD's?"

"The career nurses will have you doing all sorts of menial chores—scrubbing bedpans and so on. They have the idea that all VAD's are spoiled society girls."

"There's an irony there, if I can think of it."

"But why in London, Kate?"

"Because that's where I feel I'd be most useful. So many of the children are still in the city—they weren't all evacuated. Besides, I'd be closer to Tony."

"But you said you weren't able to see him or even talk to him on the phone while you were there."

"In his last letter he said they'd been flying a lot of sorties. He said most pilots are too tired to even get drunk when they're on the ground. Sooner or later he'll get a weekend pass."

Cecilia sighed extravagantly. "You had so little time together."

Kate felt her toes curl. The statement seemed to sound a death knell, as though they'd never have any more time together. How could she explain to Cecilia how she felt? It wasn't just fear for Tony's life, or even the stupefying lack of anything for Kate to do at Cardovan House, nor even the memory of the child dying in her arms, nor any of the other casualties of war she'd touched. Like a drowning person flailing arms and legs in a desperate attempt to save herself, Kate felt an equally urgent need to be busy, useful, contributing something.

"You'll come home for Ursula's wedding?" Cecilia asked, brightening. "Roderick is getting leave next month, and we hope to have lots of parties. It's tiresome trying to cater, with the rationing. And I have to keep after the servants. They're all so terribly ancient now that all the young ones have gone, but . . ."

Cecilia rattled on and Kate shut her out. The old adage about living with someone to get to know them was true. Cecilia came alive only when surrounded by people, plucking bits and pieces of their conversation and wit, and passing it on as her own. Her charm and attractiveness depended entirely upon the personality of the last person she had spoken to.

When she wound down, Kate said, "Of course I'll be back to see you often. You do understand. It's not that I don't love Cardovan House, or being with you . . ." That was true, and it wasn't necessary to add *but I can't be a drone twenty-*

four hours a day. Cecilia did some fund-raising for various charities, provided this was accomplished by means of a social function. Life was one long party. It was easy to see now why Hardie had moved out of the house.

"I must go and have a word with Cook about dinner," Cecilia said, rising. "The meat ration is going to be cut again, I hear. I don't know how we can manage with any less. I was approached about turning over part of the grounds to the Women's Land Army so they could raise pigs and grow vegetables."

"Hey, that sounds like a great idea," Kate began, then realized she'd said the wrong thing when Cecilia looked aghast.

After Cecilia left, Kate finished packing and then slipped on a coat and went downstairs. She crossed the marble hall and went out onto the terrace. The day was gray and bitingly damp. Dark purple clouds lay heavy on the horizon and the woods were stark, bare branches against a gunmetal sky. It was too cold to stand still, so she walked along the terrace, then went down the steps to the topiary garden. She planned to return to London the following day and, almost unconsciously, began to tour the grounds of Cardovan House in a farewell stroll.

Circling the house, she walked through the rose gardens, then started down the driveway, with no destination in mind, merely a need to be alone. As she reached the bend just before the gatekeeper's cottage, a car came screeching down the driveway behind her.

Startled, Kate looked back over her shoulder and, realizing the car was traveling too fast to brake in time, flung herself out of the way. Trees and sky and earth spun in dizzying circles as she rolled down the grassy bank bordering the drive.

Stunned, she picked herself up and stood unsteadily, staring at the car, which had come to a stop a few feet past where she had been walking a moment before. The driver's door opened and Ursula got out wearing a slightly wary smile. "I say, I almost didn't see you in time. Are you all right?"

Kate climbed back up the bank. "You were coming at quite a clip. Don't you think maybe a little too fast for inside the gates?"

"It's almost dusk, and I wasn't expecting anyone to be walking down the middle of the drive," Ursula said defensively, her eyes beginning to narrow.

Kate had recovered from the shock and, not wanting to start another quarrel just before leaving, said, "I'm not hurt. It's okay."

"Well I'm *not* all right. You frightened the wits out of me. Why can't you behave decently, instead of like some half-witted idiot?"

Kate felt her teeth grind. She clenched her fists inside her coat pockets. "Look, Ursula, I'm leaving tomorrow. I'm moving to London to be nearer Tony. Let's not start anything on this last evening, okay? If we can't be friends, can't we at least try to tolerate one another? After all, by the time I move back here you'll be married and in your own home. This is the last day we'll be under the same roof."

Unexpectedly, Ursula's mascaraed eyes brimmed with tears. "How perfectly hateful of you to tell me that I must live somewhere else."

Kate blinked. "Isn't that usually the case when you get married?"

"If it weren't for you, Roderick and I would live here. Anthony promised us he'd never get married, never bring a wife to take Cardovan House away from us. He only married you out of a sense of obligation, you know. Because you'd been so hopelessly compromised by him when you both escaped from France."

Kate wanted to slap the carefully made-up face, to pull the sleek blond hair out by the roots. She drew a deep breath. "I don't believe that. And if you weren't a spoiled brat who doesn't know what she's talking about, I'd turn you over my knee and spank you."

"Oh, you're such a fool. It's true. Why else would a man like Anthony marry a nobody like you? He felt sorry for you, that's all. He always said that marriage was one trap that would never catch him. He *never* believed in it. You can ask him yourself, if you don't believe me. Good Lord, you've only to look at our parents to see how Anthony and I have *always* regarded marriage. He told me once he'd see Hardie in hell before he'd spawn any little Winfields just to keep the Winfield name going. Anthony knew the only reason Hardie adopted him was so there wouldn't be a break in the line. You—you trapped him."

Kate turned away and began to walk back to the house. There was a ring of truth in what Ursula had said. Kate didn't doubt that at one time Tony had felt that way about marriage and children. But to marry her because he pitied her? Because of the nights they'd shared sleeping quarters in France? Surely he hadn't told Ursula about them? That had to be a shot in the dark on her part—a rationalization of their marriage.

She heard the car start up again but didn't look back.

Minutes later she went into the hall and saw Cecilia coming down the staircase. She looked surprised to see her. "Kate! Oh, no. Didn't Ursula find you? We just got a message from Anthony to pick him up at the station. He has a three-day pass. Ursula was going to look for you so you could go with her to get him."

[25]

Kate ran down the stairs to fling herself into Tony's arms. She clung to him and kissed his lips and his cheeks, held him tightly; and he kissed her and murmured her name over and over again. At last, breathless, they pulled apart to devour one another with their eyes.

He looked exhausted, his eyes bloodshot and smudged with fatigue, but it was he who searched her face and body anxiously and asked, "Are you all right? You didn't hurt yourself too badly? Ursula said you took a tumble while you were out walking and couldn't come to the station because you felt faint."

Behind him, Ursula stood staring defiantly at Kate, challenging her to deny the explanation. Kate whirled on her. "Damn it, why didn't you tell me you were going to pick Tony up? I'd have gone with you. Why didn't you even tell me he'd called? You miserable, conniving little—"

Ursula dissolved into tears. Perplexed, Tony looked from one woman to the other.

"I *tried* to tell you," Ursula sobbed. "But you were too busy screaming like a fishwife because you thought I was driving too fast. Anthony, I'm sorry I didn't tell you all that happened. I didn't want to spoil your homecoming."

And neither do I, Kate thought, resisting an almost overwhelming urge to belt Ursula in the chops. Slipping her arm through Tony's, Kate said, "I guess it was all a misunderstanding. Let's forget it, shall we? Come on, your mother's waiting in the drawing room. We've got a huge fire going in there, and the rest of the house is like a mausoleum with the fuel rationing."

The waiting butler took Tony's bag and welcomed him home. They walked into the drawing room, and Cecilia hugged her son excitedly. "I've called everyone to tell them you're home. Now I know you'll want to rest tonight, but I thought tomorrow we could have a party."

Kate's heart sank. She met Tony's gaze over Cecilia's shoulder, willing him to say, No, no parties, we want to be alone. But he didn't.

Clive joined them for dinner, and Kate found herself watching him and wondering. Did he bear any physical resemblance to Tony? They were almost the same height, but then Cecilia went out of her way to collect tall men. Had Tony himself ever considered the possibility?

Tony was quiet, preoccupied. He looked so desperately tired that Kate wanted to drag him from the table and up to bed, and contemplating what Ursula would think about that brought a grin to her face. Ursula, watching her, said nastily, "Do let us in on the joke, Kate. I'm sure we need a giggle to take our minds off what Anthony's been going through."

"Uh . . . nothing," Kate mumbled, flushing.

Cecilia said, "I'm so glad you're home, Anthony. You must talk Kate out of this foolish plan of hers."

Kate thought, Oh, terrific. She'd hoped to tell him herself about her plans. He looked at her expectantly.

"Your father kindly offered me the use of his flat. I . . . uh . . . visited it a few days ago. In fact, I phoned you while I was there. I guess you didn't get my message."

"Actually, I'm surprised a personal call got through. We've been . . . busy."

"Your father gave me a number to use. I'm sorry, I shouldn't have bothered anybody, especially since you were coming home anyway. What your mother is referring to is my plan to volunteer for nursing service in London."

Tony glanced at his mother, then said, surprisingly,

"There's a desperate need for nurses." There was a slight edge to his voice.

Clive raised his glass in a toast, "To our own Florence Nightingale—who will sing in Berkeley Square for us." He winked broadly. "Nightingale . . . Berkeley Square . . ."

"No need to hit us over the head with it," Tony said shortly. He stood up. "Excuse me, I'm rather tired." He looked at Kate, his glance both questioning and slightly wounded. She said, "I'll come up with you."

They went up the staircase silently, not touching, and Kate began to feel uneasy. In their bedroom he walked slowly to his dressing table and began to empty his pockets. It wasn't the scene Kate had imagined, where he kicked the bedroom door shut, hurled himself into her arms, flung her on the bed, and made passionate love to her. She said uncertainly, "Tony, what is it? What's wrong?"

In the mirror his eyes moved in her direction, observing her reflection without turning around. "I'm very tired, a little on edge. It's probably not the right time to discuss your plan to move to London."

"From the tone of your voice, I think we'd better. I thought you'd understand why I need to get out of here."

He turned and looked at her, his expression unreadable. "Are you really going to volunteer to work in a hospital?"

"Yes. What are you driving at?"

"It isn't that you're bored here and want to go up to London so you'll have more freedom and excitement?"

"I see," Kate said grimly as the penny finally dropped. "Ursula did a little whispering in your ear on the way back from the railway station. That lying little—"

He crossed the room swiftly and put his arms around her. "Forgive me, Kate. I should have known better than to listen to her. I knew she wasn't exactly in favor of our getting married. But she's never lied to me in her life. And the evidence did seem to back up what she said."

"Evidence? Am I on trial?"

"I'm sorry. That was a poor choice of words. What I meant was that I *did* receive your phone message from the Berkeley Square flat. I didn't want to say anything in front of the others at dinner, but I spent the entire evening and most of the night trying to call you back at my father's flat. You didn't spend the night there, Kate."

Kate sat down on the bed abruptly, remembering the pub, the air raid, the demolished house, the hours she'd walked the streets before being ushered into the public shelter. She wasn't sure what her expression might have been, but Tony stood watching her intently.

"Look, Kate, I'm not accusing you of anything, and God knows, I'm no angel myself. I know it's going to be lonely for you, but a lot of people get lonely in a war. I need to know that you haven't had second thoughts about our marriage. I need to know you didn't make that vow to forsake all others lightly. I need you to be faithful."

Kate stood up and threw her arms around him. "Oh, Tony, I *am* faithful. I'll always be. Our marriage is important to me too. I just want to work—to do something useful. And I'd like to see you a bit more often. That's the reason I want to move to London. And you couldn't get me on the phone that night because I was in an air-raid shelter. I had this crazy idea of coming to you at Biggin Hill, and the taxi driver couldn't make it to the station—"

He cut off her explanation with a kiss, but in the second before she yielded her mouth to his she thought that the most insidious of lies were those that contained a grain of truth.

Tony buried his face in her neck, inhaling her scent, his hands caressing her back. "I've been longing to hold you all evening. Oh, Kate, I've missed you so."

"I've missed you too, but Tony, we have to trust one another." She bit her lip, still angry that Ursula had managed to spoil his homecoming, but wanting to regain the closeness they'd had on their honeymoon.

"I know," he said. "I do. But I'm worried about your going to London. Couldn't you find a nice quiet country hospital?"

"I want to be near you," she said stubbornly. "Don't try to talk me out of it."

"All right, I won't. I just wish you weren't so damn brave."

"I'm not! If I were, I'd have suggested to your mother that we'd rather not have a big party tomorrow night."

He started to unbutton his uniform jacket. "Shall I have a word with her? After all, you are the new mistress of Cardovan House."

"Hey, wait up! I don't want to usurp her position."

"She hasn't told you?" He looked surprised. "One of the conditions my father made before he moved out was that the house was to remain in the Winfield family, that immediately upon my marriage my mother was to turn everything over to me. It was that or a scandalous divorce."

Kate was astonished. "And knowing that, she still did everything she could to encourage us to get married."

He gave a wry smile. "Cecilia carries a great load of guilt on her shoulders, perhaps more than is really necessary. Besides, she knew she'd always have a home with me. If her constant parties get on your nerves—and frankly they get on mine—then we'll renovate the old east wing and she can move in there, turn it into a salon."

Kate was so relieved she hugged him. He said, "Kate, forgive me. I shouldn't have doubted you. I suppose I'm so afraid of losing you. I love you so much . . . want you so desperately. Being away from you is hell." He crushed her in his arms, kissed her eyelids and nose and lips, then drew back so that he could look at her face. "I wanted to fling you on the dining table and make love."

Kate's eyes twinkled. "You know what amazes me most about this grand old house of yours? The sheer size of the bathtubs! I swear you could do the backstroke in them. Think we could both fit into that one next door?"

He pursed his lips, giving the matter serious consideration, then laughed. "I'd certainly like to try."

With much giggling and tickling, they piled into the big old tub, soaped each other's backs, kissed and nibbled, splashed the entire bathroom, soaked the towels, and finally, still damp, rushed back into the bedroom and collapsed onto the bed. Arms and legs entwined in a frenzy of need, their joining was swift and urgent as they sought to recapture the intimacy they had enjoyed on their honeymoon. After a moment, Kate lost herself in their lovemaking, forgetting their first married quarrel, and the reason for it.

With the first urgency of their passion satisfied, they then made love tenderly, lingering to explore each nuance of feeling, each breathtaking step of the journey toward a new pinnacle of desire. Kate sighed, marveling that each time they made love it could get better, but it did, because they learned something new about the other each time they kissed and touched, so in tune with their responses that words were unnecessary.

When at last they lay quietly in each other's arms, Tony said, "I knew—even before—that you would be warm and passionate. Perhaps that's why I worry about not being near to satisfy that passion that I've awakened in you."

She placed her fingertips on his lips. "You make it sound like a sleeping dragon!"

He chuckled and kissed her forehead. She said, "I couldn't ever feel this close to anyone else."

He whispered against her hair, "I love you, Kate."

And, she thought wonderingly, I love you. She was so surprised to realize it that she didn't say anything, just quietly reveled in the knowledge for a moment. Then she said softly, "Tony . . ."

But he had fallen asleep.

When she awakened the following morning, Tony was sitting on the bed with a breakfast tray in his hands. He kissed her and said, "Just cereal and toast. Cook says the bacon ration is saved for dinner."

"Oh, spoil me!" Kate exclaimed, sitting up.

"I've had a word with Cecilia. I told her that since you're moving into the flat, we're going up there today so I can help you get settled."

Kate almost upset the tray. She let out a small whoop of joy, clapped her hand over her mouth, and said, "We'll have two whole days all alone. We can make love every hour on the hour."

His face fell. "What's wrong with every minute?" He climbed back into bed with her.

Later, when Cecilia was bidding them a tearful farewell, she reached out and fingered the locket Kate wore. "You must put a picture of Anthony and yourself in the two compartments. The first part of the legend has already come true; now you must make the second part happen."

Kate said, "Tell me the legend, please."

"The locket has been in the family since the Crusades, they claim. It's always given by the son and heir to the woman he'll marry. It's supposed to keep her safe until he returns to make her his wife. When the pictures are placed inside, then she will bear the next heir."

Kate looked from Cecilia to Tony. "You sent me the locket, not your mother."

He smiled. "I knew a long time before I asked you that I wanted you to marry me."

It was only when they were on the train speeding toward the city that Kate remembered that Cecilia had not given birth to a male heir—at least not one who was the Earl's son.

[26]

The ward sister walked briskly up to Kate as she was depositing linen into a cupboard. "I need assistance," Sister said. "Do you think you can keep from fainting while I change the dressings on a burn patient?"

Kate nodded. "Yes, ma'am."

"Ah, you're the American. Husband in the RAF." Sister bustled off down the corridor, her uniform bristling with starch. "I wouldn't personally ask a VAD to do this, but beggars can't be choosers. Come on, he's in here."

Kate clenched her nostrils against the smell of ether. A bandage-swathed young airman lay loosely hung on straps just above the bed. He moaned as Sister bent over him, and Kate saw him feebly try to raise his arms. He whispered hoarsely, "Nurse? What have they done to me?"

"We've put something on your face and hands to stop them from hurting. You won't be able to see for a while, but don't worry. You're not blind."

Kate quickly prepared a tray and held it as Sister began to cut the bandages around the eyes. His face and hands had been sprayed with tannic acid, which hardened and became black as pitch, while his eyes were coated with a layer of gentian violet.

Sister went on: "You're going to get some nice ginger ale through a tube, soon as we get these bandages away from your lips."

He had no lips, Kate saw, feeling her stomach contract, just a slit in the charred and horribly swollen lower part of his face.

The pilot, floating in pain, moaned again.

"Stop that now. You're not due for morphia for another hour." Looking up at Kate, Sister said, "Put the tray down. You'll have to hold his arms to keep him still while I get this off."

Kate held his arms grimly, although he didn't try to fight her. His body movements were involuntary, reactions to his agony. She saw her tears splash down on the clean white gauze Sister was placing over his distorted parody of a chin. She frowned ferociously at Kate, who managed to keep from weeping aloud.

Afterwards, Kate stood in the corridor partially hidden by a linen cupboard door, shaking uncontrollably and crying unashamedly.

The ward sister patted Kate's shoulder as she went by. "Well done. Some of my best nurses can't handle the burned pilots."

Two days later Kate was called in to assist when another burn patient had the hardened tannic acid chipped from his skin with a scalpel. The theory was that the hard crust kept the air out and allowed the skin underneath to heal. However, doctors were discovering the treatment caused secondary infections and septicemia. An RN newly transferred from a burn center had mentioned in the nurses' common room that some hospitals had already discontinued the use of tannic acid.

As a lowly VAD, Kate knew better than to mention this to the doctor, who cursed under his breath when he discovered the rampant infection under the black crust. Kate silently wondered if the burned pilot's agony would have been lessened had he known he was suffering in the cause of science, that new and better treatments were emerging from the injuries of the war.

When the doctor departed, Kate whispered to the burned airman, whose eyes were bandaged, "You won't have to go through that again. You were very brave."

Kate had little energy left at the end of a long and grueling hospital shift, and usually went back to the flat, had a quick meal, read for a while or wrote to Tony, then collapsed into bed and slept through all but the most severe of the bombing. She even became accustomed to the roar of the big anti-aircraft guns in Berkeley Square. A couple of times when the bombs fell close enough to shake the apartment building and break windows, her neighbor had to pound on her door to get her to go to the safer ground floor.

The weeks sped by, and with each passing one the consensus was that the threat of invasion grew less. The Battle of Britain, everyone agreed, had taken place in the skies over England, and despite being hopelessly outnumbered, the RAF were beating back the Luftwaffe.

Kate listened to the BBC news and each day waited with dread for those chilling words, "One of our aircraft is missing . . ." or two, or three, and wonder if Tony was one of them. She would be nervous and jittery until she heard from him.

She tried to keep a diary, mostly because of a vague feeling that at some future time she wouldn't be able to recall exactly what had happened to her during the winter of 1940–41. Some of the entries were brief, others more detailed.

> *Finished VAD training today. Phew!*
>
> *The flag flies over Buckingham Palace when the King is in residence. Londoners have noticed it's always flying nowadays. A dusty old Daimler passed me the other day and in the back seat was a lovely woman dressed in pale blue. I couldn't believe my eyes—it was the Queen. No motorcycles, nothing but a chauffeur.*
>
> *Neville Chamberlain died. I suppose he'll only be remembered for that sadly wrong declaration, "Peace in our time."*
>
> *Tony here on a weekend pass!!!*
>
> *Damn it, I couldn't get much time off. We made love so feverishly that the other nurses kidded me all day about the bags under my eyes.*
>
> *We dined in style at the Savoy (the big dining room is closed, so we ate in the River Room—it's underground and you can't hear the guns there). You get a choice of*

fish or meat now, not both, and wine is scarce and expensive. The Luftwaffe really shellacked us last night, and Tony was amazed how we can put up with it night after night. He says he feels safer in his airplane.

We walked for a little while. Men were placing new sandbags around the statue of Eros in Picadilly Circus. Tony looked up at Lord Nelson, still standing bravely atop his column in Trafalgar Square, and remarked that he hoped Hardie's ship returns safely. He said, "I never told him how much I admire him. He was more than a father to me, really."

How I miss him now he's gone back to Biggin Hill!

Cecilia called. Ursula has called off her wedding. Poor old Roderick—or perhaps he had a lucky escape? Now, now, Kate, be nice.

A battered parcel arrived from Mom and Dad—been en route since our wedding. A silver platter engraved with our names as a wedding gift and a supply of underwear for me—silk teddies and panties and stockings. Mom is probably worrying about me being dug out of the smoking rubble wearing frayed underpants.

We've been having smothering, freezing winter fogs . . . with the blackout, it's like trying to find your way about under a heavy, icy-wet blanket. So many of the patients have bronchitis in addition to their injuries.

Not much to do in the evenings, thanks to Goering's boys. (Did I really once shake that man's hand?) Movies close at seven and theatres mainly play matinees, except for the Windmill, which boasts it has never allowed the blitz to shut down the show (bare breasts get a little tedious after a while, however). I'm too tired to go out anyway, except when Tony's here; then we don't need outside entertainment.

A nice letter came from Hardie, warning me that the refrigerator is temperamental (I'd already found out) and to be sure to go to an underground shelter during air raids, as he'd heard they'd been heavy. (His ship must be far away.) And that I shouldn't take anything Ursula says too seriously. (I know she used to stay here *in the flat when she came to London to give piano concerts, but I doubt she'll come while I'm here.)*

Shipping losses are terrible. Bad enough I have to worry about Tony, but I worry about Hardie too. He's such a nice man. I can't help blaming Cecilia for the situation between them. What happened? I wonder.

Churchill says it will take the Luftwaffe ten years to destroy half the city. Sure hope he's right.

Kate hadn't been feeling well. She was excessively tired and her stomach felt constantly queasy. One day a badly injured pilot arrived, and upon hearing his name Kate fainted. She came to in the nurses' common room, with a senior nurse bending over her. "Win*gate*—not Winfield. It isn't your husband. You haven't been looking well. Why don't you take the afternoon off? Go home and rest."

Still shaken, Kate didn't need any further persuasion.

Letting herself into the flat, she stopped dead on the threshold, a prickly sense of something not quite right assailing her.

She prowled around the living room, paused at the study door. Had she left the desktop in such disarray? Perhaps she'd been writing a letter and had to give up when it was time to go to the shelter.

Her bedroom door opened suddenly and Kate gave a small cry of alarm. Ursula appeared, still dressed in her fur coat and hat. "I didn't think you'd be home. I let myself in. I'm giving a recital later on."

Of course she had as much right to be there as Kate, perhaps more, but why had she gone into a bedroom obviously being used by Kate? Had she been spying on her? The disarray of the desk—her half-written letter to Tony and her diary—all flashed through Kate's mind. She said, "I'm using the spare room. There's clean linen on your father's bed, if you're staying overnight."

Ursula pulled off her hat and shook her blond hair into place. She flashed Kate a malevolent glance and went into the main bedroom. Kate went into her room to change out of her uniform. Two of the dresser drawers were slightly open, as was the mahogany wardrobe. Feeling invaded, Kate decided to eat at home rather than giving Ursula free run of the flat while she went out.

Kate put on her warmest sweater and a pair of slacks and went into the kitchen. There was a tin of beans, some bread, and plenty of coffee, which wasn't rationed but might as well have been, because the heavy doses of chicory in it nauseated her. She was heating the beans and had toast under the grill when Ursula walked into the room.

"Don't bother to prepare anything for me. I've already had lunch."

"It's just beans on toast," Kate said, pouring the rather pallid beans from pan to toast. She took her plate to the dining table, not sure she was going to be able to get the food down, but afraid if she didn't she might faint again. She hadn't been able to get breakfast down either.

Ursula made herself some coffee and brought it to the table. The aroma added to Kate's queasiness. Ursula said petulantly, "There's a waiting list now for all of the women's services. Can you believe it? They simply don't want any more volunteers."

"Oh? Did you try to get in one of the services?"

"Yes. The WAAF."

The women's branch of the air force, of course. She would choose the WAAF, since Tony was in the RAF. Kate wondered about Ursula's obsessive bond to her brother. It was more than sisterly love. Perhaps what she really wanted was to *be* Tony. Kate had a mouthful of beans that didn't want to go down. She swallowed and tried desperately not to bring it back up.

Ursula stirred saccharin into her coffee. "Roderick was killed last week. He was shot down over the French coast."

"Oh, my God! I'm sorry." Kate didn't know what to say.

"Yes, I'm certainly glad I called off the wedding. I'd have been widowed immediately, and there's something so . . . *ancient* about being a widow."

Kate put her hands on the table and pushed herself slowly to a standing position. She felt the room spin, her stomach churn, and didn't know if it was caused by her own malaise or by Ursula's utter callousness and self-absorption. "Excuse me, I don't feel well." She raced to the bathroom.

When she returned, Ursula continued as if nothing had happened. "I really feel wartime weddings are a mistake. So many of them are going to end disastrously. I mean, not only if one partner gets killed, but when everything settles down again, so many people will have rushed into completely unsuitable marriages, don't you think?"

"I think," Kate said, "you're about as subtle as a sledgehammer."

One of the other VAD's stuck her head into the ward as Kate collected bedpans. "You're wanted in the common room. You've got a visitor."

Kate's heart leapt. Tony! It had to be. It had been weeks since he'd had any time off.

She dashed into the lavatory and straightened her cap. Her hair was growing out and, remembering Marie Allegret's advice, Kate had it expertly shaped by the best hairdresser she could find. She didn't bother to put on lipstick, since she expected Tony to kiss it all off anyway. Besides, it brought back the nausea that she was learning to control by eliminating certain tastes and smells—now that she suspected the cause of it. *Oh, Tony, have I got wonderful news for you!*

Dashing down the corridor, she burst into the common room, prepared to hurl herself into her husband's arms.

In the center of the room, a crumpled trench coat slung over one shoulder, hat pushed to the back of his head, stood Wade Lowery.

[27]

For a minute neither of them spoke. Wade's lively dark eyes went from her jaunty nurse's cap to her uniform, then back to her face. His look said she had changed more than he had. His was a face made for cheeky grins and devil-may-care expressions, but also written on the ruggedly appealing features was keen intelligence and a restless, searching curiosity, a need to experience everything life had to offer. She'd forgotten the way his presence could light up a room. She stood perfectly still, staring at him.

"Hi, Kate," he said softly. "You look terrific. What have you done to yourself? You look . . . very attractive in that uniform. A regular angel of mercy."

"Hello, Wade. How are you?" If she'd ever for a moment contemplated this meeting, perhaps she could have prepared a more scintillating line for herself.

"Fine, great. You?"

"I'm fine too. I'm . . . I'm on duty."

"I know. I got permission from the matron to interview you. You know, human interest stuff for the papers back home. American woman nursing burned pilots and blitzed kids."

"I'm only an auxiliary, a nurse's aide. Why did you do this, Wade? Look me up, I mean."

"I just told you, human—" He broke off as she gave an

exasperated sigh. He spread his hands, palms upward, in a gesture of helplessness. "I never could put one over on you, could I? I wanted to see you again. I guess you're the main reason I took this assignment."

"I married an Englishman."

"Yeah, I know. I still wanted to see you."

"You're over here reporting the war for your father's newspapers?"

"No, as a matter of fact I'm working for International News Service. Dad didn't take kindly to only son and heir exposing himself to danger."

"You should have listened to him. If you really did come to see me, which is hard to believe, in view of our last conversation . . ."

He had the grace to look uncomfortable. "Kate, I'm sorry. You'll never know how sorry I truly am. It was a case of pre-wedding jitters—nerves—nothing more. I realize that now. But you took off for Europe. I never got a chance to see you, talk to you."

"I was in New York most of that summer, I just did that one tour. I don't remember any phone calls or letters."

"I went to Germany to report on the situation there. When I got back I called and Evans Tours told me you'd left again. Listen, let's not talk here. You've got the rest of the day off, to give me my interview. Let's get outta here. I can't stand the sinister smell of this place."

"No, Wade. I'm *married*."

"So give me a human interest story about a nurse in wartime London." He placed his hand solemnly over his heart. "I swear I won't make any passes. Come on, Kate, as one expatriate to another."

The door behind her opened and two student nurses, giggling and chattering, came into the room. They stopped at the sight of Wade, uncertain whether to stay or not. He gave them a typically endearing Wade Lowery smile, winked, and said, "Afternoon, ladies. I'm here for a complete physical. Shall I undress now?"

The two nurses blushed and stammered and Kate said, "Come on, I'll get my coat."

They walked along the Embankment in the frosty late

afternoon and Kate tried to keep foremost in her mind what this man had done to her, the hurt and humiliation, the complete loss of her self-esteem. But all the while it was easier to remember the old magic. His quick grin, his habit of greeting complete strangers as though they were old friends, his tomfoolery if something struck him as funny or ridiculous or pompous. The way he liked to make physical contact. He claimed it was impossible for two people to stroll side by side without lurching into one another unless an arm was placed around a waist, or hands held, or arms linked. When he tried to draw her arm through his, she pulled away and he said, "Okay, but we're going to collide, I guarantee it. We'd better at least get in step—hut, hut, three, four."

"We were never in step, Wade."

"Kate, honey, I know I hurt you. I wish I hadn't. I'm sorry. God, you'll never know how sorry. I panicked. I felt trapped. No, listen, I'm not making excuses for myself. What I did was unforgivable. I was a first-class heel and I paid for it. God, I missed you. It wasn't you, Kate, don't you see. It was the *idea* of marriage—forever and ever, world without end. It was only after I lost you I realized what we had going for us. All I needed was a little more time. I should have asked if we could postpone the wedding, instead of—"

"Stop it, Wade! I don't want to hear any more of this. You wanted a story about an American nurse in London. Okay, I'll give you one. I'm not a real nurse. In fact, real nurses look down their noses at us. We get to empty bedpans and scrub equipment, change linen and clean up all the blood and gore and excrement. Once in a great while, if we're very good, we get to help with dressings. If you really want to get inside this story, why don't you tour the wards? Talk to the kids with missing limbs, the pilots with their faces burned off." Her voice was quivering and she stopped walking, feeling dizzy.

He slipped his arm around her shoulders. "Hey, kid, it's okay, let it out. This is Uncle Wade, remember? I've got a pretty good idea of what you've been through. I've been sending stories home about British soldiers knitting socks for beleaguered Londoners. Listen, it's freezing out here.

Let's have dinner and I'll make some notes and then, if you want me out of your life, I'll go and not look back. I promise."

The feeling of faintness passed, but Kate knew she'd better sit down and she did need to eat. She didn't argue when he hailed a cab and told the driver to take them to the Savoy. She'd made an appointment to see one of the doctors at the hospital, but she didn't really need a gynecologist to tell her she was pregnant. It was ironic that Wade should come back into her life now, just as she was carrying Tony's child.

Only when they entered the River Room did Kate remember that she and Tony had dined there on his last weekend pass—probably the night she conceived his child. She hoped there wouldn't be a table available, but of course, in typical cocksure fashion, Wade had already made a reservation.

She refused his offer of wine. He ordered Niersteiner and commented that it was typical of the British to continue to enjoy German wine despite the war. Several dinner parties were in progress. Wade pointed out Lord Beaverbrook's party and, at another table, the Duke and Duchess of Kent. "Every editor in town seems to be here," he added, raising his glass to her in a silent toast. "I guess because it's close to Fleet Street. The music is great, isn't it? Carol Gibbons is an American. He came over here years ago and became so popular he stayed. Though if Quentin Reynolds comes in and requests 'Lullaby of Broadway' I may start a brawl. Hey, kid, what did you think about Roosevelt getting re-elected? That gladden your little Democratic heart?"

The soup was served and Kate began to thaw out a little. She said, "Wade, I've a question I'm dying to ask."

He leaned forward eagerly. "Anything, kid."

"Who played in the Rose Bowl this year, and who won?"

It was like old times. The back-and-forth banter, the bursts of laughter, the sudden seriousness. His was a voice from home, and whether she admitted it to herself or not, she'd been damned homesick. Tony was her husband and she cared deeply about him, but there were some things he couldn't give her. A long conversation about things familiar and dear, about America—a little visit home, to a past and a

ECHOES OF WAR

childhood Tony hadn't shared and probably could never understand.

By the time they reached the entrée, Wade had begun to tell her about some of the articles he'd sent back home. "I'm small potatoes compared to the likes of Murrow and Reynolds, but I think maybe I'm letting the American people see a different angle to the suffering here. I spent a week sleeping in the tube with people who don't have fancy underground rooms like this, and I lived on a workingman's ration of food—a couple of ounces of meat a week, a single egg. I ate the herring and mackerel and turnips of people who can't afford to dine out and save their rations for an occasional dinner party. Did you know that better than half of the houses in the East End have already been destroyed? The people who can afford to, pay for the removal of any furniture left and rent a place. The rest have to rely on the 'poor law' and move into an overcrowded rest center. Shades of *Oliver Twist!*"

"You sound like a page from the *Daily Worker*," Kate said.

"I'm certainly not a communist. Maybe I'm sniping at the insulated peerage you married into. Even in a war it's a bit more comfortable for people like the Winfields than for the working class."

"You forget, I'm working class myself."

Wade's glance held hers for a moment. "What's he like?"

Kate silently considered the eternal curiosity of rivals. Tony had asked the same question about Wade. She replied, "About your height, but not as husky as you. Light brown hair, gray eyes, educated, gentle, thoughtful, considerate. Brave. Nice—I mean really nice. He's a Spitfire pilot."

Wade gave an exaggerated grimace. "Well, hell, he sounds too good to be true. All that and a title too."

"No, no title. He's plain Mr. Winfield. He won't inherit his father's title. He's adopted. But enough personal stuff. What do you want to know about my life at the hospital?"

"Not a hell of a lot." He chuckled. "Sorry. I just want to talk to you, be with you. Hearing a voice from home makes me realize America is still there waiting for us. But tell me about the hospital anyway."

She spoke of the dedication of the staff, the uncomplaining bravery of the patients, the medical profession's fumbling for better treatments for the appalling mutilations caused by bombs and bullets and fire. She stopped speaking when she saw his eyes drifting over her face and body again and knew he wasn't listening.

He said, "I can't figure out what's different about you. The short hair, I guess, changes your face. You've got a sort of grandeur, Kate. I always loved that big happy grin of yours, the vivacity of your features, but there have been subtle changes since I last saw you. You, kid, are a knock-out."

Maybe what Wade is seeing is my love for Tony reflected from my face, or that glow of pregnancy, Kate thought. She felt a certain satisfaction in the knowledge that Wade was seeing a poised, attractive woman, whose nurse's uniform added a touch of gallantry.

When she didn't comment on his compliments, he said, "I'd like to get a picture of you to use with the article."

"No! No pictures."

He seemed about to argue, but met her gaze and thought better of it. "Okay, tell me, why did you decide to go into nursing?"

She started to tell him about helping to nurse Marie, then stopped. "I suppose the decision was made for me one night when I was caught in a cab after an air raid started." She told him of being in the pub, of the death of the barmaid and mother and child, of her feelings and reactions, of how the little girl's last words had haunted her.

He didn't make any notes. He simply listened.

When she couldn't bear to recall her emotions of that night any longer, she asked, "Can the British win the war, do you think? I don't believe they'll lose it, but I sure don't see how they can win it."

"Not without American help. At least credit to buy weapons and food from us, rather than the present cash-and-carry arrangements. I think Roosevelt will get it for them before long. Not that I approve of the man or of American involvement in this mess."

"What would happen to the world if Hitler won? Did you

ever think of that? There'd be an end to all independent thought. Everyone would be afraid to follow his heart or any of his intellectual inclinations. All spontaneous acts would disappear because people would be afraid of the consequences."

Wade raised his eyebrows. "That comment sounds more like something your husband would say."

Kate flushed, wondering if she had quoted Tony unknowingly, thinking about Cecilia's habit of parroting other people's remarks. She snapped, "Why? Was it too profound a thought for Kate of PS Thirty-two? You'd be surprised how much of an education can be picked up from travel and public libraries, Wade."

"Sorry, I didn't mean that the way it sounded. Were you suggesting that America should enter the war?"

"No! I wouldn't want my brothers to die on some foreign battlefield. But I worry sometimes about what's going to happen to England."

"Yet you married an Englishman. Kate Kieron—I remember seeing her drop her last dollar in a collection cup in the Blarney Stone bar to help free the Counties." He clucked his tongue. "Married the enemy and chose to stay here."

"Yes, I did marry an Englishman," she answered shortly, no longer sure of her reasons. Sitting here with Wade, it would be easy to imagine herself as she was before the war, when her future plans were centered entirely around him. Sometimes the enormity of the decision to marry Tony overwhelmed her, and all she could do was to tell herself she felt doubts only because he wasn't with her.

"I must say, when I first came here," Wade said, "I wasn't exactly crazy about the English. You know, they don't take the Nazi rantings about being the master race seriously, simply because the English *know* that *they* are the master race. It's a view that's made them disliked in a lot of places. But I do admire their guts—and sheer tenacity. Still, much as I dislike dictatorships, I'm not sure the British way of life is worth fighting for."

She was shocked. "You *are* a communist. A rich communist."

"Nuts to that. I mean the British aristocracy has to go, the hedonistic existence of the few."

She thought about Cecilia and Clive and was silent.

Wade went on: "A lot of things have to change in this country. I just hope your husband's family doesn't come apart at the seams when the old order dies."

"In view of the way you feel about the British, I'm surprised you're here reporting on the war."

"I wouldn't have missed it. There may never be another war like this one."

"Amen to that."

"And as regards your noble husband, what's he fighting for, do you suppose? He's a landowner, right? That's what he wants to protect. Don't let him kid you that he's making the world safe for humanity. Hell, he's making his land safe for his dependents."

"All right, Wade, enough! Tony isn't here to defend himself. Besides, I've got to go home or I won't be fit for work in the morning. Get the check, will you?"

Wade motioned to their waiter. "I'll bring you a copy of the piece I do on you."

"Mail it to me in care of the hospital." She remembered something she'd meant to ask him earlier. "By the way, how did you know I was there?"

"Your mother placed a large wedding announcement in the papers back home. I looked up the Winfields in Debrett's Peerage, then I called your mother-in-law on the phone."

"Did you give her your name, tell her who you were?"

"Sure. I said I was an old friend from back home. Why— uh-oh, she knew about us?"

Kate didn't answer as, having risen to her feet, she now had a view of a table near the door. She had been so engrossed in her conversation with Wade she had no idea how long Ursula had been sitting there watching them.

[28]

Below, the shadow of the plane moved across winter-bare fields. Above and all around, the skies were unexpectedly clear. A halo of sunshine rimmed the earth. On other such days Tony had enjoyed the sheer pleasure and unfettered freedom of light. Today he flew automatically, hands on controls, eyes ahead, barely seeing, as he gave in to the dangerous emotions of anger and hurt.

The words of Ursula's letter had been burned into his mind as if with a flaming brand.

. . . and Anthony, dear, I've really weighed the pros and cons of whether to tell you this, but there's just too much of it going on and I feel you have a right to know. I was in town recently and went to the Savoy for dinner, and guess who should be there in the company of a very dashing-looking chap? Sorry, Anthony, but it was Kate.

Now, had it been a casual date, I might have kept quiet, for your sake rather than hers, but I inquired of the headwaiter and he told me that the gentleman in question was an American war correspondent named Wade Lowery. The very same Wade Lowery who phoned Cardovan House recently inquiring about Kate, and, according to Cecilia, the very same one she was going to marry just before you met her in Berlin.

A word to the wise, Anthony . . .

Tony's thumb moved up and down in simulated attack. Where the hell was that German formation they were supposed to intercept? He wanted very badly to blast somebody out of the sky. The Luftwaffe now concentrated their attacks at night, and it was becoming a rarer treat to get a shot at them in the daylight. They were probably heading for the London docks before the early winter dusk set in.

All right, damn it, think about it then. Lowery is in London and knows Kate is married to me. If he called Cardovan House, then it was all open and aboveboard. He merely wanted to pay his respects.

Oh, damn it all, what about dining at the Savoy with her? What about the fact that Kate has never mentioned him in any of her letters or conversations with me? She was in love with him, admitted to being in love with him when I met her. Kate is different now than he remembered her. Living in Pairs changed her, added a gloss that wasn't there before. She was always a vibrant woman, but now she has a style, a flair.

She also has a husband, and perhaps Lowery feels safe in moving in again. What was it she once said—that she lost him because she wouldn't sleep with him?

The squadron was over the coast now, he could see the cliffs below, and still no sign of bogies. Tony, recently promoted to squadron leader, gave the order to turn for home.

A squadron of Hurricanes, returning after presumably engaging the Luftwaffe formation Tony's squadron had missed, flew into view. They were several planes short and there was no "arse-end Charlie" to watch their rear. Tony maneuvered his Spitfire into position behind them to weave a protective path behind and above and around.

Within seconds he recalled the warning "Beware of the Hun in the sun." A yellow-nosed Messerschmitt 109 came out of the sun right at him and, momentarily blinded, Tony had no time to go into an evasive roll or even to flip the button to the "fire" position. He watched, mesmerized, as bullets ripped along the starboard wing of his machine, felt the jolt of impact; then everything went crazily awry.

His plane was a blurred shape vanishing toward the dark blue of the channel below like a great wounded fish returning to the deep. Sunlight, and a sky scratched with tracers like the mindless scribbling of a child, spun into a dizzying kaleidoscope. The flash of flame and sudden agony of hands and face. Seared flesh meeting a welcome blast of cool air; then he was tumbling through space.

Wind rushing in his ears, falling, dropping down endlessly. Somewhere some last center of control in his brain was issuing an order: *Pull the ripcord*.

Fingers touched the chromium ring, jerked away in agony. *Pull the bloody ripcord or you'll hit the water at two hundred miles an hour. Go on, do it. One second of pain now, or . . .*

The pain in his fingers was unbearable. He thought perhaps he screamed into the whistling air as he grabbed the ring again with the livid flesh; then his shoulders were almost wrenched from their sockets as the parachute opened with a sound like the crack of a whip.

Silk billowed overhead. Sun, sky, cliffs, and water resumed their normal positions. His nostrils recoiled at an evil stench that now assailed them and he retched, realizing that what he could smell was his own burned flesh.

He was going down over the water. His swollen eyelids were as puffy as clouds and his vision rapidly fading. He recalled no boats, just an empty expanse of water, in the minutes before he was hit.

Shaking now, as shock took hold, he told himself, Don't panic. Try to think. Water will be cold. Once you're in, you have to get rid of the chute within seconds or it'll pull you under.

A small metal release box fitted over his stomach held the four ends of his harness. All he had to do was turn a disc ninety degrees and bang on it. Easy enough—if your fingers weren't blackened and blistered. He'd never be able to turn that damned disc.

He hit the water feet first, went under. Gasping for breath, he surfaced and immediately began to struggle as his arms were wrapped in the shrouds of the parachute. He spat a mouthful of water and grabbed at the metal disc, feeling flesh flake from his fingers and blood pour from the raw tissue.

The blackness that obscured his eyes now squeezed at his brain. His body was numb, shivering violently, teeth chattering. The waterlogged chute tugged him relentlessly toward the murky depths below.

[29]

Perhaps the change in her was due to some natural instinct of self-preservation, or perhaps it was the strain of early pregnancy, but Kate found it harder to get up in the morning and face the day at the hospital. She spent most nights underground and had begun to cringe at the banshee wail of the sirens and the crack of gunfire. She couldn't breathe during the whining fall to earth of bombs. When she slept, her nightmares were worse than the reality of her waking hours. She thought perhaps the night shifts were slightly easier to take. At least then she had to wear a brave face for the sake of the patients and was kept too busy to stop and cower at each detonation.

One morning she moved in a trance down Ward Five. The Polish airman with messy stumps where his hands used to be smiled at her. The little bombardier from Lancashire was having his face rebuilt with strips of flesh grafted from his legs and he couldn't talk, but he raised a blackened hand in salute at the sight of the nurses coming on the day shift. A new patient was lying waiting beside the saline bath. The blinded airman was talking to his neighbor, who had lost both legs, trying to cheer him up.

Kate's thoughts weren't noble or caring and she didn't like what she felt. The patients irritated her with their uncomplaining acceptance of the fumbling efforts of the staff to alleviate their pain and mend their broken bodies. Their humble gratitude made her feel guilty, like an impostor pretending she could help them when all she did was stand by and watch while the doctors added to their misery. She could no longer feel the suffering of the patients, and that troubled her deeply.

The day passed as they always did—time marked by the endless chores, the feeble attempts to brighten the pain-wracked hours of the victims of the hellish madness of war.

A couple of weeks had passed since she dined with Wade. There had been calls for her, messages left at the hospital, which she never answered. That night when he took her home to Hardie's flat she hadn't invited him in and had told him there wasn't a phone there. A week had passed also since she'd heard from Tony, who usually called or wrote frequently. That was a constant knifelike worry that pierced all her other thoughts and actions. She hadn't told him about the baby yet, wanting to see his face when she did, rather than tell him in a letter or over the phone.

A steady drizzle of rain was falling when she reached Berkeley Square. Wade was pacing up and down in front of her apartment building, a bulging briefcase in his hand. Catching sight of her, he snapped to attention. "Miss Nightingale, I presume?"

"What are you doing here?"

"Now is that any kind of a greeting for a man who comes bearing gifts extravagant and rare?"

"Beware of Greeks bearing gifts."

"How about a first glimpse at the article I wrote about you, which, I might add, has not only been picked up by a score of newspapers but has also gained the attention of *Collier's*."

"You're kidding!"

Placing his hand over his heart, he solemnly shook his head. Rainwater ran from the brim of his hat. "Or, if that fails to move you, let me appeal to your nursing instincts. Help! Save me from double pneumonia."

"Okay, come on up. But you're not staying. My in-laws have keys to this place, and I don't want any of them interrupting what they might misinterpret as a tête-à-tête."

She had been intending to visit Cardovan House, but didn't want to do so until she'd seen Tony and told him about her pregnancy. Perhaps when Cecilia learned she was to be a grandmother she would dismiss as unimportant the fact that Wade Lowery had called about her daughter-in-law. Kate already regretted not telling Tony and his mother that Wade was in London. That little omission was going to look bad in view of his openness in calling Cardovan House.

Unlocking the door to the flat, Kate gestured for Wade to go in. Looking around, he said, "Nice. Real nice. Though it's still a man's apartment."

"I'm only a temporary guest. I couldn't very well change it. I guess I really should find a place of my own, but—" She stopped herself from adding that in a few months she'd go home to Cardovan House to have her baby.

Wade tossed his coat and hat onto the hall stand, walked into the living room, and put his briefcase on the table. *"Voilà!"* He produced a bottle of bourbon. "Tell me where the glasses are and I'll fix us a warming solution while you get out of that uniform. It's dashing as hell, but I'm sick and tired of uniforms, and I'd like to see you in a pretty dress."

"I'll change because my clothes are damp, but I don't want a drink and you're not staying. The glasses are in that cabinet. One drink for you while I read your article, then out you go."

In her bedroom she contemplated her clothes with a frown. The wool jerseys and close-fitting suits would surely reveal the increased plumpness of her breasts, and besides, those tight waistlines wouldn't fasten. She settled for a man-tailored pair of slacks and a silk blouse.

Wade was sitting on the couch when she returned. He whistled. "Nice, kid. I know those pants are supposed to dampen my ardor, but as a matter of fact they're having the opposite effect."

"Where's the article? I'm tired and I just want to write a letter to my husband and then go to bed."

He'd discarded his jacket and now rolled up the sleeves of a wool pullover he wore over his shirt. "For my next trick, ladies and gentlemen, I will produce from this here briefcase—dah, dah—note that my hands never leave my body . . ." His hand came up holding a small bunch of bananas.

Kate sat down, laughing in spite of herself. Bananas hadn't been seen in England since the onset of the war. A moment later he fished out a trio of oranges and two Hershey bars, spreading the offering across the smoked-glass surface of the coffee table.

Kate shook her head disbelievingly. "Candy . . . oranges! Gad, don't you know there are people who would kill for— No, don't open that chocolate! I want it for a couple of kids at the hospital."

"Kate, my Kate. Okay, be unselfish if you must, but don't be so damn long-suffering! I'll get you some more candy for the kids. This is for you. Now." He pulled a newspaper tear sheet from the briefcase, fashioned it into a glider, and sailed it across the table to her.

Unfolding the paper, Kate read the headline: AMERICAN NURSE BRAVES BLITZ AND TERROR OF SIEGE OF LONDON.

Wade said hastily, "I didn't write the headline. Ignore it and read the rest."

She read on.

Nothing has stopped Hitler's Nazis so far. Not apeasement, nor tact and diplomacy, nor verbal threats, promises, or compromises. The swastika now flies over all of Europe, and only this one small island remains free. But there is something that's going to stop Hitler. You've been reading about it in every dispatch from London. It's the incredible valor and morale of the people of this country—their will to win this war in spite of the odds against it.

A handful of Americans have joined the British in their struggle. There's the Eagle Squadron that was formed in the RAF during the Battle of Britain last summer, and individual soldiers, sailors, and airmen who came via Canada. Now meet Kate Kieron, an American nurse in beleaguered Britain.

Kate groaned and looked up. "Couldn't you just have let me be anonymous? And if you had to use my name, it should have been Winfield, not Kieron."

"You know what the first rule of good reporting is? Be specific rather than general. Of course I had to use your name, and I wanted to use your American name, not your English one. The public can identify more readily with the struggles and hardships of one person than with a group of nameless, faceless beings."

Kate scanned the rest of the article. "Oh, God, Wade, you've made me out to be a heroine. I'll never live this down. I'm no heroine, believe me. If you could have read my mind today—what I was thinking and feeling—you wouldn't have written this. Sure, I know I told you how I felt when I held that dying child, maybe then I did feel a bit noble and self-sacrificing. But not any more. You get hardened to the suffering. You have to, or you'd go mad. This picture you've painted of me—it just isn't accurate."

"You're too modest, Kate. You always were. It used to infuriate me, that inferiority complex of yours. Why are you so damned hard on yourself?"

"Maybe because I wish I were better than I am. Maybe self-complacency is the greatest sin. You ever consider that? Oh, no, look at this!"

Despite the fearful din of blitzkrieg raging outside the hospital walls, the flickering of lights and falling plaster from the blast of high explosives, Kate moves calmly among maimed and mutilated men, women, and children; her healing hands touching a terrified child, soothing the agony of a disfigured pilot. . . .

"Wade, how could you write this? Which newspapers bought it? All the yellow rags that print with purple ink? I don't believe *Collier's* would even read this."

"Oh, no? They've asked for a longer article about you."

Kate gasped as she came to the next paragraph.

Although as the wife of a British nobleman Kate could have remained at the family estate, safe in the country, she chose to place herself on the front line of battle in London while her husband's Spitfire defends the skies against the might of the Luftwaffe.

She looked up angrily. "I never gave you permission to write anything like that! I thought you'd do a piece about the terrible toll of the air raids and . . ." Her voice trailed off as she came to a detailed description of what she looked like. Some of the thoughts Wade had expressed over dinner that night were here, polished and revised now, along with a rather touching tribute to her inner qualities of warmth and compassion that glowed in her eyes and shone from her face. She flung the paper down wordlessly. She should have let him use a photograph.

"Kate, don't get mad. This is the stuff heroines are made of. No matter how you belittle your own efforts, it's articles like this that will bring the war home to Americans. Hell, you said yourself there's no way for England to win without at least some material help from us. Don't you realize that this kind of reporting will sway public opinion and get it? Christ, you act like I'd sent you a poison pen letter. You think I care one way or the other if England wins or loses? Maybe I'd even prefer that they lose. If they did, you might come home and forget this crap about being an English lady. I did this for you, babe, because I thought—"

"I don't care what you thought. Take your damned article and get out of here. Leave me alone. I don't want to see you or hear from you again, do you understand?"

"Sure, okay. Don't start throwing things. I'm going."

After he'd gone, Kate stared moodily at the fruit and candy he'd left on the coffee table, wondering why she'd reacted so violently to the piece. Was it that she knew in her heart she didn't live up to his opinion of her, or was it that she was afraid Tony would read and misunderstand—especially that description of her. She'd seen less romantic ones on Valentine cards. But Tony couldn't read it. It wouldn't be published here. Or would it? Wade had said a string of newspapers bought it, but he didn't say where.

Seconds later there was a knock on her door, and Wade's voice called plaintively, "So much for my grand exit. Hey,

Kate, I forgot my hat and it's raining elephants and kangaroos out there."

She opened the door and let him in. He was reaching for his hat when the telephone rang on the table behind the couch. He looked at Kate. "No phone, huh?" and in three quick strides reached the telephone, picked it up and said, "Duffy's Tavern."

Kate clapped her hand to her mouth and prayed it wasn't Tony on the line. Wade was silent, listening, then he said, "Uh . . . yes, just a minute." He held out the receiver to her, mouthing the words *I'm sorry*.

She snatched it from him and heard Ursula's perfectly enunciated words. "Kate? I take it that was your American friend, Mr. Lowery. He didn't have the decency to introduce himself."

"What is it, Ursula? What do you want?"

"Keep your bonnet on, old thing, I had no idea I was interrupting anything. I just wanted to tell you that Cecilia is ill. We haven't been able to get hold of Tony and thought if you heard from him you could ask him to come home to see her."

[30]

Tony fought for his life on the choppy surface of the English Channel, battling the pain of his burned hands and the inexorable pull of the waterlogged parachute.

Batting at the metal disc to try to release the harness, the agony went screaming from fingers to brain. A red haze veiled his eyes, and he had no idea how far from shore he was. Suddenly the disc jerked around and he was free, beating off the tentacles of the chute and floating clear.

Unscrewing the valve of his Mae West life jacket with his teeth, he tried to clamp his mouth around the tube to inflate the life jacket, but his lips felt like charred rubber. He rested for a moment on his back, gulping in air and salt water, then tried again. This time he got some air into the tube but felt a surge of bubbles trail away in the water. Damn, the flames must have seared a hole in the Mae West.

All right, keep calm. Someone will have radioed air-sea rescue. A boat will be on the way. Just keep floating. God, the salt water stings. Helmet strap cutting into my chin . . . never mind, not enough strength to wrench it off. Water so cold . . . Strange how similar extreme cold and extreme heat are. Can't tell the difference between burning flesh and freezing water. Why can't I see? A wave sucked him up, turned him over, and his face went under the surface, immediately easing the livid flesh.

ECHOES OF WAR

He came up coughing and choking, in time to hear the zooming roar of a plane. A sense of unreality swept over him, and for an instant he thought either that he had imagined the sound or that he was inside the plane soaring skyward.

His eyelids felt like lead, pressing down on his useless eyes in an unnecessary effort at protection. He felt the water splashing into mouth and nostrils, and he thought he could hear the engines of a motor launch but wasn't sure. He didn't know how long he hung in the freezing water, moving his feet up and down to stay afloat, flailing weakly with his arms, more because they hurt so horribly than in any real effort to swim.

Then a voice cut through the last ounce of consciousness, telling him they were going to pull him into their boat and he shouldn't fight them, they merely wanted to help him. The voice spoke to him in fractured German. Tony wanted to laugh hysterically that they'd mistaken him for a downed German pilot, but instead hurled a barrage of oaths in the direction of his rescuers.

Vaguely he was aware of helping hands, of being laid on deck, rolled to a stretcher, hands peeling off clothing, wrapping him in blankets. He began to curse again, then blacked out.

Sounds intruded: the wail of an air-raid siren, the hideous shriek of diving Stukas; explosions. He drifted toward the sound, then tumbled again into oblivion. Hands, voices, pain. Stukas? No, they'd been withdrawn after fearful losses. He remembered thinking about the deaths of the pilots he'd shot down, trying to imagine their last moments. He was dreaming, that was it.

A voice broke through the darkness. Not young, not kindly, but businesslike. "I'm Staff Nurse Pickett. I'll be looking after you. I'm going to change the dressings on your face now. We'll do your hands later."

"Turn on . . . lights." His words came out as a series of croaks. "Bring . . . mirror."

"Not now. Later, when we pretty you up a bit."

He felt the bandages being unrolled, mummy-style, and gasped with pain when the last layer was taken. It was very dark, he supposed because his eyelids were stuck down.

"Eyes . . . can't see."

"We're keeping them covered because of your burned eyelids. The doctors are hoping your corneas aren't burned."

"How long . . . since . . ."

"You were quite poorly when they brought you in. Don't worry about anything now. I'll be giving you something for the pain in just a moment."

She placed gauze pads over his cheeks, and the pain in his hands seemed to immediately get worse. He felt a needle prick his skin, then merciful oblivion.

"Ah, there you are. Feeling better this morning?"

"No, I feel bloody worse. I want you to uncover my eyes."

"Not yet. Be patient."

"Listen, Pickett, I don't want anyone to send for my wife or my mother and sister, understand? I don't want them to see me like this."

"Squadron Leader Winfield, I'm afraid that's out of the question. Your family has already been notified. You'll be having visitors this afternoon. Don't worry, we'll cover your face with gauze and just leave a slit for your mouth."

"No . . . visitors."

"Hush. Rest now, so we'll be up to receiving our visitors."

"You receive our bloody visitors."

Morphia-induced relief from the pain. Sounds, sensations, fading away. The dark shape of a Dornier falling to earth, tracers following him like cobwebs in the wake of a giant spider. The Me 109 coming out of the sun and then the flash of fire, someone falling, someone screaming. . . .

Arms held him. "You're having a nightmare. Come on, wake up. Your visitors are in the waiting room."

The gauze was lifted from his eyes. Shadows and vague shapes stirred, all indistinguishable. "Better get some fresh." It was the staff nurse's voice. He tried to lift his eyelids, but nothing happened. Pickett said, "This is Polly, she's a VAD. She helps me with your dressings."

A very young voice said, "I thought they'd never let me do anything but empty bedpans and polish bed tables."

Kate was a VAD. *Oh, Kate* . . . Kate and Wade Lowery.

"There, now you look much better. Shall I send in your visitors?"

"If you let my wife in here I'll climb out the window."

"Now, now, Anthony—"

"Don't call me Anthony. You're not my bloody mother. Now listen carefully. *I . . . don't . . . want . . . to . . . see . . . any . . . visitors*. Do you understand that, Nurse? Or do I have to hit you to get your bloody attention?"

"Very well, Squadron Leader. I'll tell them you're sleeping."

"Tell them to go to hell," Tony roared at the top of his lungs. "Tell them I'm dead. Tell the whole fucking world to leave me alone. *Do you read me?*"

There was a gasp from somewhere near his head, he presumed from the young VAD. At the same instant a sharply in-drawn breath of outrage from the staff nurse and the rustle of starched aprons marching from the room. He gave a small manic chuckle. He had committed the inexcusable sin of using an Anglo-Saxon word in the presence of a member of the opposite sex. He shouted it again into the ether-drenched air, along with a stream of curses in German and French. He wasn't sure why. It certainly didn't help the torture of his burned flesh.

The timid voice of the VAD whispered, "I brought something to read to you, sir. I wanted you to hear it before your wife came to visit you. It was in the paper yesterday, and you'll be ever so proud of her."

He stopped ranting and said, "Polly? Is that your name? Has the old dragon gone?"

"Yes, sir."

"Very well. Read me the piece about my wife."

The article she read was reproduced from an American newspaper syndication. Tony listened and knew long before she'd finished reading who had written it.

ECHOES OF WAR

He lay still, not speaking, simply picturing Kate and Lowery together. This article could have been the reason for that dinner at the Savoy, of course, but that thought didn't alleviate either his jealousy or his anger. The piece may have been designed as propaganda for American readers, but whatever Lowery's motives for writing it were, whatever purpose it was supposed to serve, one thing came through with the clarity of a clarion call. The man who wrote that article about Kate still loved her.

"Sir . . . are you all right? Can I get you anything?"

"No, nothing. Polly, listen, nip out to the waiting room and if my sister is there, tell her I'll see her. Just my sister, understand? And get her out of here after five minutes."

Waiting, he lay as still as his tortured flesh would allow. He had no illusions about how grotesque he looked, or would continue to look. He'd visited other pilots with less severe facial burns than his.

His mind played what-if games with him. What if Kate had never stopped loving Wade Lowery? What if Lowery now loved her? Damn, that wasn't a what-if; it was a certainty. Just as an artist depicted his love for his model in his brush strokes, so had Lowery shown his for Kate in the words he'd written about her.

But Kate would take one look at her burned husband, and for her, loyalty would come first. No, damn it all to hell, he wouldn't accept pity from her.

A stifled sob close to his bed announced the arrival of Ursula. "Please," Tony said, "don't cry, for God's sake. I've heard enough whimpering from the student nurses."

"Cecilia . . . couldn't come. She's been ill, but she's getting better." The words were punctuated by more sobs. "I brought some flowers . . . but you . . . can't s-s-see them."

"Ursula, when we were children we made a solemn vow to each other, do you remember?"

"Y-yes. We swore we'd never lie to each other. And I never have lied to you, Anthony."

"What about not telling Kate I was coming home that weekend?"

"That wasn't a lie. It wasn't even an omission really. She

wouldn't give me a chance to tell her. She was so angry that I hadn't seen her on the driveway. I just got back in the car and drove on. Otherwise I'd have missed meeting your train."

"Very well. So you did actually *see* her and the American war correspondent together at the Savoy?"

"More than that, Anthony. I called Hardie's flat late one night, and Wade Lowery answered the phone. I swear I'm telling the truth. I could hardly mistake his American accent, could I?"

Tony listened to the sound of his own labored breathing for a moment, then said, "Keep Cecilia away from here until I look a little more presentable, will you? And Ursula, I don't want to see Kate either."

"She won't believe me. You know how she is. If you don't want to see her, you'll have to tell her yourself."

Ursula was right, of course. But he wasn't up to any sort of confrontation with Kate right now. He needed time to think. "Tell her I've just been given a sedative and I'm asleep. Ask her to come back tomorrow."

Kate paced the waiting room, unable to sit or even stand still. She pressed her fingers to her brow, trying to drive away the tension.

A middle-aged woman sat quietly weeping in a corner of the room. A young woman in ATS uniform pretended to read a magazine. An elderly man sat with his hands cupped around a walking stick, staring straight ahead at a blank wall.

Outside, snowflakes drifted out of a leaden sky. Only a couple of minutes had passed since Ursula was summoned to Tony's room. She had given Kate a triumphant glance before departing in a swirl of sable.

They had been told only that Tony had sustained burns and a broken ankle. His eyelids had been so badly burned that it was possible his corneas were damaged, but it was too early to tell. Perhaps the damage was only to the skin surrounding the eyes. They weren't to expect to find him looking quite . . . normal at this stage of his treatment.

Kate had heard the same words at the hospital across

town where she worked. Sometimes they meant that the poor devil had no face left and was permanently blind. Other times it was the medical profession's Godlike judgment that families prepared for the worst usually were grateful to find their loved one could still see and had some semblance of humanity left in his ravaged features. She was tempted to go storming after Ursula, but had no idea where Tony was.

Five minutes later Ursula was back, her face tear-streaked. Kate said, "How is he? Can I go in now?"

"No, no, he's asleep. You're to come back tomorrow."

"I'll wait. For God's sake, tell me how he is."

"His poor face . . . is all covered with gauze, except for his lips, and they're horribly swollen and blackened. His arms and hands are bandaged too." She began to cry again, her shoulders heaving.

Kate tried to put her arms around her, but Ursula pulled free and muttered, "I must get back to Cecilia. There's really no point in your waiting. The doctor won't let you in until tomorrow." She went through the open door and ran down the corridor toward the exit.

Kate went to the reception desk and told the nurse on duty that she would be in the waiting room when her husband awakened. The fact that Tony had asked for Ursula instead of her confirmed Kate's worst suspicions about his injuries. Although she thought he knew her better than to expect her to go to pieces.

She returned to the waiting room. An hour later a nervous-looking young VAD came to the door and asked for Mrs. Winfield, then motioned for Kate to step outside. She held a sheet of paper. "I'm sorry, Mrs. Winfield. It was embarrassing for me, but he can't write himself, you see." Red-faced, she thrust the note into Kate's hands and fled.

The words were written, incongruously, in a childishly round script:

Kate: This has nothing to do with my present condition. I was going to tell you, but didn't get a chance. I've been doing a lot of thinking since the last time I saw you and I realize that like many other people in wartime we were a little hasty in our actions. We can sort out the legal ramifications later, but meantime, I'm asking you to release me from promises made. As I release you from yours.

Kate swayed, blinking as the corridor suddenly shrank, closing in on her like a coffin.

[31]

"Feeling better?" A lined, gray-mustached face came into focus. Kate was lying on a leather couch in what appeared to be a doctor's office. She said, "Yes, thank you, Doctor—"

"Mr. Derwent. I'm the resident orthopedic surgeon."

Of course, Fellows of the Royal College reverted from doctor back to mister. Kate had been intrigued that they studied for years to earn the right to call themselves doctor and then for more specializing years to call themselves mister again.

"I guess I fainted."

"Often the shock of seeing a burned patient—"

"I haven't seen my husband yet." She sat up, looking around. "Mr. Derwent, I must see him, talk to him . . ." She felt her lip quiver and bit down on it, hard.

Derwent regarded her with sympathetic eyes. "I'll be back in a moment. Stay here; no one will disturb you."

Kate leaned back against the cool smooth leather, silently rationalizing that Tony was in shock. He couldn't have meant what he had dictated in that note. Or was it that he was afraid his burns had turned him into a monster? That he couldn't bear her pity? She made a vow never to show any.

Ten minutes later Derwent returned with a surgical-gowned man he introduced as Dr. Bradley, who had been treating Tony's burns.

Bradley seated himself behind the desk, and Kate wondered if he felt he needed a barrier between himself and distraught wives. He had a thin, reedy voice, and an unfortunate habit of addressing his remarks to the space over a person's head. "You must understand, Mrs. Winfield, that often men who undergo the trauma, that is, the shock, of being shot down, the pain and, ah, uncertainty . . . This sometimes causes irrational behavior. He refuses to see you. I understand you haven't been married very long. Perhaps he wishes to spare your feelings."

"I'm a nurse, Doctor Bradley. Will you please tell me how badly my husband has been burned?"

"Ah, yes, someone mentioned you're a VAD." He emphasized the initials slightly. "Well, he'll be scarred, of course. We don't know how badly. We shall have to reconstruct his eyelids, upper and lower. As to his sight, we hope his corneas haven't been seriously damaged, but it's too early to tell."

Tony might be blind, Kate thought, terrified for him. Her fingernails dug into the leather upholstery. "Can I go to him?"

The doctor picked up a pen and scribbled something on the desk pad, although it was clearly Derwent's desk, not his. "I'm sorry, but your husband is quite firm. He doesn't wish to have you visit him just now. He becomes quite agitated. Perhaps if you would return in a few days—or better still, give us a ring first."

Kate stood up. "Is there a phone in his room?" The doctor shook his head. Kate asked, "How about a phone I can use to call his mother?"

Standing quietly on the sidelines, Mr. Derwent said, "Use mine. Come along, Bradley, let's give her a moment of privacy."

Waiting for the call to go through to Cardovan House, Kate felt drained, unable to think. She thought longingly of the quiet peace of the gracious old house, the tranquillity of the grounds, and wished she could go there to curl up and await the arrival of better times.

Cecilia's voice, slightly hoarse, came on the line. Kate

said, "He's going to be fine. Ursula's on her way home. Don't worry, he'll be good as new. How are you feeling?"

There was a long relieved sigh. "Much better now. They didn't take him to your hospital, did they?"

"No, he's at the Masonic Hospital. I'm going to stay here for a while."

"Well, tell him he's lucky. He'll have his own nurse to look after him when he comes home. I'm so proud of you, Kate. I just read the article your American friend wrote about you."

Kate wasn't sure what was said during the rest of the conversation.

"I don't care what he says, I intend to see him." Kate squared her shoulders and stared Dr. Bradley down. "Please, just for a moment. I promise I won't upset him. I'm his wife; I must have some rights. I've been here for fourteen hours—"

"You must understand, my patient comes first. I can't let domestic problems enter into the case."

"What domestic problems? I don't know what you're talking about."

"Bradley"—Mr. Derwent's voice came from just behind her left shoulder—"give Mrs. Winfield five minutes with her husband. You can have a nurse accompany her if you must."

"Wait here. He may be having his dressings changed," Bradley said, his face pink with disapproval.

Derwent gave Kate a sympathetic smile. "You'll make yourself ill, if you continue to live in that waiting room. As soon as you've seen your husband I want you to go home and rest. And keep in mind that severe injuries often cause temporary emotional problems. Be as patient as you can. Don't force any decisions just now."

Kate was too tired to figure out what was going on. Minutes later a middle-aged nurse came to take her to Tony's room.

The room was in semi-darkness, as the window shades had been dropped to a couple of inches above the ledges. Tony was an immobilized gauze-swathed figure in the shadows. The nurse held up five fingers and closed the door, but Kate knew she was probably waiting just outside. She whispered, "Tony . . ."

"Did you get the note I had the girl write you?"

"Yes, but—"

"I was going to tell you when I saw you again. We made a mistake, Kate. Let's admit it and not ruin our lives over it."

"Tony, I love you. What are you saying? You don't mean it."

"I'm sorry. There's someone else. Don't make this any harder than it is already."

"Someone else?" Her knees shook. She placed her hand on the bed rail to steady herself. "I don't believe you. Is it because of your burns . . . do you think—"

"It's a WAAF officer. She's in the operations room at Biggin Hill. I'd prefer you didn't visit me again, in case your visits coincide with hers."

The cloying smell of ether, her early-pregnancy nausea, and the strain of the past hours were overwhelming her, but still her mind struggled to accept the unthinkable.

I love you. You can't fall in love with someone else, not now. Oh, Tony, not now that I know how much I love you.

She turned and stumbled blindly toward the door. "I'll be back . . . when you're more rational."

"Kate"—his voice bore the imprint of physical pain but was surprisingly strong—"I've no intention of ever living the kind of marital farce my parents endure. I know you're seeing Wade Lowery again—not only in public but also at my father's flat, which seems rather unsporting of the pair of you. So please don't play the outraged wife when I tell you there's someone else in my life too."

Kate spun around. "No! No. You've got it all wrong about Wade and me."

"Did you dine with Lowery at the Savoy? Has he visited you at my father's flat?"

"Yes, but—"

"Please go, Kate. And don't come back here, or I swear I'll get out of bed and leave. Probably break my neck, because I can't see a bloody thing."

"No, no, I won't go until you hear the whole story." Her voice rose to a small scream.

Tony called, "Nurse!"

"I was going to tell you—Please, Tony, listen to me."

The nurse, grim-faced, opened the door, grabbed her by the arm, and yanked her outside. "Really, Mrs. Winfield. I shall have to report this to the doctor."

Kate nodded wordlessly, knowing she must get out into the fresh air or she would probably pass out.

The flat in Berkeley Square was in darkness. Outside, the night was shattered by gunfire, the whine of falling bombs, explosions. Kate, bundled up in his lordship's eiderdown quilt, was curled in an armchair in front of an empty fireplace. She'd been there since before the dusk crept through the city streets, rising only to close the blackout shutters. But she hadn't turned on the lights. Somehow the darkness felt deserved, a form of penance for sins of omission, or perhaps a shield to hide behind as protection from any more accusations.

She shivered and pulled the quilt closer. Probably be warmer in bed, but she felt no inclination to undress and go there. She had been given a leave of absence from the hospital because of the seriousness of Tony's condition. She had cancelled her own appointment by telling the doctor it was a false alarm. She wasn't sure why she felt she should keep her pregnancy secret, but was too miserable and angry to analyze reasons for any of her actions any more. The trouble was, even though she told herself she hadn't done anything to deserve this treatment, there was that one little bit of guilt—the fact that Wade was still attractive to her, despite what he'd done, and the knowledge that she had been with him while Tony was fighting for his life. But damn it, how did you make amends to a man who refused to see you? And was there in fact another woman in his life?

Someone banged loudly on her door. She ignored it. No doubt her nosy neighbor had noticed she wasn't in the shelter and had come looking for her. Another reason to stay in the dark, so a chink of light didn't appear under the hall door.

Wade's voice called, "Open up, Kate. I know you're in there."

When she didn't reply, he shouted, "God damn it, open up or I'll bust the door down."

She was on her feet moving toward the door before she realized what she was doing, feeling almost grateful that someone issued an order. She blinked as Wade came in and flipped on an overhead light. His face was angry and his quick glance took in her creased dress, the quilt she'd trailed across the floor behind her. He closed the door, grabbed her hand, and yanked her across the room, switching on lamps as he went.

Shoving her into the fireside chair, he stood, arms folded, and looked down at her. "Okay, what the hell is going on? I called the hospital and they said you'd been given a furlough because your husband's plane was shot down. I called your ancestral home and got some hysterical female telling me you were no longer a part of their family and that I shouldn't bother them again regarding you." He paused for breath, looked her over again, and added, "And you look like hell. Are you sick?"

"Sit down, Wade, for God's sake. You're giving me a crick in my neck. I guess I might as well tell you, since it's all your fault, this whole rotten mess. You and your damn dinners at the Savoy, you and your fooling around on my phone. Not to mention that stupid article."

He shrugged off his coat, pulled a chair close to hers so that their knees were touching. Somewhere a bomb exploded, in concert with a burst of ack-ack fire. Wade said, "Shoot. You might as well; everybody else is."

Kate sighed. "I think I let you come around just to hear an American voice. I got kind of homesick and scared sometimes. You know sometimes I feel like such a foreigner here. That stiff-upper-lip stoicism drives me crazy. I want to run screaming through the streets when the bombs fall. I just hope they don't bomb this place while you're here. If they find our dead bodies together, Tony will never believe me."

Wade laughed and Kate gave a wry grin. She told him about Tony's letter, his refusal to see her. Wade listened silently and when she finished he said, "I remember that night at the Savoy you said little sis was there, but she ducked out before we got to her table. And as regards answering your phone, I was mad at you because you'd told me you didn't have a phone here. I'm sorry, Kate. What can I do to square things for you?"

"Do you really mean that?"

"Of course I do. What sort of heel do you take me for?"

"If there was just some way to make Tony understand that we just got together to do the story . . . But how do I explain you being here in the flat?"

"Tell him the truth, for Pete's sake. We didn't do anything." He paused. "Hey, maybe now we might as well."

Kate ignored him. "Besides, he told me there's someone else."

He reached over and picked up her hands, gripping them tightly. "Do you love him? He didn't just catch you on the rebound? Don't ruin your whole life if—"

"Wade, I'm pregnant."

He was silent, his face immobile. After a moment he asked, "Does he know?"

She shook her head. "I never got a chance to tell him."

"You still haven't answered my question. Do you love him?"

She wanted to look him straight in the eyes and say, Yes, yes I love my husband; but the words of Tony's cruel dictated note, the callous refusal to see her or discuss the situation, the sheer injustice of being accused, condemned, and sentenced without a trial, stopped her. She thought of the brittle charade of Cecilia's life, the loneliness of Hardie exiled to this flat. Then she cast her mind back over her relationship with Tony. He'd been patient, loving, courteous, and considerate to the point of saintliness; yet he had turned on her with a fury on the basis of a hearsay accusation. Almost as if he'd been expecting something like this to happen, had tried too hard to prevent it by being damn near the perfect companion, lover, husband.

Had he perhaps tried as hard as a child to be "good" so that he wouldn't cause a rift between his parents and, having failed, in some way expected his own marriage to fail— perhaps as punishment? Even if his plane hadn't been shot down and he hadn't suffered so terribly, could he—could anyone—have maintained such perfection?

Kate ran her hands through her hair despairingly. Trying to analyze Tony's actions and motives was almost as difficult as sorting out her own feelings toward him and their marriage. There had been an abrupt shift in the equity of their relationship; and Kate felt that the major burden for its continuance, formerly carried by Tony, had now fallen on her shoulders. But she wasn't sure if she had the power to make things right again, no matter how much she loved him. And she did love him, more than ever.

She was unaware of her long silence until Wade said softly, "So you refuse to answer on grounds that it might tend to incriminate you."

"Shut up," Kate said. "Who needs you here, anyway? Why don't you go write a piece of propaganda?"

"What are you going to do? You can't sit here in the dark indefinitely."

"I'm going to have to find a flat of my own, for starters. That's the last time Ursula's going to come rifling through my things. Then I'll go back to work for as long as I can. Maybe when Tony's burns heal a little, he'll be more reasonable."

"You said he told you there was someone else. That's not the kind of thing a guy would make up. Kate, in wartime it's hard to live by the old rules when every day might be your last."

"No! No, don't you see, he was making that up to let me off the hook. He thought you and I . . . And his burns might be disfiguring."

"But you're not really sure about that," Wade said softly, "or you wouldn't have told me about his someone else."

"I tell you too damn much. I always did."

"I know of an apartment that's going to be vacant soon. A correspondent is going home."

Interested, she looked up. "Would you . . . ?"

"Sure. Now how about coming down to the shelter until things quiet down outside? I admire stoics, but this is getting ridiculous."

ECHOES OF WAR

Another burst of gunfire rattled the windows. Kate said, "Okay, let me get my coat. It's cold down there."

He helped her into her coat, then kept his hands on her shoulders and turned her around to face him. "Kate . . . nothing's irrevocable. Not marriage, not even a baby. I know you're Catholic, but I checked and found out that you can get an annulment through the Church, especially since he isn't Catholic."

Kate was speechless for a moment. "You . . . checked? What right did you have—"

"None," he said quickly. "Except that I still love you. I guess I always will."

[32]

Tony's entire squadron visited him in twos and threes, regaling him with stories of their exploits. A couple of WAAF officers also dropped in, and he forced himself to make small talk with them, thinking perhaps their visits would be reported to Kate, who had made several attempts to see him.

Thoughts of Kate tormented his mind as much as his burns ravaged his body. At times he even considered allowing her sense of obligation and pity to bring her back into his life, but he loved her too much to suffer that kind of travesty. No, better to let her go to Lowery. Hadn't she been carrying the proverbial torch for Lowery when they met—even when they were married? After all, she'd never pretended she loved him. Not until she visited him in the hospital and saw the extent of his injuries.

Dusty Miller was a frequent visitor. He claimed to have spoken over his radio to a German Me 109 pilot, offering a few choice epithets in German, and had been informed in return that he was a filthy Englishman who would learn proper German one of these days.

"Called me a bloody pommie!" Dusty declared indignantly. "I mean, is there a worse way to insult an Aussie? Anyway, they were about two thousand feet below us, and our leader yelled, 'Tally-ho,' and we spread fanwise and peeled off. I had him in my sights at three hundred yards, and at two hundred I opened up with a long burst and saw the tracers go right into his nose."

Under the protective gauze over his eyes Tony relived some of his own dogfights and felt a savage need to be back in the sky, making Germans pay for the pain he suffered. It had become an obsession. He didn't dare consider it might also be a death wish, putting an end to his misery over the loss of Kate.

"Hey, sorry, mate. I'm supposed to be cheering you up, not making you wish you were back in your Spit," Dusty said, with his usual perception. "Listen, you remember when I tried to land on that flamin' decoy airfield?"

Tony nodded. In the early days of the Battle of Britain, before Goering's Luftwaffe switched to terror bombings of cities, the RAF airfields had taken a terrible pounding, and to relieve the pressure decoy targets had been set up. The ruse worked, and the Germans dropped their bombs on fake runways. The trouble was, the decoys looked so realistic at night that several RAF pilots, particularly those with crippled planes, tried to land on them. Dusty had been fortunate to walk away from his aircraft after cracking it up on a decoy field.

"Well, I was talking to a bloke who told me the Jerries found out about our decoys and decided to build one of their own in Holland. They built it entirely out of wood, see, with typical bloody meticulous Jerry attention to detail. Anyway, the day the last wood plank was in place, a lone RAF plane crossed the channel, went in low, circled the field once, and dropped a large wooden bomb."

Tony had little recollection of the early weeks he spent cursing and blaspheming, refusing to see anyone but Dusty and his fellow pilots. Even Ursula's visits were infrequent. After the first few times that he flew into a rage when someone tried to bring Kate in, her name was no longer mentioned. Perversely, he was then angry because she had given up.

A calm-voiced orthopedist named Derwent told him he was in the Masonic Hospital, part of which had been donated for service casualties, but owing to its vulnerable location few were kept there for long, and he would probably be moved to the main Air Force Hospital when he was stronger.

"I'll keep you here as long as I can," Derwent told him, after setting his broken ankle. "You'll like it here better. It hardly resembles a hospital at all, and the nursing staff are very carefully chosen."

Cecilia visited him, and although Tony warned the nurses to keep the room dark, Cecilia had wept at the sight of him. She was still weak from her bout with pneumonia; and her husky voice, muffled by sobs, had castigated first the Germans and then, for some reason, herself, for Tony's condition.

She cried out, "Oh, my darling, what have I done to you? What have I done to *him?*" Then Ursula and the nurses managed to get her out of the room.

Tony thought about her last statement, unsure if the "him" his mother referred to was his real father or his adoptive father. He cursed women for their infidelities, wondering if any of them were capable of being faithful, or if they simply marked time waiting for a better prospect to come along.

He didn't understand why it was, when he could catalogue so thoroughly all of the reasons not to love a woman, that her leaving tore his life to shreds, that he still ached for Kate's presence, her touch, her laughter.

A couple of days later Cecilia returned. She was more composed, but she asked reproachfully, "Anthony, what's all this about you not wanting to see your wife?"

"Kate and I made a mistake. We shouldn't have married in haste. What's the old saying? We're repenting at leisure. Please, Mother, I don't want to discuss it."

"Mother," Cecilia repeated. "How strange to hear you call me that."

"But you *are* my mother, aren't you? Or did you adopt me too?"

"No, of course not. Anthony, you sound so . . . different."

"I *am* different. I intend to stay different."

A nurse's voice interrupted to say it was time to irrigate

his eyes, and he was glad to be left alone again. He appreciated the visits from the squadron, but afterwards they left him restless and impatient and furious at the slow healing process of human flesh. Besides, each time they came there were always one or two missing. One night he persuaded Dusty Miller to smuggle in a bottle of brandy and managed to get roaring drunk.

He found that with his eyes covered, his other senses became more acute. He always knew when someone was in the room with him, even if they didn't speak, and would angrily demand to know who was present. Staff Nurse Pickett informed him icily that he was the worst patient she'd ever had and she could have understood any other reaction to his injuries except his vocal rage.

After a month he was considered out of danger and moved to a ward where he would await the reconstruction of his eyelids and some skin grafting on his hands. Mr. Derwent told him he was lucky that the bones of his hands appeared undamaged, and he should regain full use of them, although the scars would probably be permanent. Derwent was a lot more honest and inclined to give him the facts than Dr. Bradley, who talked in circles whenever Tony asked whether he would see again.

With his hands heavily bandaged, Tony had to suffer the indignity of having everything done for him, of being completely helpless. It was maddening, humiliating, and his state of mind, as well as the constant pain, turned him into a growling bear feared by every nurse and VAD. He was, Pickett reminded him, the terror of the wards, and nobody knew why they put up with him.

Most of all he hated being fed like a baby. Having gone through every VAD in the wing, Pickett claimed that the nurses now drew lots to see who would get the job.

"Good," Tony retorted. "Then you'll all hurry up and get the damn skin grafts done and get me out of here."

Then one morning at breakfast he sensed a different touch, and when he demanded to know which VAD was shoving that putrid slop in his mouth, instead of a reply he felt a gentle hand on his shoulder, massaging slightly, and the spoonful of porridge was offered again. Later, when Pickett came to change his dressings, he asked about the silent nurse who'd shown superhuman patience.

"Oh, that's Anna. She's a Dutch refugee. Her English isn't very good yet, but she's an excellent worker. Mr. Derwent found her. She was a student nurse before the war in Rotterdam. Don't bully her, do you hear? She's had a bad time of it."

"Is she pretty?"

"Of course. We don't allow ugly girls to take care of RAF officers," Pickett said sarcastically.

After that the Dutch nurse was permanently assigned to feeding him. He tried to behave himself at mealtimes for her sake, feeling her loneliness and isolation mirror his own. He tried to speak to her in French and in German, but evidently she didn't speak either language.

Still, he found himself talking to her occasionally in English, thinking perhaps it would help her pick up the language and also because the silence, except for his slurping of food, became ridiculous to him. She would respond by touching his upper arm or shoulder or neck, and there was great tenderness in her touch that made him recall the "laying on of hands" referred to in the Bible. He mentioned this one day in English, then, slightly embarrassed, added for his own benefit, "Not that I'm a religious person. I read the Bible as a child as one would read any other interesting piece of literature."

She stroked his neck gently, almost as if she understood the ambivalent emotions of an agnostic snatched back from death and not at all sure he had accomplished it all on his own.

Anna was spooning soup into his mouth early one evening when the Luftwaffe again decided to try to knock out Hammersmith Bridge. Since their aim wasn't too good, the crump of bombs inched closer to the hospital. A stick of bombs screamed overhead and the next second he felt a soft body sheltering his.

The building shook with the detonation, but remained intact. For a second or two Anna didn't move. Tony's feelings were fragmented, obscured by his own sense of helplessness, but he thought for an instant he recalled how it was to lie with a woman. He felt no physical response to the young nurse's nearness, but rather the memory of desire. At the same time he was deeply moved that she would try to protect his body with her own, and then angry again at his own impotence. Then they both relaxed and she resumed feeding him.

He said testily, "Isn't it about time you were learning a few English phrases?"

He heard a whispered, "Yes," and immediately felt ashamed of himself.

A few days later when his eyes were being irrigated he said, "Why, Pickett, you old battleaxe, you never told me you had green eyes."

The nurse's face broke into a delighted smile. She had silver hair, like Cecilia, and a skin like faded rose petals. She exclaimed, "I'll fetch Dr. Bradley right away. He'll be so pleased with you."

Tony looked around slowly as other shapes came into focus. His bed was screened from the rest of the ward. The daffodils Ursula had brought were in a glass vase on his table, a cheerful yellow splash against the monotones. There was also a tiny pot of violets. He'd thought a couple of times he could smell the scent of violets, but their subtle fragrance had been overwhelmed by the stronger hospital smells.

Dr. Bradley appeared around the screen, bent over him, and peered into his eyes. Tony said, "Boo!" Bradley gave him a pained glance and said, "We'll be transferring you to another hospital for your new eyelids. They'll take the skin graft from inside your left arm. A 'Thiersch' graft—thin as cigarette paper. Later on they'll take skin from your legs to do your hands. By the way, when you go to the Air Force Hospital the nurses there won't tolerate any more swearing, so I suggest you control yourself and behave like a gentleman."

"Just get on with it is all I ask," Tony said.

Bradley stared at the wall above his bed. "By the way, I'm afraid I have some bad news. A message came for you from your squadron. Your friend Dusty Miller was killed. Apparently he was seen to climb out of his plane, but it was only a thousand feet over a densely populated area, so he got back in and crashed it into the Thames."

Tony would have closed his eyes for a moment, if he could. Instead he barked, "Isn't it time to feed the bloody animals? I want my little Dutch girl in here."

Nurse Pickett, who had apparently been hovering behind the screen, popped her head into view and said, "Lunch will be along in a few minutes."

Tony turned his head away from them, wishing all at once for the comforting touch of the Dutch nurse so that the image of Dusty's Spitfire crashing into the Thames would go away.

They removed the screen, and now he could see a window. Fragile sunlight gilded the glass. There was a single tree within view, festooned with tiny green buds. Perhaps he'd be flying again by summer.

He heard the rattle of the lunch trolleys but didn't turn to watch their approach. All at once he wasn't sure he wanted to see his Dutch angel of mercy. Women had a terrible habit of not living up to your expectations.

A quiet voice said, "Please don't be angry, Tony."

Turning his head, he looked at Kate, wearing her VAD uniform, holding his lunch tray. For an instant he merely looked at her, thinking that despite everything that had ever been written on the subject of beauty, no one had ever captured in words that inner glow of a woman who loves deeply.

For one wrenching moment he would have given the rest of his life to know that he was the object of that love, even if he were only aware of it in the fleeting seconds left to him. But, of course, as Ursula had reported, Kate was now seeing Lowery on a regular basis. "Dutch?" Tony asked casually.

"I knew it was a language you didn't speak." She bit her lip. "Mr. Derwent arranged for my transfer here. He's been very kind. He kept you here too. Every time the Air Force Hospital called, he told them you were too ill to be moved. At first I thought of posing as deaf and mute, but I figured a VAD would at least need to hear the patients."

"I see. So Pickett and all the others—Everybody was involved in the little deception, obviously. What a good laugh you must all have had at my expense."

"Tony, please—"

"I'm surprised Ursula didn't give the game away."

"I'm sure she would have, had she known. I kept out of the way during her visits. Tony, she lied to you about Wade and me."

"Are you telling me you didn't dine with him at the Savoy? That he hasn't visited you at my father's flat?"

"No, but—"

"This is neither the time nor the place for personal matters. I'm being transferred out of here tomorrow. When I'm able to go home for my convalescent leave perhaps you could come to Cardovan House and we'll discuss what's to be done. In the meantime, I'd appreciate it if you would kindly send someone else in to feed me."

He turned his head to the window again.

There was a moment's silence, and then Kate said quietly, "Seeing Wade again was probably the best thing that could have happened to me, because it made me realize how much I love you."

"Sorry, old girl, that declaration comes a little late in the day. I'm neither physically nor mentally in the mood for it. Now for God's sake get someone else in here to spoon that slop to me."

"Tony, I'm pregnant."

"How very nice for you and Mr. Lowery. Why don't you run along and talk to Cecilia and Clive about how to find a way to bring up your bastard at Cardovan House?"

He heard her swiftly indrawn breath, then the sound of her running footsteps fading away. The scent of violets intruded for a second into the aching void of his emotions, and he knew that she had brought them.

It wasn't until the following day, when he was being prepared for his move to the Air Force Hospital, that a VAD found a card stuck to the bottom of the pot of violets. She handed it to him and he read: "Forgiveness is the scent of violets on the heel of he who crushed the petals."

[33]

Kate visited Tony every day, but he was now in a crowded ward that offered no privacy and the visits were painfully impersonal. When she tried to talk about their relationship, Tony changed the subject or pretended to sleep.

Once when she said quietly, "Tell me it was only because of your agony that you made that accusation about Wade being the father—"

Tony interrupted. "Please, old girl, there are two gents less than three feet away from my bed on either side. Let's save the theatrics for later, shall we?"

There was nothing to do but to await his release from the hospital and hope they'd be able to talk things out then. But one evening Kate arrived a little later than the scheduled time for the visiting hour, and saw that a slender, dark-haired WAAF officer was at Tony's bedside.

Kate stopped at the door, turned, and went back to the waiting room. She felt physically ill, beaten. Her body hurt as if from a blow.

All of Kate's joy that she was carrying Tony's child had vanished. Her pregnancy was now further proof to him that she was having an affair with Wade. In return, he flaunted his WAAF. Damn him, damn everything. She went outside before giving in to tears.

ECHOES OF WAR

The following day she called Wade and he helped her move into a smaller flat. He called to see her frequently. She felt comfortable with him, almost like a family member.

She realized now that it was possible for love to die; hers for Wade had faded without her noticing. In its place was a feeling of friendship and camaraderie not unlike that she had enjoyed with Tony before their marriage. Kate decided she could go crazy trying to figure out human emotions.

So was there any reason not to have a friendship with Wade? Not just out of rebellion at Tony's unjust accusations, but simply because Wade was another American voice raised in good old Yankee anger and bravado in a sea of British stiff-upper-lip stoicism. Although sometimes his articles revealed his changing attitude toward the British.

Wade's friendship eased her loneliness, but not her anguish over Tony. She alternated between hurt and resentment that he'd turned to someone else, and a fierce longing for him that brought determination not to let that damned WAAF officer have him. When he got out of the hospital . . . Everything was in abeyance until then.

On one of her days off in early March she lay in bed reading the first draft of Wade's latest dispatch home. He had written:

> *London is like an aristocratic old lady who's just been beaten up and hasn't had time to clean herself up yet. She's still proud, queenly, but she shows gutted buildings, open scars where whole blocks have been razed to rubble, and a desperate need for paint, repair, and scrubbing clean.*
>
> *Yet there is a cheerful willingness here to keep on living as decently and honorably as possible under harrowing conditions that I'm not sure any other race on earth is capable of.*
>
> *The blackout is a darkness that swallows you up like a tar pit. The lights of home are remembered and longed for like—*
>
> *N.B. to Kate: Hey, babe, you love this gutsy old town. How about thinking up some similes, meta-*

phors—anything that will make this piece come together for me.

When the doorbell rang she got up and slipped on a robe, knowing that the chances were that it would be Wade. She saw no reason to discourage his visits, since apart from that one wistful declaration that he still loved her, he'd been a model of decorum. Perhaps because of her pregnancy, she reasoned.

Opening the door, she was confronted by a bouquet of narcissus and a large cardboard carton. Wade peered at her between his burdens. "Manna from heaven, untold treasures from the great land of plenty across the sea, sustenance for ladies who are *enceinte*."

"Shhh! Don't tell the world," Kate said, giggling. She took the flowers from him and sniffed their fragrance. "Oh, lovely. Thank you. It amazes me that we can still get flowers in the midst of all the nightly mayhem."

Wade kissed her cheek, then staggered to the dining table with his cardboard box. She watched him fondly, appreciating the companionship and almost reverent concern for her welfare he offered. Perhaps friendship was best, after all.

With a flourish he withdrew a large can of chicken, then dumped canned fruits, nuts, dried fruit, and some slightly whitish chocolate bars. "The chocolate doesn't travel too well. It gets that gray bloom, but it still tastes okay, 'specially when you're eating for two. Now, pass me the curry and ginger and I'll make my famous chicken à la Lowery. And lookee here, Kate, a can of pumpkin. Wrong season, but what the hell." Carrying the cans to her cupboards, he added, "You read that last piece I wrote?"

Kate ran her fingers through her hair to untangle the knots, rubbed the sleep from her eyes, then reached for a vase for the flowers. "Yes, I did. It's good, Wade. I mean, really good. Your style is changing, you know that? There's a deep vein of compassion underlying what you write nowadays that wasn't there before. What's happening to you?"

He glanced at her, his eyes dark and unexpectedly serious, and quoted, " 'Any man's death diminishes me, because I am involved in mankind.' "

"I should know that quotation, but—"

"Donne's *Devotions*. I was talking to a young air force gunner one night in a bar who reminded me of it. He was killed a few days later, I found out. I guess I can't get it off my mind. It's . . . having people you know—have talked to and swilled beer with—having them blasted to kingdom come. I guess you can't help getting personally involved. What's new about your husband?"

"His new eyelids are healing nicely, according to the doctor, and thank God they didn't get infected. He can use his hands again. I think they'll probably send him home on convalescent leave soon."

"I have an irresistible urge to meet him. A burning curiosity—"

"Whoa! Down, boy. I don't think that would be a good idea. He's in no condition to get into a punching match with you, and I'm afraid that's what would happen. He's changed. . . . Well, maybe he was always like this under the surface and showed me a gentler side. But there's a fury in him now that astonishes me. When Mr. Derwent first got me transferred to the Masonic Hospital, I couldn't believe the stories I heard about Tony. About his cursing and ranting and raving, or having members of his squadron smuggle booze in to him, and terrorizing the nurses. Honestly, he was the last man on earth to act like that, in spite of his terrible burns."

"The ravages of love and war. He wouldn't be the first man to discover a darker side to himself."

"The strange thing is I didn't know how much I loved him until I saw that other side of him. Maybe I just felt he was too good for me—too perfect—before. I believe even the scars from his burns will humanize him." She smiled sadly. "He was just too damned good-looking before."

Wade was examining the contents of her cupboards. He pulled out a package of powdered eggs and shook it. "I don't want to hear that, Kate. I want to hear that you made a big mistake, and as soon as he's back on his feet you'll come home where you belong."

She smiled. "You don't mean that. You're just trying to make up for past sins."

His eyes held hers for a moment. "How about some scrambled eggs for breakfast? I don't think you're getting enough to eat. You know you've got to see a doctor. I found out pregnant ladies can get extra rations. How come you're not putting on any weight?" He looked down at the powdered eggs again. "And as far as me not meaning what I say, just wait till after your baby's born and your husband's back on his feet. Then I start to fight dirty."

"Wade."

"Yeah?"

"I really don't hold a grudge against you any more, you know. It was better that you called off the wedding rather than went ahead with doubts. And I've been grateful for your friendship these past weeks. You've been a link to home, and I don't know how I'd have handled what happened with Tony if you hadn't been around."

He paused, frying pan in one hand, and gave her a rueful grin. "Isn't it the damnedest thing the way it worked out? When people talk about the impetuousness of youth, I begin to see what they mean. You and me and Winfield—we made some hasty decisions, didn't we? But do we have to spend the rest of our lives paying for them?"

"Wade, don't! I know it's hard for you to believe, but I do love my husband. I want him back. I want my marriage to work. I'm not going to let a spoiled, jealous kid wreck it. Or another woman."

He brought her the scrambled eggs and two hefty slices of toast. "Okay, Kate. I can wait." He took a bite of her toast. "After all, not many people tell me I write with compassion."

The telephone rang in the living room and Kate jumped to her feet. "Don't you dare touch that! I'll get it."

Cecilia's voice came over the wire. "Kate? Wonderful news. I just spoke with Anthony's plastic surgeon, and he said we can bring him home. Kate, darling, I know you and he had a spat, and I thought, wouldn't it be marvelous if you were to go to the hospital to bring him home. The doctors don't want him to travel alone, and I thought maybe you knew someone who would lend you a car. Ours are all in the garage for the duration now the civilian petrol ration has been taken away. Otherwise, I suppose you'd have to come by train. Only . . . I don't know how he'd feel about people staring at his scars, and then too, you wouldn't be able to talk privately. Ursula's up north and I told the doctor that you were the only one who could go, so Anthony can't refuse."

Kate said, "I'll go get him and bring him home, one way or another. When is he to be released?"

"The day after tomorrow. He can leave any time after nine. You'll be there? Oh, splendid. Good luck, dear. I'll see you when you get here."

Replacing the receiver, Kate looked up to see Wade standing in the doorway. "I take it he's getting out of the hospital?"

She nodded. "I need a car and gasoline desperately. Is there any way . . . Can you . . . ?"

He rolled his eyes, and Kate said, "I know it's a lot to ask, but you really owe me, Wade. It's all your fault I'm at odds with him."

He walked over to the telephone. "If ever a guy had to pay for his sins, and pay, and pay . . . I'll see what I can do. One of the big wheels at International has the use of a car. He owes me a favor."

Wade's friend, along with his car, was staying with English friends in Surrey. Kate could pick up the car the following day, then return it later to London. This was more driving than she bargained for, but she quickly agreed. Wade was concerned about the distances and the possibility of her getting caught in an air raid.

"I'll stop and get into a shelter, I promise, and I won't drive after dark."

"I wish I could go with you—at least down to Surrey to pick up the car," Wade said. "But I have to go home."

"Home?" she repeated blankly.

"To America, babe. I got a cable last night. My mother is seriously ill. I'm leaving for Shannon this afternoon. I'm hoping to connect to a clipper out of Lisbon."

"Oh, Wade, I'm so sorry about your mother. I hope she'll be all right." Kate instinctively extended her arms to him in sympathy and found herself unexpectedly crushed into a fierce embrace. She felt him tremble, then bury his face in her hair.

He whispered, "Oh, Kate . . ."

The strange thing was that all of her passion had gone. It was difficult to recall how once he'd been able to drive her wild just by holding her. She said, "I don't suppose you'll be coming back?"

"Oh, yes I will. Meantime, you take care of yourself, hear?" He ran his fingertips lightly across her cheek. For a moment his expression was stripped of all pretense. "Are you ever going to give me a second chance?"

"Please, Wade. You know we can't ever go back."

"Promise me that if anything comes up you'll send me a cable if you need me, for anything."

"I promise."

He said sadly, "I hope he's good to you, Kate. You deserve the best."

She took an early train down to Surrey. She was due to pick up Tony at the hospital that afternoon. After inquiring about getting a taxi from the station to the address Wade had given her and being told the only cab driver had been called up, she waited an hour for a bus.

The bus deposited her on a country lane, and the conductor gave her instructions to take the next right turn, follow her nose, and she'd come to the house she wanted.

The walk took forty-five minutes, and she began to worry about making it to the hospital in time.

Neither the family nor the American gentleman was home, an elderly servant informed her, but he had the car keys and could offer her some tea and scones.

She was hungry but declined politely. With luck she could drive back to London and be at the hospital before the arrival of the German bombers for the nightly raids.

The car proved to be an elderly MG. She'd never driven a sports car before, and shifting gears with her left hand was disconcerting at first; but armed with a map of her route and the warning that there were no street signs or village names, since they'd been removed in preparation for the expected German invasion, she set off. There were only winding hawthorne-bordered lanes to contend with, and she soon became accustomed to the reversed controls.

An hour later she was hopelessly lost. The lanes all looked the same and it had begun to rain, the skies darkening rapidly. Okay, no need to panic. Just keep going until you reach a village or a farm, then stop and ask directions.

She slowed down as she saw a gate ahead. That surely led to a farmhouse. On the other side of the narrow lane was a wooded area, shadowed and vaguely sinister.

The dark figure seemed to rise up out of nowhere. Kate braked abruptly, startled by the apparition that lurched into the middle of the lane, one hand raised to flag her down.

Rain now pelted the steamy windshield, cutting her visibility, but she could see that the man moved as though sick or injured. As the car rolled to a halt, she pulled the snaps on the side curtains. A ride in return for directions. At worst the man was someone in need of a doctor, at best a motorist who'd run out of gas or broken down.

Instead she looked into the muzzle of an automatic pistol, recognized the flying suit of the man holding it, and thought incredulously, He's a Luftwaffe pilot. He must have bailed out. In heavily accented English, the man said, "You will drive us to the south coast." A moment later a second man, also wearing a flying suit, emerged from the trees.

[34]

Tony looked up as his mother entered the study, where he sat moodily staring at the dying embers of the fire. She said, "She isn't at Hardie's flat, nor the flat she took for herself. I phoned the hospital where she worked, and they said she'd told them she was coming home. I'm getting quite worried. Do you think we should call the police?"

His new eyelids itched unbearably, but he'd seen skin grafts become infected and simply fall off other patients, so he kept his hands away from his face. He picked up the brass poker and stirred the fire. Flames flickered to life, sending tall shadows dancing on the walls. "What do you suggest we tell them? That my wife has run off with her lover? That in all probability they're at this moment somewhere over the Atlantic? To please dispatch the marines to fetch them back?"

"You don't know they're together." Cecilia sat on the arm of his chair and ran her hand lightly across the top of his head in the way she used to when he was a small boy. The gesture hadn't comforted him then either. Cecilia's gestures, like her conversation, had always seemed contrived, as though she were still on stage following direction. He'd always felt isolated from her, despite their desperate charade of closeness.

He said, "No? Isn't it just too much of a coincidence that

Lowery left England on the same day Kate disappeared? According to the International Press people in London, he's returned to the States."

"But darling, Kate wouldn't tell me she was coming to pick you up at the hospital and then suddenly decide to go home with Lowery."

"She would if he suddenly decided to ask her." Tony thought of the hours he'd waited for Kate to arrive, the sympathetic glances and excuses the hospital staff made as he paced anxiously, eyes fixed on the door. The stupid thing was, he'd been prepared to make almost any kind of compromise with her in return for a new beginning. Eventually he'd told his doctor he could take a train home alone and they'd better damn well sign him out or he'd simply walk out of there.

"Something's happened to her," his mother insisted. "Kate wouldn't leave without a word to anyone. Don't you think you're magnifying the whole Lowery thing out of all proportion? You saw the article he wrote about her. Perhaps there was no more to their meeting again than that. I told you he called here quite openly about her."

Irritated, Tony stood up and walked stiffly to the sideboard to pour himself a drink. His ankle no longer required a cast, but the recent rains caused havoc with the newly mended bones. "I require fidelity in my marriage, Mother. I can't imagine any other kind of relationship working for me. Unlike my father, I might add."

She bit her lip and stared at him with drowning eyes. He couldn't summon any sympathy for her. "Incidentally, while I'm home, I'd rather you didn't invite Clive over. I don't give a damn if he *is* my father."

Cecilia stood up, her face white. She walked to the door, and he was reminded of Marie Antoinette going to the guillotine. He felt a momentary twinge of conscience. He supposed he was lashing out at his mother because of his own agony over Kate, over the general unfaithfulness of the female population. Or perhaps a lonely and hurt-filled childhood, filled with bewildering memories, needed to be cleansed from his system.

He called after Cecilia, "That's right, walk away. Just as

you always did when I asked questions you didn't want to answer. My God, can you imagine what goes through a child's mind when his own mother won't tell him about his father? I used to have nightmares that he was a deformed monster—perhaps criminally insane. And you know, come to think of it, perhaps that would have been better than him turning out to be that fatuous ass Clive."

Cecilia stopped, her hand on the doorknob, and turned to look at him. She said with quiet dignity, "You're quite wrong about Clive. Just as you're quite wrong about Kate."

Tony called, "Come in," in response to the tentative tap on his bedroom door. He had taken his dinner in his room that evening, his first day home, not wanting to face any guests Cecilia might have invited. He assumed the maid had returned to pick up his tray, but instead it was Cecilia who appeared. She twisted a long chiffon scarf between nervous fingers, and he thought of the dancer Isadora Duncan, whom his mother had spoken of and greatly admired during her theater days. Isadora had loved long, floating scarves and had ultimately been strangled by one. "Anthony . . ."

"Would you mind not calling me that? It makes me feel six years old, and about to be reprimanded for some misdeed."

"I'm sorry."

"I am too. About this afternoon. I had no right to speak to you the way I did, to insult you and Clive."

"Oh, yes, I think you had every right. Tony, I called the local constable and he's coming over to talk about Kate."

"If it will make you feel better, so be it."

"I hope you're not angry."

"No, I'm not. I just feel it's a wasted effort. You'll have to bear with me. I'm afraid I've been acting rather selfishly. There's something about looking death in the face that does that. It isn't the ennobling experience some people claim. As soon as I'm fit for duty I'll take my anger out on Germans."

"I haven't been a very good mother, have I? I was no better as a mother than a wife. They were the two roles I couldn't quite master. Perhaps because there was no Ella Fontaine around to emulate. I spoiled Ursula and hurt you—"

"No, no you didn't." He gave a ghost of a smile. "You may have killed us both with kindness, in fact."

But there was no depth to our relationship, was there? I always had the feeling when I was a child that as soon as I left the room I ceased to exist for you. I remember coming home from boarding school and you looking at me in a vague, querying sort of way, as though you were wondering who I was.

"I always tried. . . . You were such a well-behaved child, but we never knew what you were thinking. You kept everything inside. Except when—"

"I asked about my father."

She looked at him with sudden fire in her eyes. "Wasn't Hardie everything a father could possibly be to you?"

"Oh, yes, he had no trouble casting me in the role of his son. I remember once he took me up to the top of the bell tower in the old church. He said from there we could look out over most of the land that had been in his family for four hundred years. He said, 'I'd like to think the Winfields will be here another four hundred years. I want you to take my name, Tony. Be my link to the future.' "

"And what did you say?" She leaned forward eagerly, like someone listening to a story whose outcome is in doubt.

"I asked what choice did I have. Not very gracious of me, was it, in view of my origins."

Cecilia closed her eyes, as though willing her past away, but he knew she wouldn't have changed any of it. She had reveled in the flaming-youth-free-love-defy-convention role written for her by that female Svengali Ella Fontaine. "Hardie loves you, Tony. I know he was rather cold—distant—but he does love you."

"God knows I tried to make him proud of me. But there was always that fear that one day he would have a real son, of his own flesh and blood. If not by you, then—Oh, Christ, I'm sorry."

She pressed her hand to her forehead. "He couldn't have any more children after Ursula. I suppose you were too young to remember or realize the implications, but he contracted mumps and—"

Some half-forgotten memory flickered. "Please don't tell me that he caught mumps from me!"

"I'm afraid so. Oh, it doesn't matter now, Tony. It never mattered really. If only . . . if only we hadn't become so entangled in deception, the three of us. If only I could have believed that it was possible for one love to die and another to be born."

"What do you mean?"

Her long, tapered fingers brushed across her eyes. "Kate loves you, Tony. She may not even know it herself yet, but she does. It doesn't matter that she thought she loved the American once. That's over. Don't make the same mistakes your father and I made."

"Why don't you tell me about those mistakes? Fill me in on all the missing pieces of my life. *Tell me who I am.*"

She stared at him, her lips slightly parted, and he could see her inner turmoil written in the tight lines of her face, the pulse that fluttered in her throat. After an interminable minute she said, "I'm not terribly proud of the life I've lived. I know I've never accomplished anything really worthwhile. I'm about as useful as a piece of bric-a-brac. But I made a solemn promise to someone I loved long ago, and I'm proud of the fact that I've never broken that promise. Please don't ask me to now."

They sat quietly for a while, Tony unable to say anything for fear of unleashing emotions he'd kept tethered for years. Then there was a knock on the door and a disembodied voice announced, "The constable is here to see you, mum."

Cecilia looked at Tony. "Shall we see him downstairs?"

"Why don't you talk to him? You can give him one of the wedding pictures of Kate. You know as much about her movements as I do. Tell the constable I'm not feeling well."

She picked up a framed photograph of Tony and Kate which was standing on his dresser and took it with her.

After she left, he stared at the place where the picture had stood and for some unaccountable reason thought of the album his father kept in the drawer of the writing table in his bedroom at the Berkeley Square flat.

There were photos of Cecilia and Hardie and Ella Fontaine and her brother, Neil. Tony remembered hearing stories about the legendary Ella, his mother's best friend and idol of her youth.

He supposed his father kept the album because of the pictures of Cecilia with Ella, since the only time he had ever heard them mention the names of the Fontaines had been in the heat of argument, when Hardie had said in a voice that chilled Tony's blood, "Don't ever mention her name to me again." Ella and her brother had both been killed in Spain during the Civil War.

Half an hour passed before Cecilia returned, looking more downcast than ever. She closed the bedroom door and said, "The constable will file a report, but he says . . . He seems to agree with you, that Kate disappeared of her own free will. He also pointed out that we're at war. Lord, if anyone else says to me, Don't you know there's a war on, I swear I don't know what I'll do. He says the police and everyone else have their hands full, what with air raids and fires and people without homes. He said a number of the children who were evacuated from the cities to the country have run away from their foster parents and tried to find their way home. He doesn't know who can be spared to look for a runaway wife. At least not until we're really sure she's missing. We're to wait a few days. Oh, Tony, he hinted at another possibility—that her name may turn up on an air-raid casualty list."

Tony felt his breath stop in his throat. "All right, calm down. There's one person who might be able to help us. At least he can find out if she's on her way to America. I'll call Charles Morcambe. He has an office on Baker Street now."

[35]

Kate drove slowly, wedged behind the wheel of the MG with two Germans in their bulky flight suits jammed into the two-seater car beside her. The rain was heavier now, with a cloud cover so low it seemed to press down on the tops of the trees bordering the narrow country lane. Tony would have left the hospital hours ago. He'd have called the police by now. She just had to stay alive until they found her.

The two men spoke to each other in their own language. Kate hadn't let them know she understood and she listened carefully, gathering from what they said that they were members of a bomber crew. They didn't mention when their plane had crashed, or how long they'd been hiding in the woods. One of them was the second pilot and the other was the navigator. The navigator had injured his leg, she didn't know how. They had concealed their parachutes under branches and dead leaves, but were worried about the rest of the bomber crew being captured. Apparently they were the first to bail out.

She wondered if they would believe her if she told them she had no idea where they were, which direction they were heading, or where the south coast was. Probably not. Perhaps they would come to a town or village soon and she could get some help. Whenever she slowed down too much she was prodded with the automatic pistol.

The rain rippled down the windshield in solid sheets. She said in English, "Why don't you let me take you to a hospital? You're hurt. You need a doctor."

"*Nein*. Drive to the coast."

"What will you do when you get there—swim across? Oh!" She gasped as he shoved the gun viciously against her ribs.

Gritting her teeth to keep them from chattering, she drove on. They no doubt planned to steal a boat and leave her body on the beach.

The man next to her was obviously in considerable pain. Unfortunately he was the one who spoke English and who wielded the gun. She couldn't help thinking of Tony being shot down in France, and all the other RAF pilots she and Annette and Jean-Louis had helped to escape. The two Luftwaffe men were a lot worse off. No one in this bomb-battered island was going to help them.

The engine sputtered and coughed. "We're running out of gas—petrol," she announced, relieved. They coasted to a standstill.

There was another quick conference between the Germans. They felt they had traveled enough distance from the probable crash sight now to be out of immediate danger. The pilot said, "Find out where she was going—where she lives."

Kate managed to keep from replying until the question was translated into English. "I live in London. I'm an American, as much a stranger here as you are. I was visiting friends and got lost. I have no idea where we are."

She waited uneasily while he translated, praying that another car would come by, or even a constable on a bicycle. The navigator said, "Get out and walk. You lead the way."

Luckily she'd worn a raincoat. Turning up the collar and pulling on a sou'wester, she stepped into the driving rain and started to walk through deepening puddles.

About half a mile down the lane there was a break in the hedge and a farmer's gate. Kate slowed down hopefully, but she heard the pilot say, "Can you go a little farther, Hans? We're too close to the abandoned car."

ECHOES OF WAR

Looking back, she saw the pilot supporting the injured man with his arm pulled over his shoulder. She remembered to wait until she was ordered to walk on.

Another quarter mile brought a fork in the road, and they took a rutted dirt path. The silhouette of a barn came into view and Kate felt a ray of hope. They were coming to a farm; there would be other people.

Dogs started to bark as they reached a paddock containing a couple of bedraggled horses. A small farmhouse hugged the side of a hillock just ahead. She could just distinguish the shape of the house in the misty rain. No chink of light showed.

Two border collies came bounding around the corner of the house, growling a warning. At the same time a faint yellow glow appeared at the door. A woman's voice called, "Is anyone there?"

The gun was jammed into Kate's side. "Tell her your car ran out of petrol."

Kate hesitated, wondering how she could warn the woman. There was an ominous click from the gun's safety catch. She shouted, "My car ran out of petrol. Do you have a phone?"

"No, but come in out of the rain."

The two dogs herded them toward the house. Kate prayed, Please let her have an enormous husband and half a dozen equal-sized farm laborers.

She was shoved ahead of the men into the house. The woman said, "There's not another house for miles, I'm afraid—" then broke off, her eyes widening as she saw the two Germans. She was young, with a toddler clinging to her skirts. Kate's heart sank. The woman and child appeared to be alone.

"Where is your husband?" Hans demanded. He leaned against the wall, waving the gun at the two women. The pilot moved cautiously across the room to an inner door.

The woman stared at the gun, shaking her head in disbelief. Kate said, "I'm sorry, I think we'd better do as they say. My name's Kate. What's yours?"

"Beryl. Who . . . what . . . ?"

ECHOES OF WAR

"German airmen," Kate began, but the navigator snapped, "Where are the others?"

Beryl said, "Only me and Billy here. My husband's gone and won't be back until"—she caught Kate's wildly rolling eyes, but didn't get their message—"tomorrow." She clutched the child's head as the pilot kicked open the door and disappeared into the next room.

"Bang!" Billy said, mischievous blue eyes peering over his mother's arm at the gun.

The navigator was young, probably no more than twenty, with fair skin and wheat-colored hair. Pain was evident in the clenched lines of his face and dulled eyes. Kate was wondering what her chances of grabbing the gun would be when the pilot came back. "There's no one else here, Hans. Give me the gun now, you must rest. Tell the women to boil water and tear a sheet to make bandages."

Kate stared at the torn and bloody flight suit Hans wore, illuminated now by the kitchen light, and knew that the German's injuries were caused by more than an unluckly parachute landing.

Hans translated, handed the gun to the pilot, then slid to the floor. He rolled to his back, his lips moving as he summoned his last strength to speak again. The pilot had moved to the table and was stuffing Beryl's dinner into his mouth hungrily. He waved the gun at them, indicating that they should go to the man on the floor.

"Oh, my God!" Beryl exclaimed, as full realization hit her, "What are we going to do? They're going to kill us."

Hans whispered raggedly, "We . . . don't kill women."

Kate dropped to her knees to unzip the flight suit. She looked up at Beryl, who was pretty and sturdily built, but obviously terrified for her child, whom she now picked up and held protectively in her arms. Kate said, "You go and find something to use for bandages. And put Billy to bed, if you can. I've had a little nursing experience. I'll see what I can do."

When she tried to ease the flight suit off the navigator's shoulders he moaned and turned deathly pale. The pilot leaped across the room, brandishing the gun. Kate yelled,

"You're going to have to help me. I can't get it off him by myself." She pantomimed undressing the navigator and putting him to bed, wondering if she should speak to him in German, but deciding against it. She wanted them to discuss their plans without fear of being understood.

When they had laid Hans on Beryl's bed and peeled off the flight suit, Kate surveyed his wounds with dismay. His right leg was peppered with shrapnel. The pilot prodded her with the gun, and she said, "Okay, okay. First we'll have to clean the wounds, try to stop the bleeding. But I'm no doctor. I can't probe for shrapnel."

The pilot muttered under his breath that if Hans died, she died. Kate took off her raincoat and sou'wester. It was going to be a long night.

[36]

Charles Morcambe wore the uniform of an army major and the same steel-rimmed glasses. He accepted the brandy Tony offered and then stood with his back to the fireplace. Tony sat down and said, "I didn't really expect you to drive all the way out here. A phone call would have done."

Charles was studying Tony's face with unabashed interest. "Extraordinary what the plastic surgeons can do nowadays, isn't it? Your face isn't half bad. What about your hands? Can they do anything about those scars? And when do the bandages come off your left hand?"

"As soon as the graft heals. Tell me, when did the army grab you?"

"The PM decided we'd be less conspicuous in khaki."

"So you're part of the SOE now?"

Charles blinked. "You've heard of the new organization? What makes you think I'm part of it?"

"Your past experience for one thing. Your Baker Street address for another. You forget I flew some of de Gaulle's people out of France; I'm still in touch with a few of them. I understand Churchill's Special Operations Executive is causing a battle royal among the Foreign Office, the War Office, the Secret Service, and de Gaulle's people. But I'm not really interested in what you're doing, Charles. Tell me, have you learned anything about Kate?"

"Too soon, old chap. She's only been missing for a day and a half. If she's en route to New York, as you suspect, then she'll probably go via Shannon, Lisbon, possibly Portuguese Guinea, then perhaps Brazil, north to Trinidad, on to Puerto Rico, Bermuda. Three or four days in the air, at the very least, before we can inquire in New York about her. That is, if she's able to fly all the way. Very difficult for civilians. Most clipper passages are reserved for diplomats and generals."

"What if she's still in this country?" Tony asked carefully, not wanting to give away to Charles how desperately he hoped that she was.

"We're making inquiries. Nothing yet."

"Then why the hell are you here?"

Charles' smile was deceptively bland. Tony felt his irritability turn to curiosity. Charles was up to something. He had the look of a professor about to spring a surprise quiz on his unsuspecting students. "To see you, old man. I'd been intending to come and visit ever since I learned of your little run-in with the Me 109."

"And instead of popping into the hospital while I was in London, you waited until now so you could waste petrol by driving all the way to Cardovan House. Or was it that you thought I'd be able to fly again soon and you had another job for me?"

"Actually, I did know that the last of your dressings come off in a few days. The doctors tell me you'll need very little in the way of therapy for your hands. You're a quick healer, Tony. You're very fortunate."

"Oh, yes, damn lucky. Why don't you sit down? I keep expecting you to rap my knuckles with a ruler. You didn't come here to talk about my wife, did you?"

Charles sat down in the armchair on the other side of the fireplace. "Of course, I did want to reassure you that I'll do everything I can to find her." He sipped his drink. "The doctors also say your scars will fade somewhat, in time."

"Charles, what is it you want?"

"We're no longer in danger of invasion, you know. Your fighter command pilots have nipped that little problem in the bud. I wonder if instead of going back to Biggin Hill and a new Spitfire or Hurricane, whether you'd like to fly Lysanders instead. When you're fit, of course."

"Lysanders," Tony repeated. "They're made of canvas or wood or cardboard or something—propelled by elastic bands. Ugly squat little machines. Why would I—"

"They have a rugged undercarriage and can land and take off in about four hundred yards. Fitted with an extra fuel tank and stripped of armament, they have a range of up to four hundred and fifty miles."

"So?"

"Very useful for transporting SOE agents to and from France. The pilots call themselves the Moon Squadron, since they fly the week before and the week after the full moon."

"Tell me, are you offering me this assignment because you think I've probably lost my nerve, that I won't be any good in a dogfight in future?"

Charles looked pained. "My dear fellow, you'll need an equal amount of nerve—perhaps even more—to land in enemy territory in the dead of night with contraband cargo and a spy or two aboard. If you're caught, I doubt you'll be given prisoner-of-war status. You'll be turned over to the Gestapo and they'll want to know everything you know about our operations. I don't have to remind you of their methods of obtaining information, do I?"

"I'll think about it, Charles. I take it the job would be strictly voluntary?"

"We thought," Charles said, as though Tony hadn't spoken, "that since there's a bit more training involved, that you could get started on some of it while you're waiting for your hands to finish healing. We'd like to send you up to Scotland."

Tony stared into the fire for a moment, considering. Perhaps that's what he needed to take his mind off Kate. With each passing hour, it seemed more likely that she had gone with Lowery.

There was a sudden burst of conversation in the hall and Ursula flung open the door. She snapped at someone behind her, "Take her up to her room. Go *on*. I'll be there in a minute. Tony, I'm sorry to interrupt, but we've just had terrible news."

Tony felt the room spin. He came out of his chair like a drowning man. "Kate?"

"It's Hardie," Ursula said, her lip quivering. "His ship has been sunk."

[37]

Kate and Beryl surveyed one another across the kitchen table. Billy was still asleep as a watery dawn broke. The German pilot, Günther, leaned wearily against the door, still holding the gun.

Beryl's eyes were smudged with fatigue and fear. "Is the other one going to be all right?" she asked in a whisper.

Kate glanced in Günther's direction, wondering if he understood any English. "I sure hope so. But he needs to have the shrapnel removed or his leg will get infected." She brought up her hand to cover the side of her mouth exposed to Günther and mouthed the words, "When is your husband due back?"

Beryl glanced at the wall clock and held up five fingers.

Kate blew out her breath in a long sigh. Anything could happen in that length of time.

"Günther." A muffled cry came from the bedroom. The pilot motioned with the gun for the two women to precede him. At the same time Billy awakened and called for his mother.

Beryl darted into her son's room and scooped him into her arms before being herded with Kate into the room where Hans lay in bed. His pain had dulled his eyes and settled like a caul over his face. He struggled to try to sit up, but couldn't. Kate felt a stirring of compassion. He may have been guilty of dumping bombs on defenseless civilians, but right now he was a twenty-year-old kid with a mangled leg who would probably bleed to death if he didn't get proper medical attention.

Hans spoke to Günther in hoarse, pleading whispers, trying to persuade him to leave for the coast alone. Günther, however, was sure that if he left his wounded companion behind he would immediately be turned over to the authorities, who would then quickly catch up with Günther.

"Beckfust, Mummy," Billy said plaintively, rubbing his eyes.

"Hush," Beryl said.

Hans whispered in German, "Leave the gun with me. I won't let them go until I'm sure you're safe."

Günther muttered, "You want the gun because you think I'll kill a few Englishmen on the way. I should kill these three right now, then we wouldn't have to bother with them."

"Mein Gott! They're women—a baby."

"They're *enemies*. This is enemy territory. It's our duty as Luftwaffe officers to use any means necessary to escape."

Listening and understanding, Kate stifled a shiver. Billy was tugging at Beryl's hair and becoming hungrier and more restless by the minute.

Kate moved toward the bed, despite Günther's warning gesture with the gun to back away. She said, "Hans, please let her go and feed the child."

Hans translated. He added, "I got a little sleep last night. When you've eaten, I'll guard them while you rest for a couple of hours."

Günther, his eyes almost closed with exhaustion, agreed.

While Beryl took care of Billy, Kate cooked eggs and made toast. When Beryl handed her a bowl of new-laid eggs, Kate exclaimed, "I guess you don't have to worry about the one-a-week ration when you live on a farm."

There was a mournful mooing sound outside and Beryl grimaced. "And that's a disadvantage to living on a farm. We've a couple of cows. The dogs have brought them in for their morning milking. Now what am I going to do?"

Kate placed a plate of eggs on the table. "You eat first,

then go do the milking." Günther reached for the food, but Kate held up her hand to stop him. "No—*nein*—she has to take care of cows." She pointed to the window and imitated the cows' mooing.

Somehow they got through the early part of the morning. Everyone was fed, the cows were milked, and Günther lay down to sleep.

Beryl played nervously with Billy on the floor, building with wooden blocks. Kate sat on the foot of the bed, assessing Hans's condition and wondering if she'd have the nerve to grab the gun.

Perhaps if she talked to him, lulled him into believing she wouldn't try anything? She asked, "Where are you from?"

"Dresden," he answered. "Have you ever been to Germany?"

"Yes, and to Dresden. A lovely city."

Homesickness flickered briefly in his light gray eyes. "I think about home when I—" He stopped, remembering where he was. *When I drop my bombs on English cities and worry about retaliation.* The words didn't have to be spoken, they hung in the air like smoke.

Kate inched imperceptibly closer to him. "Do you have a family there?"

"Parents and two sisters." He blinked rapidly. Kate thought, He's wondering if he'll ever see them again. Damn it, you weren't supposed to be so human, Hans. What if I grab your gun? What if it goes off and I kill you? Why couldn't it have been Günther who got wounded? I could probably blast him without a second thought. But you, you're just an ordinary kid who has to follow orders.

She forced herself to think of prewar Berlin, of what had appeared to be massed millions of Germans endorsing Hitler with their *Sieg heil*. Her hand crept across the quilt toward the motionless shape of his leg. A horrifying thought struck her—that if she were to smash her fist into that wounded leg, taking the gun would be easy.

"Bang, bang!" Billy said suddenly, tiring of the building blocks and pointing his finger at Hans.

Beryl said, "No, no, love. Come here." She grabbed the child and held him, giving Hans a reproachful look.

Hans said to Kate, "Were you on holiday in Dresden?"

Kate thought quickly. Better not say she'd been a tour guide. He might wonder why she didn't speak German. She said, "Yes, I was there just before the war."

A gust of wind sent raindrops pattering against the window, and the room darkened as black clouds raced across the sky. Beryl looked up, her expression anxious. "If we get much more rain, the road turns to mud."

She's thinking her husband might not make it back. Where did he go? Into town probably. I've got to do something now, while Günther is asleep. I'd never be able to get the gun away from him. Kate said, "I visited the Hofkirche. I'm Roman Catholic myself, and I went to the Frauenkirche too. I'd always wanted to see the Ladies' Church—so beautiful, eighteenth-century . . . uh . . . baroque."

Babbling on, she positioned her feet on the floor, tensing her muscles ready to spring, eyes fixed on the gun.

At the last second she couldn't bring herself to attack his wounded leg. Every mangled patient in the hospital seemed to flash through her mind, begging with piteous eyes for her to heal, not hurt. Instead she dived for the hand holding the gun.

The element of surprise, and his weakness, worked for her. The pistol flew from his hand and went skittering across the floor.

Hans struggled to get out of bed as Kate went after the gun, tripping over Billy and falling heavily to the floor. Beryl gave a small scream. Billy gurgled with delight and snatched up the gun. He pointed it at Kate. "Bang!"

Holding her breath, Kate eased herself up on her knees. "Give it to me, Billy. No, don't point it at me."

Beryl cried, "Oh, my God, oh, please!"

Ghastly pale, Hans flopped back weakly onto the pillow, unable to get out of bed. There was blood on the quilt covering his leg.

Before Kate could react to the gun in the child's hand, Günther burst into the room. He grabbed Billy from behind and pulled the gun from small fingers. Beryl screamed, and Kate scrambled to her feet.

Günther spun around to face the sobbing Beryl, then he

deliberately placed the muzzle of the gun to Billy's head. "Tell the mother we want to know exactly when her husband will return. Tell her that if *anyone* appears unexpectedly, I'll kill the boy."

Hans looked at Beryl's fear-stricken face and said, "Don't worry. He won't harm your son if you tell us when your husband will be back. Will anyone else come today?"

"No, nobody will come in that rain." Beryl's voice verged on the shrill edge of hysteria. "Please don't hurt Billy. Oh, God, please don't! Jack—my husband—he won't be here before five o'clock. He'll be on the four o'clock bus from town."

After Günther received the translation, he nodded. "Good. We'll have time to rest, then change into his civilian clothes. I'm going to lock these three in a shed behind the house so we won't have to worry about them. When we leave, we'll take the boy."

"*Nein!*" Kate cried. "Not the boy. If you must take somebody, take me." She had spoken in German. Everyone stared at her.

"So . . ." Günther said.

"You speak German." Beryl's statement sounded like an accusation. "Ask him to put Billy down. Tell him we'll do anything he wants." But Günther was already striding from the room, the boy in his arms, flinging an order to follow him over his shoulder.

There were several outbuildings behind the house, but the shed to which he led them was stoutly built of wood against the sloping side of the hill. Inside there were farm tools and milk cans. Kate gave a small shriek as she came face to face with a pair of dead chickens, strung upside down from the ceiling. Beryl said, "We like to hang them a couple of days before we cook them."

Günther dropped Billy to the floor and slammed the door on them. They heard the padlock click. Billy flew to his mother's arms, and Kate shivered, looking around. "Is there a light?"

"No, there's a lamp somewhere, but we've no paraffin. We should've got coats."

There was some light seeping in through the cracks in the

wood, and rain found its way through the holes in the roof. Kate paced the plank floor, looking at spades, hoes, and forks. She felt the walls, rattled the door. There was no window. It was no use; they'd never break out.

"Maybe the Jerries won't be able to leave before Jack gets home. If this rain keeps up, the road will be nothing but a river of mud," Beryl said helpfully.

"How do we warn him?" Kate asked. "He wouldn't hear us yell. We wouldn't hear him coming. The house is between us and the road."

Beryl wrapped her arms around her child.

They were silent for a moment, listening to the steady downpour of rain. Kate picked up a spade and tried to insert the steel between the door and wall, thinking perhaps she could dislodge the padlock. After a few tries she flung the spade down on the floor in frustration. The floor planks rattled.

"Wait a minute." Kate peered through the scant light at the spade lying on the floor. "Those floor planks look pretty loose." She lifted one of the floor planks. It came up easily, revealing the framing supporting it and dirt and rock beneath.

Beryl said, "We can't get out that way. It's nearly solid rock in the hill; and what bit of clay there is, that'll be harder to shift because it's wet."

Kate picked up the spade. "Maybe we could make enough of a hole under the wall to put Billy through."

"Billy can't go! He's too little," Beryl said in alarm.

"Calm down. Come on, help me get these planks up and start digging. At least it will give us something to do and keep our circulation going. Come on, Billy boy. You can use this trowel, but for Pete's sake don't bop me with it, okay?"

Billy chuckled. "You talk funny."

"Yeah, well, you may hear some funnier words yet when we start hacking at the dirt."

They chipped away bits of rock and clay all morning, making a pathetically small pile of dirt.

Kate's watch had stopped and Beryl didn't wear one, so they had no idea what time it was. They were hungry and miserably cold by the time they heard a key rattle in the padlock. Quickly they dragged milk cans and tools to cover the hole in the floor, then grouped themselves in front of it.

The door opened, swinging wildly in the wind. Günther braced it with his shoulder. He was now dressed in civilian clothes that were slightly too large for him. He flung a child's coat and a tiny pair of Wellington boots on the floor, then shut the door. They heard the padlock snap.

Beryl stared at the coat and boots. "Billy's things. What . . . why . . . ?"

Kate felt a wave of dizziness. The rain continued to pound the roof, and the strong gamy smell of the bloodied chickens assaulted her nostrils.

Beryl clung to her son, crying. "I won't let them take him. I won't."

Kate flung herself at the hole in the floor again with renewed frenzy, banging the rock with her spade. "For God's sake, help me." She punctuated each word with a thrust of the spade, and suddenly a large rock split down the middle.

Dropping to her knees, she began to scoop the sticky clay with her hands. "Look, this stuff has bonded the rocks together like mortar. If we can get these two chunks of rock out of here . . ."

She gave a low whoop of triumph as one piece came free. Beryl came to help her, and minutes later they could see daylight under the shed wall.

Eyeing the opening, Kate then looked at Billy. Beryl drew him into her arms. "No, he's too little. He'd go right into the house."

Kate looked at the small hole. Although she was much taller than Beryl, she wasn't nearly as big around, despite being pregnant. "Okay, I'll go. You may have to push from behind."

Lowering herself to lie on her stomach, she reached into the hole with outstretched arms, feeling the wet ground outside.

It was like going through the neck of a toothpaste tube, feeling jagged rock and sodden wood close around shoulders, squeezing, bruising; then the sticky ooze of wet clay sucking at her. When her head was clear she felt the rain soak her hair, run down her forehead into her eyes. The narrow opening gripped her breasts and she wanted to scream with pain as Beryl tried to shove her through.

"No! Wait, I'm stuck."

Okay, keep calm. Breathe in. No, deflate lungs. Let the air out. There! Her upper body was free. The sense of panic and claustrophobia subsided. Beyond her Beryl was offering words of encouragement and guiding her hips.

Sorry, little baby in there, if I'm squashing you, Kate thought as she came to the most difficult part—hips and stomach. Panic began to choke her again. Oh, God, what if I hurt the baby? No, don't be silly, you're only in the fourth month. How big can it be? And anyway, it's floating in a protective sac of fluid.

She was out! She stood up uncertainly, shaking the rain from her hair. Now what? She looked at the rear of the house. She couldn't simply walk around the house and go back down the road. They might see her, or the dogs would alert the Germans. Nor did she know which direction led where.

Crouching beside the shed again, she called to Beryl, "Which way to the nearest house?"

"Half a mile down the lane you turned off to our road." There was a pause. "You could take the horse. Would you know how to harness it? They can't see the paddock from the house."

"Horsey," Billy's voice piped up.

Kate considered. She'd never been on a horse in her life, but—No, she wouldn't know how to get on the damn beast, or guide it.

Beryl said, "The mare's gentle, she'd let you ride her." A length of rope was shoved through the hole. "Slip it around her neck and tie it. Pull whichever way you want her to go."

Kate picked up the rope. *Why me, Lord?* She crossed the wet grass carefully, dodging from the outbuildings to the orchard.

It seemed to take forever to skirt the house and, when she emerged, as Beryl had predicted, the road was under water. The paddock was on a slight rise and was dry, she could see.

There was an open expanse, a muddy field, to cross. She went as quickly as the disintegrating ground would allow.

She had just reached the paddock gate when the dogs began to bark excitedly. Two black forms came hurtling toward her. Muttering a prayer for help, she yanked open the gate and went inside the paddock.

One of the horses backed away skittishly, but the other stood placidly as Kate approached. "Nice horse . . . whoa . . . be good now." The mare gave her a docile stare.

She slipped the rope around the mare's neck and fumbled with cold fingers to tie it. The rope was tied. Now, how to mount? Oh, Lord, if I ever complain about nice warm subways again, please strike me dead! She tugged on the rope, leading the horse over to the fence.

She climbed onto the fence, still holding the rope, pulled until the mare came close, then threw her leg across the wide back. God, it was *wide*. She felt as though she were doing the splits. And so high—the ground was a dizzying distance below.

A wave of nausea went through her as she smelled the wet animal odor and they lurched forward.

The other horse bolted through the open gate. Kate's mount followed, at a faster pace than she would have chosen.

She was rocking from side to side alarmingly and tried to dig her knees into the mare's flanks to keep her balance. Oh, Lord, this was never going to work. The mare simply went in the direction she chose, ignoring Kate's frantic rope-pulling.

Luckily the mud slowed her gallop, or perhaps it was only a canter. Whatever it was, it was too fast for Kate's liking. She clutched the mane in terror, letting the rope dangle.

The rain came down in torrents, black clouds hugging the tops of the trees, it seemed. At least the mare seemed to be heading for the lane.

Okay, girl, go wherever you want. But how am I going to stop her or get off her?

There was a harsh shout from behind her. "Stop! Come back or I'll shoot." Günther's voice, yelling in German, seemed a fitting accompaniment to all of Kate's other terrors. She froze, lying along the horse's neck, her arms welded to the animal, unable to look back at the German or urge the mare forward, or even to stop.

A shot pinged past her, gone in an instant, quickly followed by a second one that grazed the mare's rump. She whinnied in pain and shock and bolted.

Now Kate clung for dear life, fingers tangled in the coarse mane, prayers tumbling from her lips.

Ahead was the lane, bordered by hawthorne hedges. The mare, feeling her hooves strike more solid ground, galloped even faster.

Kate caught only a glimpse of the approaching lorry, heard the squeal of brakes and honking of the horn—then the mare reared and plunged, and Kate went down, tumbling into a vortex of jolting pain, feeling the hard wet ground, hearing her own cry of fear and agony.

[38]

Tony stood at the top of the bell tower of the ancient church that overlooked Winfield land. Misty rain borne on an early dusk obscured his view, but still he stared in the direction of Cardovan House, remembering the man who had chosen to be his father, even during all those lost years when Tony had thought of him as a stranger.

He wasn't sure when he had begun to think of Hardie as "my father." Perhaps long before his conscious mind dared admit the fact. How very ironic, but how very human, that he should realize only after his father's death how much they had loved one another.

His father's ship was confirmed sunk, lost to enemy action somewhere in the South Atlantic, hit by at least two torpedoes while en route to her home port after delivering troops to Egypt by the long Cape of Good Hope way. The route around the tip of South Africa had been used because the Mediterranean and Suez Canal waters were too hazardous to risk valuable men and supplies.

Tony supposed, knowing his father, that he would have been glad at least that his ship was sunk on the way back, after delivering men and supplies to the beleaguered Eighth Army in North Africa.

Strange how, on looking back, Tony was able to remember so many times when his father had been there—to dispense advice, to explain something baffling or frightening, to lean on. And, except for rigid discipline, which was probably necessary in view of Cecilia's indulgences, there had been few real hurts or injustices at his adoptive father's hands.

Now that he was irrevocably gone, Tony realized that most of their estrangement had been his own doing. He'd been a prisoner of his own fear that his father would replace him or cast him out. With a sick sense of futility it came to him that he'd waited all his life for something that would never happen. Tony supposed that regrets went hand in hand with bereavement, but still couldn't help wishing passionately for another chance to make amends.

Oddly, it was he who secretly hoped that his father would be found alive, floating in a life jacket, or cast up on some reef; while Cecilia, once her initial grief subsided, accepted the Admiralty's final word, that Hardie was not among the survivors picked up by the troop carrier's escort ships.

When the memorial service concluded, Tony couldn't bear to return to the house with the mourners. He had surprised himself by attending the service in the first place. He wasn't sure how long he had stood here beside the great bells that had remained silent since the onset of the war, waiting to ring out either the news that German invaders had landed or that victory was won.

Tony ran his hand over the cold surface of the nearest bell, the image of his father so clear in his mind that he felt he could almost touch him.

Blue shadows had crept like silent invaders across the land, and the stillness of evening had settled almost unnoticed upon the stone and stained glass of the medieval church. Caught in that fleeting moment between day and night, beset by memories, Tony wished he could believe in a hereafter.

"Anthony, are you still up there?"

He jumped, startled. Ursula's voice rang with hollow echoes.

He called back, "Yes. Don't come up; I'll come down. The steps are treacherous at dusk."

She still wore her black mourning dress. Her fair hair gleamed silvery against the stark contrast of her dress. She watched him come down the stone staircase, and he cringed inwardly at the look in her eyes that told him she couldn't bear the sight of his scarred face. Reaching her side, he took her hand and led her to the nearest pew. "Sit with me for a minute. I'm not ready to go back to the house."

"Clive's with Cecilia. She's all right. I don't know how she could put on such a show of grief when she and Hardie hadn't lived together for years." Ursula dabbed her eyes with a sodden handkerchief. "I'm going to miss him so. You know I was planning to go and live with him in London when the war's over. First I lose you and now him."

"I'm still here."

"But you're married to that woman."

The knife twisted in his heart again. Kate, oh, dear beloved Kate, can you know how I miss you? How I still feel the imprint of your body on mine, how my mind refuses to let you go?

"Anthony . . ."

"Yes?"

"What will you do if she comes back? You surely can't forgive this—"

"Let's wait and see, shall we?"

"I don't think you should forgive her, no matter what. I practically caught them in the act at Hardie's flat, you know. I mean, there's no doubt whatsoever that they were lovers."

"Please drop it, will you? At the moment it's all I can do to cope with Father's death."

"It sounds so funny to hear you call them Mother and Father. I don't think Cecilia likes it, but she's afraid to say anything to you. I used to think she insisted on us using their first names because it made her feel younger, but now I'm not so sure. I thought I understood them—I mean, that Hardie found out about her and Clive and that was why he moved out."

"He did think they were having an affair, but I'm not so sure. Father might not have been entirely blameless either."

She sighed and leaned her head against his shoulder. "I didn't mind when I was little how she was always so wrapped up with her parties and her strange friends, because I had my music and I had you. I used to daydream that we were left all alone in the world and you'd promised to take care of me forever."

"One of these days the right man will come along for you."

"I always compare them to you and they fail miserably. Oh, I know you've been hard to get along with lately, and it's not as much fun being with you, but when your scars fade and this business of your marriage to that woman is settled, you'll be your old self again."

"No, love, I'll never be that self again. My scars are with me for life. Just as my love for Kate will be with me for as long as I live, whether I see her again or not."

She stood up abruptly. "I came to tell you that Charles Morcambe has to leave, and he wants to talk to you before he goes." She ran down the aisle away from him and he heard her crying as she went.

He met Charles halfway through the topiary garden, his slight frame dwarfed by a rearing privet horse. Charles peered through his glasses, as though assuring himself that Tony was still the same man. "Got to get back to Baker Street. Just wanted to say *au revoir*. You'll get your orders in a few days. Unless you need compassionate leave? Though I'd say Cecilia is bearing up rather well."

"Don't post me anywhere until I know for certain Kate is back in the States."

"Yes. I'll be in touch as soon as I hear."

Tony had just finished picking at his breakfast the following morning when Cecilia appeared. She wore a suit and hat, her gloves and handbag in her hand. She was a little pale, but otherwise composed. "Tony, I want you to come somewhere with me."

"Now?"

"Yes, please. You don't have to dress up. Just put on a jacket and bring your mac. It looks like we're in for more rain."

"I'm not sure I feel like—"

"Please. It's frightfully important. I've got to talk to you and I can't do it here. If we don't do it today, I'm afraid we never will."

Curious, he put down the newspaper he'd been reading. Cecilia was quiet, almost childlike in her expression and movements. He asked, "Where are we going?"

"Stoke Poges. To St. Giles Church."

Thomas Gray had written his "Elegy" here and was buried in the churchyard. The church dated back to sometime before the fourteenth century. Cecilia wandered among the ancient tombstones, her head bent in silent contemplation.

Tony waited, studying barely discernible epitaphs. He supposed his mother was going through some private ritual of death, and although he would have preferred to stay near a phone in case some word of Kate came, he waited patiently.

The rain had stopped, but the spring day was overcast, heavy with the threat of another cloudburst. To pass the time, he tried to recall the lines of Gray's "Elegy Written in a Country Churchyard" as Cecilia paused for a moment beside a mottled tombstone, then moved on. Perhaps if they'd had a body to bury, his father's death would have seemed more real to him.

How did it go? "The curfew tolls the knell of parting day, The lowing herd wind slowly o'er the lea, The ploughman homeward plods his weary way, And leaves the world to darkness and to me."

Cecilia came back toward him, raising her eyes sadly to meet his. "What are you thinking? That I've gone mad?"

"I was trying to remember the 'Elegy.' " He was glad she hadn't worn black. It would have seemed hypocritical. He said, "The verse I like best is, 'Full many a gem of purest ray serene The dark, unfathom'd caves of ocean bear: Full many a flower is born to blush unseen, And waste its sweetness on the desert air.' "

She gazed up at the church and quoted, " 'The struggling pangs of conscious truth to hide, To quench the blushes of ingenuous shame, Or heap the shrine of Luxury and Pride, With incense kindled at the Muse's flame.' "

"Very good. You say the lines with all of your old theatrical skill."

"They're both dead now. I think that releases me from my promise. I used to wonder how I'd tell you—*if* I'd tell you when the time came."

She looks like a sleepwalker, he thought. She needs Clive's shoulder to lean on more than mine. I probably should have asked him to come along.

Cecilia said softly, "She loved it here. That's why I wanted you to come. Even though she and Neil are buried in Spain, somehow I can feel close to her here."

"Ella Fontaine?" Tony asked, surprised. He'd believed it was his father's death ritual Cecilia performed, and all the time she was grieving for her friend—dead since the Spanish Civil War, but lost to Cecilia long before that. He felt a stirring of curiosity again. He thought of the photo album, the pictures of Cecilia and Ella and . . . *Neil Fontaine?* Could it have been . . . ?

"She was such a brilliant, mystical creature. No one like her ever walked the earth before or since, and I . . . I looked a little like her, they said, but of course I was a pale shadow, only a reflection on a still pond. While she . . . she was flash and fire and truth and beauty." She was silent for a moment, her eyes drifting over Tony's face. He wondered if she was seeing it without the scars. Then she said, "There's a bench over there. Let's go and sit down, shall we?"

She arranged herself on the bench with her customary attention to pose. Legs crossed at the ankles, hands folded on her lap. She always seemed to be sitting for an unseen portrait artist. She didn't look at Tony as he sat beside her.

"I simply couldn't keep up. Oh, she swept me along with her for a while. I don't think she meant to hurt us—either of us, really. It was just her way, but then it was time for her to move on, to devote all of that mercurial energy of hers to something else, someone else. People said, after they died, that the Fontaines had been looking for a way to die dramatically from the day they were born. They were twins, you know, but not alike, not really. Neil turned his genius inward, created his plays, wrote essays, while Ella—" Overcome, Cecilia buried her face in her hands.

Tony slipped his arm across her shoulders, wondering

why they were sitting on a damp bench talking about a man and woman long dead, unless . . . "Mother, was Neil Fontaine my father?"

She looked up, her mouth dropping open. "Your father? Oh, no! Oh, Tony, dear, no! Perhaps I'd better begin at the beginning. It was 1912 or perhaps early 1913 when I met Hardie. He came backstage after I had a small speaking part in a forgettable play. How can I describe him in those days? A lot like you, I suppose, a man whom women both desire and fear because of that intensity he seems to radiate. You look at such a man and know there'll be no going back once you're committed to him. I fell completely, irrevocably, wildly in love with James, Earl of Hardmoor. There was nothing I wouldn't have done to get him. But . . . There was Ella."

"He disapproved of your friendship? She was a bit of a female rouée, from what I hear. If you loved him so much, why didn't you end your friendship with her?"

"You're jumping to conclusions again. Hear me out. I loved Ella too. I'd known her much longer. She was the shining light in my life, even though she dominated me in every way. I needed to be with her. She was my friend, and I don't think men are as deeply committed to friendship as women are. Losing a close woman friend can be much more devastating than the loss of a lover—or even a husband."

"But she was a bad influence on you, with her views on women's rights and free love, I take it."

Cecilia said quickly, "You still don't understand! He didn't love me. He loved *her*. Your father fell madly in love with *Ella*. How could he not? Everyone did. She was a blazing comet streaking across the heavens. She could have achieved so much if she hadn't wanted everything. She ran for Parliament, you know, but lost the seat to a little fat man whose name I've forgotten. Furious, she went with Neil to Addis Ababa. Neil was always traveling to exotic places. While they were gone, Hardie was lonely. I was lonely. We saw one another. Oh, I knew it was only because I looked a little like her, but it was enough. I tried so hard to make myself into her image. Then all at once 1914 was upon us, and the Kaiser's troops were massing for war."

She was silent for a moment, one tapered finger smoothing an invisible wrinkle in her skirt as though tracing the direction their lives had taken. "There was such a restlessness in the young men that year. Ella felt it too. She came back to London to try to work for peace. Before that she never really encouraged Hardie. But, I don't know, when he joined the navy, I suppose . . . I don't think their affair lasted more than a few days, perhaps only hours. Ella would have made love to him as another woman gives a man a farewell kiss. How could she have known that for him the commitment was forever?"

Tony searched his mind for the memory of those photos in the album, trying to bring the elusive Ella Fontaine into focus. Cecilia had never visited the flat in Berkeley Square. His father had kept those pictures because Ella was on them. Now that he thought about it, except for the portrait in oils his father had commissioned of Cecilia, most of the old photographs were of both women. Poor Cecilia, no wonder her life had been such a masquerade.

She went on: "I was heartbroken. His ship sailed, and Ella took up with a very famous actor. They went to America together. Then a few months later she was back in London and called me. She was all alone in a mews house the actor owned. I can see her now, a stunning woman, enormous expressive eyes, a wild lion's mane of tawny hair. She wore scarlet, I remember, and she walked back and forth, the chiffon whispering about her body. I wanted to comfort her and I wanted to kill her. I suppose I wanted to *be* her. She said, 'Did you sleep with James just before he sailed?' And I said, No, I'd never slept with him."

Tony eased his arm to the back of the bench. Sometimes the new skin pulled and twitched like a shrinking piece of cloth.

"Ella was astonished, contrite, amused in a way. She said, 'Well, that dishes that little plan.' I said, 'I love James. Why did you take him away from me?' She said, 'I didn't intend to, Cecie, honestly. And you know, for a minute I thought I had a way to solve both of our dilemmas.' Then she told me she wished she hadn't let passion sweep them away. She said, 'I don't know where my wits were, to get caught like this. Listen, Cecie, a woman I know just died having an abortion. She bled to death in some filthy back street, and I'm not going to risk it.' "

Everything dropped neatly into place. "Nineteen-fourteen," Tony said, his voice echoing around the tombstones. "The year I was born."

The rest of the story was at once simple and complex. Ella Fontaine, pregnant with the Earl's child; Cecilia, madly in love with him. Ella had hatched a vague plan to go away, have the baby, then pass it off as Cecilia's, in order to induce him to marry her. Cecilia could write and tell him while he was away at sea and unable to make an honest woman of her. The flaw in Ella's plan had been that Cecilia had never slept with him.

Ella had laughed, shrugged it off, and said she'd simply never tell him. She'd have the child and put it up for adoption. Cecilia couldn't bear the thought of this. The baby belonged to the two people she loved most in the world. She begged Ella to allow her to adopt the child, and, characteristically, Ella then went ahead with the charade of pretending the baby was born to Cecilia, even registering her name on Tony's birth certificate. The price she extracted from Cecilia was a promise never to let the Earl know that Tony was Ella's and his child.

How could poor Cecilia have foreseen that when he returned from the war he would court her? Three years had passed, and Ella was again abroad. Cecilia thought, wrongly, that her small son was a badge of honor, that bearing a child out of wedlock somehow put her into the same class as the flamboyant Ella, and that was why James, Earl of Hardmoor, suddenly found her irresistible. After all, Cecilia was something of a heroine to the Bohemian crowd of friends she had inherited from Ella and Neil.

Tony felt his breath slowly leave his lungs, draining away like air from a punctured balloon. Had his father taken up with Cecilia because of her physical resemblance to the woman he loved and then, having married her, found he couldn't live with the vacuous shell she proved to be? Or had he genuinely cared for her? Tony didn't know whether to laugh or cry. "You never told him?"

"I promised. I swore to Ella I wouldn't." Cecilia's voice trembled.

"All those years, all those wasted years, you let us both believe—Good God, you even let him *adopt* me!"

She was weeping now. "How could I tell him? He would have left me, gone searching for Ella. You don't understand how I loved him. I would have done anything to get him and to keep him."

"I remember once hearing him say he didn't want to hear her name again. I thought because he disliked her."

"He loved her. I suppose when I talked about her he couldn't bear it. He told me we were both to forget her. Then, after we were married and Ursula was born, I think the pain eased a little. He told me he loved me. I didn't believe him. She was always there between us. I used to be terrified he would see her in you."

"Did she ever come to see me?"

"Oh, yes. Before James came home from the war, yes, many times. When you were a small baby, she'd scold me for spoiling you, make me promise I'd let you grow up to be strong and brave. But she disappeared on one of her jaunts just before James came home. He never let me invite her to Cardovan House after we were married."

Was there any point in pondering the imponderables? Tony wondered. How different everyone's lives might have been had they been stripped of deception. How Cecilia, so weak in other respects, had maintained a lifelong loyalty to her friend. And the wild, doomed Ella Fontaine, what of her, the mother he'd never known?

"I always wondered," Tony said. "Whose son did he believe I was? You'd never tell me who my father was—I see why now—but surely you must have had to tell him?"

"I told him it was Ella's brother. I thought it might explain any Fontaine family likeness you might have."

"You know, Cecilia, I believe my father did love you. But you shut him out, surrounded yourself with hangers-on—Clive."

"Clive accepted me for what I was," Cecilia said with

sudden spirit. "The incident that caused your father to move out of the house was so unjust. Your father had been away on business, and I'd heard he was seeing another woman. I don't know if it was true, but I called Clive, and, like the dear friend he is, he came. We were in my bedroom because I was hiding the ravages of a day of crying from the servants. Clive has never been more than a dear friend. He's not even capable of being a lover."

Tony thought about Clive and wondered why no one had realized that before now, when it suddenly seemed so obvious.

Cecilia turned and looked at him, touched his scarred cheekbone. "Your father did love you, you know. I think perhaps, if he hadn't, I might have told him the truth. But he couldn't have loved you more than he did. And even when he moved out, still he didn't insist on a divorce. I could always hope he'd come back, but not if he knew Ella and I had deceived him."

Tony stood up and extended his hand to her. "Come on, let's go home. Your bombshell has detonated, but the blast hasn't really registered yet."

[39]

There were moments when the smothering veil was snatched away and she saw and heard clearly what was going on, but the price she paid was unbearable pain, and Kate begged them to let her go back to that shadowland where nothing was real.

Faces came and went. Some of them she recognized, some were strangers. A young woman and a little boy, a florid-faced man at her side, cap in hand. Doctors. Nurses. Tony . . . He was a stranger too, of course, now.

Brisk medical voices gave orders, chastised, cajoled. "Drink this. Turn over. Lie still. Swallow this tablet. Wake up."

She dreamed she was running endlessly through the topiary garden at Cardovan House, only instead of bushes trimmed into the shape of animals, they were now all carved into human forms. Some had missing parts. Arms and legs gone, faces burned off. The smaller ones were children, babies. The mutilations were awful.

Someone sobbed piteously. Someone called for her husband. A blitz victim, probably. Well, there was nothing Kate could do. She was only a BAD. Not that the doctors did all that much. God in heaven, when they said they practiced medicine, that sure as hell was what they meant—practiced. *BAD?* No, Kate wasn't bad. She hadn't been unfaithful to

Tony. She loved him. But he'd tried to kill her. Why? Was this all a horrible dream? Where was she, anyway?

Kate opened her eyes to bright sunshine flooding a hospital ward. She looked down at the outline of her body under a threadbare sheet, starched within an inch of its life. She looked shrunken somehow. A screen separated her bed from the others in the ward. All she could see was a window and one empty bed opposite hers. The British didn't believe in putting anyone who wasn't in critical condition in a private room. That was a good sign.

She slid her arms cautiously from under the sheet and held them up for inspection. Some ugly bruises and lacerations, but no casts, thank God. Her legs were stiff, but she moved her feet and found to her great relief that neither of her legs was encased in plaster. She'd been lucky—no broken bones.

Lying still for a minute, she recalled all that had happened until the moment she saw the approaching army lorry. She wasn't aware at first of the bulky pads between her legs. Or of the telltale stickiness.

Oh, no! Oh, dear God, please no!

She sat up, clutching her stomach, and screamed, "Nurse!"

Scurrying footsteps, the screen snatched back. A young VAD appeared, her expression sympathetic. "I'm sorry, Mrs. Winfield, I didn't know you were awake."

"My baby." Kate's voice cracked. "What have they done to me?"

The VAD bit her lip. "I'll fetch the doctor." She turned and fled.

Kate waited, running her hands over her abdomen, feeling tears prick her eyes. She knew even before the doctor came what he was going to say.

An older man, with a soft Scottish burr. "So very sorry, Mrs. Winfield. We did what we could, but the fall . . . The horse kicked you too, we think. It could have been even worse. You could have been killed if the driver hadn't seen you in time to swerve. You're a healthy young woman. There'll be other babies. Ironic, wasn't it, that the lorry was loaded with Home Guards searching for the Germans.

They'd been combing the countryside all day, going house to house."

Funny how unimportant even the most critical matters can become when all's said and done. Kate didn't care about the Home Guards, or the Germans, or anything else. She wanted to know about her baby. Had it been a boy or a girl? Would it have been incredibly good-looking like Tony, or perhaps just impulsive like herself? Tears slipped down her cheeks and she began to weep.

The doctor patted her shoulder. "Your husband is waiting outside. I'll send him in."

"No!" Kate scrubbed at her eyes. "Not yet. Let me wash my face and comb my hair."

The VAD said, "I'll help you."

A few minutes later Kate looked at herself in a hand mirror. She looked haggard, as bereft as she felt. It didn't matter. "All right, send him in."

She wondered if she'd have the strength to talk to Tony. She felt empty, hollow almost, and so inwardly focused that she doubted she'd be able to comprehend what he might be feeling or thinking, even if he were to tell her in great detail. Her own body and mind had been so completely geared toward the child she had been carrying that her sense of loss obliterated all other feelings.

Kate watched with dulled eyes as Tony walked the length of the ward toward her. He was in uniform again. His scars were less livid. Strange how his face was both the same and different. She observed him almost impersonally, as one would an interesting stranger.

When he reached her bed, he put the screen back to give them privacy, then stood looking at her with unspoken questions in his eyes as he asked, "How are you feeling?"

She tried to hide a wince of pain as a violent cramping began, accompanied by another rush of blood. Tony bent as though to kiss her, and she said, "Please, don't touch me."

He straightened up at once, turned to reach for a chair. When he faced her again his expression was unreadable. "Kate, I'm sorry about the baby—and everything that happened to you."

"Where were you when I needed you?" She closed her eyes, sighed. "I know, you were in the hospital waiting for me. But damn it, couldn't you have called out the fire brigade, sent a posse after me—something, anything?"

His eyes were filled with his own suffering. "I'm sorry," he said again helplessly. "We thought— We didn't know. Your friend Lowery had left the country, and we thought—"

Her eyes flew open angrily. "You thought I'd gone home with Wade?" she asked incredulously. "Without a word to anyone? Just like that? Poof, Kate's gone. Oh, Tony, if you don't know me any better than that, what hope is there for us?"

"Kate, nothing I say now is going to make any sense to you. I think perhaps we both need time to lick our wounds. Too much happened too quickly to both of us. Perhaps it's the accelerated pace of everyone's life in wartime."

She lay still, trying not to think of the grinding pain in her abdomen, ignoring those other, sharper pains.

He said, "My father was killed."

"I'm sorry, he was a fine man," she said automatically.

But not as sorry as I am that our baby was killed and our marriage was killed, and, oh, Tony, has our love been killed too? How did it happen to us? Disaster crept in almost unnoticed, and we let it tear apart all we'd built. It came disguised as Wade and Ursula and a war.

"His ship was torpedoed," Tony said, looking beyond her for a moment into space. "I've a rather unusual story to tell you about my father and Cecilia and me, sometime when you're feeling better and we've both had time to reflect. Is there anything you need?"

Yes, she wanted to say. I need your love and support. I need your baby back inside me. I need the world to be at peace. She shook her head, too drained to really care.

"I'm not going back to Biggin Hill. I've been transferred to another squadron. You can live at Cardovan House, of course, or wherever you choose. I've instructed my bankers to place funds at your disposal. However, if you're thinking of going home to the States, the transfer of funds could get tricky—"

"No," she interrupted. "I won't be leaving England just yet."

His eyes searched her face, and she knew he wanted to ask her about Wade, but she was damned if she was going to make it easy for him. He said, "Some newspaper reporters have been hanging about wanting to interview you about your experience with the Germans."

"Get rid of them, would you?"

"Cecilia and Ursula were here earlier. I told them I'd let them know when you were up to having visitors."

"Ursula? What does she want—to gloat?"

"She's quite contrite, as a matter of fact. Kate, you were very ill. We nearly lost you. Ursula's sorry about what happened to you and—"

"Our baby?" she finished for him, feeling the knife twist in her insides again. "It was *our* baby, you know."

The grafted skin on his face was very white, or perhaps the color had drained away, like the imprint of a slap. He said, "I never really believed it was Lowery's child. I suppose I wanted to hurt you, as you'd hurt me. Oh, God, Kate, how can I tell you how sorry I am?"

"And now you expect the background violins will rise to a crescendo and I'll say I'm sorry too, and all the hurt will be wiped away? Sorry, Tony, I'm not quite that forgiving. It's strange, but right now I don't give a damn what you thought, or Ursula thought, or Wade thought. I can't do anything about any of that. At this moment I'm just concerned with myself."

"I just want you to know that I made up my affair with the WAAF. There's never been another woman in my life since I met you. I . . . it wasn't just Lowery. I was afraid you'd pity me." There was desperation in his voice now and raw pleading in his shattered eyes. "Kate, I love you."

Her cramping abdomen felt as if it were on fire. She clutched her body under the sheets, trying to press away the pain. Perspiration was forming in stinging droplets under the hair hanging over her forehead. "We seem to have a hell of a time getting our declarations of love in sync, don't we?" The words came out in a breathless rush, torn from a sense of unutterable loss and physical agony and a need to remove herself from the perceived source of it all.

"Perhaps . . ." Tony began, his face stricken.

"On your way out," Kate said, beginning to pant, "would you please ask the nurse to come to me. I'm hemorrhaging."

She really wanted to laugh at the look on his face as he raced away shouting for doctors and nurses, but when she opened her mouth the laughter sounded like muted sobs.

[40]

The special-duty Lysander skimmed apple trees and blackberry brambles and bumped down gently on a buttercup-dotted meadow. Tony looked over his shoulder at his passenger, a gaunt man with cadaverous hollows around his eyes. "England, home, and glory," Tony announced in English, then told him in French that he was safely on British soil.

This particular "Joe" was too frail to show any visible signs of enthusiasm as Tony helped him from the "Lizzie." The man had spent months in Gestapo hands and his face seemed to be set in a permanent wince, while his undernourished body carried scars far worse than Tony's burns. The French agent had told Tony he'd been unable to use his lethal capsule because the Gestapo had found it first. He'd begged them to kill him.

As they walked across the airstrip together, the Joe looked around him in dazed interest. Tony wondered again if the man were a Gestapo plant. His escape from them seemed too fantastic to be true, but the SOE was pretty canny about such matters. He'd leave it to Charles and the others in Baker Street to worry about that.

"We call this place Gibraltar Farm," Tony said. "Wonderful sense of history here—the Roman road, the great white way that starts from *Ad Pontes* on the Thames, passes through the village to reach Godmanchester and Ermine Street. When the Romans left, the Danes came. The Viking conquerors constructed fortifications, and now here we are."

Several months had passed since Tony was posted to Tempsford for "special duties." Flying SOE agents in and out of occupied Europe had become almost routine, but never ordinary. Tony had as many narrow escapes to relive as any other pilot in the Moon Squadron.

He also knew that he had received training above and beyond what was required of most of the pilots who flew the Lysanders, Halifaxes, and Hudsons over Nazi territory. He understood that he was probably biding Charles Morcambe's time until that special training would be useful. When Charles sent him to Scotland, he'd said it was a time filler until his burns healed, but Tony knew better.

After delivering the silent Joe to the debriefing room, Tony went back to his quarters. He paused for a moment before going inside, savoring the poignance of the summer day. A bird twittered on the roof, a breeze passed by on its way to cool distant woods. It was a lazy summer day when the world should have been at peace. In the daylight, Gibraltar Farm might indeed have been only rich farmland, but on moonlit nights airplanes emerged from camouflaged hangars to carry anonymous men and women into hostile territory; and all the ghosts of the Roman legions and ancient Vikings stirred and proudly remembered a thousand years of history.

Tony was due for leave. The week of the moon was now over, and he could go up to London for a few days. He'd seen Kate only once since her release from the hospital. She'd been accepted as a student nurse at a teaching hospital in London and had only a couple of hours to spare to see him.

They had a meal together and talked like polite strangers. He couldn't tell her anything about the Moon Squadron, and perhaps she misinterpreted his reticence. She had said merely, "I work on the wards, as well as studying, and don't have much time. If there's anything special you want to tell me . . ."

Anything special. He'd studied the menu. Most of the items had been scratched out as food shortages grew more severe. *Yes, Kate, I want to tell you that I love you, need you, and want you with a yearning that transcends death itself, but you sit there wearing that businesslike expression that stops me cold.* Aloud, he said, "I just wondered how you were. If you had fully recovered from—"

"The miscarriage? Oh, yes." She gave him a cool smile. "How about you? Do you like your new assignment?"

"Uh, yes, it's interesting." He looked up as an elderly waiter approached. "I suppose the shepherd's pie?"

He took her back to her flat afterwards, but she didn't invite him in. She said, "Tony, I'm still Catholic. I don't believe in divorce. But, of course, you do whatever you like."

What he would have liked was to take her in his arms and kiss her until that icy composure melted. He wanted to embrace her so much that he had to knot his hands into fists behind his back. "Oh, Kate, how did we ever make such a mess of things? I don't suppose you'd want to try again?"

For a moment she'd stared at him, her lovely eyes searching his face. Hers was one gaze that didn't make him instantly conscious of his scars. She said, "The way things are right now, I don't think it would be a good idea to even try. We both have too many other things on our minds. We'd have a couple of hours together, like tonight, or maybe a few days' leave. We'd be lucky to even get our time off together. I don't want to go through that again. The not knowing what's happening when we're apart, the endless goodbyes. I can't take that again just now."

He'd stood staring at her closed front door long after she'd gone inside. Her scars weren't as visible as his, but perhaps would be slower to heal. He wrote to her. Friendly notes, cards. He tried phoning her at the hospital, but she asked him not to do that.

Now the summer had almost passed, and surely it was time to try again. He loved Kate, forever and irrevocably. He no longer even cared that once she had loved Wade Lowery. Life was simply too damned short for meaningless pride. He felt a surge of hope, confidence that enough time had now passed to repair the damage.

For one thing, his own private ghosts had been laid to rest—his father, the beautiful reckless mother he'd never known. He even got along better with Cecilia nowadays. It was so much easier to accept her now. And Ursula, having at last realized that he was not going to be magically transformed back into the adoring and unscarred brother she had worshipped, even she released her hold on him. She was being energetically courted by a senior naval officer, years older than she.

Too excited to sleep when he thought about seeing Kate again, he tossed and turned and finally gave up. Dressing again, he peered into the mirror, fingering scars and alien eyelids. A summer tan had left the stitchery of the grafts more pronounced, but he disliked the pallor of those who avoided the sun. Kate wouldn't find the scars repulsive, he was sure.

When he walked into the officers' mess he saw Charles Morcambe alone at a table, waiting. Tony went over to him, unsuspectingly, he thought later. "Hello, Charles, what are you doing here? Waiting for Miss Muffet to sit down beside you?"

"I believe it was the *spider* who sat down beside *her*," Charles said with his usual humorless preciseness. "I was waiting for you. Will you take a stroll with me so we can talk privately?"

Warning signals were flashing in Tony's mind. The training in Scotland, his knowledge of both French and German, his familiarity with Hitler's territory. Charles and his cohorts at the SOE would be foolish to keep him on merely as a Lysander pilot, as essential as that service was. He said, "Very well. But I must tell you, I'm going up to London on leave, and whatever you want me for will have to wait until I get back."

Charles' eyes were crystal beads behind his glasses. "Naturally you can have your weekend in London. You can't go until the next moon, in any event."

* * *

ECHOES OF WAR

It was one of those oversights that seem impossible, but Tony found his letter to Kate, unsealed and unstamped, stuck into the pocket of his dress uniform. The train was on the outskirts of the city, packed as usual with servicemen and women. Oh, well, he could call her at either her flat or the hospital, as soon as he reached the station.

He was told at the hospital that Kate was on her way home; she'd just left. A shawl-wrapped woman was selling flowers from a basket at the entrance to the station. He stopped, searching among the daisies and gladioli. "Do you have any violets?"

"Oh, yes, guv, 'ere yer are." The small bunch of violets was slightly wilted, but Tony took it. Kate was now living in Hampstead, and her address was respectability itself. In the taxi on the way he wrote a note to attach to the violets: "Forgiveness is the scent of violets on the heel of he who crushed the petals."

He blinked away a sudden misting of his eyes, so overcome at the prospect of seeing her again, touching her, that he had to back away from the intensity of his own thoughts. He studied instead the city passing in review. Poor old London was looking battered but not forlorn. Workmen were clearing away debris from last night's raid; shopkeepers swept their broken glass, raised defiant signs on boarded-over windows.

A young woman wearing a WRNS uniform was coming down the front steps of the three-story house where Kate lived. He asked, "Could you tell me which flat Kate Winfield has?"

"Top floor, three flights of stairs steeper than Everest. Sorry." The girl gave him an engaging grin and waved frantically to stop his taxi driver from leaving.

He ran up the stairs, hoping Kate had arrived home, that she hadn't stopped to do any shopping en route. Breathless, he came to the top landing. There was a faded red carpet on the floor, two doors. One was open and there were a couple of cardboard boxes standing outside. He could hear somebody whistling a tune and recognized the jaunty American melody. "Mr. Whatcha-callit, whatcha doin' tonight? Hope you're in the mood because I'm feelin' just right." A male voice began to sing the words.

A civilian appeared in the doorway, bent to pick up one of the boxes, then caught sight of Tony. His song died on his lips. Black-haired, dark-eyed, shoulders straining at a well-tailored jacket. He straightened up, jaw moving slightly to one side in a way that said without words, Okay, the game's up. For a second or two neither of them spoke, then the black-haired man said, "Tony Winfield, I presume?"

Tony had imagined such a confrontation, of course, many times. Sometimes he thought it would be a fast and furious battle of wits, verbal thrusts and parries that would leave his opponent looking and feeling foolish. Scathing comments about honor and decency would reduce him to an incoherent, blustering wreck. Other times Tony imagined they would simply set about one another with fists, and when the usurper was taught a proper lesson he would walk away, the righteous victor, bloody and unbowed, leaving behind a whimpering cur who would never again look at another man's wife. But Tony had never prepared himself for the sick sense of everything lost, of humiliated defeat, that he actually felt at the sight of Wade Lowery at home in Kate's flat. Tony felt too emotionally battered to say or do anything but simply stare.

"Kate isn't here," Lowery said. "She'll be home soon, if you'd care to wait. Or I could give her a message for you."

Tony still stood rooted to the spot, his mouth dry.

Lowery said, "Look, I'm sorry, I hate like hell to be the one to do this to you, but, well, she was never really yours, you know."

"Just tell her . . . I was here," Tony said. "And if you want my blessings or congratulations on your success in stealing my wife, I'm afraid you won't get them. There's nothing honorable in what you're doing. My wish for you is that one day you'll acquire a conscience."

"Hey, fella, if it would make you feel any better to take a swing at me, feel free. I don't like this situation any better than you do, but I'm not about to give up Kate because you stepped in and caught her on the rebound."

"Settling matters with one's fists seems a somewhat adolescent way of handling things," Tony said, turning away.

He ran down the stairs and out onto the street. As he walked he tore the violets and his note to shreds and sent them flying on a rising wind that already carried a hint of winter.

[41]

Kate turned the key in her door and paused, surprised that she'd left the lights on this morning when she left for the hospital. The aroma of meat cooking in a rich wine sauce surely wasn't coming from *her* kitchen?

She sniffed her way into the room just as Wade finished setting the table. A quick glimpse of fresh fruit, the stack of books on nursing she'd written him about, and what looked like a dress box all registered briefly, overshadowed by her surprise at seeing him back in England after all these months.

He bounded across the room and pulled her into a bone-crushing hug. "Hi, babe, you look terrific. Aw, c'mon, just a little welcoming kiss couldn't hurt."

"How did you get in here? Why didn't you write me that you were coming?" She turned her cheek for his kiss, but he chased her mouth until he caught it, and gave her a long exploratory kiss. It had been a long time since anyone had kissed her so thoroughly, and she was too startled to object quite as strenuously as she probably should have.

"Told your landlady I was your brother from America and wanted to surprise you. She asked me if your hair was naturally that color, and I said no, it was black like mine and you dyed it that red-gold."

Kate shook her head. "I'd tell you you're incorrigible, but

ECHOES OF WAR

you'd take it as a compliment. Look, Wade, I know I wrote you, but I thought you could just mail me the books I wanted. I certainly don't want to start up anything with you again."

His face assumed an expression of exaggerated dismay. "After I cooked beef burgundy for you, slaved over a hot stove all afternoon. Come on, kid, ease up. I've got drinks in the living room. Let's go put our feet up and hash this out."

She gave an exasperated sigh and went into the living room. It looked smaller, slightly shabby, now that Wade was here. He brought the dress box with him. She said awkwardly, "I thought maybe the U.S. nursing manuals might be easier to follow. Biology is killing me."

He handed her a glass of wine, then the dress box. "This is for you too." His eyes went over her slender figure. "You never mentioned the baby in your letter."

"I lost the baby. I'd rather not talk about it."

"I wondered why your letter sounded like a cry for help."

Damn, why had she written him that stupid letter? Another of her sudden impulses that couldn't be recalled once in motion. "It did not. You've got an overactive imagination."

He handed her a glass of wine, then raised his own in a toast. "To you, Kate, the most desirable woman I know. And before you start protesting about the impropriety, you'd better know that I'm aware you haven't lived with your husband for some time. In fact, you spent the whole summer here, alone."

"You had somebody check up on me? You've got nerve."

"Open your present," he said softly.

"Whatever it is, I'm going to donate it to the blitz victims' relief." She broke off as he raised the lid of the box and pulled out a filmy nightgown and matching negligee trimmed with black swansdown.

Kate said an unladylike word. Placing the glass down on the coffee table, she added, "And my marriage is none of your business. If you must know, I was pretty sick after I lost the baby. Sick enough that it took all of my strength to get back on my feet. I'm studying to be a nurse, as you know, and Tony's still in the RAF. The fact that we don't get together very often—"

"Oh, come off it, Kate. You know what they say about fooling some of the people some of the time."

"—and when I make it as a nurse, I'll probably try to get into a college and maybe later on try for medical school."

He gave a one-sided grin. "You're really taking this Florence Nightingale stuff seriously, aren't you?"

"Yes, I am. Call it exasperation at the bumbling of the medical profession, or call it horror at the frailty of the human body. I just feel, if one portion of humanity has to inflict such pain and suffering on another, then somebody better care about alleviating that suffering. And before you write another of those maudlin articles about me, let me tell you that, yes, it's a form of penance on my part. I was getting hardened to it when I was a VAD. Then when I was hurt, when I lost my baby and was so ill, being on the other side of the fence taught me quite a lesson."

"Kate, I understand. Honest I do. I remember how I was myself when I first came over here. I expected to be untouched by it all too. But it gets to you after a while. Talking to kids—young air force pilots, soldiers, sailors—listening to their plans for their lives, or what their plans were before the war came along and fixed it so that nobody can even make any plans for the future, knowing that some of them are brilliant, gifted. Christ only knows what they might contribute if they could be allowed to live. Maybe we just killed off the researcher who'd have come up with a cure for cancer."

Kate remembered his mother. "I was sorry to hear about your mother." He nodded, drained his glass. She said quickly, "I read the *Collier's* piece you did. It was good."

"I hope you noticed that although I'm still at the mercy of machete-wielding editors, my articles are no longer the pure propaganda you accused me of writing. I think maybe I'm sneaking in a message, below the surface at least, that war is hell and probably very unnecessary. I just hope to God we don't get sucked into it."

Kate regarded him curiously. "If we did, what would you do?"

"I'm not sure. Probably wouldn't have the guts to refuse to fight, so I'd go against my convictions and no doubt die a warrior hero. But I'd hate like hell to be cut down in my prime and never get a chance at a Pulitzer." He flashed her a smile. "Now, let's lighten the heavy load of this conversation. It's getting too serious. Put on the negligee and let's talk about you and me, kid."

"You can take that and undoubtedly find someone willing to wear it. I sure never will. Forget the 'you and me' too."

He had been wandering restlessly around the room, but now he dropped down beside her and put his arm around her. His other hand went to her face, turned her toward him. His mouth covered hers and there was no subtlety or finesse; his lips took hers in a bruising demand that was as much suppressed anger as passion. For a moment she fought, but her struggles aroused him even more and now his hands traveled over her body in feverish search for a response. "Kate, don't you know how much I want you?"

She forced herself to go limp. She sagged against him, letting her arms dangle at her sides. When he stopped kissing her unresponsive lips she said quietly, "What do you intend to do, rape me? Don't force yourself on me, Wade, I'm warning you."

He let go of her, but his eyes were both defiant and still hungry. "I'm sorry. I guess I came on a little strong. It's just that I want you so much. I've waited for you for a very long time."

"Shall we talk about that for a minute?"

He relaxed. "You bet. You know I love you. I never stopped."

Her voice was very soft. "Tell me, what's your definition of love?"

He leaned forward, dazzling her with the intensity of his dark eyes. She wondered if he could actually make them smolder at will. He said, "Love is not being able to think about anything else but the person you want to be near. It's closeness and magic and . . . I guess Hemingway said it better—it's the earth moving."

"No, you're wrong." She looked down at the third finger of her left hand, with its plain gold wedding band. "Love isn't a sudden all-consuming passion. Love is staying, no matter what, for better, for worse."

"Sure, that too."

"You mentioned once that the Catholic Church will grant annulments when one partner isn't Catholic. Do you think I could get a civil annulment too? Maybe on the grounds that Tony and I never really lived together? That way I wouldn't have to worry about divorce or excommunication or being a social outcast or anything." She controlled her expression very carefully, showing only, she hoped, an eager wistfulness.

Wade drooped visibly. "Why I, uh, I'm not sure."

She smiled sweetly. "I see. You checked on the situation with the Church, to salve my religious conscience. But you didn't really want me *legally* free to marry again, did you, Wade? In fact, the reason you find me so desirable now is precisely because I *am* married. You haven't changed your spots, have you, you old leopard you. You'd walk out and leave me waiting at the altar again tomorrow, just like last time."

His grin was frank, engagingly easy. "What is it with you women and that damn piece of paper—legalizing what comes naturally?"

"It's a sense of continuity, Wade. A commitment to a union that's more than sexual coupling, a commitment to humanity itself, to bring children into the world and nurture a family. It's what I want with Tony, what I'm going to fight for. I didn't even know it myself until now. I've been so busy wallowing in self-pity and lost pride and outrage at the injustice of everything, I lost sight of what I really want."

He stood up slowly. "Bully for you, kid. There's just one thing I guess you should know. Your husband was here earlier tonight. He left when he saw me making myself at home. He was kinda in a huff."

Kate flew at him with fingernails and a stream of curses she hadn't been aware she knew.

[42]

In the operations room at Tempsford it was noted that a Lysander had taken off. In the country house not far from the airfield, two code names were erased from the chalk-smeared blackboard, and the others who awaited their turn realized that two of their number were in transit. They concentrated on rehearsing their own cover stories, checking their clothes for telltale labels, forgotten bus tickets to Baker Street, anything that might give them away to the enemy. For the two now flying across the channel, it was too late to worry or wonder or rehearse. For those two, the mission had begun.

In the plane over the channel, Tony felt strange in his new role of "Joe." He studied the back of the pilot, mentally going through the motions of flying the plane with him. Beside Tony, his companion sat silently, methodically pulling threads from the worn cuffs of his French-made trousers. His code name was Maurice. Tony was now Jules.

He tried to think like Jules, who had been burned in a car accident, who was a bachelor, who'd never known Kate. The pain was still there, but he'd learned to hide it, sometimes even from himself. In retrospect, he was sorry he hadn't flattened Wade Lowery. It would have been stupid, adolescent, and probably immensely satisfying.

* * *

ECHOES OF WAR

The minute he had arrived back in Tempsford, Charles Morcambe had had him transferred to the country house where the SOE agents were kept in seclusion. Tony had had no contact with the outside world since. "What is it I'm to do when the moon rises again?" he'd asked Charles.

"Fetch our old friend Wolf out of the occupied zone."

"*Wolf?* Good lord, when did you hear from him?" Tony recalled their old contact in Berlin. Wolf of the hooded eyes and inexhaustible supply of magic tricks. But Wolf had told them many times that although he felt the Nazi persecution of the Jews was wrong, he nevertheless felt that Germany needed Hitler's leadership.

"We received word last month from the French underground," Charles said, "that a German officer had picked up one of their people and, instead of taking him in, had asked that they contact us and arrange to fly him here. That he had valuable information to offer in return for political asylum."

"How do you know it's Wolf? How do you know it isn't a trap?"

"If we were sure about that, we wouldn't need to send you in, would we? We could simply send in a Lizzie to pick him up. Trouble is, there's been radio silence from that sector ever since we got that last message. We don't know what's happening there. We're sending in another radio operator with you."

"But why risk it? Wolf helped us with some civil service paperwork to get a few Jews out of Germany. He's been serving in the army, presumably, ever since. Didn't you tell me that Hitler himself is aware of the Moon Squadron? That he ordered his intelligence service to find that vipers' nest and destroy it?"

"It's true we don't know for certain what Wolf's been doing since the Germans invaded Poland. But the hint he gave us about the type of intelligence he has to offer . . . Well, it makes the risks worthwhile if it's true."

"Another of Hitler's 'secret weapons,' I suppose?"

"This time it's no myth. We were aware of where the experiments were being conducted. Wolf was stationed there, guarding the facility, before being transferred to garrison duty in France."

"What type of experiments?"

"Deuterium oxide—heavy water. It's essential we know just how far along they are. If Wolf has anything at all to give us, the PM feels it's a risk worth taking, especially if we're absolutely sure that the German turncoat is our old friend Wolfgang von Klaus."

"And the only way to be certain is to send someone after him who would recognize him. When do I leave?"

"Next moon. The radio man going in with you is a French agent from that part of the country. He risked de Gaulle's wrath to volunteer for an SOE mission instead of going to work for Colonel Passy. You can have your pick of the Lysander pilots."

Charles had studied him intently for a moment, then added, "You can turn this one down if you wish."

Surprised, Tony asked, "You're surely not developing a conscience at this stage of the game? Afraid you're sending me to my death or worse and all that rot?"

"You're probably the closest thing to a friend I've ever had, Tony. I'm not a demonstrative man, but I admire your courage, and I might as well tell you, knowing Wolf wasn't the only criterion for choosing you. We needed a man who, if the situation warranted it, would either take his lethal capsule or would not, under any form of torture, tell the Gestapo anything about our operations. Oh, damn it all."

Tony watched incredulously as Charles blinked furiously, then blew his nose. From beneath the folds of his handkerchief he added, "They picked you because they're sure you'd never break."

Later Tony realized that he had been so deeply moved by Charles' apparent concern for his welfare that he never questioned in his own mind whether the entire conversation could have been a clever way of making certain that he fulfilled Charles' expectations of him.

The pilot was now circling back over what appeared to be a forest. On the ground below, three lights blinked at them. Cutting his engine speed, the pilot put down his flaps and skimmed the tops of the trees. Tony checked his gear, maps, money, Colt revolver, L-capsule, and wondered about the reception committee on the ground. Were they beleaguered resistance fighters grateful to see RAF wings silhouetted against the moon, or perhaps a more vicious welcoming group? The SOE had to arrange this drop by means of radio contact with another sector and then hope the message would be delivered overland.

The Lysander bounced, settled down again, then careened like a drunken dragonfly along a rutted path. Two shadowy figures waited. Maurice and Jules threw down their gear, then jumped from the plane. The four men walked quickly toward the trees. Behind them the engines of the Lysander revved up again and roared up over the trees with a couple of inches to spare.

There was no conversation until they had crossed a field, wended their way through a dense grove of pines, then come at last to a stone cottage.

Inside, a slim young woman with dark close-cropped hair and watchful eyes waited. She and Maurice embraced, kissed cheeks, as the two guides vanished into the night. Turning to Tony, Maurice said, "This is Lise. She is the daughter of the local gendarme, who is a collaborator. She has as much to fear from her father as from the Boche if she is caught helping us."

Lise shook his hand, her face pinched with worry. Maurice placed his cheap fiber suitcase on the table and began to check the radio equipment that filled the case. Lise was avoiding looking at Tony's scars. Her eyes were fixed somewhere in the region of his neck. She said, "I'm sorry, m'sieur. Until Maurice came with the radio, we did not know how to divert you. Even now, we don't know if we can get a message out to bring back a plane for you. The new company of the Wehrmacht, they are much more efficient than the last one. They brought in a Gestapo radio-detection van."

"What do you mean? What happened to Wolf von Klaus? Why isn't he here?" Tony asked.

Lise's lip trembled. "When they found our radio, they executed ten of our people in retaliation. Just random choices. They weren't involved in the underground."

No wonder Wolf was getting disillusioned. He'd always

been outraged at the persecution of innocent victims. Tony asked, "What about Captain von Klaus? What arrangements have you made?"

"None. He's under heavy guard in the big house on the hill where the Boche are stationed. A village girl who cooks for them brought word that he was arrested yesterday. They found out he had released two of our people with a warning. They don't know he planned to defect. But the commandant has ordered a Gestapo investigation."

Tony swore under his breath in several languages.

Maurice was unraveling yards of aerial. "I can ask for a Lysander for tomorrow night."

Tony considered for a moment. "How many men do you have in the hills?" he asked Lise. "How many Sten guns and hand grenades? How much ammunition?"

Maurice snapped, "They don't have enough to take on a Boche company. You know how much the British have sent. But we can't waste all of our people to get one turncoat out of here."

Tony drummed his fingers on the edge of the fiber suitcase. "A diversion was all I had in mind."

Lise said, "I can go to the men in the hills."

Tony said, "First I want you to go to the village curé. See if he'll lend you a Bible, a crucifix, his stole, perhaps a hat and clerical collar. I'll also need a brush-up course in Latin and the words to a certain service."

"You're mad," Maurice said. "Even if you get inside, one man can't get him out."

"He won't be interrogated by the Gestapo here," Tony said. "Bad for the morale of the rest of the garrison to treat one of their own the same as any French resister. They'll take him back to Germany. Probably right away." He turned to Lise. "Can your cook find out when he's to be picked up by the Gestapo?"

Lise nodded. "I think so. The commandant is afraid of the Gestapo himself. He always orders special meals and much spit and polish when they're coming."

"Good. The whole operation will require exact timing. We need that Lysander as soon as Wolf is free, which means if they plan to move him in the daylight, we'll have to delay their leaving until the moon rises. I'll go in and see him first thing in the morning, so he'll be prepared."

Lise bit her lip. "My father told me that anyone who goes in is searched very thoroughly. No weapons, of course. It's up to you whether you want to take a chance on leaving your lethal capsule here or not. The Boche have become adept at finding them, no matter how carefully hidden. Oh, yes, they'll check the fillings in your teeth too. And you know having one of those capsules on you is as good as saying you're an agent."

"I won't take my L-capsule," Tony replied. "It makes me more nervous than the Gestapo."

Two sentries barred his way. Tony tried not to sweat under the clerical collar and heavy coat of the village priest as he stood at the gates of the chateau that had been commandeered as headquarters of the German garrison. He explained in halting German that he was the newly arrived priest, come to assist the old curé. "I must see Monsieur le Commandant at once, on a matter of extreme urgency."

"Get away from here, priest," one sentry said.

Tony said, "I can assure you, young man, that your commandant will be most interested in what I have to tell him."

The sentries exchanged glances. Tony read their minds. They were thinking that this was no simple village priest, and maybe they'd better let a superior take over.

One of the sentries said, "All right, come with me."

Tony followed into the chateau, where he was thoroughly searched. He expressed what he hoped was appropriate outrage, protesting that he was a man of God. When they prodded his teeth and looked under his tongue, as well as examining other more private places, he was glad he hadn't brought his lethal capsule. When they were finished, he was taken to a small room to wait.

Half an hour later a noncommissioned officer took him to the office of the commandant.

A major sat behind a cluttered desk. Behind him stood a

man in a civilian suit, rigidly erect, a hard, blank look on his face. Damnation, Tony thought, the Gestapo are already here.

The major studied Tony's scarred face with detached interest. "What happened to you?"

Tony was prepared for the question. "I was an army chaplain—a car overturned, there was a fire. Fortunately for me, the surgeons had improved their skin grafting techniques. So many war casualties to practice on—"

"Why have you come to me? What do you want?" the major interrupted impatiently.

"Ah . . . um, yes, I have come to you Monsieur le Commandant, as one honorable man to another, on a matter of extreme delicacy."

"Get to the point, will you please?"

"The local gendarme, M'sieur Chabot, he has a daughter, Lise."

"So?"

"The unfortunate girl is . . . *enceinte*."

The Gestapo man smirked. The commandant waited, his eyes like frozen steel. Tony continued: "I beg permission to speak with the young officer who is the father. I must persuade him to do the honorable thing."

"What? Do you think we're running a marriage bureau here?"

The Gestapo man placed his hands on the desk and leaned forward. "Who is the father?"

Tony looked him straight in the eye. "Captain Wolfgang von Klaus."

The commandant and Gestapo man exchanged glances. Tony went on: "The father of the girl does not know of her condition yet. I understand from the curé that her father has been most cooperative with your soldiers. Surely, you will at least allow me to speak with Captain von Klaus?"

The Gestapo man threw back his head and laughed. "Why not, Herr Major? What possible difference can it make to von Klaus now? You can pay back the gendarme's favor. Let the local people see how reasonable we Germans can be when they cooperate with us."

There was an open file on the major's desk. Tony could see Wolf's name on it.

All right, Wolf, we're going to need a magic trick or two now.

Wolf sat on a wooden chair in a small locked room, with a sentry posted at the door. As Tony entered, Wolf's melancholy eyes swiveled slowly in his direction. His face was ashen, devoid of expression, and his uniform had a slept-in appearance.

"I've come on behalf of Mademoiselle Lise Chabot, and it's no use pretending you don't know why," Tony said quickly, before the door was closed on them. "She's with child and I've come to ask you to do the honorable thing by her and your child. Your commandant has graciously permitted us to perform a wedding ceremony this afternoon at the church, since I understand you are to leave here today for posting to Germany."

Wolf stood up, recognition and amazement registering in his hooded eyes. He smiled faintly. "You priests astonish me. One never knows where you're going to show up next."

Tony said, "Lise is upset that you didn't keep your rendezvous with her and the curé at the church yesterday. Of course, when I explain about the trouble you're in, I'm sure she'll understand."

Moving closer, Wolf examined Tony's scars with interest. Tony said, "A car accident. There was a fire."

There was a flicker of sympathy in Wolf's glance. "Of course, I intend to marry Lise. You say you have my commandant's permission?"

"Good, good, my son. Now, the old curé is ill, and I have a number of things to do today—baptisms, confessions to hear. It will be late this afternoon, possibly even early this evening, before I can schedule the ceremony." Tony's eyes moved briefly in the direction of the closed door, sure that their conversation was being monitored. "Lise tells me you're an amateur magician, that you can make things appear and disappear. We must hope you don't make yourself disappear before you become a married man."

From the sudden gleam in Wolf's eyes, Tony was sure the message had been understood.

Lise and her father, who looked surprised and angry, stood in front of the altar in the village church. Tony, wearing the priest's robes, waited in the vestry. Sentries with rifles in hand were posted at the back of the church, armed guards were at the doors, and the Gestapo car waited for the completion of the ceremony. A motorcycle and sidecar stood ready as an escort.

Inside the church there was silence, except for the shuffling of feet. The scent of incense was heavy in the air.

Tony went into the sanctuary and lighted the candles, then left again. If they didn't bring Wolf soon, they wouldn't make it to the field in time for the Lysander pickup, and it would be too dangerous to keep the plane on the ground for more than minutes.

The rear door creaked open, and there was the clatter of more boots at the back of the church. Wolf, flanked by two guards, came slowly down the aisle.

Tomorrow morning the real priest would be found by his housekeeper, bound and gagged. As a precaution against retaliation, he would tell the Germans that the men responsible were thugs from a nearby city, hired by Wolf to help him escape. The priest would be most cooperative, giving detailed descriptions of the men. He would laugh at any suggestion that any of the villagers were involved, pointing out that they would hardly risk their lives to help a German officer escape.

Tony glanced at Lise, willing her to turn and watch the approach of her prospective bridegroom. She was the most vulnerable member of the cast, and Tony feared for her safety. For Lise the charade would have to continue. She would have to play the part of a deserted, pregnant, fraternizing woman and face the wrath of her father as well as the contempt of the villagers. He had tried to persuade her to leave, but she insisted she must stay and continue her work with the resistance. "Don't worry," Lise had said, "I can always go into the hills with the Maquis. Besides—the

Boche motorcycle and sidecar we plan to steal for the getaway won't carry four people."

As Wolf and the two guards reached Lise and her father, Tony put the priest's stole around his neck and went to the altar. In the dimly lit church, the stiffly erect soldiers, the livid-faced father of the bride, and Wolf's nonchalant expression all registered briefly. But it was Lise, gravely composed but pale, who made Tony wish he'd devised another plan. He felt like some pagan priest about to offer a human sacrifice.

"*In nomine Patris, et Filii, et Spiritus Sancti.*" Tony found he actually was praying, that he remembered the hastily taught words of the ceremony. None of the Germans were Catholic; they—and Lise's father—would not connect her with the escape plot. Tony stumbled over the words, his voice a breathless mumble: "*Uxor tua sicut vitis abaundans in lateribus domus tuae. . . .*"

The Nuptial Mass ended. Wolf, who had been giving Lise sidelong glances throughout, tried to take her in his arms. The Gestapo man said, "Forget about that. You've already consummated this marriage. Come on, move out."

Wolf and his guards marched back up the aisle. Tony followed. "Please, wait. I understood from M'sieur le Commandant that the young couple were to have a little time together."

They reached the back of the church; the doors were opening. One guard turned and said, "This farce is over, priest." He stepped outside, into a barrage of gunfire and exploding grenades.

Wolf dropped to the ground as two of the Germans clutched their stomachs and pitched forward. Shouted orders punctuated the bursts of Sten gun fire. The Gestapo car burst into flames. Tony grabbed Wolf's shoulder and pointed to the motorcycle and sidecar as the Germans dived for cover.

Maurice materialized from the shadows and climbed onto the motorcycle. Wolf flung himself into the sidecar as the engine roared to life. Tony was about to climb into the sidecar when Lise came flying out of the church, her face white in the darkness. She screamed, "My father, he knows!" Behind her, silhouetted against the church doors, Tony saw her father. His pistol was pointed squarely at the middle of Lise's back.

Tony picked her up and dropped her into the sidecar on top of Wolf. Maurice yelled, "You fool," and roared off into the night, bullets whistling after him. Tony felt the sickening crunch of a rifle butt striking the back of his head, then slipped into oblivion.

Seated between two burly Gestapo men in the back seat of a Citroen, Tony stared at the shaved neck of the driver as the dark countryside flashed by the windows, wondering if they had any idea of their great good luck in capturing him alive.

The exact location of Gibraltar Farm, the Moon Squadron's operations, everything that went on at Tempsford, and the nature of the SOE training in Scotland had thus far been one of the best-kept secrets of the war, known only to the War Cabinet and those members of the SOE who were directly concerned with the operation of the squadron. Even the pilots who flew the aircraft and their crews saw only bits and pieces of the whole picture.

Speculating what the Gestapo would do if they knew they were about to interrogate a man who probably knew more about the SOE than anyone else, and about their transportation to and from resistance groups from Yugoslavia to the Arctic Circle, brought to Tony's mind one implacable fact. That no matter what they did to him—and he knew well what that might be—*no matter what, he couldn't talk.*

[43]

Tony had vanished into the maelstrom of war. Kate frantically searched his letters for a clue to his whereabouts, but he'd given no address on those brief notes and cards of last summer. She called Cardovan House, and Cecilia said she didn't have his address either, not since he left Biggin Hill. "He's been so withdrawn, acted so strangely, since his father's death, since you and he—"

"The War Office," Kate interrupted. "Somebody must know how we can find him. We're his next of kin, for pity's sake."

"I did see his name in *The Times*," Cecilia said helpfully. "He was awarded a DFC and a DSO. I don't know what to tell you, Kate. I think he just wants to be left alone. Tell me, dear, how are you?"

"Fine. I'm studying for my first exam. Please, if you hear from him, ask him to call me. And tell him . . . tell him I love him."

In December, Japan attacked the American navy base at Pearl Harbor in the Hawaiian Islands, and a few days later Hitler declared war on America. Germany was already at war with its former ally, having invaded the Soviet Union earlier that year. Now the war was global. Wade called Kate to tell her he was going home to enlist.

"Kate, I'm sorry about that day I barged into your apartment and loused things up for you with your husband. He seemed like a pretty nice guy. I just called to say goodbye. When push came to shove, I got as mad as anybody else about Tojo stabbing us in the back. I had some friends at Pearl."

She wished him Godspeed and prayed that he wouldn't come back into her life.

The war dragged on, with the Allies retreating on every front, and the German, Italian, and Japanese dictators expanding their conquered territories in every direction.

Kate ran into a blank wall every time she tried to find out where Tony was. She was given polite assurances that someone would be in touch, then never heard from them again. She visited Cecilia whenever she could, putting in brief appearances at the inevitable parties. She had wondered if Cecilia, now that her widowhood was of proper duration, would marry Clive. She didn't. They seemed more like affectionate brother and sister than anything else, Kate decided, wondering why Hardie had walked out because of poor old Clive.

She knew now about Ella Fontaine. Cecilia had shown her some yellowing newspaper clippings about the Fontaines, and Kate studied the picture of Tony's real mother, becoming more convinced than ever that civilization needed the sacrament of marriage. It was the only system that really worked. All those free spirits who couldn't recognize the social value of marriage for themselves should at least have the decency to forgo having children.

By the time the telegram arrived informing her officially that Tony was "missing in action" Kate had already concluded as much.

"We mustn't give up hope, dear," Cecilia said, embracing her. "We'll hear that he's a prisoner of war one of these days."

But they didn't and it tormented Kate that no one would, or could, tell her any details of *how* he became missing in action. She alternated between periods of deep depression when she was sure he was dead, and moments of almost manic hope and joy that he couldn't be, because if he were she wouldn't go on longing for him so. Finding that the only antidote to her anguish was not to give herself time to think, she filled every moment of her time with work and study.

Ursula married her naval officer and sought out Kate just before they were to leave for his estate in Scotland, tiptoeing into Kate's bedroom at Cardovan House with the air of a little girl about to make amends. "I just wanted you to know that I'm sorry if I caused any trouble between you and Tony. I'm not going to take all the blame, because you *were* seeing that American correspondent, but I suppose I shouldn't have told Tony."

Kate was packing to return to her London flat. She'd been bombed out of her previous one—luckily while she was at the hospital—and now had an even smaller flat. "It's all water under the bridge now, Ursula."

"Then you won't bear a grudge?"

"No, of course not. What would be the point? I guess wherever Tony is, he's probably given up on all the crazy females in his life, and who'd blame him?"

"It's awful for you, not knowing."

Kate sighed. "I don't know who else to go and badger for information. I've tried everyone. I'd ask Churchill himself if I could find him."

Ursula patted a strand of cornsilk hair into place under the pink confection of tulle and roses that was her "going away" hat. She had splurged her entire year's clothing ration on a pink coat that wasn't quite as ugly as most of the "utility" clothing that was now issued. Kate felt almost guilty in the stylish emerald green suit her mother had sent from unrationed America. Ursula said, "You know, I've been wondering if Charles Morcambe doesn't know something about where Tony went."

Kate dropped the lid of her suitcase. "What do you mean?"

"Well, we had a memorial service for Hardie, and Charles came for it. Afterwards we all went back to the house for the usual sherry and sandwiches, but Tony stayed at the church. Charles was obviously there to see Tony about something other than the memorial. In fact he had to get back to London right away and insisted he must speak privately to

Tony first. I had to stop him from going back to the church. I said I'd go and see if Tony was up to one of Charles' conversations. He isn't the most tactful person, as you know. I never understood how he could be an embassy official, I always thought diplomats were supposed to be diplomatic."

"But he's in the army now," Kate pointed out. "He wouldn't have anything to do with an air force posting."

"Clive told me Charles is with the SOE. Old Clive isn't quite as stupid as he seems, you know."

"What's the SOE?"

"Special Operations Executive. Churchill founded the group himself. He told them to 'set Europe ablaze.' It's all very hush-hush."

"Commandos?"

"No, agents, guerrillas, and partisans in occupied countries. Winnie knew it would be years until we could invade the continent, and in the meantime he wanted the Germans harassed at every turn. I think Charles Morcambe was up to something in Germany even before the war. Perhaps Tony too."

Kate slapped her forehead with the palm of her hand. "Of course. Of *course!* Do you think Clive knows where I'd find Charles?"

Ursula smiled. "He said he thinks they're headquartered on Baker Street. Kate . . ."

"Yes?"

"You know, I never realized before what a terribly nice person you are, or how much I secretly admire you. Do you think we could ever be friends?"

"Maybe more than that—maybe sisters." She was startled to find herself the sudden recipient of a tearful hug.

The new year was upon them before Kate finally managed to meet and talk with Charles Morcambe. She was never allowed into the Baker Street address and eventually simply camped outside until Charles arrived. He blinked at her nearsightedly, then invited her to get into his car. He asked for her address, gave it to the driver, and said, "Been intending to get in touch, but so busy—"

"Where's Tony? And before you give me any diplomatic double-talk or brush-off, I'm warning you that if I don't get some straight answers about my husband, I'm going to take the whole story of the SOE to the American press. I'm sure you're aware of my connections to a certain war correspondent." She let her voice trail off, hoping the bluff would work.

He gave her a glacial stare. "He disappeared in occupied France. His name never appeared on any prisoner-of-war lists, so he's listed as missing in action. He helped us get a very valuable agent out."

Kate felt the interior of the car close in on her. "Is he dead? Please, you've got to tell me."

"My dear, I wish I could. I honestly don't know. We don't know what happened to him."

Kate looked into his fishy stare and wanted to feel her fingernails on his face, ripping out the secrets he concealed. That he knew more than he was saying was certain. If only she'd known about this before December 7, while there were still American correspondents in London who could get information out of Nazi Germany.

Charles said, "I shall, of course, let you know immediately, if we learn he's still alive."

From the tone of his voice, he thought it extremely unlikely. For Kate everything was dissolving—his face, the car, the city—blurring into a flood of tears she knew would never end.

She got through the days, and the endless nights. Work was a great healer, and being busy made the time pass. There were times when she still acted too impulsively and spoke her mind when she probably shouldn't have, especially when it came to the nursing care and medical attention given the sick and wounded. More than one doctor was startled to hear a lowly nurse clatter instruments on a tray and mutter, "No wonder we call them *patients*. They've got to have superhuman *patience* to put up with this."

As the British Isles began to fill up with American troops gearing for the expected invasion of the European continent, Kate sought out the nurses and medics in their midst to exchange knowledge, grievances, ideas—anything that might help their patients.

She was outraged to hear that Sir Ian Fleming's discovery, penicillin, which had recently been stabilized into a usable preparation, was being given only to those American soldiers in North Africa deemed capable of returning to the front lines. She went storming back to the hospital to inquire of the doctors there if the same was true in the British army medical services. The civilian doctors didn't know. They knew that penicillin was extremely scarce, that it took nearly a hundred liters of the mold to brew sufficient penicillin to treat a single patient.

"So the soldiers who catch a venereal disease in Cairo or Alexandria get the penicillin, and a man too badly wounded to fight again goes without? God in heaven!"

One of the doctors, an expatriate Frenchman, observed with a shrug, *"C'est la guerre."*

A letter came from Kate's mother in the summer of 1943.

Dear Kate:
Just a few lines to let you know Dad and I are fine. The two boys are still together—in the South Pacific on something called a PT boat. Hope you're well and not working too hard. We're still not sure why you wanted to work in a hospital. I'd have thought being the wife of a big landowner with a large house would have been enough to keep you busy. But anyway, congratulations on becoming a full-fledged nurse.

We read some sad news some months ago. I wondered whether to tell you or not, but think I should. There was a piece in the paper—an obituary. Wade Lowery was killed in action at a place called Guadalcanal. . . .

Kate had gone for a walk, alone, thinking about some of the later articles Wade had written, wondering sadly what he might have accomplished in the field of journalism had he been spared. She remembered his lively dark eyes, his sense of humor and sheer joy at being alive. She didn't recall any of his faults or weaknesses. She went into the nearest still-standing church to pray for his soul. Churches had been demolished at an alarming rate by the Luftwaffe, because they made such good targets with their tall steeples.

In the spring of 1944 all civilian travel between Britain and Eire was suspended, reportedly because of the presence of German agents in the Irish Republic, and the possibility of "something big" about to happen. The British government also banned visitors from their own coastal areas; the movement of foreign diplomats and their couriers into and out of the United Kingdom was prohibited; censorship laws were extended; and a delay was imposed on the forwarding of mail to the United States.

The reason for all of these extraordinary precautions became obvious when in June the long-awaited invasion of the continent began.

Kate listened to the news of the Allied landings on D-Day and prayed for their success without too much loss of life.

That night she kept watch over a badly wounded RAF pilot who had crash-landed his fighter-bomber after a near suicide mission to blow up a dam in occupied Europe. Sitting beside his bed in the dimly lit ward that was packed with war casualties, she thought of the thousands of prisoners of war held by the Germans. Was Tony one of them? Please, God, yes. Wouldn't she have known if he were dead? Wouldn't she have felt it long ago?

The pilot moaned softly and she picked up his wrist again to take his pulse, willing him to live. She had stopped agonizing over what might have transpired between Tony and Wade that day they met at her flat. Tony would naturally have assumed the worst, and Wade would have let him. At first she had been torn between anger that Tony had simply gone away with never a word, and guilt that it was her fault Wade even knew where she lived. She should have realized when she wrote to him that he'd do exactly what he did—try to move back into her life. Then she decided there was no use in brooding on what couldn't be changed. Tony had been

ECHOES OF WAR

Tony, Wade had behaved like Wade, and yes, Kate had been true to form too. She wondered despairingly if Tony would ever believe that she loved him and only him.

The pilot she was caring for slipped away from her just before dawn, and she went home and spent the day crying—for him, for Wade, for Tony, for herself.

A couple of days later Hitler unleashed his "secret weapon" against London. A rocket-powered missile that resembled a small pilotless plane was launched against southern England. The V-1 was relatively slow, and many were brought down by anti-aircraft fire or intercepted by fighters; but with a warhead of one ton of high explosives, the ones that got through managed to kill nearly six thousand people and injure another sixteen thousand or so. Kate and her fellow nurses were kept busy.

Everyone in London learned to live with this new terror. The frightening sound of the buzz bomb, as Londoners dubbed it, the holding of your breath until it passed overhead, or the heart-stopping wait after its engines died and it plunged to earth—all became one more part of the Londoner's daily life.

The V-2 rockets, which were invulnerable to either AA defenses or fighters, came later that year. Since the V-2s couldn't be stopped, all anyone could do was to hope the advancing Allied forces would soon overrun the launching fields. Kate started to make one of her bargains with the Almighty: *Please, God, don't let me be killed with victory this close . . . or at least until I know whether Tony is alive.*

Cecilia called on a warm August day. "Kate? Have you heard the wonderful news? Paris has been liberated! Can you come home for the weekend? I thought we'd have a little celebration party, and I know how you loved Paris."

Kate's mind traveled back among her Paris memories, to those wonderful days with Marie Allegret when Kate emerged from her cocoon to find Jean-Louis and every other young male wanting to court her—and Tony risking his life to come to her. She recalled prewar Paris and the way ethereal vapors floated over the Seine, and the trees seemed to have their leaves and blossoms painted on a sky of delicate blue; and there were the honking cars and thronging pedestrians, the packed sidewalk cafes, and above all the wonderful joie de vivre of the French. Funny how the rest—the German occupation, everything that was ugly—suddenly became indistinct in her mind.

She declined Cecilia's invitation because, fortunately, she was working that weekend.

Ursula called to say she'd be in London to meet her husband, whose ship had recently returned from the Mediterranean, and she asked whether they could have lunch together.

Kate was immediately aware that marriage had changed the spoiled young society girl into, if not exactly a kindly matron, at least a more mature woman.

"You look a wee bit tired, Kate, but those circles under your eyes are quite attractive, even a wee bit sexy." Ursula giggled over a glass of sherry. "You're a marvel, you really are. I'd have gone mad if I'd been in your shoes. I mean, you work so hard in those dreadful hospitals, and it can't be any fun, not knowing whether or not you're a widow—"

"He's alive," Kate said quickly, a shade too emphatically. "I feel it in my bones."

"If he is, have you faced the possibility that he may be horribly disfigured? Or his mind may be gone?"

Kate's hand shook as she put down her fork.

Ursula went on hurriedly. "I don't mean to be a pessimist or try to frighten you, but it's been so long. If by some remote chance he's still alive, then God knows what condition he's in."

"It wouldn't matter to me. Nothing would matter except having him back with me."

In April 1945, Charles Morcambe telephoned. "Kate? I have news for you. A concentration camp called Buchenwald was liberated."

Kate slid into a chair, gripped the receiver tightly. "Tony? He's alive—they found him?"

"Yes. We think so."

"What do you mean, you think so? Is he alive or not?"

Charles said, "The first reports from Buchenwald are horrifying. The camp was packed with Jews and political prisoners, most of them awaiting execution, apparently. There were also a number of SOE agents. The Germans were executing the SOE people up to the last minute, and all of the prisoners were in such emaciated condition that—"

Kate screamed into the phone, "Is he *alive?*"

"Yes, barely. At least a man who gave his name as Tony Winfield has been found. He'd been tortured by the Gestapo, but apparently told them nothing, and eventually they gave up on him and sent him to the concentration camp. If it is indeed Tony . . . well, I gather he's in rather poor condition. I couldn't get any more details, but they're sending him home and you'll be able to see him in a few days."

It had rained that morning and the sky was a dark sea filled with restless billowing sails as the storm lingered, churning the air in tremulous promise. Kate walked up and down the platform of the small country railway station waiting for the train bringing Tony home. She thought about the first time she had come to Middle Knole. She and Michelle and a grumbling bevy of elderly tourists, already worn out from being shown too much in too short a span of time. It seemed an eon ago.

She heard the rumble of the approaching train far down the tracks and felt all of her senses quicken. A misty rain had again begun to fall, blurring all of the images. Unfurling her umbrella, she walked to the edge of the platform as, heralded by a great burst of steam, the train came squealing to a halt.

About half a dozen people were meeting the train from London. As the doors opened young servicemen and women leaped down to be engulfed in hugs and smiles and greetings, then were whisked away to be restored, briefly, to the bosoms of their families.

Kate's eyes covered every one of the doors. No one emerged from the first-class section. She watched all of the second-class doors until they were closed by the conductor moving briskly along the length of the train. There was no sign of Tony.

The platform emptied of everyone but Kate and the conductor. He tipped his cap to her as he made his way back to the baggage car, paused, and looked at her searchingly, as though waiting for her to depart too. When she didn't, he opened the baggage car doors and beckoned to someone inside.

Kate began to walk slowly toward the back of the train, a sick sense of something horribly wrong growing with each step.

Air force uniforms were coming out of the baggage car. They scarcely registered on her frozen brain. She stopped, her mouth open but her throat too dry to scream, as the conductor wheeled a cart into position to receive a flag-draped coffin.

[44]

She stood perfectly still, afraid to move in case movement caused the nightmare to continue. The men with the coffin, intent on their somber business, ignored her. She thought, If I'm awake, I'm going to die too. Oh, Tony, oh, no, not so close to being liberated.

Someone tapped her on the shoulder and she jumped. The stationmaster said politely, "Excuse me, but are you Mrs. Winfield?"

She nodded, not taking her eyes off the coffin.

"I'm sorry, Mrs. Winfield. I wasn't sure until the others had gone. I've a gentleman on the phone wanting to speak to you. My office is over there."

When she didn't move, he took her arm and led her. His tiny office overlooked the platform, but the windows were steamy with the rain. Someone put a telephone receiver into her hand and Charles Morcambe's voice came calmly over the wire. "I'm sorry, Kate. I tried to get you at the house, but you'd already left. I just found out that Tony is being kept in London for a few days—debriefing and a good going-over by the doctors."

She found her voice again only after a couple of promptings on Charles' part. "God damn you! The train came in and there was a coffin with a flag—and RAF people—" Her voice sounded as though it were shattering like glass.

"I'm sorry. I had no idea someone would be sending a body home on that train. I only found out he was being kept here half an hour ago."

"How is he? Have you seen him? When will he be here?"

"I haven't seen him, but from what I've been told, his physical condition isn't . . . I mean, his physical injuries have more or less healed. He's suffering from malnutrition, of course. Unfortunately, there seem to be some other problems. Shock, amnesia . . . Kate, in view of this, I'll drive him home myself. You go on back to Cardovan House and wait for him there."

Kate walked through the topiary garden at Cardovan House feeling the springy turf under her feet, the warm caress of a mellow late-afternoon sun on her bare arms. The scent of roses crept by, borne on a slight breeze. What did it matter that the topiary shrubs were badly in need of pruning and had lost their forms, or that the roses were going to seed because a pair of elderly gardeners now concentrated all of their efforts on growing vegetables for the household? Kate had insisted and Cecilia had acquiesced. Now, as she looked at the straggly shrubs, Kate wondered if there wasn't a place on earth for lovely useless things too, because beauty was as necessary for the human soul as food was to the body.

She had been too tense to wait in the drawing room, where Cecilia and Clive and Ursula and about half the county awaited Tony's arrival.

A car came slowly up the drive. Kate drew back behind a bush that had once been trimmed into the shape of a charging elephant but was now resuming its natural form. Her heart beat rapidly, in her throat, it seemed. She fought a sudden impulse to run away and hide more completely. She couldn't even bring herself to look at Charles and Tony getting out of the car, and remained motionless for several minutes after she heard the doors slam.

Gradually the panic subsided. She smoothed her yellow dress over her hips, bent to straighten her stocking seams. Both were gifts from her mother. The stockings were of nylon, a miraculous synthetic that had all of the qualities of silk but was less fragile.

Kate's hair had grown back to shoulder length, enough now to sweep into a coil on top of her head, the way Tony liked it. She fingered the locket around her neck and hoped that all those other Winfield women who had worn it would rally around her now, at least in spirit.

Barely five minutes passed before she heard footsteps on the terrace, coming down the steps toward her. A voice both strange and dear called, "Kate . . . ?"

Swallowing a great lump of emotion, Kate stepped out from her hiding place and looked at her husband.

He was about five yards away from her. Her first thought was that he had been restored to her whole and complete and somehow untouched by war. But then she saw how loosely his civilian suit hung on his emaciated frame, and how haunted his eyes were. They were the eyes of a man who has looked into hell. The clumsy reconstruction of his burned eyelids added a slightly puckered wrong-size look to those eyes but perhaps it would go away in time. The plastic surgeons had learned a great deal since the early days of the war. It wasn't right that great progress should be made at a cost of such human misery.

She whispered, "Oh, Tony . . . thank God!" and took a tentative step toward him. He closed the distance between them and took her in his arms. She felt nothing but bones, and his heart pounding against hers.

They held one another, trembling, not speaking. Kate felt her tears soak his shirt and thought briefly that she was glad he hadn't worn his uniform. When at last she raised her face to his, she saw there was more than hideous memories in those shattered eyes. There was love and hope there too. He said, "Thinking about this moment is what kept me going."

"Tony, oh, my dear, dear . . ." Her endearment was lost in the blending of their lips, which came together so gently, so carefully, that each might have been afraid of breaking some fragile thread that held them together.

He touched her hair and it came loose and he said, "I'm sorry." She laughed and said, "It's all right, really." And they kissed again, more firmly, conviction returning. It wasn't a dream, it was real.

Kate pulled away to look at him again, ran her hands

lightly over his face, down shoulders that had no flesh, and pulled his arms back around her. Oh, how she'd longed for, yearned for, those arms. His fingers drifted to her locket and he snapped it open. Inside were two miniatures she'd had made from their wedding photograph.

He said, "I'm glad you did that," and kissed her again.

She thought, Thank God, his mind is intact. He even remembers the foolish legend of the locket. The sun had slipped behind the trees and she shivered with the loss of its warmth. He said, "Come on, let's go back to the house."

She hesitated and he added softly, "No, not that crowd in the drawing room. They can celebrate without us. I want to be alone with my wife." He slipped his arm around her waist and they walked back up the steps to the terrace.

Ursula was waiting for them in the hall. She put one finger to her lips conspiratorially and whispered, "Go on up to your room. I'll have someone bring your dinner to you."

Tony kissed the top of his sister's head, then seized Kate's hand and they ran up the stairs, dashed along the landing, and, laughing, breathless, went into their room.

Closing the door, Tony wrapped his arms around her again. She pressed her body close to his, feeling the comfort of his nearness, overwhelmed at how great her need for him was. At the same time she felt as shy as any bride. To cover her confusion, she said, "I've got a whole month before I have to go back to the hospital."

He pulled back slightly and gave her a puzzled look. "Hospital?"

Startled, she looked into a blankness in his gaze that hadn't been there before. She cleared her throat. "I'm a fully qualified nurse now. I . . ." Her voice trailed off as he continued to give her his polite but baffled attention.

At length she said, "Tony, why am I all at once very frightened?"

He buried his face in her hair, his lips warm. "Don't be. It will be all right in time, I promise. I love you. I love you so much. If you love me even half as much, then everything will work out." Then he was kissing her again with a desperate urgency, and she responded as every numbed nerve in her body came back to life.

"Tony, do you remember your first leave?" she asked when at last they had to stop for breath. "We took a bath together in that big old bathtub—"

She felt a tremor pass through him. He seemed to fall back, away from her. Then abruptly he turned away and went to his dressing table, leaning on it with his hands. "Kate, not yet. I don't want you to see me completely naked . . . yet."

A hammering, nagging suspicion took hold. "Tony—"

"The Gestapo left a few marks on me, Kate." He turned to look at her, attempting a smile. "Besides, I'm scrawny as a starved chicken. Give me a little time."

She couldn't bear to have any distance, however slight, between them, so she went to him and slipped her arms around him again. "Oh, my darling, what did they do to you?"

"Do you remember when we were trying to leave France, we went to that bistro, large as life, and drank wine under the noses of three Gestapo agents? And they noticed us, and I pretended we were having a domestic quarrel and pulled you over my knee?"

"Yes, of course. You were so nonchalant about the whole episode I was convinced you were carrying a safe conduct pass."

"Do you remember the inn where we stayed on our wedding night?"

She sighed. "Oh, yes. Yes, I do."

"I used to relive that night, every second of it, in my mind while I was a prisoner. I used to send my thoughts back over our mad dash out of France and over the mountains. When the Gestapo came at me with rubber truncheons and fists and boots, I used to think about finding the rum in the Basque's hut and how Kate got tipsy and tried to seduce me."

Kate demurred. "I did not!" She kissed his cheek, cradled his face in her hand, and tried not to imagine what they had done to him.

"When I didn't tell them what they wanted to know, they tried other methods. Sodium Pentothal. Electric shocks."

She felt her insides shrivel into a tiny solid mass. "Don't think about it now, darling. Later, when you've been home

ECHOES OF WAR

for a while. Oh, you're shaking like a leaf. Come on, lie down. Here, let me take your shoes off."

They lay together on the bed, wrapped in each other's arms. Kate knew that men who had been deprived of contact with women for long periods of time were often temporarily impotent, and she was careful not to make any sexual overtures.

Tony said, "It's possible to convince your own mind that you actually don't know anything." He shivered again, less violently. "At least I don't fear burning in hell any more."

"You never did. I was the one who worried about hellfire and purgatory, remember?"

He stroked her hair back from her forehead, traced the curve of her cheek, touched her lips. "How I love that face."

"Tony, you didn't say anything when I told you I was a nurse. You aren't going to be one of those husbands who— I mean, I'll quit when we start our family, of course. Oh, yes, the doctors say there's no reason we can't have lots of healthy little Winfields. I didn't do myself any real damage when I made my famous Paul Revere ride."

Shadows flickered in his eyes; a pulse beat in his temple. "Kate, you don't know? Charles didn't tell you? He said he would."

She felt faint and realized she was holding her breath. "Tell me what?"

"I can't remember anything of the time after we were married and I went to Biggin Hill. Just vague images of flying, the dogfights. Then everything becomes blurred, fragmented, after that. I remember being a prisoner and concentrating on specific memories, trying to keep them alive in my mind, but they're isolated, without connecting threads or sequence. The doctors in London told me it's probably a result of the electric shocks. They said in time my memory may come back completely, or there may be things I'll always block from my mind. Be patient with me, my darling. Help me fill in all the missing pieces. I take it from what you said that you've been trained as a nurse?"

Everything was crashing down in Kate's mind, breaking into shards that cut deeply into hopes and dreams. In Tony's mind there had been no Wade Lowery, no misunderstandings or jealousies or estrangement. But what would happen when his memory returned?

He tried to make love to her that night but faltered, and she held him and comforted him and whispered that they had the next sixty years or so to get to know one another again, body and mind.

In the following days they walked together in the grounds, explored the woods, sat in the cool dimness of the ancient church, and watched the setting sun bring the stained-glass figures in the windows to life. Tony even accompanied her to services one Sunday morning, and she saw him brush a tear from his eyes at the sheer fleeting beauty of the voices of the young choirboys. The stirring notes of the organ echoed about granite walls, and Kate slipped her hand into Tony's and prayed with all of her might that he'd never remember anything but the good times.

After they shook hands with the vicar and began to walk down the lane toward Cardovan House, Kate said, "I could have been real sneaky and taken you to a Catholic church. You wouldn't have known the difference, would you?"

He drew her arm through his, their fingers entwined. "I remember that I wasn't particularly religious before the war. I'm probably not now, either. Your God is a little cruel for my liking. But I want to do the things you enjoy doing. I feel we never had a chance to do simple, ordinary things. The world was in such a mess when we met, it colored our lives, our marriage, I think. It must have—the partings, the other obligations. I want to go boating on the river, picnicking in the park. I want to stroll down a windswept beach with you, feeling the sand and shells between our toes."

He stopped suddenly and pulled her into his arms, oblivious of a pair of farmers who pedaled sedately past on their bicycles. With lips poised to kiss, Tony added softly, "I'm beginning to feel like a man again. My blood has started to churn every time I see my wife."

That night when Kate came out of the bathroom he was sitting up in bed. He hadn't worn pajamas. She'd seen the marks left by electricity burns on his chest and thighs as he dressed or undressed, but after the first surreptitious glimpses she forgot about them, they became just a part of him.

Kate slipped off her nightgown and slid into bed. As soon as she lay beside him she felt his desire surge back to life. They strained together, fusing into dearly remembered patterns, and for Kate everything was melting, running away in molten floods. She felt his mouth and tongue, his hands caressing her body, finding breasts and inner thighs. His breath mingled with hers, sweet and filled with promise, and she touched him tenderly and fiercely and with all of the pent-up need of their long absence.

When he entered her it was like the first time, yet even more fulfilling. She lost herself in the magic of being one with the man she loved, feeling her heart pound against his, feeling his joy match her own; and for those precious moments there was nothing in the world that could touch them or harm them or destroy the love they felt for one another.

With passion spent, they lay in each other's arms and talked softly, recapturing their ecstasy in the words of lovers, making plans, promises, dreaming of the future, reveling in the knowledge that they had found each other. Of all the millions of souls on earth, they had managed to find each other; and more than that, they had not lost their love, in spite of the terrible times in which they lived.

Just before dawn, as Tony slept, Kate lay close to him and realized that not once during the night's lovemaking had she worried about him regaining his memory of the early part of their marriage, when everything had gone disastrously wrong.

As their hours together expanded into days, their intimacy was honed to a fine point where they found themselves able to express thoughts and feelings without speaking. Their eyes would meet across the dinner table, and they'd give one another the secretive smile of lovers who know that they must quickly escape to a private place and make love. Or one would start to say something, and the other laughingly would finish the sentence. Their time together was so perfect that Kate prayed nightly that Tony's memory would never come back, even though it was clear that bits and pieces were taking shape and dropping into place for him.

Kate had been afraid he would ask about his father and then they'd have to reopen all of those old wounds, but one day as they strolled through the woods together he said, "I'm surprised at how well Cecilia has taken over the running of the estate since Father died."

"Yes," Kate said cautiously. "I guess it was a case of having to. There was no one else. Clive has been a big help, of course. I was so busy with my studies and nursing, it didn't occur to me that I probably should have helped in some way. But she really did have everything under control."

"The war has changed all of us, hasn't it? I suppose none of us really knew our own hidden strengths. It's a pity it has to take a cataclysm to get us to use all of our resources."

"Tony . . ."

"Yes?"

"You knew your father had been killed."

"Charles filled me in on those events he felt I should know before I came home. He thought it would spare you and Cecilia."

Charles Morcambe visited them, just before the Allied troops overran Germany and Berlin fell. Cecilia gave a small dinner party, and at one point during the evening Charles drew Kate to one side. "Your husband is a very brave man, Kate. I don't want to say anything to him about it just now, but, well, when the war is over and we can talk about things that must remain secret for now, I believe there may be a decoration of the highest order forthcoming for him."

Kate was both proud and uneasy. "He should get his country's honors, of course, Charles. But I can't help worrying about what it might do to him if he's forced to relive the nightmare of being caught by the Gestapo."

Chares blinked behind his glasses. "His memory hasn't come back? The doctors were sure that after he'd been home for a time he'd recover completely. That some recollections of certain events might perhaps be vague, but no real amnesia."

Kate looked across the room at Tony. He stood with Cecilia and Clive and was smiling at something they'd said. There had been a change in his attitude toward both of them. A more tolerant, forgiving atmosphere seemed to pervade the entire family. Even Cecilia's parties weren't quite so frequent nowadays. Kate thought that Cecilia had been something like the topiary shrubs, pruned and trimmed and cut to fit a certain mold, obscuring the real shape of the shrub, which had a resilient beauty of its own when the gardeners left it alone. Perhaps Cecilia would have been a different person if she hadn't loved two dynamic and dominant people.

And Tony . . . Despite all he'd been through, watching him, Kate felt the old thrill of pride. With it came another stab of fear that every day that passed brought her closer to the moment when the ghost of Wade Lowery would again rise up and smash her hopes for happiness.

[45]

Kate opened her eyes and saw Tony standing beside the bed watching her. He bent over, smiling. "Sorry, did I wake you?"

She put her arms around his neck and murmured against his mouth, "You can wake me like this anytime." Her hand slid down his arm. "You're dressed. What time is it?"

"Very early on the morning of the day designated as V-E Day. I thought we might go up to London and see a little of the victory celebration."

Kate nibbled his lower lip. "Mmm . . . wonderful idea."

"Then I thought I'd better go through my father's things—clear them out of the flat. We may want to use it occasionally, and, well, it has to be done. You don't have to come if it would distress you."

"You think I'm going to let you out of my sight for a minute, you're nuts."

He nuzzled the warm hollow of her throat, placed a kiss on her chin. "I had an early-morning call from Charles too. They're wondering what to do with me, I think. I've been offered a medical discharge, or if I wish I can have a desk job until we finish off Japan. I've been thinking about what I'll do when you go back to the hospital, and I've decided to take the demobilization offer."

She hugged him. "Oh, thank God! I've been hoping you would. You've more than done your share. I've got some news for you too, but you're not getting it yet. Not until I'm bathed and dressed and looking pretty."

"You always look pretty, and never more than when you're all sleepy and tousled, like now."

"Oops, excuse me." She pushed him aside and fled to the bathroom.

"Are you all right? You look a little green around the gills," he said when she emerged a little later.

She nodded mysteriously and flipped through the hangers in her wardrobe for her prettiest dress. The occasion seemed to call for the sunny yellow one.

They had breakfast alone, as the rest of the household was still in bed. Tony watched her closely, a concerned frown hovering. "What is it, Kate? I usually know what you're thinking, but today you're wearing an expression that's a combination of kitten-who-got-the-cream and . . . I don't know, you look a little like Cecilia did in those photos of her aboard Father's ship—both proud and seasick."

Kate gave him a wide grin. "You're altogether too perceptive for an amnesia case. And you, my wonderful husband, are gaining a little weight and looking more like the man I married. Tell me, have you thought about what you'll do when you get discharged?"

"Assume my duties here—relieve Cecilia's burden. It's time I took over, not only running the estate, but various political functions Father fulfilled. I've been considering becoming even more politically active than he was. The next few years are going to bring about vast changes in this country—probably in the whole world—and I'd like to have a say in the direction we take. And, thank God, I won't be hampered by a title, as he was, since although I did inherit it, I intend to renounce it."

"Maybe I'd better start paying attention to British politics," Kate said. "I was just thinking about those old pictures your father kept of Ella—your mother. She ran for political office too. I guess it was in your blood."

"She was a little too radical for her time, I suspect. There's something else I should tell you. Do you remember the first time you came to Cardovan House? I managed to divert your tour group here."

"Yes, indeed I do. It was a rather romantic method of getting to see me again. I was impressed."

"Well, there may come a time soon when such tours will be an everyday occurrence. We may have to move into one wing and keep the rest of the place for show. We're probably going to have to sell off most of the tenant farms too."

"Cecilia's managing—" Kate began.

"No, no, she's done splendidly. The simple fact of the matter is this country has damn near bankrupted itself winning the war. We're going to be faced with staggering taxes. I'm afraid very few people will be able to pay those taxes and live in the way we did prewar."

Kate made a small sound that was partly a sigh, partly an expression of ironic recognition.

"What is it?" Tony asked.

"I was just thinking about something." She broke off just in time.

Something Wade said—the British aristocracy has to go . . . the hedonistic existence of the few . . . he's fighting for his land, not to save the world for democracy.

She quickly changed the subject. "I want to tell you— Have you finished breakfast?"

"I have now. Tell me before I burst."

"Okay, come on. We're going for a little walk."

Twenty minutes later they were climbing the winding stone staircase up the bell tower of the church. Tony was still thoroughly baffled. Kate took his hand and led him to the side of the tower that overlooked the rolling acres of Cardovan House. "Is this where you stood with your father that day when he told you he wanted you to be his link to the future?"

"Yes." Tony stared at the gentle green countryside, bathed in wisps of morning mist, so achingly beautiful as the sun rose and clear silver light spilled over the edge of the earth. "It took me a long time to forgive Cecilia for what she did. I had to strive to understand her motives, to tell myself we're all basically self-interested creatures, bent on our own goals. I suppose that's the miracle of humanity, really. That sometimes we're able to overcome our inherent selfishness and do something for the common good."

"Your father wanted continuity—immortality—we all do. I don't believe it had anything to do with the house and the land. He wanted to stay alive in your memory. He wanted you to have a son to love as he'd loved you. He knew there was no way for you to know how much he loved you until you had a child of your own. And it didn't matter to him one bit that he thought you weren't his own biological creation, because he knew that everything you were, you were because of his love and guidance."

Tony looked down at her, reached out to place his hand on her cheek. "How did you ever get to be so wise?"

"I think it comes with pregnancy. We're going to have a child."

"Oh, Kate! Oh, my darling."

They were in each other's arms without being aware of having moved. He rained kisses on her lips, eyelids, hair. He held her tightly, then relaxed his arms and said, "Oh, my God, am I hurting you?"

She laughed. "I won't break, I promise."

He said, "There aren't words to tell you how I feel at this moment. I'm so filled with love and pride."

"Come on, let's go tell Cecilia before we leave for London. We can call Ursula from the flat later."

"Do you think we should go?" He looked doubtful, worried, and she kissed him again to drive away his concern. He said, "There'll be throngs of people. I don't want to risk you getting crushed in a mob."

"I am going with you, Tony. I have this burning need to be with you all the time. I want to be there when—"

"When what?"

She'd been going to say, *when your memory comes back completely,* but substituted, "When you have to pack up your father's belongings. It's going to be harder than you think. I remember when my grandmother died."

In London the crowds were already dancing in the streets, laughing, singing, rejoicing. Flags and bunting had appeared like magic. British and American uniforms mingled with those of every Allied country, and the civilians had donned their threadbare best. A pearly king and queen, hundreds of

ECHOES OF WAR

pearl buttons sewn to their finery, led a group doing the Lambeth Walk down the middle of the street. A cheering crowd was bearing down on Buckingham Palace. All the way into the capital they had heard the church bells ringing, and Kate had cried with sheer joy.

When at last they reached the flat in Berkeley Square, they were both infected by the exuberance and excitement of the packed city.

Tony went to find the bottle of vintage champagne he knew his father had been saving for this day. They toasted the end of the war, they drank to victory over Japan, to the King and Queen, and they toasted each other. Kate sipped the champagne, not really needing it to keep her spirits soaring.

Below their window in the square the crowd was chanting as Tony took her in his arms and kissed her tenderly. They heard the popping of firecrackers, and Kate looked up at Tony and grinned. "The firecrackers have to be coming from the Yanks in the crowd. I can't imagine Londoners setting them off after what they've been through in the blitz."

Tony nibbled her nose playfully. "I'll ask you not to make any disparaging remarks about Yanks. I happen to be married to one, and I love her very much." He began to unfasten the buttons of her dress.

"Mmm, that's nice," Kate murmured as he bent to deliver a kiss to the hollow between her breasts. "Have I explained to you, husband mine, about how very sexy being pregnant makes me feel? Better watch out, or I'll devour you."

"Please don't make any promises you don't intend to keep." He slipped his arms under her and carried her into the bedroom.

Kate lay back and let him remove her clothes, watched as he discarded his and lay beside her. He ran his hands gently over her breasts and abdomen, then bent and kissed the place where their child was growing. Kate sighed and clasped his head in her hands, holding him close to her. "I love you so much, Tony. I wish I knew how to tell you just how much."

He raised his head and his eyes answered her even before he spoke. "You've shown me your love, Kate, in so many ways. These past weeks have been the happiest of my life, a time of perfection. If I never had such happiness again, I believe it would be enough to last the rest of my life. But now, now that we're going to be a family, I think my heart is going to burst, that it can't contain all the love I feel for you."

All that afternoon, as the crowds danced and sang under their windows, Tony made love to her. When at last she fell asleep, it was to the sounds of the celebrations and to Tony's whispered words of love.

She awoke sometime in the evening, surprised that the blackout shutters were open, the drapes drawn back, and a blaze of lights glowed where formerly only black glass had been. The blackout was over. The city lights were on again. She stared, fascinated, at the windows, marveling at the pleasure of that bright glow. A fitting end to the darkness of the past five years.

She was alone in the bed, but heard Tony moving about in the next room. Something scraped over the floor; a wardrobe door closed. He was packing his father's things, of course. She slipped out of bed and put on her negligee.

He looked up as she came to the study door. He was standing by the writing table holding the leather-bound photograph album. When she crossed the room toward him she saw that there was something else in his hand. She recognized it instantly. It was a page torn from the journal she'd kept when she lived here.

She froze, her heart beginning to hammer. *Oh no, not now, please. Don't let it be a page from the lost time. Don't let it uncork all those bitter memories for him. Oh, dear God, don't let Wade come between us again.*

Tony held out the torn page to her. "I suppose it must have got caught between the pages of the album when you lived here."

She took the page with icy fingers and read what she had written:

Some thoughts on the subject of Wade Lowery coming back into my life. . . . I'm sitting here listening to the sound of the all-clear and thinking that it's signaling more than just the departure of the bombers. It's an all-clear, in a way, for me too. Maybe there was a me of long ago who was dazzled by Wade, but now I see that those first fumbling attempts on my part to love a man were just a trial run—practice for the real thing. That wouldn't come until I met Tony. I love my husband with all my heart and mind and soul and body, and if all my atoms were exploded and scattered, each tiny individual bit of me would still love him more than I love life itself.

Kate remembered writing the words, and that she'd torn the page out of her journal because the mention of Wade's name meant she couldn't keep it for her grandchildren, and that was the whole purpose of a diary. She looked up at Tony as she crumpled the page in her fist, wanting to weep. She stared at him, her eyes beseeching, because there was nothing to say.

He picked up her clenched fist in his hands, brought it to his lips, and kissed the white bones of her knuckles. Then he gently uncurled her fingers and withdrew the sheet of paper. "Please don't destroy that, Kate. I found it earlier, soon after you fell asleep, and I've been coming back to read it every ten minutes or so since."

"You remember . . . you know all about Wade?"

"Yes. Everything." His arms went around her. He kissed her, then closed her eyes with his lips. She was trembling and clung to him for support. He whispered, "Forgive me, Kate."

Her eyes flew open. "Forgive *you?* I'm the one who made such a hash of things. It seemed like the more I struggled, the deeper into the mire I got with Wade. I didn't want to hurt you, Tony, and ended up hurting you more than if I'd been honest."

"Forgive me for not being secure enough in my love for you to trust you. Forgive me for doubting you—for all of the things I could have done, should have done, but didn't. Kate, I didn't just suddenly regain my memory this afternoon. It's been gradually coming back each day since I came home. Oh, there were gaps, but even when I was in Bu-

ECHOES OF WAR

chenwald I knew about Wade Lowery. You know, when you're faced with a struggle simply to survive, it's easier to put things into proper perspective. I knew that I loved you, that I'd never be happy if you weren't by my side. I wanted to look forward to growing old with you, to seeing our love mature and grow. We'd had time only to plant a frail and tender little shoot, easily buffeted by gales. I knew that if we were to give it a chance, it would become a sturdy oak that nothing could touch. But, God help me, I weakened again when I knew the waiting was over and I was coming home to you. I was afraid of confrontations and explanations and postmortems, so to those gaps in my memory I added everything I simply didn't wish to remember."

"You mean you've known all about Wade ever since—"

"Yes. He was no longer a threat to me, but I thought it would be easier for you if you thought I didn't remember. It would give us time to just love one another. Then when I found that page from your diary, I realized that there was no need for pretense."

Kate laid her head on his shoulder and whispered a prayer of thanks. Some day she'd tell him that Wade had been killed in a place called Guadalcanal and she wasn't even sure where it was. Perhaps she'd show her husband some of the articles Wade had written—they'd be in the archives of newspapers and magazines somewhere. She thought Tony would be as glad as she was that Wade had perhaps left behind a legacy for future generations, warning them of the everlasting peril of war.

But not now. For now it was enough that she was in Tony's arms, feeling their love for one another surround them, as outside in the city the bells chimed, the lights blazed, and peace had come at last.

Outstanding Bestsellers!

____ 61446	**COPS** by Mark Baker	$4.50
____ 83612	**THE GLORY GAME** by Janet Dailey	$4.50
____ 61702	**THE COLOR PURPLE** by Alice Walker	$3.95
____ 61106	**AT MOTHER'S REQUEST** by Jonathon Coleman	$4.50
____ 50692	**THE TITAN** by Fred Mustard Stewart	$4.50
____ 55813	**MOSCOW RULES** by Robert Moss	$3.95
____ 60776	**SILVERWOOD** by Joanna Barnes	$3.95
____ 50268	**SMART WOMEN** by Judy Blume	$3.95
____ 49837	**LOVESONG** by Valerie Sherwood	$3.95
____ 55386	**VIRGINS** by Caryl Rivers	$3.50
____ 50468	**FIRST AMONG EQUALS** by Jeffrey Archer	$4.50
____ 55797	**DEEP SIX** by Clive Cussler	$4.50
____ 54101	**POSSESSIONS** by Judith Michael	$4.50
____ 55773	**DECEPTIONS** by Judith Michael	$4.50

POCKET BOOKS, Department OBB
1230 Avenue of the Americas, New York, N.Y. 10020

Please send me the books I have checked above. I am enclosing $_____ (please add 75¢ to cover postage and handling for each order. N.Y.S. and N.Y.C. residents please add appropriate sales tax). Send check or money order—no cash or C.O.D.'s please. Allow up to six weeks for delivery. For purchases over $10.00, you may use VISA: card number, expiration date and customer signature must be included.

NAME _____

ADDRESS _____

CITY _____ STATE ZIP _____

892

Janet Dailey
America's Bestselling Romance Novelist

Why is Janet Dailey so astonishingly successful? That's easy—because she is so remarkably good! Her romance is passionate, her historical detail accurate, her narrative power electrifying.

Read these wonderful stories and experience the magic that has made Janet Dailey a star in the world of books.

- __THE PRIDE OF HANNAH WADE 49801/$3.95
- __THE GLORY GAME 83612/$4.50
- __THE SECOND TIME 61212/$2.95
- __MISTLETOE AND HOLLY 60673/$2.95
- __SILVER WINGS, SANTIAGO BLUE 60072/$4.50
- __FOXFIRE LIGHT 44681/$2.95
- __SEPARATE CABINS 58029/$2.95
- __TERMS OF SURRENDER 55795/$2.95
- __FOR THE LOVE OF GOD 55460/$2.95
- __THE LANCASTER MEN 54383/$2.95
- __HOSTAGE BRIDE 53023/$2.95
- __NIGHT WAY 47980/$3.95
- __RIDE THE THUNDER 47981/$3.95
- __THE ROGUE 49982/$3.95
- __TOUCH THE WIND 49230/$3.95
- __THIS CALDER SKY 46478/$3.95
- __THIS CALDER RANGE 83608/$3.95
- __STANDS A CALDER MAN 47398/$3.95
- __CALDER BORN, CALDER BRED 50250/$3.95

POCKET BOOKS, Department CAL
1230 Avenue of the Americas, New York, N.Y. 10020

Please send me the books I have checked above. I am enclosing $_____ (please add 75¢ to cover postage and handling for each order. N.Y.S. and N.Y.C. residents please add appropriate sales tax). Send check or money order—no cash or C.O.D.'s please. Allow up to six weeks for delivery. For purchases over $10.00, you may use VISA: card number, expiration date and customer signature must be included.

NAME _____

ADDRESS _____

CITY _____ STATE/ZIP _____

Herman Wouk

All these titles are available at your bookseller from Pocket Books

"Wouk is first and last a top-notch storyteller!" —*Time*

___ **THE WINDS OF WAR** 46319/$4.95

___ **WAR AND REMEMBRANCE** 46314/$5.95

___ **THE CAINE MUTINY** 60425/$5.95

___ **MARJORIE MORNINGSTAR** 46016/$5.95

___ **YOUNGBLOOD HAWKE** 45472/$5.95

___ **CITY BOY** 46013/$4.95

___ **DON'T STOP THE CARNIVAL** 60544/$4.50

___ **AURORA DAWN** 46012/$2.95

"Herman Wouk has a tremendous narrative gift."
—*San Francisco Chronicle*

POCKET BOOKS, Department HWT
1230 Avenue of the Americas, New York, N.Y. 10020

Please send me the books I have checked above. I am enclosing $_____ (please add 75¢ to cover postage and handling for each order. N.Y.S. and N.Y.C. residents please add appropriate sales tax). Send check or money order—no cash or C.O.D.'s please. Allow up to six weeks for delivery. For purchases over $10.00, you may use VISA: card number, expiration date and customer signature must be included.

NAME _____

ADDRESS _____

CITY _____ STATE ZIP _____